ARE THEY ON THEIR WAY TO OUR
EARTH—OR ARE THEY ALREADY HERE?

**"The Alien Rulers" by Piers Anthony**—Someone
was abducting Earth's finest—and wasn't about
to give them back!

**"For I am a Jealous God" by Lester del Rey**—If
his own people no longer heed God's word,
there are always alien races ready to become the
new Chosen People.

**"Asylum" by A.E. van Vogt**—On the run from
those they had once hungrily preyed upon,
would they find a new start on a blood-rich Earth?

**"Don't Look Now" by Henry Kuttner**—He knew
the Martians had taken over the Earth, but
could he keep anybody's attention long enough
to prove it?

These are just a few of the entertaining and cau-
tionary tales that will have you looking at friends
and strangers in a whole new light, as you search
for aliens among us in—

### INVASIONS
### ISAAC ASIMOV'S WONDERFUL
### WORLDS OF SCIENCE FICTION #10

# INVASIONS

## Isaac Asimov's Magical Worlds of Science Fiction #10

Edited by
**Isaac Asimov   Martin H. Greenberg
and Charles G. Waugh**

A ROC BOOK

ROC
Published by the Penguin Group
Penguin Books USA Inc., 375 Hudson Street,
New York, New York 10014, U.S.A.
Penguin Books Ltd, 27 Wrights Lane,
London W8 5TZ, England
Penguin Books Australia Ltd, Ringwood,
Victoria, Australia
Penguin Books Canada Ltd, 2801 John Street,
Markham, Ontario, Canada L3R 1B4
Penguin Books (N.Z.) Ltd, 182-190 Wairau Road,
Auckland 10, New Zealand

Penguin Books Ltd, Registered Offices:
Harmondsworth, Middlesex, England

First published by Roc, an imprint of New American Library, a division
of Penguin Books USA Inc.

First Printing, August, 1990
10  9  8  7  6  5  4  3  2  1

Acknowledgments

*(For permissions to reprint the following stories, please see page 383.)*

 Roc is a trademark of Penguin Books USA Inc.

PRINTED IN THE UNITED STATES OF AMERICA

# CONTENTS

# INTRODUCTION

Invasion is undoubtedly as old as humanity. Hunting groups must occasionally have encountered each other, if only by accident. Each side must have felt the other was invading. The obviously weaker side would have had to decamp. If the matter were not obvious, there might have been threats or even a brief struggle to settle the matter.

Once agriculture became a way of life and farmers were pinned in place by their farms and food stores, these same food stores became an overwhelming temptation to surrounding nomads; invasions were more terrible because farmers could not flee but had to stand and fight.

We begin to have records of early civilizations suddenly inundated and taken over by raiders. The Sumerians were taken over by Gutian invaders as early as 2200 B.C. The Egyptians fell under the grip of the Hyksos invaders soon after 1700 B.C. We can go through an endless list of such things.

Considering that those people who were invaded (until quite recent times) had little knowledge of the world outside the boundaries of their own cultures, the invasions must usually have come as unbelievable shocks, as a sudden influx of the unknown from the unknown. This would be especially so when the invaders spoke strange language, wore strange clothes, had strange ways, and even, perhaps, have *looked* odd.

As the most recent example of our cultural ancestors being subjected to the horror of an unexpected invasion, we need only go back to 1240, when the Mongols (short, squat, slant-eyed) swept into Europe on their hardy desert mounts. Europe knew nothing about them, had no way of knowing they were on the way (they had been ravaging Asian kingdoms for twenty years). All they

7

knew were that these terrible horsemen, moving with incredible speed and organization, winning every battle, smashed Russia, Poland, Hungary, and were penetrating Germany and reaching for Italy, all in a matter of a single year. And then they left and raced eastward again, smashing Bulgaria en route. (They had left because their khan had died back in Mongolia and the army had to be there for the election of a successor. Nothing the Europeans could have done would have stopped them.)

But the Mongols were "the last of the barbarians." Partly because of the Mongolian empire that was set up, communications between China and Europe became smoother. Such things as printing, the magnetic compass, and (most of all) gunpowder, leaked westward from China, and these things—for some reason not exploited by the technologically more advanced Chinese—were put to amazing use by Europeans.

And beginning about 1420, the tide of invasion was reversed. The "civilized" Europeans, with their ships and their guns, fell upon the coastlines of all the continents and, eventually, penetrated the interiors until Europe dominated the world politically and militarily (and as it still does, even today, culturally.)

But how did the non-Europeans feel about it? How about the Africans who watched the Portuguese ships come from nowhere and carry them off as slaves; the Asians who watched Portuguese, Dutch, and English ships come in, set up trading posts, skimming off profits and treating them as inferiors; the Native Americans watching the Spanish ships come in and take over and destroy their civilizations? There must have been the feeling of monsters arriving from some other world.

All invasions, however, at least of the kind I'm discussing, were by human beings. However strange they might have seemed—Mongols to Europeans, or Spaniards to Incas—they were clearly human beings. (There were also invasions or infestations of non-human types—rats, locusts, the plague bacterium of the Black Death, the AIDS virus—but these fall outside the subject matter of this introduction, and even they were forms of terrestrial life.)

What if, however, the invaders were intelligent beings who were not human and, in fact, not earthly. The possibility did not seriously arise until the time when it was thoroughly recognized that the planets were other worlds and that the universe might be full of still other planets outside the domain of our own sun.

At first, other worlds were the subject of "travel tales." Human beings went to the moon (as early as the A.D. second century in fiction and more frequently as time went on), but there are no tales I can think of in which the inhabitants of the moon came to Earth.

In 1752, the French satirist Voltaire wrote *Micromegas*, in which visitors from Saturn and Sirius observe the Earth, but this cannot be taken literally. The visitors are merely Voltaire's device for having Earth viewed with apparent objectivity from without in order to have its follies and contradictions made plain.

But then in 1877, there was the discovery of thin, dark markings on Mars. This was interpreted by some as "canals" and the American astronomer Percival Lowell was convinced that they were artificial waterways built by intelligent beings trying to use the ice of the polar caps to maintain agriculture on their increasingly desiccated planet. He wrote books on the subject in the 1890s that created quite a stir.

The British science fiction writer Herbert George Wells proceeded to make use of the notion and, in 1898, published *The War of the Worlds*, the first significant tale of the invasion and attempted conquest of Earth by more advanced intelligences from another world (in this case, Mars). I have always thought that Wells, in addition to wanting to write an exciting story with an unprecedented plot, was also bitterly satirizing Europe. At the time he wrote, Europeans (the British, particularly) had just completed dividing up Africa without any regard for the people living there. Why not show the British how it would feel to have advanced intelligences treat them as callously as they were treating the Africans?

Wells's novel created a new sub-genre—tales of alien invasion. The manner in which Wells made the Martians unpitying exploiters of humanity (for the sake of excitement and, I believe, satire); the memory, perhaps, of the Mongol invasion; the feeling of guilt over the European despoliation of all the other continents; combined to make it conventional to have the alien invaders unfeeling conquerors, for the most part.

Actually, we have no reason to think this would be so. As far as we know, no invaders from without have ever reached Earth and, for a variety of reasons, it might be argued that none ever will. However, if they do come, there is no a priori reason to suspect they won't come in friendship and curiosity, to teach and to learn.

Yet such is the power of humanity's own shameful history and the conventions of fiction that very few people would be willing to consider alien invaders coming in peace as a real possibility. In fact, when plaques and recordings were placed on rocket probes designed to leave the solar system and go wandering off into interstellar space, in order that alien intelligences (if any) might find them someday, millions of years in the future, and that they might thus learn that Earthmen had once existed—there were not lacking those who thought it a dangerous process. Why advertise our existence? Why encourage ferocious aliens to come here in order to ravage and destroy?

Here, then, in this collection, are stories of alien invasion. We have selected a variety of contemporary treatments of the problem, some a matter of excitement, some thoughtfully philosophic, some even funny. They view the possibility from all angles and stretch our minds on the matter, as good science fiction should.

—Isaac Asimov

# LIVING SPACE

## BY ISAAC ASIMOV

Clarence Rimbro had no objections to living in the only house on an uninhabited planet, any more than had any other of Earth's even trillion of inhabitants.

If someone had questioned him concerning possible objections, he would undoubtedly have stared blankly at the questioner. His house was much larger than any house could possibly be on Earth proper and much more modern. It had its independent air supply and water supply, ample food in its freezing compartments. It was isolated from the lifeless planet on which it was located by a force field, but the rooms were built about a five-acre farm (under glass, of course), which, in the planet's beneficent sunlight, grew flowers for pleasure and vegetables for health. It even supported a few chickens. It gave Mrs. Rimbro something to do with herself afternoons, and a place for the two little Rimbros to play when they were tired of indoors.

Furthermore, if one *wanted* to be on Earth proper; if one insisted on it; if one *had* to have people around and air one could breathe in the open or water to swim in, one had only to go out of the front door of the house.

So where was the difficulty?

Remember, too, that on the lifeless planet on which the Rimbro house was located there was complete silence except for the occasional monotonous effects of wind and rain. There was absolute privacy and the feeling of absolute ownership of two hundred million square miles of planetary surface.

Clarence Rimbro appreciated all that in his distant way. He was an accountant, skilled in handling very advanced computer models, precise in his manners and clothing, not much given to smiling beneath his thin, well-kept mustache and properly aware of his own worth.

11

When he drove from work toward home, he passed the occasional dwelling place on Earth proper and he never ceased to stare at them with a certain smugness.

Well, either for business reasons or mental perversion, some people simply had to live on Earth proper. It was too bad for them. After all, Earth proper's soil had to supply the minerals and basic food supply for all the trillion of inhabitants (in fifty years, it would be two trillion) and space was at a premium. Houses on Earth proper just *couldn't* be any bigger than that, and people who had to live in them had to adjust to the fact.

Even the process of entering his house had its mild pleasantness. He would enter the community twist place to which he was assigned (it looked, as did all such, like a rather stumpy obelisk), and there he would invariably find others waiting to use it. Still more would arrive before he reached the head of the line. It was a sociable time.

"How's your planet?" "How's yours?" The usual small talk. Sometimes someone would be having trouble. Machinery breakdowns or serious weather that would alter the terrain unfavorably. Not often.

But it passed the time. Then Rimbro would be at the head of the line; he would put his key into the slot; the proper combination would be punched; and he would be twisted into a new probability pattern; his own particular probability pattern; the one assigned to him when he married and became a producing citizen; a probability pattern in which life had never developed on Earth. And twisting to this particular lifeless Earth, he would walk into his own foyer.

Just like that.

He never worried about being in another probability. Why should he? He never gave it any thought. There were an infinite number of possible Earths. Each existed in its own niche; its own probability pattern. Since on a planet such as Earth there was, according to calculation, about a fifty-fifty chance of life's developing, half of all the possible Earths (still infinite, since half of infinity was infinity) possessed life, and half (still infinite) did not. And living on about three hundred billion of the unoccupied Earths were three hundred billion families, each with its own beautiful house, powered by the sun of that probability, and each securely at peace. The number of Earths so occupied grew by millions each day.

And then one day, Rimbro came home and Sandra (his wife) said to him, as he entered, "There's been the most peculiar noise."

Rimbro's eyebrows shot up and he looked closely at his wife. Except for a certain restlessness of her thin hands and a pale look about the corners of her tight mouth, she looked normal.

Rimbro said, still holding his topcoat halfway toward the servette that waited patiently for it, "Noise? What noise? I don't hear anything."

"It's stopped now," Sandra said. "Really, it was like a deep thumping or rumble. You'd hear it a bit. Then it would stop. Then you'd hear it a bit and so on. I've never heard anything like it."

Rimbro surrendered his coat. "But that's quite impossible."

"I *heard* it."

"I'll look over the machinery," he mumbled. "Something may be wrong."

Nothing was, that his accountant's eyes could discover, and, with a shrug, he went to supper. He listened to the servettes hum busily about their different chores, watched one sweep up the plates and cutlery for disposal and recovery, then said, pursing his lips, "Maybe one of the servettes is out of order. I'll check them."

"It wasn't anything like that, Clarence."

Rimbro went to bed, without further concern over the matter, and wakened with his wife's hand clutching his shoulder. His hand went automatically to the contact patch that set the walls glowing. "What's the matter? What time is it?"

She shook her head. "Listen! *Listen!*"

Good Lord, thought Rimbro, there *is* a noise. A definite rumbling. It came and went.

"Earthquake?" he whispered. It did happen, of course, though, with all the planet to choose from, they could generally count on having avoided the faulted areas.

"All day long?" asked Sandra fretfully. "I think it's something else." And then she voiced the secret terror of every nervous householder. "I think there's someone on the planet with us. This Earth is *inhabited*."

Rimbro did the logical things. When morning came, he took his wife and children to his wife's mother. He himself took a day off and hurried to the Sector's Housing Bureau.

He was quite annoyed at all this.

Bill Ching of the Housing Bureau was short, jovial and proud of his part Mongolian ancestry. He thought probability patterns had solved every last one of humanity's problems. Alec Mishnoff, also of the Housing Bureau, thought probability patterns were a snare into which humanity had been hopelessly tempted. He had originally majored in archeology and had studied a variety of antiquarian subjects with which his delicately poised head was still crammed. His face managed to look sensitive despite overbearing eyebrows, and he lived with a pet notion that so far he had dared tell no one, though preoccupation with it had driven him out of archeology and into housing.

Ching was fond of saying, "The hell with Malthus!" It was almost a verbal trademark of his. "The hell with Malthus. We can't possibly overpopulate now. However frequently we double and redouble, Homo sapiens remains finite in number, and the uninhabited Earths remain infinite. And we don't have to put one house on each planet. We can put a hundred, a thousand, a million. Plenty of room and plenty of power from each probability sun."

"More than one on a planet?" said Mishnoff sourly.

Ching knew exactly what he meant. When probability patterns had first been put to use, sole ownership of a planet had been powerful inducement for early settlers. It appealed to the snob and despot in every one. What man so poor, ran the slogan, as not to have an empire larger than Genghis Khan's? To introduce multiple settling now would outrage everyone.

Ching said, with a shrug, "All right, it would take psychological preparation. So what? That's what it took to start the whole deal in the first place."

"And food?" asked Mishnoff.

"You know we're putting hydroponic works and yeast plants in other probability patterns. And if we had to, we could cultivate their soil."

"Wearing space suits and importing oxygen."

"We could reduce carbon dioxide for oxygen till the plants got going and they'd do the job after that."

"Given a million years."

"Mishnoff, the trouble with you," Ching said, "is you read too many ancient history books. You're an obstructionist."

But Ching was too good-natured really to mean that, and Mishnoff continued to read books and to worry. Mishnoff longed for the day he could get up the courage necessary to see the Head of the Section and put right out in plain view—bang, like that—exactly what it was that was troubling him.

But now, a Mr. Clarence Rimbro faced them, perspiring slightly and toweringly angry at the fact that it had taken him the better part of two days to reach this far into the Bureau.

He reached his exposition's climax by saying, "And *I* say the planet is inhabited and I don't propose to stand for it."

Having listened to his story in full, Ching tried the soothing approach. He said, "Noise like that is probably just some natural phenomenon."

"What kind of natural phenomenon?" demanded Rimbro. "I want an investigation. If it's a natural phenomenon, I want to know what kind. I say the place is inhabited. It has life on it, by Heaven, and I'm not paying rent on a planet to share it. And with dinosaurs, from the sound of it."

"Come, Mr. Rimbro, how long have you lived on your Earth?"

"Fifteen and a half years."

"And has there ever been any evidence of life?"

"There is now, and, as a citizen with a production record classified as A-I, I demand an investigation."

"Of course we'll investigate, sir, but we just want to assure you now that everything is all right. Do you realize how carefully we select our probability patterns?"

"I'm an accountant. I have a pretty good idea," said Rimbro at once.

"Then surely you know our computers cannot fail us. They never pick a probability which has been picked before. They can't possibly. And they're geared to select only probability patterns in which Earth has a carbon dioxide atmosphere, one in which plant life, and therefore animal life, has never developed. Because if plants had evolved, the carbon dioxide would have been reduced to oxygen. Do you understand?"

"I understand it all very well and I'm not here for lectures," said Rimbro. "I want an investigation out of you and nothing else. It is quite humiliating to think I may be sharing my world, my own world, with something or other, and I don't propose to endure it."

"No, of course not," muttered Ching, avoiding Mishnoff's sardonic glance. "We'll be there before night."

They were on their way to the twisting place with full equipment.

Mishnoff said, "I want to ask you something. Why do you go through that 'There's no need to worry, sir' routine? They always worry anyway. Where does it get you?"

"I've got to try. They *shouldn't* worry," said Ching petulantly. "Ever hear of a carbon dioxide planet that *was* inhabited? Besides, Rimbro is the type that starts rumors. I can spot them. By the time he's through, if he's encouraged, he'll say his sun went nova."

"*That* happens sometimes," said Mishnoff.

"So? One house is wiped out and one family dies. See, you're an obstructionist. In the old times, the times you like, if there were a flood in China or someplace, thousands of people would die. And that's out of a population of a measly billion or two."

Mishnoff muttered, "How do you know the Rimbro planet doesn't have life on it?"

"Carbon dioxide atmosphere."

"But suppose——" It was no use. Mishnoff couldn't say it. He finished lamely, "Suppose plant and animal life develops that can live on carbon dioxide."

"It's never been observed."

"In an infinite number of worlds, anything can happen." He finished that in a whisper. "Everything *must* happen."

"Chances are one in a duodecillion," said Ching, shrugging.

They arrived at the twisting point then, and, having utilized the freight twist for their vehicle (thus sending it into the Rimbro storage area), they entered the Rimbro probability pattern themselves. First Ching, then Mishnoff.

"A nice house," said Ching, with satisfaction. "Very nice model. Good taste."

"Hear anything?" asked Mishnoff.

"No."

Ching wandered into the garden. "Hey," he yelled. "Rhode Island Reds."

Mishnoff followed, looking up at the glass roof. The sun looked like the sun of a trillion other Earths.

He said absently, "There could be plant life, just starting out. The carbon dioxide might just be starting to drop in concentration. The computer would never know."

"And it would take millions of years for animal life to begin and millions more for it to come out of the sea."

"It doesn't have to follow that pattern."

Ching put an arm about his partner's shoulder. "You brood. Someday, you'll tell me what's really bothering you, instead of just hinting, and we can straighten you out."

Mishnoff shrugged off the encircling arm with an annoyed frown. Ching's tolerance was always hard to bear. He began, "Let's not psychotherapize——" He broke off, then whispered, "Listen."

There was a distant rumble. Again.

They placed the seismograph in the center of the room and activated the force field that penetrated downward and bound it rigidly to bedrock. They watched the quivering needle record the shocks.

Mishnoff said, "Surface waves only. Very superficial. It's not underground."

Ching looked a little more dismal, "What is it then?"

"I think," said Mishnoff, "we'd better find out." His face was gray with apprehension. "We'll have to set up a seismograph at another point and get a fix on the focus of the disturbance."

"Obviously," said Ching. "I'll go out with the other seismograph. You stay here."

"No," said Mishnoff, with energy. "*I'll* go out."

Mishnoff felt terrified, but he had no choice. If this were *it*, he would be prepared. He could get a warning through. Sending out an unsuspecting Ching would be disastrous. Nor could he warn Ching, who would certainly never believe him.

But since Mishnoff was not cast in the heroic mold, he trembled as he got into his oxygen suit and fumbled the disrupter as he tried to dissolve the force field locally in order to free the emergency exit.

"Any reason *you* want to go, particularly?" asked Ching, watching the other's inept manipulations. "I'm willing."

"It's all right. I'm going out," said Mishnoff, out of a dry throat, and stepped into the lock that led out onto the desolate surface of a lifeless Earth. A presumably lifeless Earth.

The sight was not unfamiliar to Mishnoff. He had seen its like dozens of times. Bare rock, weathered by wind and rain, crusted and powdered with sand in the gullies; a small and noisy brook beating itself against its stony course. All brown and gray; no sign of green. No sound of life.

Yet the sun was the same and, when night fell, the constellations would be the same.

The situation of the dwelling place was in that region which on Earth proper would be called Labrador. (It was Labrador here, too, really. It had been calculated that in not more than one out of a quadrillion or so Earths were there significant changes in the geological development. The continents were everywhere recognizable down to quite small details.)

Despite the situation and the time of the year, which was October, the temperature was sticky warm due to the hothouse effect of the carbon dioxide in this Earth's dead atmosphere.

From inside his suit, through the transparent visor, Mishnoff watched it all somberly. If the epicenter of the noise were close by, adjusting the second seismograph a mile or so away would be enough for the fix. If it weren't, they would have to bring in an air scooter. Well, assume the lesser complication to begin with.

Methodically, he made his way up a rocky hillside. Once at the top, he could choose his spot.

Once at the top, puffing and feeling the heat most unpleasantly, he found he didn't have to.

His heart was pounding so that he could scarcely hear

his own voice as he yelled into his radio mouthpiece, "Hey, Ching, there's construction going on."

"What?" came back the appalled shout in his ears.

There was no mistake. Ground was being leveled. Machinery was at work. Rock was being blasted out.

Mishnoff shouted, "They're blasting. That's the noise."

Ching called back, "But it's impossible. The computer would never pick the same probability pattern twice. *It couldn't.*"

"You don't understand——" began Mishnoff.

But Ching was following his own thought processes. "Get over there, Mishnoff. I'm coming out, too."

"No, damn it. You stay there," cried Mishnoff in alarm. "Keep me in radio contact, and for God's sake be ready to leave for Earth proper on wings if I give the word."

"Why?" demanded Ching. "What's going on?"

"I don't know yet," said Mishnoff. "Give me a chance to find out."

To his own surprise, he noticed his teeth were chattering.

Muttering breathless curses at the computer, at probability patterns and at the insatiable need for living space on the part of a trillion human beings expanding in numbers like a puff of smoke, Mishnoff slithered and slipped down the other side of the slope, setting stones to rolling and rousing peculiar echoes.

A man came out to meet him, dressed in a gas-tight suit, different in many details from Mishnoff's own, but obviously intended for the same purpose—to lead oxygen to the lungs.

Mishnoff gasped breathlessly into his mouthpiece, "Hold it, Ching. There's a man coming. Keep in touch." Mishnoff felt his heart pump more easily and the bellows of his lungs labor less.

The two men were staring at one another. The other man was blond and craggy of face. The look of surprise about him was too extreme to be feigned.

He said in a harsh voice, *"Wer sind Sie? Was machen Sie hier?"*

Mishnoff was thunderstruck. He'd studied ancient German for two years in the days when he expected to be an archeologist and he followed the comment despite the fact that the pronunciation was not what he had been taught. The stranger was asking his identity and his business there.

Stupidly, Mishnoff stammered, *"Sprechen Sie Deutsch?"* and then had to mutter reassurance to Ching whose agitated voice in his earpiece was demanding to know what the gibberish was all about.

The German-speaking one made no direct answer. He repeated, *"Wer sind Sie?"* and added impatiently, *"Hier ist für ein verrückten Spass keine Ziet."*

Mishnoff didn't feel like a joke either, particularly not a foolish one, but he continued, *"Sprechen Sie Planetisch?"*

He did not know the German for "Planetary Standard Language" so he had to guess. Too late, he thought he should have referred to it simply as English.

The other man stared wide-eyed at him. *"Sind Sie wahnsinnig?"*

Mishnoff was almost willing to settle for that, but in feeble self-defense, he said, "I'm not crazy, damn it. I mean, *"Auf der Erde woher Sie gekom——"*

He gave it up for lack of German, but the new idea that was rattling inside his skull would not quit its nagging. He had to find some way of testing it. He said desperately, *"Welches Jahr ist es jetzt?"*

Presumably, the stranger, who was questioning his sanity already, would be convinced of Mishnoff's insanity now that he was being asked what year it was, but it was one question for which Mishnoff had the necessary German.

The other muttered something that sounded suspiciously like good German swearing and then said, *"Es ist doch zwei tausend drei hundert vier-und-sechzig, und warum——"*

The stream of German that followed was completely incomprehensible to Mishnoff, but in any case he had had enough for the moment. If he translated the German correctly, the year given him was 2364, which was nearly two thousand years in the past. How could that be?

He muttered, *"Zwei tausend drei hundert vier-und sechzig?"*

*"Ja, Ja,"* said the other, with deep sarcasm. *"Zwei tausend drei hundert vier-und-sechzig. Der ganze Jahr lang ist es so gewesen."*

Mishnoff shrugged. The statement that it had been so

all year long was a feeble witticism even in German and it gained nothing in translation. He pondered.

But then the other's ironical tone deepening, the German-speaking one went on, *"Zwei tausend drei hundert vier-und-sechzig nach Hitler. Hilft das Ihnen vielleicht? Nach Hitler!"*

Mishnoff yelled with delight. "That *does* help me. *Es hilft! Hören Sie, bitte——"* He went on in broken German interspersed with scraps of Planetary, "For Heaven's sake, *um Gottes willen——"*

Making it 2364 after Hitler was different altogether.

He put German together desperately, trying to explain.

The other frowned and grew thoughtful. He lifted his gloved hand to stroke his chin or make some equivalent gesture, hit the transparent visor that covered his face and left his hand there uselessly, while he thought.

He said, suddenly, *"Ich heiss George Fallenby."*

To Mishnoff it seemed that the name must be of Anglo-Saxon derivation, although the change in vowel form as pronounced by the other made it seem Teutonic.

*"Guten Tag,"* said Mishnoff awkwardly. *"Ich heiss Alex Mishnoff,"* and was suddenly aware of the Slavic derivation of his own name.

*"Kommen Sie mit mir, Herr Mishnoff,"* said Fallenby.

Mishnoff followed with a strained smile, muttering into his transmitter, "It's all right, Ching. It's all right."

Back on Earth proper, Mishnoff faced the Sector's Bureau Head, who had grown old in the Service; whose every gray hair betokened a problem met and solved; and every missing hair a problem averted. He was a cautious man with eyes still bright and teeth that were still his own. His name was Berg.

He shook his head. "And they speak German; but the German you studied was two thousand years old."

"True," said Mishnoff. "But the English Hemingway used is two thousand years old and Planetary is close enough for anyone to be able to read it."

"Hmp. And who's this Hitler?"

"He was a sort of tribal chief in ancient times. He led the German tribe in one of the wars of the twentieth century, just about the time the Atomic Age started and true history began."

"Before the Devastation, you mean?"

"Right. There was a series of wars then. The Anglo-Saxon countries won out, and I suppose that's why the Earth speaks Planetary."

"And if Hitler and his Germans had won out, the world would speak German instead?"

"They *have* won out on Fallenby's Earth, sir, and they *do* speak German."

"And make their dates 'after Hitler' instead of A.D.?"

"Right. And I suppose there's an Earth in which the Slavic tribes won out and everyone speaks Russian."

"Somehow," said Berg, "it seems to me we should have foreseen it, and yet, as far as I know, no one has. After all, there are an infinite number of inhabited Earths, and we can't be the only one that has decided to solve the problem of unlimited population growth by expanding into the worlds of probability."

"Exactly," said Mishnoff earnestly, "and it seems to me that if you think of it, there must be countless inhabited Earths so doing and there must be many multiple occupations in the three hundred billion Earths we ourselves occupy. The only reason we caught this one is that, by sheer chance, they decided to build within a mile of the dwelling we had placed there. This is something we must check."

"You imply we ought to search all our Earths."

"I do, sir. We've got to make some settlement with other inhabited Earths. After all, there is room for all of us and to expand without agreement may result in all sorts of trouble and conflict."

"Yes," said Berg thoughtfully. "I agree with you."

Clarence Rimbro stared suspicously at Berg's old face, creased now into all manner of benevolence.

"You're sure now?"

"Absolutely," said the Bureau Head. "We're sorry that you've had to accept temporary quarters for the last two weeks——"

"More like three."

"——three weeks, but you will be compensated."

"What was the noise?"

"Purely geological, sir. A rock was delicately balanced and, with the wind, it made occasional contact with the rocks of the hillside. We've removed it and surveyed the area to make certain that nothing similar will occur again."

Rimbro clutched his hat and said, "Well, thanks for your trouble."

"No thanks necessary, I assure you, Mr. Rimbro. This is our job."

Rimbro was ushered out, and Berg turned to Mishnoff, who had remained a quiet spectator of this completion of the Rimbro affair.

Berg said, "The Germans were nice about it, anyway. They admitted we had priority and got off. Room for everybody, they said. Of course, as it turned out, they build any number of dwellings on each unoccupied world. . . . And now there's the project of surveying our other worlds and making similar agreements with whomever we find. It's all strictly confidential, too. It can't be made known to the populace without plenty of preparation. . . . Still, none of this is what I want to speak to you about."

"Oh?" said Mishnoff. Developments had not noticeably cheered him. His own bogey still concerned him.

Berg smiled at the younger man. "You understand, Mishnoff, we in the Bureau, and in the Planetary Government, too, are very appreciative of your quick thinking, of your understanding of the situation. This could have developed into something very tragic, had it not been for you. This appreciation will take some tangible form."

"Thank you, sir."

"But, as I said once before, this is something many of us should have thought of. How is it you did? . . . Now we've gone into your background a little. Your co-worker, Ching, tells us you have hinted in the past at some serious danger involved in our probability-pattern setup, and that you insisted on going out to meet the Germans although you were obviously frightened. You were anticipating what you actually found, were you not? And how did you do it?"

Mishnoff said confusedly, "No, no. That was not in my mind at all. It came as a surprise. I——"

Suddenly he stiffened. Why not now? They were grateful to him. He had proved that he was a man to be taken into account. One unexpected thing had already happened.

He said firmly, "There's something else."

"Yes?"

(How did one begin?) "There's no life in the Solar System other than the life on Earth."

"That's right," said Berg benevolently.

"And computation has it that the probability of developing any form of interstellar travel is so low as to be infinitesimal."

"What are you getting at?"

"That all this is so *in this probability*! But there must be some probability patterns in which other life *does* exist in the Solar System or in which interstellar drives *are* developed by dwellers in other star systems."

Berg frowned. "Theoretically."

"In one of these probabilities, Earth may be visited by such intelligences. If it were a probability pattern in which Earth is inhabited, it won't affect us; they'll have no connection with us in Earth proper. But if it were a probability pattern in which Earth is uninhabited and they set up some sort of a base, they may find, by happenstance, one of our dwelling places."

"Why ours?" demanded Berg dryly. "Why not a dwelling place of the Germans, for instance?"

"Because we spot our dwellings one to a world. The German Earth doesn't. Probably very few others do. The odds are in favor of us by billions to one. And if extraterrestrials do find such a dwelling, they'll investigate and find the route to Earth proper, a highly developed, rich world."

"Not if we turn off the twisting place," said Berg.

"Once they know that twisting places exist, they can construct their own," said Mishnoff. "A race intelligent enough to travel through space could do that, and from the equipment in the dwelling they would take over, they could easily spot our particular probability. . . . And then how would we handle extraterrestrials? They're not Germans, or other Earths. They would have alien psychologies and motivations. And we're not even on our guard. We just keep setting up more and more worlds and increasing the chance every day that——"

His voice had risen in excitement and Berg shouted at him, "Nonsense. This is all ridiculous——"

The buzzer sounded and the communiplate brightened

and showed the face of Ching. Ching's voice said, "I'm sorry to interrupt, but——"

"What is it?" demanded Berg savagely.

"There's a man here I don't know what to do with. He's drunk or crazy. He complains that his home is surrounded and that there are things staring through the glass roof of his garden."

"Things?" cried Mishnoff.

"Purple things with big red veins, three eyes and some sort of tentacles instead of hair. They have——"

But Mishnoff and Berg didn't hear the rest. They were staring at each other in sick horror.

# ASYLUM

## BY A. E. VAN VOGT

### I

Indecision was dark in the man's thoughts as he walked across the spaceship control room to the cot where the woman lay so taut and so still. He bent over her; he said in his deep voice:

"We're slowing down, Merla."

No answer, no movement, not a quiver in her delicate, abnormally blanched cheeks. Her fine nostrils dilated ever so slightly with each measured breath. That was all.

The Dreegh lifted her arm, then let it go. It dropped to her lap like a piece of lifeless wood, and her body remained rigid and unnatural. Carefully, he put his fingers to one eye, raised the lid, peered into it. It stared back at him, a clouded, sightless blue.

He straightened, and stood very still there in the utter silence of the hurtling ship. For a moment, then, in the intensity of his posture and in the dark ruthlessness of his lean, hard features, he seemed the veritable embodiment of grim, icy calculation.

He thought grayly: "If I revived her now, she'd have more time to attack me, and more strength. If I waited, she'd be weaker—"

Slowly, he relaxed. Some of the weariness of the years he and this woman had spent together in the dark vastness of space came to shatter his abnormal logic. Bleak sympathy touched him—and the decision was made.

He prepared an injection, and fed it into her arm. His gray eyes held a steely brightness as he put his lips near the woman's ear; in a ringing, resonant voice he said:

"We're near a star system. There'll be blood, Merla! And life!"

The woman stirred; momentarily, she seemed like a

golden-haired doll come alive. No color touched her perfectly formed cheeks, but alertness crept into her eyes. She stared up at him with a hardening hostility, half questioning.

"I've been chemical," she said—and abruptly the doll-like effect was gone. Her gaze tightened on him, and some of the prettiness vanished from her face. Her lips twisted into words:

"It's damned funny, Jeel, that you're still O.K. If I thought—"

He was cold, watchful. "Forget it," he said curtly. "You're an energy waster, and you know it. Anyway, we're going to land."

The flamelike tenseness of her faded. She sat up painfully, but there was a thoughtful look on her face as she said:

"I'm interested in the risks. This is not a Galactic planet, is it?"

"There are no Galactics out here. But there is an Observer. I've been catching the secret *ultra* signals for the last two hours"—a sardonic note entered his voice—"warning all ships to stay clear because the system isn't ready for any kind of contact with Galactic planets."

Some of the diabolic glee that was in his thoughts must have communicated through his tone. The woman stared at him, and slowly her eyes widened. She half whispered:

"You mean—"

He shrugged. "The signals ought to be registering full blast now. We'll see what degree system this is. But you can start hoping hard right now."

At the control board, he cautiously manipulated the room into darkness and set the automatics—a picture took form on a screen on the opposite wall.

At first there was only a point of light in the middle of a starry sky, then a planet floating brightly in the dark space, continents and oceans plainly visible. A voice came out of the screen:

"This star system contains one inhabited planet, the third from the sun, called Earth by its inhabitants. It was colonized by Galactics about seven thousand years ago in the usual manner. It is now in the third degree of devel-

opment, having attained a limited form of space travel
little more than a hundred years ago. It—"

With a swift movement, the man cut off the picture
and turned on the light, then looked across at the woman
in a blank, triumphant silence.

"Third degree!" he said softly, and there was an almost incredulous note in his voice. "Only third degree.
Merla, do you realize what this means? This is the opportunity of the ages. I'm going to call the Dreegh tribe.
If we can't get away with several tankers of blood and
a whole battery of 'life,' we don't deserve to be immortal. We—"

He turned toward the communicator, and for that ex-
ultant moment caution was a dim thing in the back of his
mind. From the corner of his eye, he saw the woman
flow from the edge of the cot. Too late he twisted aside.
The frantic jerk saved him only partially; it was their
cheeks, not their lips that met.

Blue flame flashed from him to her. The burning energy seared his cheek to instant, bleeding rawness. He
half fell to the floor from the shock; and then, furious
with the intense agony, he fought free.

"I'll break your bones!" he raged.

Her laughter, unlovely with her own suppressed fury,
floated up at him from the floor, where he had flung her.
She snarled:

"So you did have a secret supply of 'life' for yourself.
You damned double-crosser!"

His black mortification dimmed before the stark
realization that anger was useless. Tense with the weakness that was already a weight on his muscles, he whirled
toward the control board, and began feverishly to make
the adjustments that would pull the ship back into normal space and time.

The body urge grew in him swiftly, a dark, remorseless
need. Twice, black nausea sent him reeling to the cot;
but each time he fought back to the control board. He sat
there finally at the controls, head drooping, conscious of
the numbing tautness that crept deeper, deeper—

Almost, he drove the ship too fast. It turned a blazing
white when at last it struck the atmosphere of the third
planet. But those hard metals held their shape; and the

terrible speeds yielded to the fury of the reversers and to the pressure of the air that thickened with every receding mile.

It was the woman who helped his faltering form into the tiny lifeboat. He lay there, gathering strength, staring with tense eagerness down at the blazing sea of lights that was the first city he had seen on the night side of this strange world.

Dully, he watched as the woman carefully eased the small ship into the darkness behind a shed in a little back alley; and, because succor seemed suddenly near, sheer hope enabled him to walk beside her to the dimly lighted residential street nearby.

He would have walked on blankly into the street, but the woman's fingers held him back into the shadows of the alleyway.

"Are you mad?" she whispered. "Lie down. We'll stay right here till someone comes."

The cement was hard beneath his body, but after a moment of the painful rest it brought, he felt a faint surge of energy; and he was able to voice his bitter thought:

"If you hadn't stolen most of my carefully saved 'life,' we wouldn't be in this desperate position. You know well that it's more important that I remain at full power."

In the dark beside him, the woman lay quiet for a while; then her defiant whisper came:

"We both need a change of blood and a new charge of 'life.' Perhaps I did take a little too much out of you, but that was because I had to steal it. You wouldn't have given it to me of your own free will, and you know it."

For a time, the futility of argument held him silent, but, as the minutes dragged, that dreadful physical urgency once more tainted his thoughts, he said heavily:

"You realize of course that we've revealed our presence. We should have waited for the others to come. There's no doubt at all that our ship was spotted by the Galactic Observer in this system before we reached the outer planets. They'll have tracers on us wherever we go, and, no matter where we bury our machine, they'll know its exact location. It is impossible to hide the interstellar drive energies; and, since they wouldn't make the mistake of bringing such energies to a third-degree planet, we can't hope to locate them in that fashion.

"But we must expect an attack of some kind. I only hope one of the great Galactics doesn't take part in it."

"One of *them*!" Her whisper was a gasp, then she snapped irritably, "Don't try to scare me. You've told me time and again that—"

"All right, all right!" He spoke grudgingly, wearily. "A million years have proven that they consider us beneath their personal attention. And"—in spite of his appalling weakness, scorn came—"let any of the kind of agents they have in these lower category planets try to stop us."

"Hush!" Her whisper was tense. "Footsteps! Quick, get to your feet!"

He was aware of the shadowed form of her rising; then her hands were tugging at him. Dizzily, he stood up.

"I don't think," he began wanly, "that I can—"

"Jeel!" Her whisper beat at him; her hands shook him. "It's a man and a woman. They're 'life,' Jeel, 'life'!"

*Life!*

He straightened with a terrible effort. A spark of the unquenchable will to live that had brought him across the black miles and the blacker years, burst into flames inside him. Lightly, swiftly, he fell into step beside Merla, and strode beside her into the open. He saw the shapes of the man and the woman.

In the half-night under the trees of that street, the couple came toward them, drawing aside to let them pass; first the woman came, then the man—and it was as simple as if all his strength had been there in his muscles.

He saw Merla launch herself at the man; and then he was grabbing the woman, his head bending instantly for that abnormal kiss—

Afterward—after they had taken the blood, too— grimness came to the man, a hard fabric of thought and counterthought, that slowly formed into purpose; he said:

"We'll leave the bodies here."

Her startled whisper rose in objection, but he cut her short harshly: "Let me handle this. These dead bodies will draw to this city news gatherers, news reporters or whatever their breed are called on this planet; and we need such a person now. Somewhere in the reservoir of facts possessed by a person of this type must be clues, meaningless to him, but by which we can discover the secret base of the Galactic Observer in this system. We must find that base, discover its strength, and destroy it if necessary when the tribe comes."

His voice took on a steely note: "And now, we've got to explore this city, find a much frequented building, under which we can bury our ship, learn the language, replenish our own vital supplies—and capture that reporter.

"After I'm through with him"—his tone became silk smooth—"he will undoubtedly provide you with that physical diversion which you apparently crave when you have been particularly chemical."

He laughed gently, as her fingers gripped his arm in the darkness, a convulsive gesture; her voice came: "Thank you, Jeel, you do understand, don't you?"

## II

Behind Leigh, a door opened. Instantly the clatter of voices in the room faded to a murmur. He turned alertly, tossing his cigarette onto the marble floor, and stepping on it, all in one motion.

Overhead, the lights brightened to daylight intensity; and in that blaze he saw what the other eyes were already staring at: the two bodies, the man's and the woman's, as they were wheeled in.

The dead couple lay side by side on the flat, gleaming top of the carrier. Their bodies were rigid, their eyes closed; they looked as dead as they were, and not at all, Leigh thought, as if they were sleeping.

He caught himself making a mental note of that fact—and felt abruptly shocked.

The first murders on the North American continent in twenty-seven years. And it was only another job. By Heaven, he was tougher than he'd ever believed.

He grew aware that the voices had stopped completely. The only sound was the hoarse breathing of the man nearest him—and then the scrape of his own shoes as he went forward.

His movement acted like a signal on that tense group of men. There was a general pressing forward. Leigh had a moment of hard anxiety; and then his bigger, harder muscles brought him where he wanted to be, opposite the two heads.

He leaned forward in dark absorption. His fingers probed gingerly the neck of the woman, where the incisions showed. He did not look up at the attendant, as he said softly:

"This is where the blood was drained?"

"Yes."

Before he could speak again, another reporter interjected: "Any special comment from the police scientists? The murders are more than a day old now. There ought to be something new."

Leigh scarcely heard. The woman's body, electrically warmed for embalming, felt eerily lifelike to his touch. It was only after a long moment that he noticed her lips were badly, almost brutally bruised.

His gaze flicked to the man; and there were the same neck cuts, the same torn lips. He looked up, questions quivered on his tongue—and remained unspoken as realization came that the calm-voiced attendant was still talking. The man was saying:

"—normally, when the electric embalmers are applied, there is resistance from the static electricity of the body. Curiously, that resistance was not present in either body."

Somebody said: "Just what does that mean?"

"This static force is actually a form of life force, which usually trickles out of a corpse over a period of a month. We know of no way to hasten the process, but the bruises on the lips show distinct burns, which are suggestive."

There was a craning of necks, a crowding forward; and Leigh allowed himself to be pushed aside. He stopped attentively, as the attendant said: "Presumably, a pervert could have kissed with such violence."

"I thought," Leigh called distinctly, "there were no more perverts since Professor Ungarn persuaded the government to institute his brand of mechanical psychology in all schools, thus ending murder, theft, war and all unsocial perversions."

The attendant in his black frock coat hesitated; then: "A very bad one seems to have been missed."

He finished: "That's all, gentlemen. No clues, no promise of an early capture, and only this final fact: We've wirelessed Professor Ungarn and, by great good fortune, we caught him on his way to Earth from his meteorite retreat near Jupiter. He'll be landing shortly after dark, in a few hours now."

The lights dimmed. As Leigh stood frowning, watching the bodies being wheeled out, a phrase floated out of the gathering chorus of voices:

"—The kiss of death—"

"I tell you," another voice said, "the captain of this space liner swears it happened—the spaceship came past him at a million miles an hour, and it was slowing down, get that, slowing down—two days ago."

"—The vampire case! That's what I'm going to call it—"

That's what Leigh called it, too, as he talked briefly into his wrist communicator. He finished: "I'm going to supper now, Jim."

"O. K., Bill." The local editor's voice came metallically. "And say, I'm supposed to commend you. Nine thousand papers took the Planetarian Service on this story, as compared with about forty-seven hundred who bought from Universal, who got the second largest coverage.

"And I think you've got the right angle for today also. Husband and wife, ordinary young couple, taking an evening's walk. Some devil hauls up alongside them, drains their blood into a tank, their life energy onto a wire or something—people will believe that, I guess. Anyway, you suggest it could happen to anybody; so be careful, folks. And you warn that, in these days of interplanetary speeds, he could be anywhere tonight for his next murder.

"As I said before, good stuff. That'll keep the story frying hard for tonight. Oh, by the way—"

"Shoot!"

"A kid called half an hour ago to see you. Said you expected him."

"A kid?" Leigh frowned to himself.

"Name of Patrick. High school age, about sixteen. No, come to think of it, that was only my first impression. Eighteen, maybe twenty, very bright, confident, proud."

"I remember now," said Leigh, "college student. Interview for a college paper. Called me up this afternoon.

One of those damned persuasive talkers. Before I knew
it, I was signed up for supper at Constantine's."

"That's right. I was supposed to remind you. O. K.?"
Leigh shrugged. "I promised," he said.

Actually, as he went out into the blaze of late afternoon, sunlit street, there was not a thought in his head.
Nor a premonition.

Around him, the swarm of humankind began to thicken.
Vast buildings discharged the first surge of the five o'clock
tidal wave—and twice Leigh felt the tug at his arm before
it struck him that someone was not just bumping him.

He turned, and stared down at a pair of dark, eager
eyes set in a brown, wizened face. The little man waved a
sheaf of papers at him. Leigh caught a glimpse of writing
in longhand on the papers. Then the fellow was babbling:

"Mr. Leigh, hundred dollars for these . . . biggest
story—"

"Oh," said Leigh. His interest collapsed; then his mind
roused itself from its almost blank state; and pure politeness made him say: "Take it up to the Planetarian office.
Jim Brian will pay you what the story is worth."

He walked on, the vague conviction in his mind that
the matter was settled. Then, abruptly, there was the
tugging at his arm again.

"Scoop!" the little man was muttering. "Professor
Ungarn's log, all about a spaceship that came from the
stars. Devils in it who drink blood and kiss people to
death!"

"See here!" Leigh began, irritated; and then he stopped
physically and mentally. A strange ugly chill swept through
him. He stood there, swaying a little from the shock of
the thought that was frozen in his brain:

*The newspapers with those details of "blood" and "kiss"
were not on the street yet, wouldn't be for another five
minutes.*

The man was saying: "Look, it's got Professor Ungarn's
name printed in gold on the top of each sheet, and it's all
about how he first spotted the ship eighteen light years
out, and how it came all that distance in a few hours . . .
and he knows where it is now and—"

Leigh heard, but that was all. His reporter's brain, that
special, highly developed department, was whirling with

a little swarm of thoughts that suddenly straightened into a hard, bright pattern; and in that tightly built design, there was no room for any such brazen coincidence as this man coming to him here in this crowded street.

He said: "Let me see those!" And reached as he spoke.

The papers came free from the other's fingers into his hands, but Leigh did not even glance at them. His brain was crystal-clear, his eyes cold; he snapped:

"I don't know what game you're trying to pull. I want to know three things, and make your answers damned fast! One: How did you pick me out, name and job and all, here in this packed street of a city I haven't been in for a year?"

He was vaguely aware of the little man trying to speak, stammering incomprehensible words. But he paid no attention. Remorselessly, he pounded on:

"Two: Professor Ungarn is arriving from Jupiter in three hours. How do you explain your possession of papers he must have written, less than two days ago?"

"Look, boss," the man chattered, "you've got me all wrong—"

"My third question," Leigh said grimly, "is how are you going to explain to the police your pre-knowledge of the details of—murder?"

"Huh!" The little man's eyes were glassy, and for the first time pity came to Leigh. He said almost softly:

"All right, fellah, start talking."

The words came swiftly, and at first they were simply senseless sounds; only gradually did coherence come.

"—And that's the way it was, boss. I'm standing there, and this kid comes up to me and points you out, and gives me five bucks and those papers you've got, and tells me what I'm supposed to say to you and—"

"Kid!" said Leigh; and the first shock was already in him.

"Yeah, kid about sixteen; no, more like eighteen or twenty . . . and he gives me the papers and—"

"This kid," said Leigh, "would you say he was of college age?"

"That's it, boss; you've got it. That's just what he was. You know him, eh? O. K., that leaves me in the clear, and I'll be going—"

"Wait!" Leigh called, but the little man seemed suddenly to realize that he need only run, for he jerked into a mad pace; and people stared, and that was all. He vanished around a corner, and was gone forever.

Leigh stood, frowning, reading the thin sheaf of papers. And there was nothing beyond what the little man had already conveyed by his incoherent word of mouth, simply a vague series of entries on sheets from a looseleaf notebook.

Written down, the tale about the spaceship and its occupants lacked depth, and seemed more unconvincing each passing second. True, there was the single word "Ungarn" inscribed in gold on the top of each sheet but—

Leigh shook himself. The sense of silly hoax grew so violently that he thought with abrupt anger: If that damned fool college kid really pulled a stunt like—

The thought ended; for the idea was as senseless as everything that had happened.

And still there was no real tension in him. He was only going to a restaurant.

He turned into the splendid foyer that was the beginning of the vast and wonderful Constantine's. In the great doorway, he paused for a moment to survey the expansive glitter of tables, the hanging garden tearooms; and it was all there.

Brilliant Constantine's, famous the world over—but not much changed from his last visit.

Leigh gave his name, and began: "A Mr. Patrick made reservations, I understand—"

The girl cut him short. "Oh, yes, Mr. Leigh. Mr. Patrick reserved Private 3 for you. He just now phoned to say he'd be along in a few minutes. Our premier will escort you."

Leigh was turning away, a vague puzzled thought in his mind at the way the girl had gushed, when a flamelike thought struck him: "Just a minute, did you say *Private 3?* Who's paying for this?"

The girl glowed at him: "It was paid by phone. Forty-five hundred dollars!"

Leigh stood very still. In a single, flashing moment, this meeting that, even after what had happened on the street, had seemed scarcely more than an irritation to be gotten over with, was become a fantastic, abnormal thing.

Forty-five—hundred—dollars! Could it be some damned fool rich kid sent by a college paper, but who had pulled this whole affair because he was determined to make a strong, personal impression?

Coldly, alertly, his brain rejected the solution. Humanity produced egoists on an elephantiastic scale, but not one who would order a feast like that to impress a reporter.

His eyes narrowed on an idea: "Where's your registered phone?" he asked curtly.

A minute later, he was saying into the mouthpiece: "Is that the Amalgamated Universities Secretariat? . . . I want to find out if there is a Mr. Patrick registered at any of your local colleges, and, if there is, whether or not he has been authorized by any college paper to interview William Leigh of the Planetarian News Service. This is Leigh calling."

It took six minutes, and then the answer came, brisk, tremendous and final: "There are three Mr. Patricks in our seventeen units. All are at present having supper at their various official residences. There are four Miss Patricks similarly accounted for by our staff of secretaries. None of these seven is in any way connected with a university paper. Do you wish any assistance in dealing with the impostor?"

Leigh hesitated; and when he finally spoke, it was with the queer, dark realization that he was committing himself. "No," he said, and hung up.

He came out of the phone box, shaken by his own thoughts. There was only one reason why he was in this city at this time. Murder! And he knew scarcely a soul. Therefore—

It was absolutely incredible that any stranger would want to see him for a reason not connected with his own purpose. He shook the ugly thrill out of his system; he said:

"To Private 3, please—"

Tensed but cool, he examined the apartment that was Private 3. Actually that was all it was, a splendidly furnished apartment with a palacelike dining salon dominating the five rooms, and one entire wall of the salon was lined with decorated mirror facings, behind which glittered hundreds of bottles of liquors.

The brands were strange to his inexpensive tastes, the scent of several that he opened heady and—quite uninviting. In the ladies' dressing room was a long showcase displaying a gleaming array of jewelry—several hundred thousand dollars' worth, if it was genuine, he estimated swiftly.

Leigh whistled softly to himself. On the surface, Constantine's appeared to supply good rental value for the money they charged.

"I'm glad you're physically big," said a cool voice behind him. "So many reporters are thin and small."

It was the voice that did it, subtly, differently toned than it had been over the phone in the early afternoon. Deliberately different.

The difference, he noted as he turned, was in the body, too, the difference in the shape of a woman from a boy, skillfully but not perfectly concealed under the well-tailored man's suit—actually, of course, she was quite boyish in build, young, finely molded.

And, actually, he would never have suspected if she had not allowed her voice to be so purposefully womanish. She echoed his thought coolly:

"Yes, I wanted you to know. But now, there's no use wasting words. You know as much as you need to know. Here's a gun. The spaceship is buried below this building."

Leigh made no effort to take the weapon, nor did he even glance at it. Instead, cool now, that the first shock was over, he seated himself on the silk-yielding chair of the vanity dresser in one corner, leaned heavily back against the vanity itself, raised his eyebrows, and said:

"Consider me a slow-witted lunk who's got to know what it's all about. Why so much preliminary hocus-pocus?"

He thought deliberately: He had never in his adult life allowed himself to be rushed into anything. He was not going to start now.

### III

The girl, he saw after a moment, was small of build. Which was odd, he decided carefully. Because his first impression had been of reasonable length of body. Or perhaps—he considered the possibility unhurriedly—this second effect was a more considered result of her male disguise.

He dismissed that particular problem as temporarily insoluble, and because actually—it struck him abruptly—this girl's size was unimportant. She had long, black lashes and dark eyes that glowed at him from a proud, almost haughty face. And that was it; quite definitely that was the essence of her blazing, powerful personality.

Pride was in the way she held her head. It was in the poised easiness of every movement, the natural shift from grace to grace as she walked slowly toward him. Not conscious pride here, but an awareness of superiority that affected every movement of her muscles, and came vibrantly into her voice, as she said scathingly:

"I picked you because every newspaper I've read today carried your account of the murders, and because it seemed to me that somebody who already was actively working on the case would be reasonably quick at grasping essentials. As for the dramatic preparation, I considered that would be more convincing than drab explanation. I see I was mistaken in all these assumptions."

She was quite close to him now. She leaned over, laid her revolver on the vanity beside his arm, and finished almost indifferently:

"Here's an effective weapon. It doesn't shoot bullets, but it has a trigger and you aim it like any gun. In the event you develop the beginning of courage, come down the tunnel after me as quickly as possible, but don't blunder in on me and the people I shall be talking to. Stay hidden! Act only if I'm threatened."

Tunnel, Leigh thought stolidly, as she walked with a free, swift stride out of the room—tunnel here in this apartment called Private 3. Either he was crazy, or she was.

Quite suddenly, realization came that he ought to be offended at the way she had spoken. And that insultingly simple come-on trick of hers, leaving the room, leaving him to develop curiosity—he smiled ruefully; if he hadn't been a reporter, he'd show her that such a second-rate psychology didn't work on him.

Still annoyed, he climbed to his feet, took the gun, and then paused briefly as the odd, muffled sound came of a door opening reluctantly—

* * *

He found her in the bedroom to the left of the dining salon; and because his mind was still in that state of pure receptiveness, which, for him, replaced indecisiveness, he felt only the vaguest surprise to see that she had the end of a lush green rug rolled back, and that there was a hole in the floor at her feet.

The gleaming square of floor that must have covered the opening lay back neatly, pinned to position by a single, glitteringly complicated hinge. But Leigh scarcely noticed that.

His gaze reached beyond that—tunnel—to the girl; and, in that moment, just before she became aware of him, there was the barest suggestion of uncertainty about her. And her right profile, half turned away from him, showed pursed lips, a strained whiteness, as if—

The impression he received was of indecisiveness. He had the subtle sense of observing a young woman who, briefly, had lost her superb confidence. Then she saw him; and his whole emotion picture twisted.

She didn't seem to stiffen in any way. Paying no attention to him at all, she stepped down to the first stair of the little stairway that led down into the hole, and began to descend without a quiver of hesitation. And yet—

Yet his first conviction that she had faltered brought him forward with narrowed eyes. And, suddenly, that certainty of her brief fear made this whole madness real. He plunged forward, down the steep stairway, and pulled up only when he saw that he was actually in a smooth, dimly lighted tunnel; and that the girl had paused, one finger to her lips.

"Sssshh!" she said. "The door of the ship may be open."

Irritation struck Leigh, a hard trickle of anger. Now that he had committed himself, he felt automatically the leader of this fantastic expedition; and that girl's pretensions, the devastating haughtiness of her merely produced his first real impatience.

"Don't 'ssshh me'!" he whispered sharply. "Just give me the facts, and I'll do the rest."

He stopped. For the first time the meaning of all the words she had spoken penetrated. His anger collapsed like a plane in a crash landing.

"Ship!" he said incredulously. "Are you trying to tell me there's actually a spaceship buried here under Constantine's?"

The girl seemed not to hear; and Leigh saw that they were at the end of a short passageway. Metal gleamed dully just ahead. Then the girl was saying:

"Here's the door. Now, remember, you act as guard. Stay hidden, ready to shoot. And if I yell 'Shoot,' you shoot!"

She bent forward. There was the tiniest scarlet flash. The door opened, revealing a second door just beyond. Again that minute, intense blaze of red; and that door too swung open.

It was swiftly done, too swiftly. Before Leigh could more than grasp that the crisis was come, the girl stepped coolly into the brilliantly lighted room beyond the second door.

There was shadow where Leigh stood half-paralyzed by the girl's action. There was deeper shadow against the metal wall toward which he pressed himself in one instinctive move. He froze there, cursing silently at a stupid young woman who actually walked into a den of enemies of unknown numbers without a genuine plan of self-protection.

Or did she know how many there were? And who?

The questions made twisting paths in his mind down, down to a thrall of blankness—that ended only when an entirely different thought replaced it:

At least he was out here with a gun, unnoticed— or was he?

He waited tensely. But the door remained open; and there was no apparent movement towards it. Slowly, Leigh let himself relax, and allowed his straining mind to absorb its first considered impressions.

The portion of underground room that he could see showed one end of what seemed to be a control board, a metal wall that blinked with tiny lights, the edge of a rather sumptuous cot—and the whole was actually so suggestive of a spaceship that Leigh's logic-resistance collapsed.

Incredibly, here under the ground, actually *under* Constantine's was a small spaceship and—

That thought ended, too, as the silence beyond the open door, the curiously long silence, was broken by a man's cool voice:

"I wouldn't even try to raise that gun if I were you. The fact that you have said nothing since entering shows how enormously different we are to what you expected."

He laughed gently, an unhurried, deep-throated derisive laughter that came clearly to Leigh. The man said:

"Merla, what would you say is the psychology behind this young lady's action? You have of course noticed that she is a young lady, and not a boy."

A richly toned woman's voice replied: "She was born here, Jeel. She has none of the normal characteristics of a Klugg, but she is a Galactic, though definitely not the Galactic Observer. Probably, she's not alone. Shall I investigate?"

"No!" The man sounded indifferent to the tensing Leigh. "We don't have to worry about a Klugg's assistant."

Leigh relaxed slowly, but there was a vast uneasiness in his solar nerves, a sense of emptiness, the first realization of how great a part the calm assurance of the young woman had played in the fabricating of his own basic confidence.

Shattered now! Before the enormous certainties of these two, and in the face of their instant penetration of her male disguise, the effects of the girl's rather wonderful personality seemed a remote pattern, secondary, definitely overwhelmed.

He forced the fear from him, as the girl spoke; forced his courage to grow with each word she uttered, feeding on the haughty and immense confidence that was there. It didn't matter whether she was simulating or not, because they were in this now, he as deep as she; and only the utmost boldness could hope to draw a fraction of victory from the defeat that loomed so starkly.

With genuine admiration, he noted the glowing intensity of her speech, as she said:

"My silence had its origin in the fact that you are the first Dreeghs I have ever seen. Naturally, I studied you with some curiosity, but I can assure you I am not impressed.

"However, in view of your extraordinary opinions on

the matter, I shall come to the point at once: I have been instructed by the Galactic Observer of this system to inform you to be gone by morning. Our sole reason for giving you that much leeway is that we don't wish to bring the truth of all this into the open.

"But don't count on that. Earth is on the verge of being given fourth-degree rating; and, as you probably know, in emergencies fourths are given Galactic knowledge. That emergency we will consider to have arrived tomorrow at dawn."

"Well, well"—the man was laughing gently, satirically —"a pretty speech, powerfully spoken, but meaningless for us who can analyze its pretensions, however sincere, back to the Klugg origin."

"What do you intend with her, Jeel?"

The man was cold, deadly, utterly sure. "There's no reason why she should escape. She had blood and more than normal life. It will convey to the Observer with clarity our contempt for his ultimatum."

He finished with a slow, surprisingly rich laughter: "We shall now enact a simple drama. The young lady will attempt to jerk up her gun and shoot me with it. Before she can even begin to succeed, I shall have my own weapon out and firing. The whole thing, as she will discover, is a matter of nervous co-ordination. And Kluggs are chronically almost as slow-moving as human beings."

His voice stopped. His laughter trickled away.

Silence.

In all his alert years, Leigh had never felt more indecisive. His emotions said—*now*; surely, she'd call now. And even if she didn't, he must act on his own. Rush in! Shoot!

But his mind was cold with an awful dread. There was something about the man's voice, a surging power, a blazing, incredible certainty. Abnormal, savage strength was here; and if this was really a spaceship from the stars—

His brain wouldn't follow that flashing, terrible thought. He crouched, fingering the gun she had given him, dimly conscious for the first time that it felt queer, unlike any revolver he'd ever had.

He crouched stiffly, waiting—and the silence from the

spaceship control room, from the tensed figures that must be there just beyond his line of vision, continued. The same curious silence that had followed the girl's entrance short minutes before. Only this time it was the girl who broke it, her voice faintly breathless but withal cool, vibrant, unafraid:

"I'm here to warn, not to force issues. And unless you're charged with the life energy of fifteen men, I wouldn't advise you to try anything either. After all, I came here knowing what you were."

"What do you think, Merla? Can we be sure she's a Klugg? Could she possibly be of the higher Lennel type?"

It was the man, his tone conceding her point, but the derision was still there, the implacable purpose, the high, tremendous confidence.

And yet, in spite of that unrelenting sense of imminent violence, Leigh felt himself torn from the thought of her danger—and his. His reporter's brian twisted irresistibly to the fantastic meaning of what was taking place:

—*Life energy of fifteen men*—

It was all there; in a monstrous way it all fitted. The two dead bodies he had seen drained of blood and *life energy*, the repeated reference to a Galactic Observer, with whom the girl was connected.

Leigh thought almost blankly: Galactic meant—well— Galactic; and that was so terrific that—He grew aware that the woman was speaking:

"Klugg!" she said positively. "Pay no attention to her protestations, Jeel. You know, I'm sensitive when it comes to women. She's lying. She's just a little fool who walked in here expecting us to be frightened of her. Destroy her at your pleasure."

"I'm not given to waiting," said the man. "So—"

Quite automatically, Leigh leaped for the open door-way. He had a flashing glimpse of a man and woman, dressed in evening clothes, the man standing, the woman seated. There was awareness of a gleaming, metallic background, the control board, part of which he had already seen, now revealed as a massive thing of glowing instruments; and then all that blotted out as he snapped:

"That will do. Put up your hands."

For a long, dazzling moment he had the impression

that his entry was a complete surprise; and that he dominated the situation. None of the three people in the room
was turned toward him. The man, Jeel, and the girl were
standing, facing each other; the woman, Merla, sat in a
deep chair, her fine profile to him, her golden head flung
back.

It was she who, still without looking at him, sneered
visibly—and spoke the words that ended his brief conviction of triumph. She said to the disguised girl:

"You certainly travel in low company, a stupid human
being. Tell him to go away before he's damaged."

The girl said: "Leigh, I'm sorry I brought you into this.
Every move you made in entering was heard, observed
and dismissed before you could even adjust your mind to
the scene."

"Is his name Leigh?" said the woman sharply. "I thought
I recognized him as he entered. He's very like his photograph over his newspaper column." Her voice grew
strangely tense: "Jeel, a newspaper reporter!"

"We don't need him now," the man said. "We know
who the Galactic Observer is."

"Eh?" said Leigh; his mind fastened hard on those
amazing words. "Who? How did you find out? What—"

"The information," said the woman; and it struck him
suddenly that the strange quality in her voice was eagerness, "will be of no use to you. Regardless of what
happens to the girl, you're staying."

She glanced swiftly at the man, as if seeking his sanc-
tion. "Remember, Jeel, you promised."

It was all quite senseless, so meaningless that Leigh
had no sense of personal danger. His mind scarcely more
than passed the words; his eyes concentrated tautly on a
reality that had, until that moment, escaped his awareness. He said softly:

"Just now you used the phrase, 'Regardless of what
happens to the girl.' When I came in, you said, 'Tell him
to go away before he's damaged.' "

Leigh smiled grimly: "I need hardly say this is a far cry
from the threat of immediate death that hung over us a
few seconds ago. And I have just now noticed the reason.

"A little while ago, I heard our pal, Jeel, dare my little
girl friend here to raise her gun. I notice now that *she
has it raised*. My entrance did have an effect." He ad-

dressed himself to the girl, finished swiftly: "Shall we shoot—or withdraw?"

It was the man who answered: "I would advise withdrawal. I could still win, but I am not the heroic type who takes the risk of what might well be a close call."

He added, in an aside to the woman: "Merla, we can always catch this man, Leigh, now that we know who he is."

The girl said: "You first, Mr. Leigh." And Leigh did not stop to argue.

Metal doors clanged behind him, as he charged along the tunnel. After a moment, he was aware of the girl running lightly beside him.

The strangely unreal, the unbelievably murderous little drama was over, finished as fantastically as it had begun.

## IV

Outside Constantine's a gray light gathered around them. A twilight side street it was, and people hurried past them with the strange, anxious look of the late for supper. Night was falling.

Leigh stared at his companion; in the dimness of the deep dusk, she seemed all boy, slightly, lithely built, striding along boldly. He laughed a little, huskily, then more grimly:

"Just what was all that? Did we escape by the skin of our teeth? Or did we win? What made you think you could act like God, and give those tough eggs twelve hours to get out of the Solar System?"

The girl was silent after he had spoken. She walked just ahead of him, head bent into the gloom. Abruptly, she turned; she said:

"I hope you will have no nonsensical idea of telling what you've seen or heard."

Leigh said: "This is the biggest story since—"

"Look"—the girl's voice was pitying—"you're not going to print a word because in about ten seconds you'll see that no one in the world would believe the first paragraph."

In the darkness, Leigh smiled tightly: "The mechanical psychologist will verify every syllable."

"I came prepared for that, too!" said the vibrant voice.

Her hand swung up, toward his face, too late, he jerked back.

Light flared in his eyes, a dazzling, blinding force that exploded into his sensitive optic nerves with all the agonizing power of intolerable brightness. Leigh cursed aloud, wildly, and snatched forward toward his tormentor. His right hand grazed a shoulder. He lashed out violently with his left, and tantalizingly caught only the edge of a sleeve that instantly jerked away.

"You little devil!" he raged futilely. "You've blinded me."

"You'll be all right," came the cool answer, "but you'll find that the mechanical psychologist will report anything you say as the purest imagination. In view of your threat to publish, I had to do that. Now, give me my gun."

The first glimmer of sight was returning. Leigh could see her body, a dim, wavering shape in the night. In spite of the continuing pain, Leigh smiled grimly. He said softly:

"I've just now remembered you said this gun didn't shoot bullets. Even the *feel* of it suggests that it'll make an interesting proof of anything I say. So—"

His smile faded abruptly. For the girl stepped forward. The metal that jabbed into his ribs was so hardly thrust, it made him grunt.

*"Give me that gun!"*

"Like fun I will," Leigh snapped. "You ungrateful little ruffian, how dare you treat me so shoddily after I saved your life? I ought to knock you one right on the jaw for—"

He stopped—stopped because with staggering suddenness the hard, hard realization struck that she meant it. This was no girl raised in a refined school, who wouldn't dare to shoot, but a cold-blooded young creature, who had already proved the metalliclike fabric of which her courage was made.

He had never had any notions about the superiority of man over woman; and he felt none now. Without a single word, almost hastily, he handed the weapon over. The girl took it, and said coldly:

"You seem to be laboring under the illusion that your entry into the spaceship enabled me to raise my weapon. You're quite mistaken. What you did do was to provide me with the opportunity to let them think that that was the situation, and that they dominated it. But I assure you, this is the extent of your assistance, almost valueless."

Leigh laughed out loud, a pitying, ridiculing laugh.

"In my admittedly short life," he said laconically, "I've learned to recognize a quality of personality and magnetism in human beings. You've got it, a lot of it, but not a fraction of what either of those two had, particularly the man. He was terrible. He was absolutely the most abnormally magnetic human being I've ever run across. Lady, I can only guess what all this is about, but I'd advise you"—Leigh paused, then finished slashingly—"you and all the other Kluggs to stay away from that couple.

"Personally, I'm going to get the police in on this, and there's going to be a raid on Private 3. I didn't like that odd threat that they could capture me any time. Why me—"

He broke off hastily: "Hey, where are you going? I want to know your name. I want to know what made you think you could order those two around. *Who did you think you were?*"

He said no more, his whole effort concentrated on running. He could see her for a moment, a hazy, boyish figure against a dim corner light. Then she was around the corner.

His only point of contact with all this; and if she got away—

Sweating, he rounded the corner; and at first the street seemed dark and empty of life. Then he saw the car.

A normal-looking, high-hooded coupe, long, low-built, that began to move forward noiselessly and—quite normally.

It became abnormal. It lifted. Amazingly, it lifted from the ground. He had a swift glimpse of white rubber wheels folding out of sight. Streamlined, almost cigar-shaped now, the spaceship that had been a car darted at a steep angle into the sky.

Instantly it was gone.

Above Leigh, the gathering night towered, a strange, bright blue. In spite of the brilliant lights of the city glaring into the sky, one or two stars showed. He stared up at them, empty inside, thinking: "It was like a dream.

Those—Dreeghs—coming out of space—bloodsuckers, vampires."

Suddenly hungry, he bought a chocolate from a sidewalk stand, and stood munching it.

He began to feel better. He walked over to a nearby wall socket, and plugged in his wrist radio.

"Jim," he said. "I've got some stuff, not for publication, but maybe we can get some police action on it. Then I want you to have a mechanical psychologist sent to my hotel room. There must be some memory that can be salvaged from my brain—"

He went on briskly. His sense of inadequacy waned notably. Reporter Leigh was himself again.

## V

The little glistening balls of the mechanical psychologist were whirring faster, faster. They became a single, glowing circle in the darkness. And not till then did the first, delicious whiff of psycho-gas touch his nostrils. He felt himself drifting, slipping—

A voice began to speak in the dim distance, so far away that not a word came through. There was only the sound, the faint, curious sound, and the feeling, stronger every instant, that he would soon be able to hear the fascinating things it seemed to be saying.

The longing to hear, to become a part of the swelling, murmuring sound drew his whole being in little rhythmical, wavelike surges. And still the promise of meaning was unfulfilled.

Other, private thoughts ended utterly. Only the mindless chant remained, and the pleasing gas holding him so close to sleep, its flow nevertheless so delicately adjusted that his mind hovered minute after minute on the ultimate abyss of consciousness.

He lay, finally, still partially awake, but even the voice was merging now into blackness. It clung for a while, a gentle, friendly, melodious sound in the remote background of his brain, becoming more remote with each passing instant. He slept, a deep, hypnotic sleep, as the machine purred on—

When Leigh opened his eyes, the bedroom was dark except for the floor lamp beside a corner chair. It illuminated the darkly dressed woman who sat there, all except her face, which was in shadow above the circle of light.

He must have moved, for the shadowed head suddenly looked up from some sheets of typewriter-size paper. The voice of Merla, the Dreegh, said:

"The girl did a very good job of erasing your subconscious memories. There's only one possible clue to her identity and—"

Her words went on, but his brain jangled them to senselessness in that first horrible shock of recognition. It was too much, too much fear in too short a time. For a brief, terrible moment, he was like a child, and strange, cunning, *intense* thoughts of escape came:

If he could slide to the side of the bed, away from where she was sitting, and run for the bathroom door—

"Surely, Mr. Leigh," the woman's voice reached toward him, "you know better than to try anything foolish. And, surely, if I had intended to kill you, I would have done it much more easily while you were asleep."

Leigh lay very still, gathering his mind back into his head, licking dry lips. Her words were utterly unreassuring. "What—do—you—want?" he managed finally.

"Information!" Laconically. "What was that girl?"

"I don't know." He stared into the half gloom, where her face was. His eyes were more accustomed to the light now, and he could catch the faint, golden glint of her hair. "I thought—you knew."

He went on more swiftly: "I thought you knew the Galactic Observer; and that implied the girl could be identified any time."

He had the impression she was smiling. She said:

"Our statement to that effect was designed to throw both you and the girl off guard, and constituted the partial victory we snatched from what had become an impossible situation."

The body sickness was still upon Leigh, but the desperate fear that had produced it was fading before the implications of her confession of weakness, the realization that these Dreeghs were not so superhuman as he had thought. Relief was followed by caution. Careful, he warned himself, it wouldn't be wise to underestimate. But he couldn't help saying:

"So you weren't so smart. And I'd like to point out that even your so-called snatching of victory from defeat was not so well done. Your husband's statement that you could pick me up any time could easily have spoiled the picking."

The woman's voice was cool, faintly contemptuous. "If you knew anything of psychology, you would realize that the vague phrasing of the threat actually lulled you. Certainly, you failed to take even minimum precautions. And the girl has definitely not made any effort to protect you."

The suggestion of deliberately subtle tactics brought to Leigh a twinge of returning alarm. Deep, deep inside him was the thought: What ending did the Dreegh woman plan for this strange meeting?

"You realize, of course," the Dreegh said softly, "that you will either be of value to us alive—or dead. There are no easy alternatives. I would advise alertness and utmost sincerity in your co-operation. You are in this affair without limit."

So that was the plan. A thin bead of perspiration trickled down Leigh's cheek. And his fingers trembled as he reached for a cigarette on the table beside the bed.

He was shakily lighting the cigarette when his gaze fastened on the window. That brought a faint shock, for it was raining, a furious rain that hammered soundlessly against the noise-proof glass.

He pictured the bleak, empty streets, their brilliance dulled by the black, rain-filled night; and, strangely, the mind picture unnerved him.

Deserted streets—deserted Leigh. For he was deserted here; all the friends he had, scattered over the great reaches of the earth, couldn't add one ounce of strength, or bring one real ray of hope to him in this darkened room, against this woman who sat so calmly under the light, studying him from shadowed eyes.

With a sharp effort, Leigh steadied himself. He said: "I gather that's my psychograph report you have in your hand. What does it say?"

"Very disappointing." Her voice seemed far away. "There's a warning in it about your diet. It seems your meals are irregular."

She was playing with him. The heavy attempt at humor

made her seem more inhuman, not less; for, somehow, the words clashed unbearably with the reality of her; the dark immensity of space across which she had come, the unnatural lusts that had brought her and the man to this literally unprotected Earth.

. Leigh shivered. Then he thought fiercely: "Damn it, I'm scaring myself. So long as she stays in her chair, she can't pull the vampire on me."

The harder thought came that it was no use being frightened. He'd better simply be himself, and await events. Aloud, he said:

"If there's nothing in the psychograph, then I'm afraid I can't help you. You might as well leave. Your presence isn't making me any happier."

In a dim way, he hoped she'd laugh. But she didn't. She sat there, her eyes glinting dully out of the gloom. At last, she said:

"We'll go through this report together. I think we can safely omit the references to your health as being irrelevant. But there are a number of factors that I want developed. Who is Professor Ungarn?"

"A scientist." Leigh spoke frankly. "He invented this system of mechanical hypnosis, and he was called in when the dead bodies were found because the killings seemed to have been done by perverts."

"Have you any knowledge of his physical appearance?"

"I've never seen him," Leigh said more slowly. "He never gives interviews, and his photograph is not available now. I've heard stories, but—"

He hesitated. It wasn't, he thought frowning, as if he was giving what was not general knowledge. What was the woman getting at, anyway? Ungarn—

"These stories," she said, "do they give the impression that he's a man of inordinate magnetic force, but with lines of mental suffering etched in his face, and a sort of resignation?"

"Resignation to what?" Leigh exclaimed sharply. "I haven't the faintest idea what you're talking about. I've only seen photographs, and they show a fine, rather sensitive, tired face."

She said: "There would be more information in any library?"

"Or in the Planetarian Service morgue," Leigh said, and could have bitten off his tongue for that bit of gratuitous information.

"Morgue?" said the woman.

Leigh explained, but his voice was trembling with self-rage. For seconds now the feeling had been growing on him: Was it possible this devilish woman was on the right track? And getting damaging answers out of him because he dared not stop and organize for lying.

Even as savage anxiety came, he had an incongruous sense of the unfairness of the abnormally swift way she had solved the Observer's identity because, damn it, damn it, it could be Professor Ungarn.

Ungarn, the mystery scientist, great inventor in a dozen highly complicated, widely separated fields; and there was that mysterious meteorite home near one of Jupiter's moons and he had a daughter, named Patricia. Good heavens, Patrick—Patricia—

His shaky stream of thoughts ended, as the woman said:

"Can you have your office send the information to your recorder here?"

"Y-yes!" His reluctance was so obvious that the woman bent into the light. For a moment, her golden hair glittered; her pale-blue eyes glowed at him in a strangely humorless, satanic amusement.

"Ah!" she said, "you think so, too?"

She laughed, an odd, musical laugh—odd in that it was at once so curt and so pleasant. The laugh ended abruptly, unnaturally, on a high note. And then—although he had not seen her move—there was a metal thing in her hand, pointing at him. Her voice came at him, with a brittle, jarring command:

"You will climb out of the bed, operate the recorder, and naturally you will do nothing, *say* nothing but what is necessary."

Leigh felt genuinely dizzy. The room swayed; and he thought sickly: If he could only faint.

But he recognized dismally that that was beyond the power of his tough body. It was sheer mental dismay that made his nerves so shivery. And even that faded like fog in strong sunlight, as he walked to the recorder. For the first time in his life, he hated the resilience of strength that made his voice steady as a rock, as, after setting the machine, he said:

"This is William Leigh. Give me all the dope you've got on Professor Garret Ungarn."

There was a pause, during which he thought hopelessly: "It wasn't as if he was giving information not otherwise accessible. Only—"

There was a click in the machine; then a brisk voice: "You've got it. Sign the form."

Leigh signed, and watched the signature dissolve into the machine. It was then, as he was straightening, that the woman said:

"Shall I read it here, Jeel, or shall we take the machine along?"

That was mind-wrecking. Like a man possessed, Leigh whirled; and then, very carefully, he sat down on the bed.

The Dreegh, Jeel, was leaning idly against the jamb of the bathroom door, a dark, malignantly handsome man, with a faint, unpleasant smile on his lips. Behind him—incredibly, behind him, through the open bathroom door was, not the gleaming bath, but another door; and beyond that door still another door, and beyond that—

The control room of the Dreegh spaceship!

There it was, exactly as he had seen it in the solid ground under Constantine's. He had the same partial view of the sumptuous cot, the imposing section of instrument board, at the tastefully padded floor—

*In his bathroom!*

The insane thought came to Leigh: "Oh, yes, I keep my spaceship in my bathroom and—" It was the Dreegh's voice that drew his brain from its dizzy contemplation; the Dreegh saying:

"I think we'd better leave. I'm having difficulty holding the ship on the alternation of space-time planes. Bring the man and the machine and—"

Leigh didn't hear the last word. He jerked his mind all the way out of the—bathroom. "You're—taking—me?"

"Why, of course." It was the woman who spoke. "You've been promised to me, and, besides, we'll need your help in finding Ungarn's meteorite."

Leigh sat very still. The unnatural thought came: He

was glad that he had in the past proven to himself that he was not a coward.

For here was certainty of death.

He saw after a moment that the rain was still beating against the glass, great, sparkling drops that washed murkily down the broad panes. And he saw that the night was dark.

Dark night, dark rain, dark destiny—they fitted his dark, grim thoughts. With an effort he forced his body, his mind, into greater stiffness. Automatically, he shifted his position, so that the weight of muscles would draw a tight band over the hollowness that he felt in his stomach. When at last he faced his alien captors again, Reporter Leigh was cold with acceptance of his fate—and prepared to fight for his life.

"I can't think of a single reason," he said, "why I should go with you. And if you think I'm going to help you destroy the Observer, you're crazy."

The woman said matter-of-factly: "There was a passing reference in your psychograph to a Mrs. Henry Leigh, who lives in a village called Relton, on the Pacific coast. We could be there in half an hour, your mother and her home destroyed within a minute after that. Or, perhaps, we could add her blood to our reserves."

"She would be too old," the man said in a chill tone. "We do not want the blood of old people."

It was the icy objection that brought horror to Leigh. He had a brief, terrible picture of a silent, immensely swift ship sweeping out of the Eastern night, over the peaceful hamlet; and then unearthly energies would reach down in a blaze of fury.

One second of slashing fire, and the ship would sweep on over the long, dark waters to the west.

The deadly picture faded. The woman was saying, gently:

"Jeel and I have evolved an interesting little system of interviewing human beings of the lower order. For some reason, he frightens people merely by his presence. Similarly, people develop an unnatural fear of me when they see me clearly in a strong light. So we have always tried to arrange our meetings with human beings with me sitting in semidarkness and Jeel very much in the background. It has proved very effective."

She stood up, a tall, lithely built, shadowed figure in a rather tight-fitting skirt and a dark blouse. She finished: "But now, shall we go? You bring the machine, Mr. Leigh."

"I'll take it," said the Dreegh.

Leigh glanced sharply at the lean, sinewed face of the terrible man, startled at the instant, accurate suspicion of the desperate intention that had formed in his mind.

The Dreegh loomed over the small machine, where it stood on a corner desk. "How does it work?" he asked almost mildly.

Trembling, Leigh stepped forward. There was still a chance that he could manage this without additional danger to anyone. Not that it would be more than a vexation, unless—as their suggestion about finding the Ungarn meteorite indicated—they headed straight out to space. Then, why, it might actually cause real delay. He began swiftly:

"Press the key marked 'Titles,' and the machine will type all the main headings."

"That sounds reasonable." The long, grim-faced head nodded. The Dreegh reached forward, pressed the button. The recorder hummed softly, and a section of it lit up, showing typed lines under a transparent covering. There were several headings.

"—'His Meteorite Home,' " the Dreegh read. "That's what I want. What is the next step?"

"Press the key marked 'Subheads.' "

Leigh was suddenly shaky. He groaned inwardly. Was it possible this creature-man was going to obtain the information he wanted? Certainly, such a tremendous intelligence would not easily be led away from logical sequence.

He forced himself to grimness. He'd have to take a chance.

"The subhead I desire," said the Dreegh, "is marked 'Location.' And there is a number, one, in front of it. What next?"

"Press Key No. 1," Leigh said, "then press the key lettered 'General Release.' "

The moment he had spoken, he grew taut. If this worked—and it should. There was no reason why it shouldn't.

Key No. 1 would impart all the information under that heading. And surely the man would not want more until later. After all, this was only a test. They were in a hurry.

And later, when the Dreegh discovered that the "General Release" key had dissolved all the other information —it would be too late.

The thought dimmed. Leigh started. The Dreegh was staring at him with a bleak sardonicism. The man said:

"Your voice has been like an organ; each word uttered full of subtle shadings that mean much to the sensitive ear. Accordingly"—a steely, ferocious smile twisted that lean and deadly face—"I shall press Key No. 1. But not 'General Release.' And as soon as I've examined the little story on the recorder, I shall attend to you for that attempted trick. The sentence is—death."

"Jeel!"

"Death!" reiterated the man flatly. And the woman was silent.

There was silence, then, except for the subdued humming of the recorder. Leigh's mind was almost without thought. He felt fleshless, a strange, disembodied soul; and only gradually did a curious realization grow that he was waiting here on the brink of a night darker than the black wastes of space from which these monster humans had come.

Consciousness came of kinship with the black rain that poured with such solid, noiseless power against the glinting panes. For soon, he would be part of the inorganic darkness—a shadowed figure sprawling sightlessly in this dim room.

His aimless gaze returned to the recorder machine, and to the grim man who stood so thoughtfully, staring down at the words it was unfolding.

His thought quickened. His life, that had been pressed so shockingly out of his system by the sentence of death, quivered forth. He straightened, physically and mentally. And, suddenly, there was purpose in him.

If death was inescapable, at least he could try again,

somehow, to knock down that "General Release" key. He stared at the key, measuring the distance; and the gray thought came: What incredible irony that he should die, that he should waste his effort, to prevent the Dreeghs from having *this minute* information that was available from ten thousand sources. And yet—

The purpose remained. Three feet, he thought carefully, perhaps four. If he should fling himself toward it, how could even a Dreegh prevent the dead weight of his body and his extended fingers from accomplishing such a simple, straightforward mission?

After all, his sudden action had once before frustrated the Dreeghs, permitting the Ungarn girl—in spite of her denials—to get her gun into position for firing. And—

He grew rigid as he saw that the Dreegh was turning away from the machine. The man pursed his lips, but it was the woman, Merla, who spoke from where she stood in the gloom:

"Well?"

The man frowned. "The exact location is nowhere on record. Apparently, there has been no development of meteorites in this system. I suspected as much. After all, space travel has only existed a hundred years; and the new planets and the moons of Jupiter have absorbed all the energies of exploring, exploiting man."

"I could have told you that," said Leigh.

If he could move a little to one side of the recorder, so that the Dreegh would have to do more than simply put his arm out—

The man was saying: "There is, however, a reference to some man who transports food and merchandise from the moon Europa to the Ungarns. We will . . . er . . . persuade this man to show us the way."

"One of these days," said Leigh, "you're going to discover that all human beings cannot be persuaded. What pressure are you going to put on this chap? Suppose he hasn't got a mother."

"He has—life!" said the woman softly.

"One look at you," Leigh snapped, "and he'd know that he'd lose that, anyway."

As he spoke, he stepped with enormous casualness to the left, one short step. He had a violent impulse to say something, anything to cover the action. But his voice had betrayed him once. And actually it might already have done so again. The cold face of the man was almost too enigmatic.

"We could," said the woman, "use William Leigh to persuade him."

The words were softly spoken, but they shocked Leigh to his bones. For they offered a distorted hope. And that shattered his will to action. His purpose faded into remoteness. Almost grimly, he fought to draw that hard determination back into his consciousness. He concentrated his gaze on the recorder machine, but the woman was speaking again; and his mind wouldn't hold anything except the urgent meaning of her words:

"He is too valuable a slave to destroy. We can always take his blood and energy, but now we must send him to Europa, there to find the freighter pilot of the Ungarns, and actually accompany him to the Ungarn meteorite. If he could investigate the interior, our attack might conceivably be simplified, and there is just a possibility that there might be new weapons, of which we should be informed. We must not underestimate the science of the great Galactics.

"Naturally, before we allowed Leigh his freedom, we would do a little tampering with his mind, and so blot out from his conscious mind all that has happened in this hotel room.

"The identification of Professor Ungarn as the Galactic Observer we would make plausible for Leigh by a little rewriting of his psychograph report; and tomorrow he will waken in his bed with a new purpose, based on some simple human impulse such as love of the girl."

The very fact that the Dreegh, Jeel, was allowing her to go on, brought the first, faint color to Leigh's cheeks, a thin flush at the enormous series of betrayals she was so passionately expecting of him. Nevertheless, so weak was his resistance to the idea of continued life, that he could only snap:

"If you think I'm going to fall in love with a dame who's got twice my I.Q., you're—"

The woman cut him off. "Shut up, you fool! Can't you see I've saved your life?"

The man was cold, ice-cold. "Yes, we shall use him,

not because he is essential, but because we have time to search for easier victories. The first members of the Dreegh tribe will not arrive for a month and a half, and it will take Mr. Leigh a month of that to get to the moon, Europa, by one of Earth's primitive passenger liners. Fortunately, the nearest Galactic military base is well over three months distant—by Galactic ship speeds.

"Finally"—with a disconcerting, tigerish swiftness, the Dreegh whirled full upon Leigh, eyes that were like pools of black fire measured his own startled stare—"finally, as a notable reminder to your subconscious of the error of trickery, and as complete punishment for past and—intended—offenses, *this*!"

Despairingly, Leigh twisted away from the metal that glowed at him. His muscles tried horribly to carry out the purpose that had been working to a crisis inside him. He lunged for the recorder—but *something* caught his body. Something—not physical. But the very pain seemed mortal.

There was no visible flame of energy, only that glow at the metal source. But his nerves writhed; enormous forces contorted his throat muscles, froze the scream that quivered there, hideously.

His whole being welcomed the blackness that came mercifully to blot out the hellish pain.

# VI

On the third day, Europa began to give up some of the sky to the vast mass of Jupiter behind it. The engines that so imperfectly transformed magnetic attraction to a half-hearted repulsion functioned more and more smoothly as the infinite complication of pull and counterpull yielded to distance.

The old, slow, small freighter scurried on into the immense, enveloping night; and the days dragged into weeks, the weeks crawled their drab course toward the full month.

On the thirty-seventh day, the sense of slowing up was so distinct that Leigh crept dully out of his bunk, and croaked:

"How much farther?"

He was aware of the stolid-faced space trucker grinning at him. The man's name was Hanardy, and he said now matter-of-factly:

"We're just pulling in. See that spot of light over to the left? It's moving this way."

He ended with a rough sympathy. "Been a tough trip, eh? Tougher'n you figgered when you offered to write up my little route for your big syndicate."

Leigh scarcely heard. He was clawing at the porthole, straining to penetrate the blackness. At first his eyes kept blinking on him, and nothing came. Stars were out there, but it was long seconds before his bleary gaze made out moving lights. He counted them with sluggish puzzlement:

"One, two, three—seven—" he counted. "And all traveling together."

"What's that?" Hanardy bent beside him. "Seven?"

There was a brief silence between them, as the lights grew visibly dim with distance, and winked out.

"Too bad," Leigh ventured, "that Jupiter's behind us. They mightn't fade out like that in silhouette. Which one was Ungarn's meteorite?"

With a shock, he grew aware that Hanardy was standing. The man's heavy face was dark with frown. Hanardy said slowly:

"Those were ships. I never saw ships go so fast before. They were out of sight in less than a minute."

The frown faded from his stolid face. He shrugged. "Some of those new police ships, I guess. And we must have seen them from a funny angle for them to disappear so fast."

Leigh half sat, half knelt, frozen into immobility. And after that one swift glance at the pilot's rough face, he averted his own. For a moment, the black fear was in him that his wild thoughts would blaze from his eyes.

Dreeghs! Two and a half months had wound their appallingly slow course since the murders. More than a month to get from Earth to Europa, and now this miserable, lonely journey with Hanardy, the man who trucked for the Ungarns.

Every day of that time, he had known with an inner certainty that none of this incredible business had gone backward. That it could only have assumed a hidden, more dangerous form. The one fortunate reality in the whole mad affair was that he had wakened on the morning after the mechanical psychologist test from a dreamless sleep; and there in the psychograph report was the identification of Ungarn as the Observer, and the statement, borne out by an all too familiar emotional tension, that he was in love with the girl.

Now this! His mind flared. Dreeghs in seven ships. That meant the first had been reinforced by—many. And perhaps the seven were only a reconnaissance group, withdrawing at Hanardy's approach.

Or perhaps those fantastic murderers had already attacked the Observer's base. Perhaps the girl—

He fought the desperate thought out of his consciousness, and watched, frowning, as the Ungarn meteorite made a dark, glinting path in the blackness to one side. The two objects, the ship and the bleak, rough-shaped mass of metallic stone drew together in the night, the ship slightly behind.

A great steel door slid open in the rock. Skillfully, the ship glided into the chasm. There was a noisy clicking. Hanardy came out of the control room, his face dark with puzzlement.

"'Those damn ships are out there again," he said. "I've closed the big steel locks, but I'd better tell the professor and—"

*Crash!* The world jiggled. The floor came up and hit Leigh a violent blow. He lay there, cold in spite of the thoughts that burned at fire heat in his mind:

For some reason, the vampires had waited until the freighter was inside. Then instantly, ferociously, attacked.

In packs!

"Hanardy!" A vibrant girl's voice blared from one of the loudspeakers.

The pilot sat up shakily on the floor, where he had fallen, near Leigh. "Yes, Miss Patricia."

"You dared to bring a stranger with you!"

"It's only a reporter, miss; he's writing up my route for me."

"You conceited fool! That's William Leigh. He's a hypnotized spy of those devils who are attacking us. Bring him immediately to my apartment. He must be killed at once."

"Huh!" Leigh began; and then slowly he began to stiffen. For the pilot was staring at him from narrowing eyes, all the friendliness gone from his rough, heavy face. Finally, Leigh laughed curtly.

"Don't you be a fool, too, Hanardy. I made the mistake once of saving that young lady's life, and she's hated me ever since."

The heavy face scowled at him. "So you knew her before, eh? You didn't tell me that. You'd better come along before I sock you one."

Almost awkwardly, he drew the gun from his side holster, and pointed its ugly snout at Leigh.

"Get along!" he said.

Hanardy reached toward a tiny arrangement of lights beside the paneled door of Patricia Ungarn's apartment—and Leigh gave one leap, one blow. He caught the short, heavy body as it fell, grabbed at the sagging gun, lowered the dead weight to the floor of the corridor; and then, for a grim, tense moment, he stood like a great animal, straining for sound.

Silence! He studied the bland panels of the doorway to the apartment, as if by sheer, savage intentness he would penetrate their golden, beautiful grained opaqueness.

It was the silence that struck him again after a moment, the emptiness of the long, tunnellike corridors. He thought, amazed: Was it possible father and daughter actually lived here without companions or servants or any human association? And that they had some idea that they could withstand the attack of the mighty and terrible Dreeghs?

They had a lot of stuff here, of course: Earthlike gravity and—and, by Heaven, he'd better get going before the girl acquired impatience and came out with one of her fancy weapons. What he must do was quite simple, unconnected with any nonsense of spying, hypnotic or otherwise.

He must find the combination automobile-spaceship in which—*Mr.* Patrick—had escaped him that night after they left Constantine's. And with that tiny ship, he must try to slip out of Ungarn's meteorite, sneak through the Dreegh line, and so head back for Earth.

What a fool he had been, a mediocre human being, mixing in such fast, brainy company. The world was full of more normal, thoroughly dumb girls. Why in hell

wasn't he safely married to one of them and—and damn
it, it was time he got busy.

He began laboriously to drag Hanardy along the smooth
flooring. Halfway to the nearest corner, the man stirred.
Instantly, quite coolly, Leigh struck him with the revolver butt, hard. This was not time for squeamishness.

The pilot dropped; and the rest was simple. He deserted the body as soon as he had pulled it out of sight
behind the corner, and raced along the hallway, trying
doors. The first four wouldn't open. At the fifth, he
pulled up in a dark consideration.

It was impossible that the whole place was locked up.
Two people in an isolated meteorite wouldn't go around
perpetually locking and unlocking doors. There must be
a trick catch.

There was. The fifth door yielded to a simple pressure
on a tiny, half-hidden push button, that had seemed an
integral part of the design of the latch. He stepped through
the entrance, then started back in brief, terrible shock.

The room had no ceiling. Above him was—space. An
ice-cold blast of air swept at him.

He had a flashing glimpse of gigantic machines in the
room, machines that dimly resembled the ultramodern
astronomical observatory on the moon that he had visited
on opening day two days before. That one, swift look
was all Leigh allowed himself. Then he stepped back into
the hallway. The door of the observatory closed automatically in his face.

He stood there, chagrined. Silly fool! The very fact
that cold air had blown at him showed that the open
effect of the ceiling was only an illusion of invisible glass.
Good Lord, in that room might be wizard telescopes that
could see to the stars. Or—an ugly thrill raced along his
spine—he might have seen the Dreeghs attacking.

He shook out of his system the brief, abnormal desire
to look again. This was no time for distractions. For, by
now, the girl must know that something was wrong.

At top speed, Leigh ran to the sixth door. It opened
into a little cubbyhole. A blank moment passed before he
recognized what it was.

An elevator!

He scrambled in. The farther he got away from the residential floor, the less the likelihood of quick discovery.

He turned to close the door, and saw that it was shutting automatically. It clicked softly; the elevator immediately began to go up. Piercingly sharp doubt came to Leigh. The machine was apparently geared to go to some definite point. And that could be very bad.

His eyes searched hastily for controls. But nothing was visible. Gun poised, he stood grim and alert, as the elevator stopped. The door slid open.

Leigh stared. There was no room. The door opened— onto blackness.

Not the blackness of space with its stars. Or a dark room, half revealed by the light from the elevator. But—blackness!

Impenetrable.

Leigh put a tentative hand forward, half expecting to feel a solid object. But as his hand entered the black area, it vanished. He jerked it back, and stared at it, dismayed. It shone with a light of its own, all the bones plainly visible.

Swiftly, the light faded, the skin became opaque, but his whole arm pulsed with a pattern of pain.

The stark, terrible thought came that this could be a death chamber. After all, the elevator had deliberately brought him here; it might not have been automatic. Outside forces could have directed it. True, he had stepped in of his own free will, but—

Fool, fool!

He laughed bitterly, braced himself—and then it happened.

There was a flash out of the blackness. Something that sparkled vividly, something material that blazed a brilliant path to his forehead—and drew itself inside his head. And then—

He was no longer in the elevator. On either side of him stretched a long corridor. The stocky Hanardy was just reaching for some tiny lights beside the door of Patricia Ungarn's apartment.

The man's fingers touched one of the lights. It dimmed. Softly, the door opened. A young woman with proud, insolent eyes and a queenlike bearing stood there.

"Father wants you down on Level 4," she said to

Hanardy. "One of the energy screens has gone down; and he needs some machine work before he can put up another."

She turned to Leigh; her voice took on metallic overtones as she said: *"Mr. Leigh, you can come in!"*

The crazy part of it was that he walked in with scarcely a physical tremor. A cool breeze caressed his cheeks; and there was the liltingly sweet sound of birds singing in the distance. Leigh stood stockstill for a moment after he had entered, dazed partly by the wonders of the room and the unbelievable sunlit garden beyond the French windows, partly by—what?

*What had happened to him?*

Gingerly, he put his hands to his head, and felt his forehead, then his whole head. But nothing was wrong, not a contusion, not a pain. He grew aware of the girl staring at him, and realization came that his actions must seem unutterably queer.

"What is the matter with you?" the girl asked.

Leigh looked at her with abrupt, grim suspicion. He snapped harshly: "Don't pull that innocent stuff. I've been up in the blackness room, and all I've got to say is, if you're going to kill me, don't skulk behind artificial night and other trickery."

The girl's eyes, he saw, were narrowed, unpleasantly cold. "I don't know what you're trying to pretend," she said icily. "I assure you it will not postpone the death we have to deal you."

She hesitated, then finished sharply: "The *what* room?"

Leigh explained grimly, puzzled by her puzzlement, then annoyed by the contemptuous smile that grew into her face. She cut him off curtly:

"I've never heard a less balanced story. If your intention was to astound me and delay your death with that improbable tale, it has failed. You must be mad. You didn't knock out Hanardy, because when I opened the door, Hanardy was there, and I sent him down to father."

"See here!" Leigh began. He stopped wildly. By Heaven, Hanardy had been there as she opened the door!

And yet earlier—

WHEN?

Doggedly, Leigh pushed the thought on: Earlier, he had attacked Hanardy. And then he—Leigh—had gone up in an elevator; and then, somehow, back and—

Shakily, he felt his head again. And it was absolutely normal. Only, he thought, there was something inside it that sparkled.

Something—

With a start, he grew aware that the girl was quite deliberately drawing a gun from a pocket of her simple white dress. He stared at the weapon, and before its gleaming menace, his thoughts faded, all except the deadly consciousness that what he had said had delayed her several minutes now. It was the only thing that could delay her further until, somehow—

The vague hope wouldn't finish. Urgently, he said:

"I'm going to assume you're genuinely puzzled by my words. Let's begin at the beginning. There is such a room, is there not?"

"Please," said the girl wearily, "let us not have any of your logic. My I. Q. is 243, yours is 112. So I assure you I am quite capable of reasoning from any beginning you can think of."

She went on, her low voice as curt as the sound of struck steel: "There is no 'blackness' room, as you call it, no sparkling thing that crawls inside a human head. There is but one fact: The Dreeghs in their visit to your hotel room, hypnotized you; and this curious mind illusion can only be a result of that hypnotism—don't argue with me—"

With a savage gesture of her gun, she cut off his attempt to speak. "There's no time. For some reason, the Dreeghs did something to you. Why? What did you see in those rooms?"

Even as he explained and described, Leigh was thinking chilly:

He'd have to catch hold of himself, get a plan, however risky, and carry it through. The purpose was tight and cold in his mind as he obeyed her motion, and went ahead of her into the corridor. It was there, an icy determination, as he counted the doors from the corner where he had left the unconscious Hanardy.

"One, two, three, four, *five*. This door!" he said.

"Open it!" the girl gestured.

He did so; and his lower jaw sagged. He was staring into a fine, cozy room filled with shelf on shelf of beautifully bound books. There were comfortable chairs, a magnificent rag rug and—

It was the girl who closed the door firmly and—he trembled with the tremendousness of the opportunity—she walked ahead of him to the sixth door.

"And this is your elevator?"

Leigh nodded mutely; and because his whole body was shaking, he was only dimly surprised that there was no elevator, but a long, empty, silent corridor.

The girl was standing with her back partly to him; and if he hit her, it would knock her hard against the door jamb and—

The sheer brutality of the thought was what stopped him, held him for the barest second—as the girl whirled, and looked straight into his eyes.

Her gun was up, pointing steadily. "Not that way," she said quietly. "For a moment I was wishing you would have the nerve to try it. But, after all, that would be the weak way for me."

Her eyes glowed with a fierce pride. "After all, I've killed before through necessity, and hated it. You can see yourself that, because of what the Dreeghs have done to you, it is necessary. So—"

Her voice took on a whiplash quality. "So back to my rooms. I have a space lock there to get rid of your body. Get going!"

It was the emptiness, the silence except for the faint click of their shoes that caught at Leigh's nerves, as he walked hopelessly back to the apartment. This meteorite hurtling darkly through the remote wastes of the Solar System, pursued and attacked by deadly ships from the fixed stars, and himself inside it, under sentence of death, the executioner to be a girl—

And that was the devastating part. He couldn't begin to argue with this damnable young woman, for every word would sound like pleading. The very thought of mentally getting down on his knees to any woman was paralyzing.

The singing of the birds, as he entered the apartment,

perked him violently out of his black passion. Abruptly marveling, he walked to the stately French windows, and stared at the glorious summery garden.

At least two acres of green wonder spread before him, a blaze of flowers, trees where gorgeously colored birds fluttered and trilled, a wide, deep pool of green, green water, and over all, the glory of brilliant sunshine.

It was the sunshine that held Leigh finally; and he stood almost breathless for a long minute before it seemed that he had the solution. He said in a hushed voice, without turning:

"The roof—is an arrangement—of magnifying glass. It makes the Sun as big as on Earth. Is that the—"

"You'd better turn around," came the hostile, vibrant voice from behind him. "I don't shoot people in the back. And I want to get this over with."

It was the moralistic smugness of her words that shook every muscle in Leigh's body. He whirled, and raged:

"You damned little Klugg. You can't shoot me in the back, eh? Oh, no! And you couldn't possibly shoot me while I was attacking you because that would be the weak way. It's all got to be made right with your conscience."

He stopped so short that, if he had been running instead of talking, he would have stumbled. Figuratively, almost literally, he saw Patricia Ungarn for the first time since his arrival. His mind had been so concentrated, so absorbed by deadly things that—

—For the first time as a woman.

Leigh drew a long breath. Dressed as a man, she had been darkly handsome in an extremely youthful fashion. Now she wore a simple, snow-white sports dress. It was scarcely more than a tunic, and came well above her knees.

Her hair shone with a brilliant brownness, and cascaded down to her shoulders. Her bare arms and legs gleamed a deep, healthy tan. Sandals pure white graced her feet. Her face—

The impression of extraordinary beauty yielded to the amazing fact that her perfect cheeks were flushing vividly. The girl snapped:

"Don't you dare use that word to me."

She must have been utterly beside herself. Her fury

was such an enormous fact that Leigh gasped; and he
couldn't have stopped himself from saying what he did, if
the salvation of his soul had depended on it.

"Klugg!" he said, "Klugg, Klugg, Klugg! So you realize now that the Dreeghs had you down pat, that all your
mighty pretensions was simply your Klugg mind demanding pretentious compensation for a dreary, lonely life.
You had to think you were somebody, and yet all the
time you must have known they'd only ship the tenth-
raters to these remote posts. Klugg, not even Lennel; the
Dreegh woman wouldn't even grant you Lennel status,
whatever that is. And she'd know. Because if you're
I. Q. 243, the Dreeghs were 400. You've realized that,
too, haven't you?"

"Shut up! Or I'll kill you by inches!" said Patricia
Ungarn; and Leigh was amazed to see that she was as
white as a sheet. The astounded realization came that he
had struck, not only the emotional Achilles heel of this
strange and terrible young woman, but the very vital
roots of her mental existence.

"So," he said deliberately, "the high morality is growing dim. Now you can torture me to death without a
qualm. And to think that I came here to ask you to
marry me because I thought a Klugg and a human being
might get along."

"You what?" said the girl. Then she sneered. "So that
was the form of their hypnotism. They would use some
simple impulse for a simple human mind.

"But now I think we've had just about enough. I know
just the type of thoughts that come to a male human in
love; and even the realization that you're not responsible
makes the very idea none the less bearable. I feel sickened, utterly insulted. Know, please, that my future husband is arriving with the reinforcements three weeks
from now. He will be trained to take over father's work—"

"Another Klugg!" said Leigh, and the girl turned shades
whiter.

Leigh stood utterly thunderstruck. In all his life, he
had never gotten anybody going the way he had this
young girl. The intellectual mask was off, and underneath was a seething mass of emotions bitter beyond the
power of words to express. Here was evidence of a life so

lonely that it strained his imagination. Her every word showed an incredible pent-up masochism as well as sadism, for she was torturing herself as well as him.

And he couldn't stop now to feel sorry for her. His life was at stake, and only more words could postpone death—or bring the swift and bearable surcease of a gun fired in sudden passion. He hammered on grimly:

"I'd like to ask one question. How did you find out my I. Q. was 112? What special interest made you inquire about that? Is it possible that, all by yourself here, you, too, had a special type of thought, and that, though your intellect rejected the very idea of such lowly love, its existence is the mainspring behind your fantastic determination to kill, rather than cure me? I—"

"That will do," interrupted Patricia Ungarn.

It required one lengthy moment for Leigh to realize that in those few short seconds she had pulled herself completely together.

He stared in gathering alarm, as her gun motioned toward a door he had not seen before.

She said curtly:

"I suppose there is a solution other than death. That is, immediate death. And I have decided to accept the resultant loss of my spaceship."

She nodded at the door: "It's there in the air lock. It works very simply. The steering wheel pulls up or down or sideways, and that's the way the ship will go. Just step on the accelerator, and the machine will go forward. The decelerator is the left pedal. The automobile wheels fold in automatically as soon as they lift from the floor.

"Now, get going. I need hardly tell you that the Dreeghs will probably catch you. But you can't stay here. That's obvious."

"Thanks!" That was all Leigh allowed himself to say. He had exploded an emotional powder keg, and he dared not tamper even a single word further. There was a tremendous psychological mystery here, but it was not for him to solve.

Suddenly shaky from realization of what was still ahead of him, he walked gingerly toward the air lock. And then—

It happened!

He had a sense of unutterable nausea. There was a wild swaying through blackness and—

He was standing at the paneled doorway leading from the corridor to Patricia Ungarn's apartment. Beside him stood Hanardy. The door opened. The young woman who stood there said strangely familiar words to Hanardy, about going down to the fourth level to fix an energy screen. Then she turned to Leigh, and in a voice hard and metallic said:

"*Mr.* Leigh, you can come in."

## VII

The crazy part of it was that he walked in with scarcely a physical tremor. A cool breeze caressed his cheeks; and there was the liltingly sweet sound of birds singing in the distance. Leigh stood stockstill for a moment after he had entered; by sheer will power he emptied the terrible daze out of his mind, and bent, mentally, into the cyclone path of complete memory. Everything was there suddenly, the way the Dreeghs had come to his hotel apartment and ruthlessly forced him to their will, the way the "blackness" room had affected him, and how the girl had spared his life.

For some reason, the whole scene with the girl had been unsatisfactory to—Jeel; and it was now, fantastically, to be repeated.

That thought ended. The entire, tremendous reality of what had happened yielded to a vastly greater fact:

There was—something—inside his head, a distinctly physical something; and in a queer, horrible, inexperienced way, his mind was instinctively fighting—it. The result was ghastly confusion. Which hurt him, not the thing.

Whatever it was, rested inside his head, unaffected by his brain's feverish contortions, cold, aloof, watching.

Watching.

Madly, then, he realized what it was. Another mind. Leigh shrank from the thought as from the purest destroying fire. He tensed his brain. For a moment the frenzy of his horror was so great that his face twisted with the anguish of his efforts. And everything blurred.

Exhausted finally, he simply stood there. And the thing-mind was still inside his head.

Untouched.

*What had happened to him?*

Shakily, Leigh put his hands up to his forehead; then he felt his whole head; there was a vague idea in him that if he pressed—

He jerked his hands down with an unspoken curse. Damnation on damnation, he was even repeating the actions of this scene. He grew aware of the girl staring at him. He heard her say:

"What is the matter with you?"

It was the sound of the words, exactly the same words, that did it. He smiled wryly. His mind drew back from the abyss, where it had teetered.

He was sane again.

Gloomy recognition came then that his brain was still a long way down; sane yes, but dispirited. It was only too obvious that the girl had no memory of the previous scene, or she wouldn't be parroting. She'd—

That thought stopped, too. Because a strange thing was happening. The mind inside him stirred, and looked through his—Leigh's—eyes. Looked intently.

Intently.

The room and the girl in it changed, not physically, but subjectively, in what he saw, in the—details.

Details burned at him; furniture and design that a moment before had seemed a flowing, artistic whole, abruptly showed flaws, hideous errors in taste and arrangement and structure.

His gaze flashed out to the garden, and in instants tore it to mental shreds. Never in all his existence had he seen or felt criticism on such a high, devastating scale. Only—

Only it wasn't criticism. Actually. The mind was indifferent. It saw things. Automatically, it saw some of the possibilities; and by comparison the reality suffered.

It was not a matter of anything being hopelessly bad. The wrongness was frequently a subtle thing. Birds not suited, for a dozen reasons, to their environment. Shrubs that added infinitesimal discord not harmony to the superb garden.

The mind flashed back from the garden; and this time, for the first time, studied the girl.

On all Earth, no woman had ever been so piercingly

examined. The structure of her body and her face, to Leigh so finely, proudly shaped, so gloriously patrician—found low grade now.

An excellent example of low-grade development in isolation.

That was the thought, not contemptuous, not derogatory, simply an impression by an appallingly direct mind that saw—overtones, realities behind realities, a thousand facts where one showed.

There followed crystal-clear awareness of the girl's psychology, objective admiration for the system of isolated upbringing that made Klugg girls such fine breeders; and then—

Purpose!

Instantly carried out. Leigh took three swift steps toward the girl. He was aware of her snatching at the gun in her pocket, and there was the sheerest startled amazement on her face. Then he had her.

Her muscles writhed like steel springs. But they were hopeless against his superstrength, his superspeed. He tied her with some wire he had noticed in a half-opened clothes closet.

Then he stepped back, and to Leigh came the shocked personal thought of the incredible thing that had happened, comprehension that all this, which seemed so normal, was actually so devastatingly superhuman, so swift that—seconds only had passed since he came into the room.

Private thought ended. He grew aware of the mind, contemplating what it had done, and what it must do before the meteorite would be completely under control.

Vampire victory was near.

There was a phase of walking along empty corridors, down several flights of stairs. The vague, dull thought came to Leigh, his own personal thought, that the Dreegh seemed to know completely the interior of the meteorite.

Somehow, during the periods of—transition, of time manipulation, the creature-mind must have used his, Leigh's, body to explore the vast tomb of a place *thoroughly*. And now, with utter simplicity of purpose—*he* was heading for the machine shops on the fourth level, where Professor Ungarn and Hanardy labored to put up another energy defense screen.

*He* found Hanardy alone, working at a lathe that throbbed—and the sound made it easy to sneak up—

The professor was in a vast room, where great engines hummed a strange, deep tune of titanic power. He was a tall man, and his back was turned to the door as Leigh entered.

But he was immeasurably quicker than Hanardy, quicker even than the girl. He sensed danger. He whirled with a catlike agility. Literally. And succumbed instantly to muscles that could have torn him limb from limb. It was during the binding of the man's hands that Leigh had time for an impression.

In the photographs that Leigh had seen, as he had told the Dreegh, Merla, in the hotel, the professor's face had been sensitive, tired-looking, withal noble. He was more than that, tremendously more.

The man radiated power, as no photograph could show it, *good* power in contrast to the savage, malignant, immensely greater power of the Dreegh.

The sense of power faded before the aura of—weariness. Cosmic weariness. It was a lined, an amazingly lined face. In a flash, Leigh remembered what the Dreegh woman had said; and it was all there: deep-graven lines of tragedy and untold mental suffering, interlaced with a curious peacefulness, like—resignation.

On that night months ago, he had asked the Dreegh woman: Resignation to what? And now, here in this tortured, kindly face was the answer:

*Resignation to hell.*

Queerly, an unexpected second answer trickled in his mind: Morons; they're Galactic morons. Kluggs.

The thought seemed to have no source; but it gathered with all the fury of a storm. Professor Ungarn and his daughter were Kluggs, *morons* in the incredible Galactic sense. No wonder the girl had reacted like a crazy person. Obviously born here, she must have only guessed the truth in the last two months.

The I. Q. of human morons wavered between seventy-five and ninety, of Kluggs possibly between two hundred and twenty-five and, say, two hundred and forty-three.

*Two hundred and forty-three.* What kind of civilization was this Galactic—if Dreeghs were four hundred and—

Somebody, of course, had to do the dreary, routine work of civilization; and Kluggs and Lennels and their kind were obviously elected. No wonder they looked like morons with that weight of inferiority to influence their very nerve and muscle structure. No wonder whole planets were kept in ignorance—

Leigh left the professor tied hand and foot, and began to turn off power switches. Some of the great motors were slowing noticeably as he went out of that mighty engine room; the potent hum of power dimmed.

Back in the girl's room, he entered the air lock, climbed into the small automobile spaceship—and launched into the night.

Instantly, the gleaming mass of meteorite receded into the darkness behind him. Instantly, magnetic force rays caught his tiny craft, and drew it remorselessly toward the hundred and fifty foot, cigar-shaped machine that flashed out of the darkness.

He felt the spy rays; and he must have been recognized. For another ship flashed up to claim him.

Air locks opened noiselessly—and shut. Sickly, Leigh stared at the two Dreeghs, the tall man and the tall woman; and, as from a great distance, heard himself explaining what he had done.

Dimly, hopelessly, he wondered why he should have to explain. Then he heard Jeel say:

"Merla, this is the most astoundingly successful case of hypnotism in our existence. He's done—everything. Even the tiniest thoughts we put into his mind have been carried out to the letter. And the proof is, the screens are going down. With the control of this station, we can hold out even after the Galactic warships arrive—and fill our tankers and our energy reservoirs for ten thousand years. Do you hear, *ten thousand years*?"

His excitement died. He smiled with sudden, dry understanding as he looked at the woman. Then he said laconically:

"My dear, the reward is all yours. We could have broken down those screens in another twelve hours, but it would have meant the destruction of the meteorite.

This victory is so much greater. Take your reporter. Satisfy your craving—while the rest of us prepare for the occupation. Meanwhile, I'll tie him up for you."

Leigh thought, a cold, remote thought: The kiss of death—

He shivered in sudden, appalled realization of what he had done—

He lay on the couch, where Jeel had tied him. He was surprised, after a moment, to notice that, though *the* mind had withdrawn into the background of his brain—it was still there, cold, steely, abnormally conscious.

The wonder came: what possible satisfaction could Jeel obtain from experiencing the mortal thrill of death with him? These people were utterly abnormal, of course, but—

The wonder died like dry grass under a heat ray, as the woman came into the room, and glided toward him. She smiled; she sat down on the edge of the couch.

"So here you are," she said.

She was, Leigh thought, like a tigress. There was purpose in every cunning muscle of her long body. In surprise he saw that she had changed her dress. She wore a sleek, flimsy, sheeny, tight-fitting gown that set off in startling fashion her golden hair and starkly white face. Utterly fascinated, he watched her. Almost automatically, he said:

"Yes, I'm here."

Silly words. But he didn't feel silly. Tenseness came the moment he had spoken. It was her eyes that did it. For the first time since he had first seen her, her eyes struck him like a blow. Blue eyes, and steady. So steady. Not the steady frankness of honesty. But steady—like dead eyes.

A chill grew on Leigh, a special, extra chill, adding to the ice that was already there inside him; and the unholy thought came that this was a dead woman—artificially kept alive by the blood and *life* of dead men and women.

She smiled, but the bleakness remained in those cold fish eyes. No smile, no warmth could ever bring light to that chill, beautiful countenance. But she smiled the form of a smile, and she said:

"We Dreeghs live a hard, lonely life. So lonely that

sometimes I cannot help thinking our struggle to remain alive is a blind, mad thing. We're what we are through no fault of our own. It happened during an interstellar flight that took place a million years ago—"

She stopped, almost hopelessly. "It seems longer. It must be longer. I've really lost track."

She went on, suddenly grim, as if the memory, the very telling, brought a return of horror: "We were among several thousand holidayers who were caught in the gravitational pull of a sun, afterward called the Dreegh sun.

"Its rays, immensely dangerous to human life, infected us all. It was discovered that only continuous blood transfusions, and the life force of other human beings, could save us. For a while we received donations; then the government decided to have us destroyed as hopeless incurables.

"We were all young, terribly young and in love with life; some hundreds of us had been expecting the sentence, and we still had friends in the beginning. We escaped, and we've been fighting ever since to stay alive."

And still he could feel no sympathy. It was odd, for all the thoughts she undoubtedly wanted him to have, came. Picture of a bleak, endless existence in spaceships, staring out into the perpetual night; all life circumscribed by the tireless, abnormal needs of bodies gone mad from ravenous disease.

It was all there, all the emotional pictures. But no emotions came. She was too cold; the years and the devil's hunt had stamped her soul and her eyes and her face.

And besides, her body seemed tenser now, leaning toward him, bending forward closer, closer, till he could hear her slow, measured breathing. Even her eyes suddenly held the vaguest inner light—her whole being quivered with the chill tensity of her purpose; when she spoke, she almost breathed the words:

"I want you to kiss me, and don't be afraid. I shall keep you alive for days, but I must have response, not passivity. You're a bachelor, at least thirty. You won't have any more morals about the matter than I. But you must let your whole body yield."

He didn't believe it. Her face hovered six inches above

his; and there was such a ferocity of suppressed eagerness in her that it could only mean death.

Her lips were pursed, as if to suck, and they quivered with a strange, tense, trembling desire, utterly unnatural, almost obscene. Her nostrils dilated at every breath—and no normal woman who had kissed as often as she must have in all her years could feel like that, if that was all she expected to get.

"Quick!" she said breathlessly. "Yield, yield!"

Leigh scarcely heard; for that other mind that had been lingering in his brain, surged forward in its incredible way. He heard himself say:

"I'll trust your promise because I can't resist such an appeal. You can kiss your head off. I guess I can stand it—"

There was a blue flash, an agonizing burning sensation that spread in a flash to every nerve of his body.

The anguish became a series of tiny pains, like small needles piercing a thousand bits of his flesh. Tingling, writhing a little, amazed that he was still alive, Leigh opened his eyes.

He felt a wave of purely personal surprise.

The woman lay slumped, lips half twisted off of his, body collapsed hard across his chest. And the mind, that blazing mind was there, watching—as the tall figure of the Dreegh man sauntered into the room, stiffened, and then darted forward.

He jerked her limp form into his arms. There was the same kind of blue flash as their lips met, from the man to the woman. She stirred finally, moaning. He shook her brutally.

"You wretched fool!" he raged. "How did you let a thing like that happen? You would have been dead in another minute, if I hadn't come along."

"I—don't—know." Her voice was thin and old. She sank down to the floor at his feet, and slumped there like a tired old woman. Her blond hair straggled, and looked curiously faded. "I don't know, Jeel. I tried to get his life force, and he got mine instead. He—"

She stopped. Her blue eyes widened. She staggered to her feet. "Jeel, he must be a spy. No human being could do a thing like that to me.

"Jeel"—there was sudden terror in her voice—"Jeel, get out of this room. Don't you realize? He's got my energy in him. He's lying there now, and whatever has control of him has my energy to work with—"

"All right, all right." He patted her fingers. "I assure you he's only a human being. And he's got your energy. You made a mistake, and the flow went the wrong way. But it would take much more than that for *anyone* to use a human body successfully against us. So—"

*"You don't understand!"*

Her voice shook. "Jeel, I've been cheating. I don't know what got into me, but I couldn't get enough life force. Every time I was able, during the four times we stayed on Earth, I sneaked out.

"I caught men on the street. I don't know exactly how many because I dissolved their bodies after I was through with them. But there were dozens. And he's got all the energy I collected, enough for scores of years, enough for—don't you see?—enough for *them*."

"My dear!" The Dreegh shook her violently, as a doctor would an hysterical woman. "For a million years, the great ones of Galactic have ignored us and—"

He paused. A black frown twisted his long face. He whirled like the tiger man he was, snatching at his gun—as Leigh stood up.

The man Leigh was no longer surprised at—anything. At the way the hard cords fell rotted from his wrists and legs. At the way the Dreegh froze rigid after one look into his eyes. For the first shock of the tremendous, the almost cataclysmic, truth was already in him.

"There is only one difference," said Leigh in a voice so vibrant that the top of his head shivered from the unaccustomed violence of sound. "This time there are two hundred and twenty-seven Dreegh ships gathered in one concentrated area. The rest—and our records show only a dozen others—we can safely leave to our police patrols."

The Great Galactic, who had been William Leigh, smiled darkly and walked toward his captives. "It has been a most interesting experiment in deliberate splitting of personality. Three years ago, our time manipulators showed this opportunity of destroying the Dreeghs, who hitherto had escaped by reason of the vastness of our galaxy.

"And so I came to Earth, and here built up the character of William Leigh, reporter, complete with family and past history. It was necessary to withdraw into a special compartment of the brain some nine-tenths of my mind, and to drain completely an equal percentage of life energy.

"That was the difficulty. How to replace that energy in sufficient degree at the proper time, without playing the role of vampire. I constructed a number of energy caches, but naturally at no time had we been able to see all the future. We could not see the details of what was to transpire aboard this ship, or in my hotel room that night you came, or under Constantine's restaurant.

"Besides, if I had possessed full energy as I approached this ship, your spy ray would have registered it; and you would instantly have destroyed my small automobile-spaceship.

"My first necessity, accordingly, was to come to the meteorite, and obtain an initial control over my own body through the medium of what my Earth personality called the 'blackness' room.

"That Earth personality offered unexpected difficulties. In three years it had gathered momentum *as* a personality, and that impetus made it necessary to repeat a scene with Patricia Ungarn, and to appear directly as another conscious mind, in order to convince Leigh that he must yield. The rest of course was a matter of gaining additional life energy after boarding your ship, which"—he bowed slightly at the muscularly congealed body of the woman—"which she supplied me.

"I have explained all this because of the fact that a mind will accept complete control only if full understanding of—defeat—is present. I must finally inform you, therefore, that you are to remain alive for the next few days, during which time you will assist me in making personal contact with your friends."

He made a gesture of dismissal: "Return to your normal existence. I have still to co-ordinate my two personalities completely, and that does not require your presence."

The Dreeghs went out blank-eyed, almost briskly; and the two minds in one body were—alone!

* * *

For Leigh, the Leigh of Earth, the first desperate shock
was past. The room was curiously dim, as if he was
staring out through eyes that were no longer—his!

He thought, with a horrible effort at self-control: "I've
got to fight. Some *thing* is trying to possess my body. All
the rest is lie."

A soothing, mind-pulsation stole into the shadowed
chamber where his—self—was cornered:

"No lie, but wondrous truth. You have not seen what
the Dreeghs saw and felt, for you are inside this body,
and know not that it has come marvelously *alive*, unlike
anything that your petty dreams on Earth could begin to
conceive. You must accept your high destiny, else the
sight of your own body will be a terrible thing to you. Be
calm, be braver than you've ever been, and pain will turn
to joy."

Calm came out. His mind quivered in its dark corner,
abnormally conscious of strange and unnatural pressures
that pushed in at it like winds out of unearthly night. For
a moment of terrible fear, it funked that pressing night,
then forced back to sanity, and had another thought of its
own, a grimly cunning thought:

The devilish interloper was arguing. Could that mean—
his mind rocked with hope—that co-ordination was impossible without *his* yielding to clever persuasion?

Never would he yield.

"Think," whispered the alien mind, "think of being
one valuable facet of a mind with an I. Q. twelve hundred, think of yourself as having played a role; and now
you are returning to normalcy, a normalcy of unlimited
power. You have been an actor completely absorbed in
your role, but the play is over; you are alone in your
dressing room removing the grease paint; your mood of
the play is fading, fading, fading—"

"Go to hell!" said William Leigh, loudly. "I'm William
Leigh, I. Q. one hundred and twelve, satisfied to be just
what I am. I don't give a damn whether you built me up
from the component elements of your brain, or whether I
was born normally. I can just see what you're trying to
do with that hypnotic suggestion stuff, but it isn't working. I'm here, I'm myself, and I stay myself. Go find
yourself another body, if you're so smart."

Silence settled where his voice had been; and the emptiness, the utter lack of sound brought a sharp twinge of fear greater than that which he had had before he spoke.

He was so intent on that inner struggle that he was not aware of outer movement until—

With a start he grew aware that he was staring out of a port window. Night spread there, the living night of space.

A trick, he thought in an agony of fear; a trick somehow designed to add to the corroding power of hypnotism.

A trick! He tried to jerk back—and, terrifyingly, couldn't. His body wouldn't move. Instantly, then, he tried to speak, to crash through that enveloping blanket of unholy silence. But no sound came.

Not a muscle, not a finger stirred; not a single nerve so much as trembled.

He was alone.

Cut off in his little corner of brain.

Lost.

Yes, lost, came a strangely pitying sibilation of thought, lost to a cheap, sordid existence, lost to a life whose end is visible from the hour of birth, lost to a civilization that has already had to be saved from itself a thousand times. Even you, I think, can see that all this is lost to you forever—

Leigh thought starkly: The *thing* was trying by a repetition of ideas, by showing evidence of defeat, to lay the foundations of further defeat. It was the oldest trick of simple hypnotism for simple people. And he couldn't let it work—

You have, urged the mind inexorably, accepted the fact that you were playing a role; and now you have recognized our oneness, and are giving up the role. The proof of this recognition on your part is that you have yielded control of—our—body.

—Our body, our body, OUR body—

The words re-echoed like some Gargantuan sound through his brain, then merged swiftly into that calm, other-mind pulsation:

—Concentration. All intellect derives from the capacity to concentrate; and, progressively, the body itself shows *life,* reflects and focuses that gathering, vaulting power.

—One more step remains: You must see—

Amazingly, then, he was staring into a mirror. Where it had come from, he had no memory. It was there in front of him, where, an instant before, had been a black porthole—and there was an image in the mirror. Shapeless at first to his blurred vision.

Deliberately—he felt the enormous deliberateness—the vision was cleared for him. He *saw*—and then he didn't.

His brain wouldn't look. It twisted in a mad desperation, like a body buried alive, and briefly, horrendously conscious of its fate. Insanely, it fought away from the blazing thing in the mirror. So awful was the effort, so titanic the fear, that it began to gibber mentally, its consciousness to whirl dizzily, like a wheel spinning faster, faster—

The wheel shattered into ten thousand aching fragments. Darkness came, blacker than Galactic night. And there was—

Oneness!

# EXPOSURE

## BY ERIC FRANK RUSSELL

The Rigelian ship came surreptitiously, in the deep of the night. Choosing a heavily forested area, it burned down a ring of trees, settled in the ash, sent out a powerful spray of liquid to kill the fires still creeping outward through the undergrowth.

Thin coils of smoke ascended from dying flames. Now adquately concealed from all directions but immediately above, the ship squatted amid towering conifers while its tubes cooled and contracted with metallic squeaks. There were strong smells of wood smoke, pine resin, acrid flamekiller and superheated metal.

Within the vessel there was a conference of aliens. They had two eyes apiece. That was their only positive feature: two eyes. Otherwise they had the formlessness, the almost liquid sloppiness of the completely malleable. When the three in the chart room consulted a planetary photograph they gestured with anything movable, a tentacle, pseudopod, a long, stump-ended arm, a mere digit, anything that struck their fancy at any given moment.

Just now all three were globular, shuffled around on wide, flat feet and were coated with fine, smooth fur resembling green velvct. This similarity was due to politeness rather than desire. During conversation it is conventional to assume the shape of one's superior and, if he changes, to change with him.

So two were spherical and furry solely because Captain Id-Wan saw fit to be spherical and furry. Sometimes Id-Wan was awkward. He'd give himself time to do a difficult shape such as that of reticulated molobater then watch them straining their innards in an effort to catch up.

Id-Wan said: "We've recorded this world from far out on its light side and not a spaceship came near to challenge our presence. They have no spaceships." He sniffed expressively and went on, "The blown-up pictures are plenty good enough for our purpose. We've got the lay of the land and that's as much as we need."

"There appears to be a lot of sea," remarked Chief Navigator Bi-Nak, peering at a picture. "Too much sea. More than half of it is sea."

"Are you again belittling my conquests?" demanded Id-Wan, producing a striped tail.

"Not at all, captain," assured Bi-Nak, dutifully imitating the tail. "I was simply pointing out—"

"You point too much," snapped Id-Wan. He turned to the third Rigelian. "Doesn't he, Po-Duk?"

Pilot Po-Duk played safe by remarking, "There are times and there are times."

"That is truly profound," commented Id-Wan, who had a robust contempt for neutrals. "One points while the other functions as a fount of wisdom. It would be a pleasant change if for once you did the pointing and let Bi-Nak be the oracle. I could stand that. It would make for variety."

"Yes, captain," agreed Po-Duk.

"Certainly, captain," endorsed Bi-Nak.

"All right." Id-Wan, turning irritably to the photographs, said: "There are many cities. That means intelligent life. But we have seen no spaceships and we know they've not yet reached even their own satellite. Hence, their intelligence is not of high order." He forced out a pair of mock hands so that he could rub them together. "In other words, just the sort of creatures we want—ripe for the plucking."

"You said that on the last planet," informed Bi-Nak, whose strong point was not tact.

Id-Wan pulled in his tail and bawled, "That was relative to worlds previously visited. Up to that point they were the best. These are better."

"We haven't seen them yet."

"We shall. They will give us no trouble." Id-Wan cooled down, mused aloud, "Nothing gives us trouble and I doubt whether anything is capable of it. We have fooled half a hundred successive life forms, all utterly different from any known in our home system. I anticipate no difficulties with another. Sometimes I think we must be unique in creation. On every world we've explored the creatures were fixed in form, unchangeable. It would appear that we alone are not the slaves of rigidity."

"Fixedness of form has its advantages," denied Bi-Nak, a glutton for punishment. "When my mother first met my father in the mating-field she thought he was a long-horned nodus, and— "

"There you go again," shouted Id-Wan, "criticizing the self-evident." Sourly, Id-Wan turned back to the photographs, indicated an area toward the north of a great landmass. "We are located there, well off the beaten tracks, yet within individual flying distance of four medium-sized centers. The big cities which hold potential dangers—though I doubt any real dangers—are a good way off. Nearer villages are too small to be worth investigating. The medium-sized places are best for our purpose and, as I've said, there are four within easy reach."

"Which we'll proceed to inspect?" suggested Po-Duk, mostly to show that he was paying attention.

"Of course. The usual tactics—two scouts in each. One day's mixing among the natives and they'll get us all we need to know, while the natives themselves learn nothing. After that—"

"A demonstration of power?" asked Po-Duk.

"Most certainly." Id-Wan extended something like a hair-thin tentacle, used it to mark one of the four near towns. "That place is as good as any other. We'll scrape it clean off Earth's surface, then sit in space and see what they do about it. A major blow is the most effective way of persuading a world to reveal how highly it is organized."

"If the last six planets are anything to go by," ventured Po-Duk, "we won't see much organization here. They'll panic or pray or both."

"Much as we did when the Great Spot flared in the year of—" began Bi-Nak. His voice trailed off as he noted the gleam in Id-Wan's eyes.

Id-Wan turned to Po-Duk: "Summon the chief of the scouts and tell him to hurry. I want action." Staring hard at Bi-Nak, he added, "Action—not talk!"

The fat man whose name was Ollie Kampenfeldt waddled slowly through the dark toward the log hut whence came the thrum of a guitar and the sound of many voices.

He was frowning as he progressed, and mopping his forehead at regular intervals.

There were other log huts scattered around in the vicinity, a few showing lights, but most in darkness. A yellow moon hung only a little above the big stockade of logs which ran right around the encampment; it stretched the shadows of the huts across neatly trimmed lawns and grassy borders.

Kampenfeldt lumbered into the noisy hut and yelped in shrill tones. The guitar ceased its twanging. The talking stopped. Presently the lights went out. He emerged accompanied by a small group of men, most of whom dispersed.

Two stayed with him as he made toward the building nearest the only gate in the heavy stockade. One of them was expostulating mildly.

"All right. So guys need sleep. How were we to know it was that late? Why don'tcha put a clock in the place?"

"The last one got snitched. It cost me fifty."

"Hah!" said the grumbler. "So time doesn't matter. What do I care about it? There's plenty of it and I'm going noplace. Make less noise and get to bed. We've got no clock because the place is full of thieves. You'd think I was back in the jug."

His companion on the other side of Kampenfeldt perked up with sudden interest. "Hey, I didn't know you'd been in clink."

"After ten years on the night beat for a big sheet you've been everywhere," said the first. "Even in a crackpotorium—even in a cemetery, for that matter." Then he stopped his forward pacing, raised himself on his toes, stared northward. "What was *that?*"

"What was what?" inquired Kampenfeldt, mopping his brow and breathing heavily.

"Sort of ring of brilliant red light. It floated down into the forest."

"Meteor," suggested Kampenfeldt, not interested.

"Imagination," said the third, having seen nothing.

"Too slow for a meteor," denied the observer, still peering on tiptoe at the distant darkness. "It floated down, like I said. Besides, I've never heard of one that shape or color. More like a plane in flames. Maybe it was a plane in flames."

"We'll know in an hour," promised Kampenfeldt, a little disgruntled at the thought of further night-time disturbances.

"How?"

"The forest will be ablaze on a ten-mile front. It's drier than I've ever known it, and ripe for the kindling." He made a clumsy gesture with a fat hand. "No fire, no plane."

"Well, what else might it be?"

Kampenfeldt said wearily: "I neither know nor care. I have to get up in the morning."

He waddled into his hut, yawning widely. The others stood outside a short time and stared northward. Nothing extraordinary was visible.

"Imagination," repeated one.

"I saw something queer. Dunno what could be out there in all that timber, but I saw something—and I've got good eyes." He removed his gaze, shrugged. 'Anyway, the heck with it!"

They went to bed.

Captain Id-Wan gave his orders to the chief of the scouts. "Bring in some local life forms. The nearest and handiest will do providing they're assorted, small and large. We want to test them."

"Yes, captain."

"Collect them only from the immediate neighborhood. There is a camp to the south which undoubtedly holds superior forms. Keep away from it. Orders concerning that camp will be given you after the more primitive forms have been tested."

"I see, captain."

"You do not see," reproved Id-Wan. "Otherwise you would have noted that I have created flexible digits upon my feet."

"I beg your pardon, captain," said the chief, hastening to create similar extensions.

"The discourtesy is overlooked, but do not repeat it. Send in the head radio technician, then get on with your task."

To the radio officer, who made toes promptly, he said: "What have you to report?"

"The same as we noted upon our approach—they fill the air."

"What?" Id-Wan pulled surprisedly at an ear which he had not possessed a moment before. The ear stretched like soft rubber. "I was not informed of that during the approach."

"I regret, I forgot to—" commenced Bi-Nak, then ceased and strained himself before Id-Wan's eyes could catch him without a rubber ear.

"They fill the air," repeated the radio technician, also dutifully eared. "We've picked up their noises from one extreme to the other. There seem to be at least ten different speech patterns."

"No common language," Bi-Nak mourned. "That complicates matters."

"That simplifies matters," Id-Wan flatly contradicted. "The scouts can masquerade as foreigners and thus avoid speech troubles. The Great Green God could hardly have arranged it better."

"There are also other impulse streams," added the technician. "We suspect them of being pictorial transmissions."

"Suspect? Don't you *know?*"

"Our receivers cannot handle them, captain."

"Why not?"

The radio officer said patiently: "Their methods do not accord with ours. The differences are technical. To explain them would take me a week. In brief, our receivers are not suitable for their transmitted pictures. Eventually, by trial-and-error methods, we could make them suitable, but it would take a long time."

"But you do receive their speech?"

"Yes—that is relatively easy."

"Well, it tells us something. They've got as far as radio. Also, they're vocal and therefore unlikely to be telepathic. I would cross the cosmos for such bait." Dismissing the radio officer, he went to the lock, looked into the night-wrapped forest to see how his scouts were doing.

His strange Rigelian life-sense enabled him to detect their quarry almost at a glance, for life burned in the dark like a tiny flame. There was just such a flame up a nearby tree. He saw it come tumbling down when the paralyzing dart from a scout's gun struck home. The flame flickered on landing but did not die out. The hunter picked it up, brought it into the light. It was a tiny animal with prick ears, coarse, reddish fur and a long, bushy tail.

Soon eight scouts struggled in bearing a huge, thickly furred form of ferocious aspect. It was big-pawed, clawed, and had no tail. It stank like molobater blood mixed with aged cheese. Half a dozen other forms were brought in, two of them winged. All were stiffened by darts, had their eyes closed, were incapable of movement. All were taken to the examiners.

One of the experts came to Id-Wan in due course. He was red-smeared and had an acrid smell.

"Nonmalleable. Every one of them."

"Bhingho!" exclaimed Id-Wan. "As are the lower forms, so will be the higher."

"Not necessarily, but very probably," said the expert, dodging the appearance of contradiction.

"We will see. Had any of these creatures possessed the power of imitative and ultra-rapid reshaping, I should have had to modify my plans. As it is, I can go right ahead."

The other responded, "So far as can be judged from these simple types you should have little trouble with their betters."

"That's what I think," agreed Id-Wan. "We'll get ourselves a sample."

"We need more than one. Two at least. A pair of them would enable us to determine the extent to which individuals differ. If the scouts are left to draw upon their own imaginations in creating differences, they may exaggcrate sufficiently to betray themselves."

"All right, we'll get two," said Id-Wan. "Call in the chief of the scouts."

To the chief of the scouts, Id-Wan said: "All your captures were of unalterable form."

"Excellent!" The chief was pleased.

"Pfah!" murmured Bi-Nak.

Id-Wan jerked around. "What was that remark?"

"Pfah, captain," admitted Bi-Nak, mentally cursing the efficiency of the rubber ear. As mildly as possible, he added, "I was considering the paradox of rigid superiority, and the pfah popped out."

"If I were telepathic," answered Id-Wan, very deliberately, "I would know you for the liar you are."

"Now there's something," offered Bi-Nak, sidetracking the insult. "So far we've encountered not one telepathic species. On this planet there are superior forms believed to be rigid—so whence comes their superiority? Perhaps they are telepathic."

Id-Wan complained to the chief scout, "Do you hear him? He points and pops out and invents obstacles. Of all the navigators available I had to be burdened with this one."

"What could be better could also be worse," put in Po-Duk, for no reason whatsoever.

Id-Wan yelled, "And this other one hangs around mouthing evasions." His fur switched from green to blue.

They all went blue, Po-Duk being the slowest. He was almost a color-cripple, as everyone knew. Id-Wan glared at him, swiftly changed to a reticulated molobater. That caught all three flat out. Id-Wan excelled at molobaters and gained much satirical satisfaction from their mutual writhings as each strove to be first. "See," he snapped, when finally they had assumed the new shape. "You are not so good, any of you."

"No, captain, we are very bad," endorsed Bi-Nak, oozing the characteristic molobater stench.

Id-Wan eyed him as if about to challenge the self-evident, decided to let the matter drop, returned his attention to the chief of the scouts. He pointed to the photographs. "There is that encampment a little to our south. As you can see, it is connected by a long, winding path to a narrow road which ambles far over the horizon before it joins a bigger road. The place is pretty well isolated; that is why we picked it."

"Picked it?" echoed the chief.

"We chose it and purposefully landed near it," Id-Wan explained. "The lonelier the source of samples, the less likelihood of discovery at the start, and the longer before an alarm can be broadcast."

"Ah," said the chief, recovering the wits strained by sudden molobating. "It is the usual technique. We are to raid the camp for specimens?"

"Two of them," confirmed Id-Wan. "Any two you can grab without rousing premature opposition."

"That will be easy."

"It cannot be otherwise. Would we be here, doing what we are doing, if all things did not come easy to our kind?"

"No, captain."

"Very well. Go get them. Take one of the radio technicians with you. He will first examine the place for signs of a transmitter or any other mode of ultra-rapid communication which cannot be detected on this photograph. If there proves to be a message-channel, of any sort at all, it must be put out of action, preferably in a manner which would appear accidental."

"Do we go right now?" asked the chief. "Or later?"

"At once, while it remains dark. We have observed how their cities dim by night, watched their lights go out, the traffic thin down. Obviously they are not nocturnal. They are most active in the daytime. Obtain those samples now and be back here before dawn."

"Very well, captain." The chief went out, still a molobater, but not for long.

Bi-Nak yawned and remarked, "I'm not nocturnal either."

"You are on duty," Id-Wan reminded him severely, "until I see fit to say that you are not on duty. And furthermore, I am disinclined to declare you off duty so long as I remain at my post."

"Example is better than precept," approved Po-Duk, currying favor.

Id-Wan promptly turned on him and bawled, "Shut up!"

"He was only pointing out," observed Bi-Nak, picking his not-teeth with fingers that weren't.

Kampenfeldt lumbered with elephantine tread to where three men were lounging full length on the grass. He wiped his forehead as he came, but it was from sheer habit. The sun was partway up and beginning to warm. The cool of the morning was still around. Kampenfeldt wasn't sweating, nevertheless he mopped.

One of the men rolled lackadaisically onto one side, welcomed him with, "Always on the run, Ollie. Why don'tcha flop down on your fat and absorb some sun once in a while?"

"Never get the chance." Kampenfeldt mopped, looked defeated. "I'm searching for Johnson and Greer. Every morning it's the same—somebody's late for breakfast."

"Aren't they in their hut?" inquired a second man, sitting up with an effort and plucking idly at blades of grass.

"Nope. First place I looked. Must've got up mighty early because nobody saw them go. Why won't guys tell me they're going out and might be late? Am I supposed to save something for them or not?"

"Let 'em do without," suggested the second man, lying down again and shading his eyes.

"Serves them right," added the first.

"They're not anywhere around," complained Kampenfeldt, "and they didn't go out the gate."

"Probably climbed the logs," offered one. "They're both batty. Most times they climb the logs when they go moonlight fishing. Anyone who wanders around like that in the middle of the night has got a hole in his head." He glanced at the other. "Were their rods in the hut?"

"Didn't think to look," admitted Kampenfeldt.

"Don't bother to look. They like to show they're tough. Let 'em be tough. It's a free country."

"Yeah," admitted Kampenfeldt reluctantly, "but they ought to have told me about their breakfasts. Now they'll be wasted unless I eat them myself."

They watched him waddle away, still worried, and mopping himself at regular intervals.

One said: "That silhouette shows there isn't much wasted."

Another said: "Hah!" and shaded his eyes with one hand and tried to look at the sun.

An examiner appeared, red-smeared and acrid-smelling as before. "They're like all the others—fixed."

"Unalterable?" insisted Id-Wan.

"Yes, captain." Distastefully he gazed down at the lurid stains upon himself, added, "Eventually we separated them, putting them in different rooms, and revived them. We killed one, then the other. The first fought with his limbs and made noises, but displayed no exceptional powers. The other one, in the other room, was already agitated but did not become more so during this time. It was obvious that he had no notion of what was happening to his companion. We then killed him after he had resisted in the same manner. The conclusion is that they are neither hypnotic nor telepathic. They are remarkably ineffectual even at the point of death."

"Good!" exclaimed Id-Wan, with great satisfaction. "You have done well."

"That is not all, captain. We have since subjected the bodies to a thorough search and can find no organs of life-sense. Evidently they have no way of perceiving life."

"Better still," enthused Id-Wan, "no life-sense means no dynamic receivers—no way of tuning an individual life and tracing its whereabouts. So those in the camp cannot tell where these two have gone."

"They couldn't in any case, by this time," the other pointed out, "since both are dead." He tossed a couple of objects onto a table. "They had those things with them. You may wish to look at them."

Id-Wan picked up the articles as the examiner went away. They were a pair of small bags or satchels made of treated animal hide, well finished, highly polished, and attached to adjustable belts.

He tipped out their contents upon the table, pawed them over: A couple of long, flat metal cases containing white tubes stuffed with herbs. Two metal gadgets, similar but not the same, which could be made to spark and produce a light. A thin card with queer, wriggly writing on one side and a colored picture of a tall-towered city on the other. One small magnifying glass. Two writing instruments, one black, the other silvery. A crude time meter with three indicators and a loud tick. Several insectlike objects with small, sharp hooks attached. Four carefully folded squares of cloth of unknown purpose.

"Humph!" He scooped the lot back, tossed the satchels to Po-Duk. "Take them to the workshop, tell them to make six reasonably good copies complete with contents. They must be ready by next nightfall."

"Six?" queried Po-Duk. "There will be eight scouts."

"Imbecile! You are holding the other two."

"So I am," said Po-Duk, gaping fascinatedly at the objects as if they had just materialized from thin air.

"There are times and there are times," remarked Bi-Nak as Po-Duk departed.

Id-Wan let it pass. "I must have a look at these bodies. I am curious about them." He moved off to the operating room, Bi-Nak following.

The kidnapped and slaughtered creatures proved to be not as repulsive as some they'd found on other worlds. They lay side by side, long, lean, brown-skinned, with two arms, two legs, and with dark, coarse hair upon their heads. Their dead eyes were very much like Rigelian eyes. Their flesh was horribly firm despite the fact that it was full of red juice.

"Primitive types," pronounced Id-Wan, poking at one of them. "It's a marvel they've climbed as high as they have."

"Their digits are surprisingly dexterous," explained the head examiner. "And they have well-developed brains, more so than I had expected."

"They will need all their brains," promised Id-Wan. "We are too advanced to be served by idiots."

"That is true," endorsed Bi-Nak, gaining fresh heart.

"Although sometimes I wonder," added Id-Wan, staring hard at him. He shifted his attention back to the examiner: "Give these cadavers to the scouts and tell them to get in some practice. I'll pick out the eight best imitators tonight. They had better be good!"

"Yes, captain."

The sinking sun showed no more than a sliver of glowing rim on a distant hill when the chief of the scouts reported to Id-Wan. There was a coolness creeping over the land, but it was not coldness. Here, at this time, the nights were merely less warm than the days.

Id-Wan inquired: "Did you have any difficulty in obtaining those two specimens this morning?"

"No, captain. Our biggest worry was that of getting there before broad daylight. It took longer than we'd anticipated to reach the place. In fact dawn was already showing when we arrived. However, we were lucky."

"In what way?"

"Those two were already outside the camp, just as if the Great Green God had provided them for us. They bore simple apparatus for trapping water game and evidently intended an early-morning expedition. All we had to do was plant darts in them and take them away. They had no chance to utter a sound. The camp slumbered undisturbed."

"And what about the message channels?"

"The technician could find none," said the chief. "No overhead wires, no underground cables, no antenna, nothing."

"That is peculiar," remarked Bi-Nak. "Why should creatures so forward be so backward? They *are* superior types, aren't they?"

"They are relatively unimportant in this world's scheme of things," declared Id-Wan. "Doubtless they serve these trees in some way, or watch for fires. It is of little consequence."

"Sitting down on their dirt is not of little consequence," grumbled Bi-Nak to himself. "I'll be happier after we've blasted one of their towns, or ten of them, or fifty. We can then get their reaction and beat it home with the news. I am more than ready to go home even if I am chosen to return with the main fleet sometime later."

"Are the scouts ready for my inspection?" Id-Wan asked the chief.

"Waiting now, captain."

"All right, I'll look them over." Going to the rear quarters, he studied the twenty Rigelians lined up against a wall. The two corpses reposed nearby for purposes of comparison. Subjecting each scout to long and careful scrutiny, he chose eight, where upon the remaining twelve promptly switched to his own shape. The eight were good. Four Johnsons and four Greers.

"It is a simple form to duplicate," commented the chief. "I could hold it myself for days on end."

"Me, too," agreed Id-Wan. He addressed the row of two-armed, brown-skinned bipeds who could be whatever he wanted them to be. "Remember the most stringent rule: In no circumstances will you change shape before your task is done. Until then, you will retain that precise form and appearance, even under threat of destruction."

They nodded silently.

He continued, "All your objectives have large parks into which you will be dropped shortly before dawn. You will then merge as unobtrusively as possible with the creatures appearing in each awakening town. After that, do as you've done many a time before—dig up all the useful data you can get without arousing suspicion. Details of weapons and power sources are especially needed. Enter no building until you are sure that your entry will not be challenged. Do not speak or be spoken to if it is avoidable. In the last resort, respond with imitations of a different speech pattern."

*"Fanziki moula? Sfinadacta bu!"* said Bi-Nak, concocting an example.

Id-Wan paused to scowl at him before he went on, "Above all, there are eight of you, and one may find what another has missed."

They nodded again, bipeds all of them, but with the Rigelian life-flame burning up within them.

He finished, "If absolutely imperative, give up the quest and hide yourselves until the time for return. Be at your respective dropping-points in the parks at the mid-hour of the following night. You will then be picked up." He raised his voice in emphasis. "And do not change shape before then!"

They didn't. They had not altered by as much as one hair when they filed impassively into the ship's lifeboat between the mid-hour and dawn. Id-Wan was there to give them a final lookover. Each walked precisely as the now-dead samples had walked, swinging his arms in the same manner, using the same bearing, wearing the same facial expression. Each had a satchel complete with alien contents, plus a midget dart gun.

The lifeboat rose among the trees into the dark, bore them away. A few creatures in the trees resented the brief disturbance, made squawking sounds.

"Not one other ship in the night," remarked Id-Wan, looking upward. "Not one rocket trail across the stars. They've got nothing but those big, clumsy air machines which we saw toiling through the clouds." He gave a sigh. "In due time we'll take over this planet like taking a karda-fruit from a nodus. It is all too easy, too elementary. Sometimes I feel that a little more opposition might be interesting."

Bi-Nak decided to let that point go for what it was worth, which wasn't much. Two days and nights on continual duty with the indefatigable Id-Wan had tired him beyond argument. So he yawned, gave the stars a sleepless, disinterested eye, and followed Id-Wan into the ship.

Making for the dynamic receivers, Id-Wan had a look at their recording globes, each of which had been tuned to a departing scout. Each globe held a bright spot derived from a distant life-glow. He watched the spots shrink with distance until eventually they remained still. A bit later the lifeboat came back, reported all landed. The spots continued to shine without shifting. None moved until the sun stabbed a red ray in the east.

Planting another filled glass on the tray, Ollie Kampenfeldt gloomed at a night-shrouded window and said: "It's been dark two hours. They've been gone all day. No breakfast, no dinner, no supper, nothing. A feller can't live on nothing. I don't like it."

"Me neither," approved somebody. "Maybe something's happened."

"If one had broken his leg or his neck, the other would be here to tell us," another pointed out. "Besides, if it were anyone else, I'd suggest a search for them. But you know those two coots. Isn't the first time Johnson and Greer have taken to the jungle. Reckon they've seen too many Tarzan pictures. Just a pair of overgrown, musclebound kids."

"Johnson's no kid," denied the first. "He's an ex-navy heavyweight who still likes to jump around."

"Aw, probably they've got lost. It's the easiest thing in the world to get lost if you wander a bit. Four times I've had to camp out all night, and—"

"I don't like it," interjected Kampenfeldt, firmly.

"O.K., you don't like it. What are you going to do about it? Phone the cops?"

"There's no phone, as you know," said Kampenfeldt. "Who'd drag a line right up here?" He thought it over, frowning fatly, and wiped his forehead. "I'll give 'em to morning. If they're not back by then, I'll send Sid on his motorcycle to tell the forest rangers. Nobody's going to say I did nothing about it."

"That's the spirit, Ollie," one of them approved. "You look after nature's children and they'll look after you."

Several laughed at that, heartily. Within half an hour Johnson and Greer were forgotten.

*        *        *

It was early in the afternoon when the tracer operators rushed into the main cabin and so far forgot themselves as not to match Id-Wan's shape. Remaining rotund, tentacular and pale purple, the leading one of the three gestured excitedly as he spoke.

"Two have gone, captain."

"Two what have gone where?" demanded Id-Wan, glowering at him.

"Two dynamic sparks."

"Are you certain?" Without waiting for a reply, Id-Wan ran to the receivers.

It was true enough. Six globes still held their tiny lights. Two were dull, devoid of any gleam. Even as he watched, another became extinguished. Then, in rapid succession, three more.

The chief of the scouts came in saying: "What's the matter? Is there something wrong?"

Slowly, almost ponderously, Id-Wan said, "Six scouts have surrendered life in the last few moments." He breathed heavily, seemed to have trouble in accepting the evidence of the globes. "These instruments say they are dead, and if indeed they are dead they cannot retain shape. Their bodies automatically will revert to the form of their fathers. And you know that means— "

"A complete giveaway," said the chief of the scouts, staring grimly at the gloves.

Both remaining lights went out.

"Action stations!" yelled Id-Wan, electrified by the sight. "Close all ports! Trim the tubes! Prepare for take-off!" He turned savagely upon Po-Duk. "You're the pilot. Don't squat there gaping like an ebelmint half-way out of its egg! Get into the control seat, idiot—we've no time to lose!"

Something whisked overhead. He caught a fleeting glimpse of it through the nearest observation port. Something long, shapely and glistening, but much too fast to examine. It had gone almost before it registered. Seconds later its noise followed a terrible howl.

The radio technician said: "Powerful signals nearby. Their sources seem to be—"

The ship's tubes coughed, spluttered, shot fire, coughed

again. A tree began to burn. Id-Wan danced with impatience. He dashed to the control room.

"Blast, Po-Duk, blast!"

"There is not yet enough lift, captain, and until the meters show that—"

"Look!" screamed Bi-Nak, pointing for the last time.

They could see what was coming through the facing port; seven ultra-rapid dots in V-formation. The dots lengthened, sprouted wings, swept immediately overhead without a sound. Black lumps fell from their bellies, came down, struck the ship and all around the ship.

The badly lagging noise of the planes never got that far. Their leading waves were repulsed by the awful blast of the bombs.

For the final change, the Rigelians became a cloud of scattered molecules.

\*     \*     \*

Settling himself more comfortably in the chair, the roving video reporter griped, "I'd no sooner shown my face in the office than the area supervisor grabbed me, told me to chase up here and give the breathless world a candid close-up of mad Martians on the rampage. I'm partway here when the Air Force chips in, holds me back a couple of hours. When I do get here what do I find?" He sniffed sourly, "Some timber smoking around a whacking big crater. Nothing else. Not a pretzel."

Dragging an almost endless handkerchief from his pocket, Kampenfeldt smeared it across his brow. "We keep civilization at arm's length here. We've no radio, no video. So I don't know what you're talking about."

"It's like this," explained the reporter. "they dumped their spies in the parks during the night. They weren't around long because they got picked up with the milk. Twenty steps and Clancy had 'em."

"Eh?"

"The cops," elucidated the other. "We put the faces of the first pair on the breakfast-time videocast. Ten people phoned through in a hurry and identified them as Johnson and Greer. So we assumed that said Johnson and Greer were nuts." He gave a lugubrious laugh.

"Sometimes I've thought so myself," Kampenfeldt offered.

"Then, half an hour later, the next station on the chain infringed our copyright by also showing Johnson and Greer. Another followed suit ten minutes later still. By ten o'clock there were four pairs of them, as alike as two of you, and all grabbed in similar circumstances. It looked like the whole cockeyed world wanted to be Johnson or, alternatively, Greer."

"Not me," denied Kampenfeldt. "Neither of them."

"The news value of that was, of course, way up. We planted the entire eight of them on the midmorning boost, which is nationwide, our only thought being that we'd got something mighty queer. Military intelligence boys in Washington saw the videocast, pestered local cops for details, put two and two together and made it four, if not eight."

"And then?"

"They clamped heavy pressure on all these Johnsons and Greers. They talked all right, but nothing they said made sense. Eventually one of them tried a fast out, got killed on the run. He was still Johnson when he flopped, but a couple of minutes later his body turned to something else, something right out of this world. Boy, it would have turned your stomach!"

"In that case, I want no description," said Kampenfeldt, defensively nursing his outside paunch.

"That was an eye-opener. Anything not of this world obviously must be of some other. The authorities bore down on the remaining seven, who acted as before until they realized that we knew what we knew. Forthwith they put death before dishonor, leaving us with eight dollops of goo and no details."

"Ugh!" said Kampenfeldt, hitching his paunch.

"Our only clue lay in Johnson and Greer. Since these creatures had copied real people, the thing to do was find the last known whereabouts of said people. Chances were good that alien invaders would be found in that vicinity. A shout went up for Johnson and Greer. Fifty friends of theirs put them here, right here. The forest rangers chipped in saying you'd just reported them missing."

"I did," admitted Kampenfeldt. "And if I'd known where they'd gone, I'd be missing myself—and still running."

"Well, the Air Force took over. They were told to

look-see. If an alien ship was down, it was to stay down. You know those boys. They swoop around yipping. They overdid the job, left not a sliver of metal as big as my finger. So what do I put on the videocast? Just a crater and some smoking tree stumps."

"Which is no great pity," opined Kampenfeldt. "Who wants to see things that could climb into your bed as Uncle Willie? You wouldn't know who was who with creatures like that around."

"You would not." The reporter pondered awhile, added, "Their simulation was perfect. They had the power to lead us right up the garden path if only they'd known how to use it. Power is never much good unless you know how to use it. They made a first-class blunder when they grabbed their models." He scratched his head, eyed the other speculatively. "It sure beats me that of all places in this wide world they had to pick on a nudist camp."

"Solar health center," corrected Kampenfeldt, primly.

# INVASION OF PRIVACY

## BY BOB SHAW

"I saw Granny Cummins again today," Sammy said through a mouthful of turnip and potato.

May's fork clattered into her plate. She turned her head away, and I could see there were tears in her eyes. In my opinion she had always been much too deeply attached to her mother, but this time I could sympathize with her—there was something about the way the kid had said it.

"Listen to me, Sammy." I leaned across the table and gripped his shoulder. "The next time you make a dumb remark like that I'll paddle your backside good and hard. It wasn't funny."

He gazed at me with all the bland defiance a seven-year-old can muster. "I wasn't trying to be funny. I saw her."

"Your granny's been dead for two weeks," I snapped, exasperated both at him and at May, who was letting the incident get too far under her skin. Her lips had begun to tremble.

"Two weeks," Sammy repeated, savoring the words. He had just discovered sarcasm and I could tell by his eyes he was about to try some on. "If she'd only been dead two days it woulda been all right, I suppose. But not two weeks, huh?" He rammed a huge blob of creamed potato into his mouth with a flourish.

"George!" May's brown eyes were spilling as she looked at me and the copper strands of her hair quivered with anger. "Do something to that *child!* Make him drop dead."

"I can't smack him for that, hon," I said reasonably. "The kid was only being logical. Remember in 'Decline and Fall' where a saint got her head chopped off, then was supposed to get up and walk a mile or so to the

104

burial ground, and religious writers made a great fuss about the distance she'd covered, and Gibbon said in a case like that the distance wasn't the big thing—it was the taking of the first step? Well . . ." I broke off as May fled from the table and ran upstairs. The red sunlight of an October evening glowed on her empty chair, and Sammy continued eating.

"See what you've done?" I rapped his blond head with my knuckles, but not sharply enough to hurt. "I'm letting you off this time—for the *last* time—but I can't let you go on upsetting your mother with a stupid joke. Now cut it out."

Sammy addressed the remains of his dinner. "I wasn't joking I . . . saw . . . Granny . . . Cummins."

"She's been dead and buried for . . ." I almost said two weeks again, but stopped as an expectant look appeared on his face. He was quite capable of reproducing the same sarcasm word for word. "How do you explain that?"

"Me?" A studied look of surprise. "*I* can't explain it. I'm just telling you what I seen."

"All right—where did you see her?"

"In the old Guthrie place, of course."

*Of course,* I thought with a thrill of something like nostalgia. *Where else?* Every town, every district in every city, has its equivalent of the old Guthrie place. To find it, you simply stop any small boy and ask him if he knows of a haunted house where grisly murders are committed on a weekly schedule and vampires issue forth at night. I sometimes think that if no suitable building existed already the community of children would create one to answer a dark longing in their collective mind.

But the building is always there—a big, empty, ramshackle house, usually screened by near-black evergreens, never put up for sale, never pulled down, always possessing a magical immunity to property developers. And in the small town where I live the old Guthrie house was the one which filled the bill. I hadn't really thought about it since childhood, but it looked just the same as ever—dark, shabby and forbidding—and I should have known it would have the same associations for another generation of kids. At the mention of the house Sammy had become solemn and I almost laughed aloud as I saw myself, a quarter of a century younger, in his face.

"How could you have seen anything in there?" I decided to play along a little further as long as May was out of earshot. "It's too far from the road."

"I climbed through the fence."

"Who was with you?"

"Nobody."

"You went in alone?"

"Course I did." Sammy tilted his head proudly and I recalled that as a seven-year-old nothing in the world would have induced me to approach that house, even in company. I looked at my son with a new respect, and the first illogical stirrings of alarm.

"I don't want you hanging around that old place, Sammy—it could be dangerous."

"It isn't dangerous." He was scornful. "They just sit there in big chairs, and never move."

"I meant you could fall or . . . *What?*"

"The old people just sit there." Sammy pushed his empty plate away. "They'd never catch me in a hundred years even if they seen me, but I don't let them see me, cause I just take one quick look through the back window and get out of there."

"You mean there are people living in the Guthrie place?"

"Old people. Lots of them. They just sit there in big chairs."

I hadn't heard anything about the house being occupied, but I began to guess what had been going on. It was big enough for conversion to a private home for old people—and to a child one silver-haired old lady could look very much like another. Perhaps Sammy preferred to believe his grandmother had moved away rather than accept the idea that she was dead and buried beneath the ground in a box.

"Then you were trespassing as well as risking . . ." I lowered my voice to a whisper as May's footsteps sounded on the stairs again. "You didn't see your Granny Cummins, you're not to go near the old Guthrie place again, and you're not to upset your mother. Got that?"

Sammy nodded, but his lips were moving silently and I knew he was repeating his original statement over and over to himself. Any anger I felt was lost in a tide of affection—my entire life had been one of compromise and equivocation, and it was with gratitude I had discovered that my son had been born with enough will and sheer character for the two of us.

May came back into the room and sat down, her face wearing a slightly shamefaced expression behind the gold sequins of its freckles. "I took a tranquilizer."

"Oh? I thought you were out of them."

"I was, but Doctor Pitman stopped by this afternoon and he let me have some more."

"Did you call him?"

"No—he was in the neighborhood and he looked in just to see how I was. He's been very good since . . . since . . ."

"Since your mother died—you've got to get used to the idea, May."

She nodded silently and began to gather up the dinner plates. Her own food had scarcely been touched.

"Mom?" Sammy tugged her sleeve. I tensed, waiting for him to start it all over again, but he had other things on his mind. His normally ruddy cheeks were pale as tallow and his forehead was beaded with perspiration. I darted from my chair barely in time to catch him as he fell sideways to the floor.

## II

Bob Pitman had been a white-haired, apple-cheeked old gentleman when he was steering me through boyhood illnesses, and he appeared not to have aged any further in the interim. He lived alone in an unfashionably large house, still wore a conservative dark suit with a watch-chain's gold parabola spanning the vest, played chess as much as possible and drank specially-imported non-blended Scotch. The sight of his square hands, with their ridged and slab-like fingernails, moving over Sammy's sleeping figure comforted me even before he stood up and folded the stethoscope.

"The boy has eaten something he shouldn't," he said, drawing the covers up to Sammy's chin.

"But he'll be all right?" May and I spoke simultaneously.

"Right as rain."

"Thank God," May said and sat down very suddenly. I knew she had been thinking about her mother and wondering if we were going to lose Sammy with as little warning.

"You'd better get some rest." Dr. Pitman looked at her with kindly severity. "Young Sammy here will sleep all night, and you should follow his example. Take another of those caps I gave you this morning."

I'd forgotten about his earlier visit. "We seem to be monopolizing your time today, Doctor."

"Just think of it as providing me with a little employment—everybody's far too healthy these days." He shepherded us out of Sammy's room. "I'll call again in the morning."

May wasn't quite satisfied—she was scrupulously hygienic in the kitchen and the idea that our boy had food poisoning was particularly unacceptable to her. "But what could Sammy have eaten, Doctor? We've had everything he's had and we're all right."

"It's hard to say. When he brought up his dinner did you notice anything else there? Berries? Exotic candies?"

"No. Nothing like that," I said, "but they wouldn't always be obvious, would they?" I put my arm around May's shoulders and tried to force her to relax. She was rigid with tension and it came to me that if Sammy ever were to contract a fatal illness or be killed in an accident it would destroy her. We of the Twentieth Century have abandoned the practice of holding something in reserve when we love our children, assuming—as our ancestors would never have dared to do—that they will reach adulthood as a matter of course.

The doctor—nodding and smiling and wheezing—exuded reassurance for a couple more minutes before he left. When I took May to bed she huddled in the crook of my left arm, lonely in spite of our intimacy, and it was a long time before I was able to soothe her to sleep.

In spite of her difficulty in getting to sleep, or perhaps because of it, May failed to waken when I slipped out of the bed early next morning. I went into Sammy's room, and knew immediately that something was wrong. His breathing was noisy and rapid as that of a pup which has been running. I went to the bed. He was unconscious, mouth wide open in the ghastly breathing, and his forehead hotter than I would have believed it possible for a human's to be.

Fear spurted coldly in my guts as I turned and ran for the phone. I dialed Dr. Pitman's number. While it was ringing I debated shouting upstairs to waken May, but far from being able to help Sammy she would probably have become hysterical. I decided to let her sleep as long as possible. After a seemingly interminable wait the phone clicked.

"Dr. Pitman speaking." The voice was sleepy.

"This is George Ferguson. Sammy's very ill. Can you get over here right away?" I babbled a description of the symptoms.

"I'll be right there." The sleepiness had left his voice. I hung up, opened the front door wide so that the doctor could come straight in, then went back upstairs and waited beside the bed. Sammy's hair was plastered to his forehead and his every breath was accompanied by harsh metallic clicks in his throat. My mind became an anvil for the hammer blows of the passing seconds. Bleak eons went by before I heard Dr. Pitman's footsteps on the stair.

He came into the room, looking uncharacteristically disheveled, took one look at Sammy and lifted him in his arms in a cocoon of bedding.

"Pneumonia," he said tersely. "The boy will have to be hospitalized immediately."

Somehow I managed to speak. "Pneumonia! But you said he'd eaten something."

"There's no connection between this and what was wrong yesterday. There's a lightning pneumonia on the move across the country."

"Oh. Shall I ring for an ambulance?"

"No. I'll drive him to the clinic myself. The streets are clear at this hour of the morning and we'll make better time." He carried Sammy towards the door with surprising ease.

"Wait. I'm coming with you."

"You could help more by phoning the clinic and alerting them, George. Where's your wife?"

"Still asleep—she doesn't know." I had almost forgotten about May.

He raised his eyebrows, paused briefly on the landing. "Ring the clinic first, tell them I'm coming, then waken your wife. Don't let her get too worried, and don't get too tensed up yourself—I've an emergency oxygen kit in the car, and Sammy should be all right once we get him into an intensive care unit."

I nodded gratefully, watching my son's blindly lolling face as he was carried down the stairs, then went to the phone and called the clinic. The people I spoke to sounded both efficient and sympathetic, and it was only a matter of seconds before I was sprinting upstairs to waken May. She was sitting on the edge of the bed as I entered the room.

"George?" Her voice was cautious. "What's happening?"

"Sammy has pneumonia. Dr. Pitman's driving him to the clinic now, and he's going to be well taken care of." I was getting dressed as I spoke, praying she would be able to take the news with some semblance of calm. She stood up quietly and began to put on clothes, moving with mechanical exactitude, and when I glimpsed her eyes I suddenly realized it would have been better had she screamed or thrown a fit. We went down to the car, shivering in the thick gray air of the October morning, and drove towards the clinic. At the end of the street I remembered I had left the front door of the house open, but didn't turn back. I think I'd done it deliberately, hoping—with a quasi-religious irrationality—that we might be robbed and thus appease the Fates, diverting their attention from Sammy. There was little traffic on the roads but I drove at moderate speed, aware that I had virtually no powers of concentration for anything extraneous to the domestic tragedy. May sat beside me and gazed out the windows with the air of a child reluctantly returning from a long vacation.

It was with a sense of surprise that, on turning into the clinic grounds, I saw Dr. Pitman's blue Buick sliding to a halt under the canopy of the main entrance. In my estimation he should have been a good ten minutes ahead of us. May's fingers clawed into my thigh as she saw the white bundle being lifted out and carried into the building by a male nurse. I parked close to the entrance, heedless of painted notices telling me the space was for doctors only, and we ran into the dimness of the reception hall. There was no sign of Sammy, but Dr. Pitman was waiting for us.

"You just got here," I accused. "What held you up?"

"Be calm, George. Getting into a panic won't help things in the least." He urged us towards a row of empty chairs. "Nothing held me back—I was driving with one hand and feeding your boy oxygen with the other."

"I'm sorry, it's just . . . How is he?"

"Still breathing, and that's the main thing. Pneumonia's never to be taken lightly—especially this twelve-hour variety we've been getting lately—but there's every reason for confidence."

May stirred slightly at that—I think she had been expecting to hear the worst—but I had a conviction Dr. Pitman was merely trying to let us down as gently as he could. He had always had an uncompromisingly level stare, but now his gaze kept sliding away from mine. We waited a long time for news of Sammy's condition, and on the few occasions when I caught Dr. Pitman looking directly at me his eyes were strangely like those of a man in torment.

I thought, too, that he was relieved when one of the doctors on the staff of the clinic used all his authority to persuade May it would be much better for everybody if she waited at home.

## III

The house was lonely that evening. May had refused sedation and was sitting with the telephone, nursing it in her lap, as though it might at any minute speak with Sammy's own voice. I made sandwiches and coffee but she wouldn't eat, and this somehow made it impossible for me to take anything. Tiny particles of darkness came drifting at dusk, gathering in all the corners and passageways of the house, and I finally realised I would have to get out under the sky. May nodded abstractedly when I told her I was going for a short walk. I switched on all the lights in the lounge before leaving, but when I looked back from the sidewalk she had turned them off again.

*Go ahead,* I raged. *Sit in the darkness—a lot of good that will do him.*

My anger subsided when I remembered that May was at least clinging to hope; whereas I had resigned myself, betraying my own son by not daring to believe he would recover in case I'd be hurt once more. I walked quickly but aimlessly, trying to think practical thoughts about how long I'd be absent from the drafting office where I worked, and if the contract I was part way through could be taken over by another man. But instead I kept seeing my boy's face, and at times sobbed aloud to the uncomprehending quietness of suburban avenues.

I don't know what took me in the direction of the old Guthrie place—perhaps some association between it and dark forces threatening Sammy—but there it was, looming up at the end of a short cul-de-sac, looking exactly as it had done when I was at school. The stray fingers of light reaching it from the road showed boarded-up windows, sagging gutters and unpainted boards which were silver-gray from exposure. I examined the building soberly, feeling echoes of the childhood dread it had once inspired. My theory about it having been renovated and put to use had been wrong, I realized—I'd been a victim of Sammy's hyperactive imagination and mischievousness.

I was turning away when I noticed fresh car tracks in the gravel of the leaf-strewn drive leading up to the house. Nothing very odd about that, I thought. Curiosity could lead anybody to drive up to the old pile for a closer look, and yet . . .

Suddenly I could see apples in a tree at the rear of the house.

The fruit appeared as blobs of yellowish luminescence in the tree's black silhouette, and I stared at them for several seconds wondering why the sight should fill me with unease. Then the answer came. At that distance from the street lights the apples should have been invisible, but they were glowing like dim fairy lanterns—which meant they were being illuminated from another, nearer source. This simple application of the inverse square law led me to the astonishing conclusion that there was a lighted window at the back of the Guthrie house.

On the instant, I was a small boy again. I wanted to run away, but in my adult world there was no longer any place to which I could flee—and I was curious about what was going on in the old house. There was enough corroboration of Sammy's story to make it clear that he had seen something. But old people sitting in big chairs? I went slowly and self-consciously through the drifts of moist leaves, inhaling the toadstool smell of decay, and moved along the side of the house towards crawling blackness. It seemed impossible that there could be anybody within those flaking walls—the light must have been left burning, perhaps weeks earlier, by a careless real estate man.

I skirted a heap of rubbish and reached the back of the house. A board had been loosened on one of the downstairs windows, creating a small triangular aperture through which streamed a wan lemon radiance. I approached it quietly and looked in. The room beyond was lit by a naked bulb and contained perhaps eight armchairs, each of which was occupied by an old man or an old woman. Most were reading magazines, but one woman was knitting. My eyes took in the entire scene in a single sweep, then fastened on the awful, familiar face of the woman in the chair nearest the window.

Sammy had been right—it was the face of his dead grandmother.

That was when the nightmare really began. The frightened child within me and the adult George Ferguson both agreed they had stumbled on something monstrous, and that adrenalin-boosted flight was called for; yet—as in a nightmare—I was unable to do anything but move closer to the focus of horror. I stared at the old woman in dread. Her rawboned face, the lump beneath one ear, the very way she held her magazine—all these told me I was looking at May's mother, Mrs. Martha Cummins, who had died suddenly of a brain hemorrhage more than two weeks earlier, and who was buried in the family plot.

Of its own accord, my right hand went snaking into the triangular opening and tapped the dusty glass. It was a timid gesture and none of the people within responded to the faint sound, but a second later one of the men raised his head briefly as he turned a page, and I recognized him. Joe Bryant, the caretaker at Sammy's school. He had died a year ago of a heart attack.

Explanation? I couldn't conceive one, but I had to speak to the woman who appeared to be May's mother.

I turned away from the window and went to the black rectangle of the house's rear door. It was locked in the normal way and further secured by a bolted-on padlock. A film of oil on its working parts told me the padlock was in good condition. I moved further along and tried another smaller window in what could have been the kitchen. It too was boarded up, but when I pulled experimentally at the short planks the whole frame moved slightly with a pulpy sound. A more determined tug brought the entire metal window frame clear of its surround of rotting wood, creating a dark opening. The operation was noisier than I had expected, but the house remained still and I set the window down against the wall.

Part of my mind was screaming its dismay, but I used the window frame as a ladder and climbed through onto a greasy complicated surface which proved to be the top of an old-fashioned gas stove. My cigarette lighter shed silver sparks as I flicked it on. Its transparent blue shoot of flame cast virtually no light, so I tore pages from my notebook and lit them. The kitchen was a shambles, and obviously not in use—a fact which, had I thought about it, would have increased my sense of alarm. A short corridor led from it in the general direction of the lighted room. Burning more pages, I went towards the room, freezing each time a bare floorboard groaned or a loose strip of wallpaper brushed my shoulder, and soon was able to discern a gleam of light coming from below a door. I gripped the handle firmly and, afraid to hesitate, flung open the door. The old people in the big armchairs turned their pink, lined faces towards mine. Mrs. Cummins stared at me, face lengthening with what could have been recognition or shock.

"It's George," I heard myself say in the distance. "What's happening here?"

She stood up and her lips moved. "Nigi olon prittle o czanig *sovisess!*" On the final word the others jumped to their feet with strangely lithe movements.

"Mrs. Cummins?" I said. "Mr. Bryant?"

The old people set their magazines down, came towards the door and I saw that their feet were bare. I backed out into the corridor, shaking my head apologetically, then turned to run. Could I get out through the small kitchen window quickly enough? A hand clawed down my back. I beat it off and ran in the direction opposite to the kitchen, guided by the light spilling from the room behind me. A door loomed up on my left. I burst through into pitch darkness, slammed it, miraculously found a

key in the lock and twisted it. the door quivered as
something heavy thudded against the wood from the
other side, and a woman's voice began an unnerving
wail—thin, high, anxious.

I groped for the light switch and turned it on, but
nothing happened. Afraid to take a step forward, I stared
into the blackness that pressed against my face, gradually
becoming aware of a faint soupy odor and a feeling of
warmth. I guessed I was in a room at the front of the
house and might be able to break out if only I could find
a window. The wallpaper beside the switch had felt loose.
I gripped a free edge, pulled off a huge swathe and rolled
it into the shape of a torch while the hammering on the
door grew more frantic. The blue cone of flame from my
cigarette lighter ignited the dry paper immediately. I held
the torch high and got a flickering view of a large square
room, a bank of electronic equipment along one wall,
and a waist-high tank which occupied most of the floor
space. The sweet soupy smell appeared to be coming
from the dark liquid in the tank. I looked into it and saw
a half-submerged *thing* floating face upwards. It was about
the size of a seven-year-old boy and the dissolving, jellied
features had a resemblance to . . .

*No!*

I screamed and threw the flaming torch from me, seeking my former state of blindness. The torch landed close
to a wall and trailing streamers of wallpaper caught alight.
I ran around the tank to a window, wadded its mouldering
drapes and smashed the glass outwards against the boards.
The planking resisted the onslaught of my feet and fists
for what seemed an eternity, then I was out in the cool
fresh air and running, barely feeling the ground below
my feet, swept along by the dark winds of night.

When I finally looked back, blocks away, the sky above
the old Guthrie place was already stained red, and clouds
of angry sparks wheeled and wavered in the ascending
smoke.

## IV

How does one assimilate an experience like that? There
were some aspects of the nightmare which my mind was
completely unable to handle as I walked homewards,

accompanied by the sound of distant fire sirens. There was, for example, the hard fact that I had started a fire in which at that very instant a group of old people could be perishing—but, somehow, I felt no guilt. In its place was a conviction that if the blaze hadn't begun by accident I would have been entitled, *obliged,* to start one to rid the world of something which hadn't any right to exist. There was no element of the religious in my thinking, because the final horror in the house's front room had dispelled the aura of the supernatural surrounding the previous events.

I had seen an array of electronic equipment—unfamiliar in type, but unmistakable—and I had seen a *thing* floating in a tank of heated organic-smelling fluid, a thing which resembled . . .

*No!* Madness lay along that avenue of thought. Insupportable pain.

What else had I stumbled across? Granny Cummins was dead—but she had been sitting in the back room of a disused house, and had spoken in a tongue unlike any language I'd ever heard. Joe Bryant was dead, for a year, yet he too had been sitting under that naked bulb. My son was seriously ill in the hospital, and yet . . .

*No!*

Retreating from monstrosities as yet unguessed, my mind produced an image of Dr. Pitman. He had attended Granny Cummins. He had, I was almost certain, been the Bryant's family doctor. He had attended Sammy that morning. He had been in my home the previous day—perhaps when Sammy had come in and spoke of seeing people in the old Guthrie place. My mind then threw up another image—that of the long-barreled .22 target pistol lying in a drawer in my den. I began to walk more quickly.

On reaching home the first impression was that May had gone out, but when I went in she was sitting in exactly the same place in the darkness of the lounge. I glanced at my watch and discovered that, incredibly, only forty minutes had passed since I had gone out. That was all the time it had taken for reality to rot and dissolve.

"May?" I spoke from the doorway. "Did the clinic call?"

A long pause. "No."

"Don't you want the light on?"

Another pause. "No."

This time I didn't mind, because the darkness concealed the fact that my clothes were smeared with dirt and blood from my damaged hands. I went upstairs, past the aching emptiness of Sammy's room, washed in cold water, taped my knuckles and put on fresh clothes. In my den I discovered that the saw-handled target pistol was never meant for concealment, but I was able to tuck it into my belt on the left side and cover it fairly well with my jacket. Coming downstairs, I hesitated at the door of the lounge before telling May I was going out again. She nodded without speaking, without caring what I might do. If Sammy died she would die too—not physically, not clinically, but just as surely—which meant that two important lives depended on my actions of the next hour.

I went out and found the atmosphere of the night had changed to one of feverish excitement. The streets were alive with cars, pedestrians, running children, all converging on the gigantic bonfire which had appeared, gratuitously, to turn a dull evening into an event. Two blocks away to the south the old Guthrie house was an inferno which streaked the windows of the entire neighborhood with amber and gold. Its timbers, exploding in ragged volleys, were fireworks contributing to the Fourth of July atmosphere. A group of small boys scampering past me whooped with glee, and one part of my mind acknowledged that I had made a major contribution to the childish lore of the district. Legends would be born tonight, to be passed in endless succession from the mouths of ten-year-olds to the ears of five-year-olds. *The night the old Guthrie place burned down . . .*

Dr. Pitman lived only a mile from me, and I decided it would be almost as quick and a lot less conspicuous to go on foot. I walked automatically, trying to balance the elements of reality, nightmare and carnival, and reached the doctor's home in a little over ten minutes. His Buick was sitting in the driveway and lights were showing in the upper windows of the house. I looked around carefully— the fire was further away now and neighbours were less likely to be distracted by it—before stepping into the shadowed drive and approaching the front door. It burst open just as I was reaching the steps and Dr. Pitman came running out, still struggling on his coat. I reached for the pistol but there was no need to bring it into view, for he stopped as soon as he saw me.

"George!" His face creased with concern. "What brings you here? Is it your boy?"

"You've guessed it." I put my hand on his chest and pushed him back into the orange-lit hall.

"What is this?" He surged against my hand with surprising strength and I had to fight to contain him. "You're acting a little strangely, George."

"You made Sammy sick," I told him. "And if you don't make him well again I'll kill you."

"Hold on, George—I told you not to get overwrought."

"I'm not overwrought."

"It's the strain . . ."

*"That's enough!"* I shouted at him, almost losing control. "I know you're making Sammy ill, and I'm going to make you stop."

"But why should I . . .?"

"Because he was in back of the old Guthrie place and saw too much—that's why." I pushed harder on his chest and he took a step backwards into the hall.

"The Guthrie house! No, George, *no!*"

Until that moment I had been half-prepared to back down, to accept the idea that I'd gone off the rails with worry, but his face became a slack gray mask. The strength seemed to leave his body, making him smaller and older.

"Yes, the old Guthrie place." I closed the door behind me. "What do you do there, doctor?"

"Listen, George, I can't talk to you now—I've just heard there's a fire in the district and I've got to go to it. My help will be needed." Dr. Pitman drew himself up into a semblance of the authoritative figure I had once known, and tried to push past me.

"You're too late," I said, blocking his way. "The place went up like a torch. Your equipment's all gone." I paused and stared into his eyes. "*They* are all gone."

"I . . . I don't know what you mean."

"The things you make. The things which look like people, but which aren't because the original people are dead. Those are all gone, doctor—burnt up." I was shooting wildly in the dark, but I could tell some of my words were finding a mark and I pressed on. "I was there, and

I've seen it, and I'll tell the whole world—so Sammy isn't alone now. His death won't cover up anything. Do you hear me, doctor?''

He shook his head, then walked away from me and went up the broad carpeted stair. I reached for the pistol, changed my mind and ran after him, catching him just as he reached the landing. He brushed my hands away. Using all my strength, I bundled him against the wall with my forearm pressed across his throat, determined to force the truth out of him—no matter what it might be. He twisted away, I grappled again, we overbalanced and went on a jarring rollercoaster ride down the stairs, bouncing and flailing, caroming off wall and bannisters. Twice on the way down I felt, and heard, bones breaking; and I lay on the hall floor a good ten seconds before being certain they weren't mine.

I raised myself on one arm and looked down into Dr. Pitman's face. His teeth were smeared with blood and for a moment I felt the beginnings of doubt. He was an old man, and supposing he genuinely hadn't understood a word I had been saying . . .

"You've done it now, George," he whispered. "You've finished us."

"What do you mean?"

"There's one thing I want you to believe . . . we never harmed anybody . . . we've seen too much pain for that . . ." He coughed and a transparent crimson film spanned his lips.

"What are you saying?"

"It was to be a very quiet, very gradual invasion . . . invasion's the wrong word . . . no conquest or displacement intended . . . physical journey from our world virtually impossible . . . we observed incurably ill humans, terminal cases . . . built duplicates and substituted them . . . that way we too could live normally, almost normally, for a while . . . until death returned . . ."

"Dr. Pitman," I said desperately, "you're not making sense."

"I'm not real Dr. Pitman . . . he died many years ago . . . first subject in this town—a doctor is in best position for our . . . I was *skorded*—you have no word for it—transmitted into a duplicate of his body . . ."

The hall floor seemed to rock beneath me. "You're saying you're from another planet!"

"That's right, George."

"But, for God's sake, *why?* Why would anybody . . .?"

"Just be thankful you can't imagine the circumstances which made such a project . . . desirable." His body convulsed with sudden pain.

"I still don't understand," I pleaded. "Why should you duplicate the bodies of dying people if it means being locked in an old house for the rest of your life?"

"Usually it doesn't mean that . . . we substitute and integrate . . . the dying person appears to recover . . . but the duplication process takes time, and sometimes the subject dies suddenly, at home, providing us with no chance to take his place . . . and there can be no going back . . ."

I froze as a brilliant golden light flooded through the hall. It was followed by the sound of wheels on gravel and I realized a car had pulled into the driveway of the house. The man I knew as Dr. Pitman closed his eyes and sighed deeply, with an awful finality.

"But what about Sammy?" I shook the inert figure. "You've told me nothing about my son."

The eyes blinked open, slowly, and in spite of the pain there I saw—kindness. "It was all a mistake, George." His voice was distant as he attempted more of the broken sentences. "I had no idea he had been around the old house . . . aren't like you—we're bad organizers . . . *nald denbo sovisegg* . . . sorry . . . I had nothing to do with his illness . . ."

A car door slammed outside. I wanted to run, but there was one more question which had to be asked. "I was in the old house. I saw the tank and . . . something . . . which looked like a boy. Does that mean Sammy's dying? That you were going to replace him?"

"Sammy's going to be all right, George . . . though at first I wasn't hopeful . . . I haven't known you and May as long as Dr. Pitman did, but I'm very fond of . . . I knew May couldn't take the loss, so I arranged a substitution . . . tentatively, you understand, *kleyl nurr* . . . not needed now . . . Sammy will be fine . . ." He tried to smile at me and blood welled up between his lips just as the doorbell rang with callous stridency.

I stared down at the tired, broken old man with—in spite of everything—a curious sense of regret. What kind of hell had he been born into originally? What conditions would prompt anybody to make the journey he had made for such meagre rewards? The bell rang again and I opened the door.

"Call an ambulance," I said to the stranger on the steps. "Dr. Pitman seems to have fallen down the stairs—I think he's dying."

## V

It was quite late when the police cruiser finally dropped me outside my home, but the house was ablaze with light. I thanked the sergeant who had driven me from the mortuary where they had taken the body of Dr. Pitman (I couldn't think of him by any other name) and hurried along the white concrete of the path to the door. The lights seemed to signal a change in May's mood but I was afraid to begin hoping, in case . . .

"George!" May met me at the door, dressed to go out, face pale but jubilant. "Where've you been? I tried everywhere. The clinic called me half an hour ago. You've been out for hours. Sammy's feeling better and he's asking to see us. I brought the car out for you. Should I drive? We're allowed in to see him, and I . . ."

"Slow down, May. Slow down." I put my arms around her, feeling the taut gratification in her slim body, and made her go over the story again. She spilled it out eagerly.

Sammy's response to drug treatment had been dramatic and now he was fully conscious and asking for his parents. The senior doctor had decided to bend regulations a little and let us in to talk with the boy for a few minutes. A starshell of happiness burst behind my eyes as May spoke, and a minute later we were on our way to the clinic. A big moon, the exact color of a candle flame, was rising behind the rooftops, trees were stirring gently in their sleep, and the red glow from the direction of the Guthrie house had vanished. May was at the wheel, driving with zestful competence, and for the first time in hours the pressure was off me.

I relaxed into the seat and discovered I had forgotten to rid myself of the pistol which had nudged my ribs constantly the whole time I was talking to the police. It

was on the side next to May so there was little chance of
slipping it into the glove compartment unnoticed. Shame
at having carried the weapon, plus a desire not to alarm
May in any way after what she had been through, made
me decide to keep it out of sight a little longer. Suddenly
very tired, I closed my eyes and allowed the mental
backwash of the night's events to carry me away.

The disjointed fragments from Dr. Pitman made an
unbelievable story when pieced together, yet I had seen
the ghastly proof. There was something macabre about
the idea of the group of alien beings, duplication of dead
people, cooped up in a dingy room in a disused house,
patiently waiting to die. The memory of seeing Granny
Cummins' face again, two weeks after her funeral, was
going to take a long time to fade. She, the duplicate, had
recognized me, which meant that the copying technique
used by the aliens was incredibly detailed, extending
right down to the arrangement of the brain cells. Presumably, the only physical changes they would introduce
would be improvements—if a person was dying of cancer
the duplicate would be cancer-free. Aging muscles might
be strengthened—Dr. Pitman and those who had been in
the house all moved with exceptional ease. But would
they have been able to escape the fire? Perhaps some
code of their own would not allow them to leave the
house, even under peril of death, unless a place had been
prepared to enable them to enter our society without
raising any alarms . . .

*The aliens may have a code of ethics,* I thought, *but
could I permit them to come among us unhindered?* For
that matter, had I any idea how far their infiltration had
proceeded? I'd been told that Dr. Pitman was the first
subject *in this town*—did that mean the invasion covered
the entire state? The country? The world? There was also
the question of its intensity. The dying man had said the
substitution technique failed when a person's death occurred suddenly *at home,* which implied the clinic was
well infiltrated—but how thoroughly? Would there come
a day when every old person in the world, and a propor-
tion of younger people as well, would be substitutes?

Street lights flicking past the car pulled redly through
my closed eyelids, and fresh questions pounded in my
mind to the same rhythm. Could I believe anything 'Dr.

Pitman' had said about the aliens' objectives? True, he had appeared kind, genuinely concerned about Sammy and May—but how did one interpret facial expressions controlled by a being who may once have possessed an entirely different form? Another question came looming— and something in my subconscious cowered away from it—why, if secrecy was so vital to the aliens' scheme, had 'Dr. Pitman' told me the whole fantastic story? Had he been manipulating me in some way I had not yet begun to understand? Once again I saw my son's face blindly lolling as he was carried down the stairs, and a fear greater than any I had known before began to unfold its black petals.

I jerked my eyes open, unwilling to think any further.

"Poor thing—you're tired," May said. "You keep everything bottled up, and it takes far more out of you that way."

I nodded. *She's mothering me,* I thought. *She's happy, serene, confident again—and it's because our boy is getting better. Sammy's life is her life.*

May slowed the car down. "Here we are. We mustn't stay too long—it's very good of Dr. Milligan even to let us in at this time."

I remembered Dr. Milligan—tall, stooped and *old*. Another Dr. Pitman? It came to me suddenly that I had told May nothing at all about the events of the evening, but before I could work out a suitably edited version we were getting out of the car. I decided to leave it till later. In contrast to the boisterous leaf-scented air outside the atmosphere in the clinic seemed inert, dead. The reception office was empty but a blond young doctor with an in-twisted foot limped up to us, then beckoned to a staffnurse when we gave our names. The nurse, a tall woman with mottled red forearms, ushered us into the elevator and pressed the button for the third floor.

"Samuel is making exceptional progress," she said to May. "He's a very strong little boy."

"Thank you." May nodded gratefully. "Thank you."

I wanted to change the subject, because Sammy had never appeared particularly strong to my eyes, and the loathsome blossom of fear was fleshing its leaves within me. "How's business been tonight?"

"Quiet, for once. Very quiet."

"Oh. I heard there was a fire."

"It hasn't affected us."

"That's fine," I said vaguely. If the aliens were constructed with precisely the same biological building blocks as humans their remains would appear like those of normal fire victims. *There'll be hell to pay,* I told myself and desperately tried to adhere to that line of thought, but the black flower was getting bigger now, unmanageable, reaching out to swallow me. Biological building blocks—where did they come from? The dark soupy liquid in the tank—was it of synthetic or natural origin? The thing I'd seen floating in there—was it a body being constructed?

Or was it being dissolved and fed into a stockpile of organic matter?

*Had I seen my son's corpse?*

Other thoughts came yammering and cavorting like demons. 'Dr. Pitman' had taken Sammy to the clinic in his own car, but he had been strangely delayed in arriving. Obviously he had taken the boy to the Guthrie place. Why? Because, according to his own dying statement, he had despaired of Sammy's life, wanted to spare May the shock of losing her son and had arranged for a substitution—just in case. Altruistic. Unbelievably altruistic. How gullible did 'Dr. Pitman' think I was going to be? If Sammy had died naturally, or had been killed, and replaced by a being from beyond the stars I was going to make trouble for the aliens. I was going to shout and burn and kill . . .

With an effort I controlled the sudden trembling in my limbs as the nurse opened the door to a small private room. The shaded light within showed Sammy sleeping peacefully in a single bed. My heart ached with the recognition of the flesh of my flesh.

"You may go in for a minute, but *just* a minute," the nurse said. Her eyes lingered for a moment on May's face and something she saw there prompted her to remain in the corridor while we went into the room. Sammy was pale but breathing easily. The skin of his forehead shone with gold borrowed from last summer's sun. May held my arm with both hands as we stood beside the bed.

"He's all right," she breathed. "Oh, George—I would have died."

At the sound of her voice Sammy's eyelids seemed to

flicker slightly, but he remained still. May began to sob, silently and effortlessly, adjusting emotional potentials.

"Take it easy, hon," I said. "He's all right, remember."

"I know, but I felt it was all my fault."

"Your fault?"

"Yes. Yesterday at dinner he made me so angry by talking that way about my mother . . . I said I wanted him to drop dead."

"That's being silly."

"I know, but I *said* it, and you should never say anything like that in case . . ."

"Fate isn't so easily tempted," I said with calm reasonableness I had no right to assume. "Besides you didn't mean it. Every parent knows that when a kid starts wearing you down you can say anything."

Sammy's eyes opened wide. "Mom?"

May dropped to her knees. "I'm here, Sammy. I'm here."

"I'm sorry I made you mad." His voice was small and drowsy.

"You didn't make me mad, darling." She took his hand and pressed her lips to it.

"I did. I shouldn't have talked that way about seeing Gran." He shifted his gaze to my face. "It was all a stupid joke like Dad said. I never saw Granny Cummins anywhere." His eyes were bright and deliberate, holding mine.

I took a step back from the bed and the black flower, which had poised and waiting, closed its hungry petals around me. Sammy, *my* Sammy, had seen the duplicate of Granny Cummins in the old Guthrie place—and no amount of punishment or bribery would have got him to back down on that point. Unlike me, my son had never compromised in his whole life.

Of its own accord, my right hand slid under my jacket and settled on the butt of the target pistol. My boy was dead and this—right here and now—was the time to begin avenging him.

But I looked down on May's bowed, gently shaking shoulders; and all at once I understood why 'Dr. Pitman' had told me the whole story. Had the macabre scenes in the Guthrie place remained a mystery to me, had I not understood their purpose, I could never have remained silent. Eventually I would have had to go to the police, start investigations, cause trouble . . .

Now I knew that the very first casualty of any such action would be May—she would be destroyed, on learning the truth, as surely as if I had put a bullet through her head. My hand moved away from the butt of the pistol.

*Sammy's life,* I thought, *is her life.*

In a way it isn't a bad thing to be the compromising type—it makes life easier not only for yourself but for those around you. May smiles a lot now and she is very happy over the way Sammy has grown up to be a handsome, quick-minded fourteen-year-old. The discovery of a number of 'human' remains in the ashes of the Guthrie house was a nine-day wonder in our little town, but I doubt if May remembers it now. As I said, she smiles a lot.

I still think about my son, of course, and occasionally it occurs to me that if May were to die, say in an accident, all restraints would be removed from me. But the years are slipping by and there's no sign of the human race coming to harm as a result of the quiet invasion. For all I know it never amounted to anything more than a local phenomenon, an experiment which didn't quite work out.

And when I look at Sammy growing up tall and straight—looking so much like his mother—it is easy to convince myself that I could have made a mistake. After all, I'm only human.

# WHAT HAVE I DONE?

## BY MARK CLIFTON

It had to be I. It would be stupid to say that the burden should have fallen to a great statesman, a world leader, a renowned scientist. With all modesty, I think I am one of the few who could have caught the problem early enough to avert disaster. I have a peculiar skill. The whole thing hinged on that. I have learned to know human beings.

The first time I saw the fellow, I was at the drugstore counter buying cigarettes. He was standing at the maga-zine rack. One might have thought from the expression on his face that he had never seen magazines before. Still, quite a number of people get that rapt and vacant look when they can't make up their minds to a choice.

The thing which bothered me in that casual glance was that I couldn't recognize him.

There are others who can match my record in taking case histories. I happened to be the one who came in contact with this fellow. For thirty years I have been listening to, talking with, counseling people—over two hundred thousand of them. They have not been routine interviews. I have brought intelligence, sensitivity and concern to each of them.

Mine has been a driving, burning desire to know peo-ple. Not from the western scientific point of view of devising tools and rules to measure animated robots and ignoring the man beneath. Nor from the eastern meta-physical approach to painting a picture of the soul by blowing one's breath upon a fog to be blurred and dis-persed by the next breath.

Mine was the aim to know the man by making use of both. And there was some success.

A competent geographer can look at a crude sketch of a map and instantly orient himself to it anywhere in the world—the bend of a river, the angle of a lake, the twist of a mountain range. And he can mystify by telling in finest detail what is to be found there.

After about fifty thousand studies where I could predict and then observe and check, with me it became the lift of a brow, the curve of a mouth, the gesture of a hand, the slope of a shoulder. One of the universities became interested, and over a long controlled period they rated me ninety-two per cent accurate. That was fifteen years ago. I may have improved some since.

Yet standing there at the cigarette counter and glancing at the young fellow at the magazine rack, I could read nothing. Nothing at all.

If this had been an ordinary face, I would have catalogued it and forgotten it automatically. I see them by the thousands. But this face would not be catalogued nor forgotten, because there was nothing in it.

I started to write that it wasn't even a face, but of course it was. Every human being has a face—of one sort of another.

In build he was short, muscular, rather well porportioned. The hair was crew cut and blond, the eyes were blue, the skin fair. All nice and standard Teutonic—only it wasn't.

I finished paying for my cigarettes and gave him one more glance, hoping to surprise an expression which had some meaning. There was none. I left him standing there and walked out on the street and around the corner. The street, the store fronts, the traffic cop on the corner, the warm sunshine were all so familiar I didn't see them. I climbed the stairs to my office in the building over the drug store. My employment agency waiting room was empty. I don't cater to much of a crowd because it cuts down my opportunity to talk with people and further my study.

Margie, my receptionist, was busy making out some kind of a report and merely nodded as I passed her desk to my own office. She is a good conscientious girl who can't understand why I spend so much time working with bums and drunks and other psychos who obviously won't bring fees into the sometimes too small bank account.

I sat down at my desk and said aloud to myself, "The guy is a fake! As obvious as a high school boy's drafting of a dollar bill."

I heard myself say that and wondered if I was going

nuts, myself. What did I mean by fake? I shrugged. So I happened to see a bird I couldn't read, that was all.

Then it struck me. But that would be unique. I hadn't had that experience for twenty years. Imagine the delight, after all these years, of exploring an unreadable!

I rushed out of my office and back down the stairs to the street. Hallahan, the traffic cop, saw me running up the street and looked at me curiously. I signaled to him with a wave of a hand that everything was all right. He lifted his cap and scratched his head. He shook his head slowly and settled his cap back down. He blew a whistle at a woman driver and went back to directing traffic.

I ran into the drugstore. Of course the guy wasn't there. I looked all around, hoping he was hiding behind the pots and pans counter, or something. No guy.

I walked quickly back out on the street and down to the next corner. I looked up and down the side streets. No guy.

I dragged my feet reluctantly back toward the office. I called up the face again to study it. It did no good. The first mental glimpse of it told me there was nothing to find. Logic told me there was nothing to find. If there had been, I wouldn't be in such a stew. The face was empty—completely void of human feelings or character.

No, those weren't the right words. Completely void of human—being!

I walked on past the drugstore again and looked in curiously, hoping I would see him. Hallahan was facing my direction again, and he grinned crookedly at me. I expect around the neighborhood I am known as a character. I ask the queerest questions of people, from a layman's point of view. Still, applicants sometimes tell me that when they asked a cop where was an employment agent they could trust they were sent to me.

I climbed the stairs again, and walked into my waiting room. Margie looked at me curiously, but she only said, "There's an applicant. I had him wait in your office." She looked like she wanted to say more, and then shrugged. Or maybe she shivered. I knew there was something wrong with the bird, or she would have kept him in the waiting room.

I opened the door to my office, and experienced an overwhelming sense of relief, fulfillment. It was he. Still, it was logical that he should be there. I run an employment agency. People come to me to get help in finding work. If others, why not he?

My skill includes the control of my outward reactions. That fellow could have no idea of the delight I felt at the opportunity to get a full history. If I had found him on the street, the best I might have done was a stock question about what time is it, or have you got a match, or where is the city hall. Here I could question him to my heart's content.

I took his history without comment, and stuck to routine questions. It was all exactly right.

He was ex-G.I., just completed college, major in astronomy, no experience, no skills, no faintest idea of what he wanted to do, nothing to offer an employer—all perfectly normal for a young grad.

No feeling or expression either. Not so normal. Usually they're petulantly resentful that business doesn't swoon at the chance of hiring them. I resigned myself to the old one-two of attempting to steer him toward something practical.

"Astronomy?" I asked. "That means you're heavy in math. Frequently we can place a strong math skill in statistical work." I was hopeful I could get a spark of something.

It turned out he wasn't very good at math. "I haven't yet reconciled my math to—" he stopped. For the first time he showed a reaction—hesitancy. Prior to that he had been a statue from Greece—the rounded expressionless eyes, the too perfect features undisturbed by thought.

He caught his remark and finished, "I'm just not very good at math, that's all."

I sighed to myself. I'm used to that, too. They give degrees nowadays to get rid of the guys, I suppose. Sometimes I'll go for days without uncovering any usable knowledge. So in a way, that was normal.

The only abnormal part of it was he seemed to think it didn't sound right. Usually the lads don't even realize they should know something. He seemed to think he'd pulled a boner by admitting that a man can take a degree in astronomy without learning math. Well, I wouldn't be surprised to see them take their degree without knowing how many planets there are.

He began to fidget a bit. That was strange, also. I thought I knew every possible combination of muscular contractions and expansions. This fidget had all the reality of a puppet activated by an amateur. And the eyes—still completely blank.

I led him up one mental street and down the next. And of all the false-fronted stores and cardboard houses and paper lawns, I never saw the like. I get something of that once in a while from a fellow who has spent a long term in prison and comes in with a manufactured past—but never anything as phony as this one was.

Interesting aspect to it. Most guys, when they realize you've spotted them for a phony, get out as soon as they can. He didn't. It was almost as though he were—well testing; to see if his answers would stand up.

I tried talking astronomy, of which I thought I knew a little. I found I didn't know anything, or he didn't. This bird's astronomy and mine had no point of reconciliation.

And then he had a slip of the tongue—yes he did. He was talking, and said, "The ten planets—"

He caught himself, "Oh that's right. There's only nine."

Could be ignorance, but I didn't think so. Could be he knew of the existence of a planet we hadn't yet discovered.

I smiled. I opened a desk drawer and pulled out a couple science-fiction magazines. "Ever read any of these?" I asked.

"I looked through several of them at the newsstand a while ago," he answered.

"They've enlarged my vision," I said. "Even to the point where I could believe that some other star system might hold intelligence." I lit a cigarette and waited. If I was wrong, he would merely think I was talking at random.

His blank eyes changed. They were no longer Greek statue eyes. They were no longer blue. They were black, deep bottomless black, as deep and cold as space itself.

"Where did I fail in my test?" he asked. His lips formed a smile which was not a smile—a carefully painted-on-canvas sort of smile.

Well, I'd had my answer. I'd explored something unique, all right. Sitting there before me, I had no way of determining whether he was benign or evil. No way of knowing his motive. No way of judging—anything. When it takes a lifetime of learning how to judge even our own kind, what standards have we for judging an entity from anther star system?

At that moment I would like to have been one of those space-opera heroes who, in similar circumstances, laugh casually and say, "What ho! So you're from Arcturus. Well, well. It's a small universe after all, isn't it?" And then with linked arms they head for the nearest bar, bosom pals.

I had the almost hysterical thought, but carefully suppressed, that I didn't know if this fellow would like beer or not. I will not go through the intermuscular and visceral reactions I experienced. I kept my seat and maintained a polite expression. Even with humans, I know when to walk carefully.

"I couldn't feel anything about you," I answered his question. "I couldn't feel anything but blankness."

He looked blank. His eyes were nice blue marble again. I liked them better that way.

There should be a million questions to be asked, but I must have been bothered by the feeling that I held a loaded bomb in my hands. And not knowing what might set it off, or how, or when, I could think of only the most trivial.

"How long have you been on Earth?" I asked. Sort of a when did you get back to town, Joe, kind of triviality.

"For several of your weeks," he was answering. "But this is my first time out among humans."

"Where have you been in the meantime?" I asked.

"Training." His answers were getting short and his muscles began to fidget again.

"And where do you train?" I kept boring in.

As an answer he stood up and held out his hand, all quite correctly. "I must go now," he said. "Naturally you can cancel my application for employment. Obviously we have more to learn."

I raised an eyebrow. "And I'm supposed to just pass over the whole thing? A thing like this?"

He smiled again. The contrived smile which was a

symbol to indicate courtesy. "I believe your custom on this planet is to turn your problems over to your police. You might try that." I could not tell whether it was irony or logic.

At that moment I could think of nothing else to say. He walked out of my door while I stood beside my desk and watched him go.

Well, what was I supposed to do? Follow him?

I followed him.

Now I'm no private eye, but I've read my share of mystery stories. I knew enough to keep out of sight. I followed him about a dozen blocks into a quiet residential section of small homes. I was standing behind a palm tree, lighting a cigarette, when he went up the walk of one of these small houses. I saw him twiddle with the door, open it, and walk in. The door closed.

I hung around a while and then went up to the door. I punched the doorbell. A motherly gray-haired woman came to the door, drying her hands on her apron. As she opened the door she said, "I'm not buying anything today."

Just the same, her eyes looked curious as to what I might have.

I grinned my best grin for elderly ladies. "I'm not selling anything, either," I answered. I handed her my agency card. She looked at it curiously and then looked a question at me.

"I'd like to see Joseph Hoffman," I said politely.

She looked puzzled. "I'm afraid you've got the wrong address, sir," she answered.

I got prepared to stick my foot in the door, but it wasn't necessary. "He was in my office just a few minutes ago," I said. "He gave that name and this address. A job came in right after he left the office, and since I was going to be in this neighborhood anyway, I thought I'd drop by and tell him in person. It's sort of rush," I finished. It had happened many times before, but this time it sounded lame.

"Nobody lives here but me and my husband," she insisted. "He's retired."

I didn't care if he hung by this toes from trees. I wanted a young fellow.

"But I saw the young fellow come in here," I argued. "I was just coming around the corner, trying to catch him. I saw him."

She looked at me suspiciously. "I don't know what your racket is," she said through thin lips, "but I'm not buying anything. I'm not signing anything. I don't even want to talk to you." She was stubborn about it.

I apologized and mumbled something about maybe making a mistake.

"I should say you have," she rapped out tartly and shut the door in righteous indignation. Sincere, too. I could tell.

An employment agent who gets the reputation of being a right guy makes all kinds of friends. That poor old lady must have thought a plague of locusts had swept in on her for the next few days.

First the telephone repair man had to investigate an alleged complaint. Then a gas service man had to check the plumbing. An electrician complained there was a power short in the block and he had to trace their house wiring. We kept our fingers crossed hoping the old geezer had never been a construction man. There was a mistake in the last census, and a guy asked her a million questions.

That house was gone over rafter by rafter and sill by sill, attic and basement. It was precisely as she said. She and her husband lived there; nobody else.

In frustration, I waited three months. I wore out the sidewalks haunting the neighborhood. Nothing.

Then one day my office door opened and Margie ushered a young man in. Behind his back she was radiating heart throbs and fluttering her eyes.

He was the traditionally tall, dark and handsome young fellow, with a ready grin and sparkling dark eyes. His personality hit me like a sledge hammer. A guy like that never needs to go to an employment agency. Any employer will hire him at the drop of a hat, and wonder later why he did it.

His name was Einar Johnson. Extraction, Norwegian. The dark Norse strain, I judged. I took a chance on him thinking he had walked into a booby hatch.

"The last time I talked with you," I said, "your name was Joseph Hoffman. You were Teutonic then. Not Norse."

The sparkle went out of his eyes. His face showed exasperation and there was plenty of it. It looked real, too, not painted on.

"All right. Where did I flunk this time?" he asked impatiently.

"It would take me too long to tell you," I answered. "Suppose you start talking." Strangely, I was at ease. I knew that underneath he was the same incomprehensible entity, but his surface was so good that I was lulled.

He looked at me levelly for a long moment. Then he said, "I didn't think there was a chance in a million of being recognized. I'll admit that other character we created was crude. We've learned considerable since then, and we've concentrated everything on this personality I'm wearing."

He paused and flashed his teeth at me. I felt like hiring him, myself. "I've been all over Southern California in this one," he said. "I've had a short job as a salesman. I've been to dances and parties. I've got drunk and sober again. Nobody, I say nobody, has shown even the slightest suspicion."

"Not very observing, were they?" I taunted.

"But you are," he answered. "That's why I came back here for the final test. I'd like to know where I failed." He was firm.

"We get quite a few phonies," I answered. "The guy drawing unemployment and stalling until it is run out. The geezik whose wife drives him out and threatens to quit her job if he doesn't go to work. The plain-clothes detail smelling around to see if maybe we aren't a cover for a bookie joint or something. Dozens of phonies."

He looked curious. I said in disgust. "We know in the first two minutes they're phony. You were phony also, but not of any class I've seen before. And," I finished dryly, "I've been waiting for you."

"Why was I phony?" he persisted.

"Too much personality force," I answered. "Human

beings just don't have that much force. I felt like I'd been
knocked flat on my . . . well . . . back."

He sighed. "I've been afraid you would recognize me
one way or another. I communicated with home. I was
advised that if you spotted me, I was to instruct you to
assist me."

I lifted a brow. I wasn't sure just how much authority
they had to instruct me to do anything.

"I was to instruct you to take over the supervision of
our final training, so that no one could ever spot us. If we
are going to carry out our original plan that is necessary.
If not, then we will have to use the alternate." He was
almost didactic in his manner, but his charm of personality still radiated like an infrared lamp.

"You're going to have to tell me a great deal more
than that," I said.

He glanced at my closed door.

"We won't be interrupted," I said. "A personnel history is private."


"I come from one of the planets of Arcturus," he
said.

I must have allowed a smile of amusement to show on
my face, for he asked, "You find that amusing?"

"No," I answered soberly, and my pulses leaped because the question confirmed my conclusion that he could
not read my thoughts. Apparently we were as alien to
him as he to us. "I was amused," I explained, "because
the first time I saw you I said to myself that as far as
recognizing you, you might have come from Arcturus.
Now it turns out that accidentally I was correct. I'm
better than I thought."

He gave a fleeting polite smile in acknowledgment.
"My home planet," he went on, "is similar to yours.
Except that we have grown overpopulated."

I felt a twinge of fear.

"We have made a study of this planet and have decided to colonize it." It was a flat statement, without any
doubt behind it.

I flashed him a look of incredulity. "And you expect
me to help you with that?"

He gave me a worldly wise look—almost an ancient
look. "Why not?" he asked.

"There is the matter of loyalty to my own kind, for one thing," I said. "Not too many generations away and we'll be overpopulated also. There would hardly be room for both your people and ours on Earth."

"Oh that's all right," he answered easily. "There'll be plenty of room for us for quite some time. We multiply slowly."

"We don't," I said shortly. I felt this conversation should be taking place between him and some great statesman—not me.

"You don't seem to understand," he said patiently. "Your race won't be here. We have found no reason why your race should be preserved. You will die away as we absorb."

"Now just a moment," I interrupted. "I don't want our race to die off." The way he looked at me I felt like a spoiled brat who didn't want to go beddie time.

"Why not?" he asked.

I was stumped. That's a good question when it is put logically. Just try to think of a logical reason why the human race should survive. I gave him at least something.

"Mankind," I said, "has had a hard struggle. We've paid a tremendous price in pain and death for our growth. Not to have a future to look forward to, would be like paying for something and never getting the use of it."

It was the best I could think of, honest. To base argument on humanity and right and justice and mercy would leave me wide open. Because it is obvious that man doesn't practice any of these. There is no assurance he ever will.

But he was ready for me, even with that one. "But if we are never suspected, and if we absorb and replace gradually, who is to know there is no future for humans?"

And as abruptly as the last time, he stood up suddenly. "Of course," he said coldly, "we could use our alternative plan: Destroy the human race without further negotiation. It is not our way to cause needless pain to any life form. But we can.

"If you do not assist us, then it is obvious that we will eventually be discovered. You are aware of the difficulty of even blending from one country on Earth to another. How much more difficult it is where there is no point of contact at all. And if we are discovered, destruction would be the only step left."

He smiled and all the force of his charm hit me again. "I know you will want to think it over for a time. I'll return."

He walked to the door, then smiled back at me. "And don't bother to trouble that poor little woman in that house again. Her doorway is only one of many entrances we have opened. She doesn't see us at all, and merely wonders why her latch doesn't work sometimes. And we can open another, anywhere, anytime. Like this—"

He was gone.

I walked over and opened the door. Margie was all prettied up and looking expectant and radiant. When she didn't see him come out she got up and peeked into my office. "But where did he go?" she asked with wide eyes.

"Get hold of yourself, girl," I answered. "You're so dazed you didn't even see him walk right by you."

"There's something fishy going on here," she said.

Well, I had a problem. A first rate, genuine, dyed in the wool dilemma.

What was I to do? I could have gone to the local authorities and got locked up for being a psycho. I could have gone to the college professors and got locked up for being a psycho. I could have gone to maybe the FBI and got locked up for being a psycho. That line of thinking began to get monotonous.

I did the one thing which I thought might bring help. I wrote up the happenings and sent it to my favorite science-fiction magazine. I asked for help and sage counsel from the one place I felt awareness and comprehension might be reached.

The manuscript bounced back so fast it might have had rubber bands attached to it, stretched from California to New York. I looked the little rejection slip all over, front and back, and I did not find upon it those sage words of counsel I needed. There wasn't even a printed invitation to try again some time.

And for the first time in my life I knew what it was to be alone—genuinely and irrevocably alone.

Still, I could not blame the editor. I could see him cast the manuscript from him in disgust, saying, "Bah! So another evil race comes to conquer Earth. If I gave the fans one more of those, I'd be run out of my office." And like the deacon who saw the naughty words written on the fence, saying, "And misspelled, too."

The fable of the boy who cried "Wolf! Wolf!" once too often came home to me now. I was alone with my problem. The dilemma was my own. On one hand was immediate extermination. I did not doubt it. A race which can open doors from one star system to another, without even visible means of mechanism, would also know how to—disinfect.

On the other hand was extinction, gradual, but equally certain; and none the less effective in that it would not be perceived. If I refused to assist, then acting as one long judge of all the race, I condemned it. If I did assist, I would be arch traitor, with an equal final result.

For days I sweltered in my miasma of indecision. Like many a man before me, uncertain of what to do, I temporized. I decided to play for time. To play the role of traitor in the hopes I might learn a way of defeating them.

Once I had made up my mind, my thoughts raced wildly through the possibilities. If I were to be their instructor on how to walk unsuspected among men, then I would have them wholly in my grasp. If I could build traits into them, common ordinary traits which they could see in men all about them, yet which would make men turn and destroy them, then I would have my solution.

And I knew human beings. Perhaps it was right, after all, that it became my problem. Mine alone.

I shuddered now to think what might have happened had this being fallen into less skilled hands and told his story. Perhaps by now there would be no man left upon Earth.

Yes, the old and worn-out plot of the one little unknown guy who saved Earth from outer evil might yet run its course in reality.

I was ready for the Arcturan when he returned. And he did return.

Einar Johnson and I walked out of my office after I

had sent a tearful Margie on a long vacation with fancy pay. Einar had plenty of money, and was liberal with it. When a fellow can open some sort of fourth-dimensional door into a bank vault and help himself, money is no problem.

I had visions of the poor bank clerks trying to explain things to the examiners, but that wasn't my worry right now.

We walked out of the office and I snapped the lock shut behind me. Always conscious of the cares of people looking for work, I hung a sign on the door saying I was ill and didn't know when I would be back.

We walked down the stairs and into the parking lot. We got into my car, my own car, please note, and I found myself sitting in a sheltered patio in Beverly Hills. Just like that. No awful wrenching and turning my insides out. No worrisome nausea and emptiness of space. Nothing to dramatize it at all. Car—patio, like that.

I would like to be able to describe the Arcturans as having long snaky appendages and evil slobbering maws, and stuff like that. But I can't describe the Arcturans, because I didn't see any.

I saw a gathering of people, roughly about thirty of them, wandering around the patio, swimming in the pool, going in and out of the side doors of the house. It was a perfect spot. No one bothers the big Beverly Hills home without invitation.

The natives wouldn't be caught dead looking toward a star's house. The tourists see the winding drive, the trees and grass, and perhaps a glimpse of a gabled roof. It they can get any thrill out of that then bless their little spending money hearts, they're welcome to it.

Yet if it should become known that a crowd of strange acting people are wandering around in the grounds, no one would think a thing about it. They don't come any more zany than the Hollywood crowd.

Only these were. These people could have made a fortune as life-size puppets. I could see now why it was judged that the lifeless Teutonic I had first interviewed was thought adequate to mingle with human beings. By comparison with these, he was a snappy song and dance man.

But that is all I saw. Vacant bodies wandering around, going through human motions, without human emotions. The job looked bigger than I had thought. And yet, if this was their idea of how to win friends and influence people, I might be successful after all.

There are dozens of questions the curious might want answered—such as how did they get hold of the house and how did they get their human bodies and where did they learn to speak English, and stuff. I wasn't too curious. I had important things to think about. I supposed they were able to do it, because here it was.

I'll cut the following weeks short. I cannot conceive of what life and civilization on their planet might be like. Yardsticks of scientific psychology are used to measure a man, and yet they give no indication at all of the inner spirit of him, likewise, the descriptive measurements of their civilization are empty and meaningless. Knowing about a man, and knowing a man are two entirely different things.

For example, all those thalamic urges and urgencies which we call emotion were completely unknown to them, except as they saw them in antics on TV. The ideals of man were also unknown—truth, honor, justice, perfection—all unknown. They had not even a division of sexes, and the emotion we call love was beyond their understanding. The TV stories they saw must have been like watching a parade of ants.

What purpose can be gained by describing such a civilization to man? Man cannot conceive accomplishment without first having a dream. Yet it was obvious that they accomplished, for they were here.

When I finally realized there was no point of contact between man and these, I knew relief and joy once more. My job was easy. I knew how to destroy them. And I suspected they could not avoid my trap.

They could not avoid my trap because they had human bodies. Perhaps they conceived them out of thin air, but the veins bled, the flesh felt pain and heat and pressure, the glands secreted.

Ah yes, the glands secreted. They would learn what emotion could be. And I was a master at wielding emotion. The dream of man has been to strive toward the great and immortal ideals. His literature is filled with admonishments to that end. In comparison with the volume of work which tells us what we should be, there is very little which reveals us as we are.

As part of my training course, I chose the worlds great liturature, and painting, and sculpture, and music—those mediums which best portray man lifting to the stars. I gave them first of all, the dream.

And with the dream, and with the pressure of the glands as kicker, they began to know emotion. I had respect for the superb acting of Einar when I realized that he, also, had still known no emotion.

They moved from the puppet to the newborn babe—a newborn babe in training, with an adult body, and its matured glandular equation.

I saw emotions, all right. Emotions without restraint, emotions unfettered by taboos, emotions uncontrolled by ideals. Sometimes I became frightened and all my skill in manipulating emotions was needed. At other times they became perhaps a little too Hollywood, even for Hollywood. I trained them into more ideal patterns.

I will say this for the Arcturans. They learned—fast. The crowd of puppets to the newborn babes, to the boisterous boys and girls, to the moody and unpredictable youths, to the matured and balanced men and women. I watched the metamorphosis take place over the period of weeks.

I did more.

All that human beings had ever hoped to be, the brilliant, the idealistic, the great in heart, I made of these. My little 145 I.Q. became a moron's level. The dreams of the greatness of man which I had known became the vaguest wisps of fog before the reality which these achieved.

My plan was working.

Full formed, they were almost like gods. And training these things into them, I trained their own traits out. One point I found we had in common. They were activated by logic, logic carried in heights of which I had never dreamed. Yet my poor and halting logic found point of contact.

They realized at last that if they let their own life force and motivation remain active they would carry the aura of strangeness to defeat their purpose. I worried, when they accepted this. I felt perhaps they were laying a trap for me, as I did for them. Then I realized that I had not taught them deceit.

And it was logical, to them, that they follow my training completely. Reversing the position, placing myself upon their planet, trying to become like them, I must of necessity follow my instructor without question. What else could they do?'

At first they saw no strangeness that I should assist them to destroy my race. In their logic the Arcturan was most fit to survive, therefore he should survive. The human was less fit, therefore he should perish.

I taught them the emotion of compassion. And when they began to mature their human thought and emotion, and their intellect was blended and shaded by such emotion, at last they understood my dilemma.

There was irony in that. From my own kind I could expect no understanding. From the invaders I received sympathy and compassion. They understand at last my traitorous action to buy a few more years for Man.

Yet their Arcturan logic still prevailed. They wept with me, but there could be no change of plan. The plan was fixed, they were merely instruments by which it was to be carried out.

Yet, through their compassion, I did get the plan modified.

This was the conversation which revealed that modification. Einar Johnson, who as the most fully developed had been my constant companion, said to me one day, "To all intents and purposes we have become human beings." He looked at me and smiled with fondness, "You have said it is so, and it must be so. For we begin to realize what a great and glorious thing a human is."

The light of nobility shone from him like an aura as he told me this, "Without human bodies, and without the emotion-intelligence equation which you call soul, our home planet cannot begin to grasp the growth we have achieved. We know now that we will never return to our own form, for by doing that we would lose what we have gained.

"Our people are logical, and they must of necessity

accept our recommendation, as long as it does not abandon the plan entirely. We have reported what we have learned, and it is conceived that both our races can inhabit the Universe side by side.

"There will be no more migration from our planet to yours. We will remain, and we will multiply, and we will live in honor, such as you have taught us, among you. In time perhaps we may achieve the greatness which all humans now have.

"And we will assist the human kind to find their destiny among the stars as we have done."

I bowed my head and wept. For I knew that I had won.

Four months had gone. I returned to my own neighborhood. On the corner Hallahan left the traffic to shift for itself while he came over to me with the question, "Where have you been?"

"I've been sick," I said.

"You look it," he said frankly. "Take care of yourself, man. Hey— Lookit that fool messing up traffic." He was gone, blowing his whistle in a temper.

I climbed the stairs. They still needed repainting as much as ever. From time to time I had been able to mail money to Margie, and she had kept the rent and telephone paid. The sign was still on my door. My key opened the lock.

The waiting room had that musty, they've-gone-away look about it. The janitor had kept the windows tightly closed and there was no freshness in the air. I half hoped to see Margie sitting at her desk, but I knew there was no purpose to it. When a girl is being paid for her time and has nothing to do, the beach is a nice place to spend it.

There was dust on my chair, and I sank down into it without bothering about the seat of my pants. I buried my head in my arms and I looked into the human soul.

Now the whole thing hinged on that skill. I know human beings. I know them as well as anyone in the world, and far better than most.

I looked into the past and I saw a review of the great and fine and noble and divine torn and burned and crucified by man.

Yet my only hope of saving my race was to build these qualities, the fine, the noble, the splendid, into these thirty beings. To create the illusion that all men were likewise great. No less power could have gained the boon of equality of man with them.

I look into the future. I see them, one by one, destroyed. I gave them no defense. They are totally unprepared to meet man as he genuinely is—and they are incapable of understanding.

For these things which man purports to admire the most—the noble, the brilliant, the splendid—these are the very things he cannot tolerate when he finds them.

Defenseless, because they cannot comprehend, these thirty will go down beneath the ravening fury of rending and destroying man always displays whenever he meets his ideal face to face.

I bury my head in my hands.

What have I done?

# IMPOSTOR

## BY PHILIP K. DICK

"One of these days I'm going to take time off," Spence Olham said at first-meal. He looked around at his wife. "I think I've earned a rest. Ten years is a long time."

"And the Project?"

"The war will be won without me. This ball of clay of ours isn't really in much danger." Olham sat down at the table and lit a cigarette. "The newsmachines alter dispatches to make it appear the Outspacers are right on top of us. You know what I'd like to do on my vacation? I'd like to take a camping trip in those mountains outside of town, where we went that time. Remember? I got poison oak and you almost stepped on a gopher snake."

"Sutton Wood?" Mary began to clear away the food dishes. "The Wood was burned a few weeks ago. I thought you knew. Some kind of a flash fire."

Olham sagged. "Didn't they even try to find the cause?" His lips twisted. "No one cares any more. All they can think of is the war." He clamped his jaws together, the whole picture coming up in his mind, the Outspacers, the war, the needle ships.

"How can we think about anything else?"

Olham nodded. She was right, of course. The dark little ships out of Alpha Centauri had by-passed the Earth cruisers easily, leaving them like helpless turtles. It had been one-way fights, all the way back to Terra.

All the way, until the protec-bubble was demonstrated by Westinghouse Labs. Thrown around the major Earth cities and finally the planet itself, the bubble was the first real defense, the first legitimate answer to the Outspacers —as the newsmachines labeled them.

But to win the war, that was another thing. Every lab, every project was working night and day, endlessly, to find something more: a weapon for positive combat. His own project, for example. All day long, year after year.

Olham stood up, putting out his cigarette. "Like the Sword of Damocles. Always hanging over us. I'm getting tired. All I want to do is take a long rest. But I guess everybody feels that way."

He got his jacket from the closet and went out on the front porch. The shoot would be along any moment, the fast little bug that would carry him to the Project.

"I hope Nelson isn't late." He looked at his watch. "It's almost seven."

"Here the bug comes," Mary said, gazing between the rows of houses. The sun glittered behind the roofs, reflecting against the heavy lead plates. The settlement was quiet; only a few people were stirring. "I'll see you later. Try not to work beyond your shift, Spence."

Olham opened the car door and slid inside, leaning back against the seat with a sigh. There was an older man with Nelson.

"Well?" Olham said, as the bug shot ahead. "Heard any interesting news?"

"The usual," Nelson said. "A few Outspace ships hit, another asteroid abandoned for strategic reasons."

"It'll be good when we get the Project into final stage. Maybe it's just the propaganda from the newsmachines, but in the last month I've gotten weary of all this. Everything seems so grim and serious, no color to life."

"Do you think the war is in vain?" the older man said suddenly. "You are an integral part of it, yourself."

"This is Major Peters," Nelson said. Olham and Peters shook hands. Olham studied the older man.

"What brings you along so early?" he said. "I don't remember seeing you at the Project before."

"No, I'm not with the Project," Peters said, "but I know something about what you're doing. My own work is altogether different."

A look passed between him and Nelson. Olham noticed it and he frowned. The bug was gaining speed, flashing across the barren, lifeless ground toward the distant rim of the Project buildings.

"What is your business?" Olham said. "Or aren't you permitted to talk about it?"

"I'm with the government," Peters said. "With FSA, the Security Organ."

"Oh?" Olham raised an eyebrow. "Is there any enemy infiltration in this region?"

"As a matter of fact I'm here to see you, Mr. Olham."

Olham was puzzled. He considered Peters' words, but he could make nothing of them. "To see me? Why?"

"I'm here to arrest you as an Outspace spy. That's why I'm up so early this morning. *Grab him, Nelson—*"

The gun drove into Olham's ribs. Nelson's hands were shaking, trembling with released emotion, his face pale. He took a deep breath and let it out again.

"Shall we kill him now?" he whispered to Peters. "I think we should kill him now. We can't wait."

Olham stared into his friend's face. He opened his mouth to speak, but no words came. Both men were staring at him steadily, rigid and grim with fright. Olham felt dizzy. His head ached and spun.

"I don't understand," he murmured.

At that moment the shoot car left the ground and rushed up, heading into space. Below them the Project fell away, smaller and smaller, disappearing. Olham shut his mouth.

"We can wait a little," Peters said. "I want to ask him some questions, first."

Olham gazed dully ahead as the bug rushed through space.

"The arrest was made all right," Peters said into the vidscreen. On the screen the features of the Security chief showed. "It should be a load off everyone's mind."

"Any complications?"

"None. He entered the bug without suspicion. He didn't seem to think my presence was too unusual."

"Where are you now?"

"On our way out, just inside the protec-bubble. We're moving at maximum speed. You can assume that the critical period is past. I'm glad the take-off jets in this craft were in good working order. If there had been any failure at that point—"

"Let me see him," the Security chief said. He gazed directly at Olham where he sat, his hands in his lap, staring ahead.

"So that's the man." He looked at Olham for a time.

Olham said nothing. At last the chief nodded to Peters. "All right. That's enough." A faint trace of disgust wrinkled his features. "I've seen all I want. You've done something that will be remembered for a long time. They're preparing some sort of citation for both of you."

"That's not necessary," Peters said.

"How much danger is there now? Is there still much chance that—"

"There is some chance, but not too much. According to my understanding, it requires a verbal key phrase. In any case we'll have to take the risk."

"I'll have the Moon base notified you're coming."

"No." Peters shook his head. "I'll land the ship outside, beyond the base. I don't want it in jeopardy."

"Just as you like." The chief's eyes flickered as he glanced again at Olham. Then his image faded. The screen blanked.

Olham shifted his gaze to the window. The ship was already through the protec-bubble, rushing with greater and greater speed all the time. Peters was in a hurry; below him, rumbling under the floor, the jets were wide open. They were afraid, hurrying frantically, because of him.

Next to him on the seat, Nelson shifted uneasily. "I think we should do it now," he said. "I'd give anything if we could get it over with."

"Take it easy," Peters said. "I want you to guide the ship for a while so I can talk to him."

He slid over beside Olham, looking into his face. Presently he reached out and touched him gingerly, on the arm and then on the cheek.

Olham said nothing. *If I could let Mary know,* he thought again. *If I could find some way of letting her know.* He looked around the ship. How? The vidscreen? Nelson was sitting by the board, holding the gun. There was nothing he could do. He was caught, trapped.

*But why?*

"Listen," Peters said, "I want to ask you some questions. You know where we're going. We're moving Moonward. In an hour we'll land on the far side, on the desolate side. After we land you'll be turned over immediately to a team of men waiting there. Your body will be destroyed at once. Do you understand that?" He looked at his watch. "Within two hours your parts will be strewn over the landscape. There won't be anything left of you."

Olham struggled out of his lethargy. "Can't you tell me—"

"Certainly, I'll tell you." Peters nodded. "Two days ago we received a report that an Outspace ship had penetrated the protec-bubble. The ship let off a spy in the form of a humanoid robot. The robot was to destroy a particular human being and take his place."

Peters looked calmly at Olham.

"Inside the robot was a U-Bomb. Our agent did not know how the bomb was to be detonated, but he conjectured that it might be by a particular spoken phrase, a certain group of words. The robot would live the life of the person he killed, entering into his usual activities, his job, his social life. He had been constructed to resemble that person. No one would know the difference."

Olham's face went sickly chalk.

"The person whom the robot was to impersonate was Spence Olham, a high-ranking official at one of the Research projects. Because this particular project was approaching crucial stage, the presence of an animate bomb, moving toward the center of the Project—"

Olham stared down at his hands. *"But I'm Olham!"*

"Once the robot had located and killed Olham, it was a simple matter to take over his life. The robot was probably released from the ship eight days ago. The substitution was probably accomplished over the last week end, when Olham went for a short walk in the hills."

"But I'm Olham." He turned to Nelson, sitting at the controls. "Don't you recognize me? You've known me for twenty years. Don't you remember how we went to college together?" He stood up. "You and I were at the University. We had the same room." He went toward Nelson.

"Stay away from me!" Nelson snarled.

"Listen. Remember our second year? Remember that girl? What was her name—" He rubbed his forehead. "The one with the dark hair. The one we met over at Ted's place."

"Stop!" Nelson waved the gun frantically. "I don't want to hear any more. You killed him! You . . . machine."

Olham looked at Nelson. "You're wrong. I don't know

what happened, but the robot never reached me. Something must have gone wrong. Maybe the ship crashed." He turned to Peters. "I'm Olham. I know it. No transfer was made. I'm the same as I've always been."

He touched himself, running his hands over his body. "There must be some way to prove it. Take me back to Earth. An X ray examination, a neurological study, anything like that will show you. Or maybe we can find the crashed ship."

Neither Peters nor Nelson spoke.

"I am Olham," he said again. "I know I am. But I can't prove it."

"The robot," Peters said, "would be unaware that he was not the real Spence Olham. He would become Olham in mind as well as body. He was given an artificial memory system, false recall. He would look like him, have his memories, his thoughts and interests, perform his job.

"But there would be one difference. Inside the robot is a U-Bomb, ready to explode at the trigger phrase." Peters moved a little away. "That's the one difference. That's why we're taking you to the Moon. They'll disassemble you and remove the bomb. Maybe it will explode, but it won't matter, not there."

Olham sat down slowly.

"We'll be there soon," Nelson said.

He lay back, thinking frantically, as the ship dropped slowly down. Under them was the pitted surface of the Moon, the endless expanse of ruin. What could he do? What would save him?

"Get ready," Peters said.

In a few minutes he would be dead. Down below he could see a tiny dot, a building of some kind. There were men in the building, the demolition team, waiting to tear him to bits. They would rip him open, pull off his arms and legs, break him apart. When they found no bomb they would be surprised; they would know, but it would be too late.

Olham looked around the small cabin. Nelson was still holding the gun. There was no chance there. If he could get to a doctor, have an examination made—that was the only way. Mary could help him. He thought frantically, his mind racing. Only a few minutes, just a little time left. If he could contact her, get word to her some way.

"Easy," Peters said. The ship came down slowly, bumping on the rough ground. There was silence.

"Listen," Olham said thickly. "I can prove I'm Spence Olham. Get a doctor. Bring him here—"

"There's the squad." Nelson pointed. "They're coming." He glanced nervously at Olham. "I hope nothing happens."

"We'll be gone before they start work," Peters said. "We'll be out of here in a moment." He put on his pressure suit. when he had finished he took the gun from Nelson. "I'll watch him for a moment."

Nelson put on his pressure suit, hurrying awkwardly. "How about him?" He indicated Olham. "Will he need one?"

"No." Peters shook his head. "Robots probably don't require oxygen."

The group of men were almost to the ship. They halted, waiting. Peters signaled to them.

"Come on!" He waved his hand and the men approached warily; stiff, grotesque figures in their inflated suits.

"If you open the door," Olham said, "it means my death. It will be murder."

"Open the door," Nelson said. He reached for the handle.

Olham watched him. He saw the man's hand tighten around the metal rod. In a moment the door would swing back, the air in the ship would rush out. He would die, and presently they would realize their mistake. Perhaps at some other time, when there was no war, men might not act this way, hurrying an individual to his death because they were afraid. Everyone was frightened, everyone was willing to sacrifice the individual because of the group fear.

He was being killed because they could not wait to be sure of his guilt. There was not enough time.

He looked at Nelson. Nelson had been his friend for years. They had gone to school together. He had been best man at his wedding. Now Nelson was going to kill him. But Nelson was not wicked; it was not his fault. It was the times. Perhaps it had been the same way during the plagues. When men had shown a spot they probably had been killed, too, without a moment's hesitation, without proof, on suspicion alone. In times of danger there was no other way.

He did not blame them. But he had to live. His life was too precious to be sacrificed. Olham thought quickly. What could he do? Was there anything? He looked around.

"Here goes," Nelson said.

"You're right," Olham said. The sound of his own voice surprised him. It was the strength of desperation. "I have no need of air. Open the door."

They paused, looking at him in curious alarm.

"Go ahead. Open it. I makes no difference." Olham's hand disappeared inside his jacket. "I wonder how far you two can run."

"Run?"

"You have fifteen seconds to live." Inside his jacket his fingers twisted, his arm suddenly rigid. He relaxed, smiling a little. "You were wrong about the trigger phrase. In that respect you were mistaken. Fourteen seconds, now."

Two shocked faces stared at him from the pressure suits. Then they were struggling, running, tearing the door open. The air shrieked out, spilling into the void. Peters and Nelson bolted out of the ship. Oldham came after them. He grasped the door and dragged it shut. The automatic pressure system chugged furiously, restoring the air. Oldham let his breath out with a shudder.

One more second—

Beyond the window the two men had joined the group. The group scattered, running in all directions. One by one they threw themselves down, prone on the ground. Olham seated himself at the control board. He moved the dials into place. As the ship rose up into the air the men below scrambled to their feet and stared up, their mouths open.

"Sorry," Olham murmured, "but I've got to get back to Earth."

He headed the ship back the way it had come.

It was night. All around the ship crickets chirped, disturbing the chill darkness. Olham bent over the vidscreen. Gradually the image formed; the call had gone through without trouble. He breathed a sigh of relief.

"Mary," he said. The woman stared at him. She gasped.

"Spence! Where are you? What's happened?"

"I can't tell you. Listen, I have to talk fast. They may break this call off any minute. Go to the Project grounds and get Dr. Chamberlain. If he isn't there, get any doctor. Bring him to the house and have him stay there. Have him bring equipment, X ray, fluoroscope, everything."

"But—"

"Do as I say. Hurry. Have him get it ready in an hour." Olham leaned toward the screen. "Is everything all right? Are you alone?"

"Alone?"

"Is anyone with you? Has . . . has Nelson or anyone contacted you?"

"No. Spence, I don't understand."

"All right. I'll see you at the house in an hour. And don't tell anyone anything. Get Chamberlain there on any pretext. Say you're very ill."

He broke the connection and looked at his watch. A moment later he left the ship, stepping down into the darkness. He had a half mile to go.

He began to walk.

One light showed in the window, the study light. He watched it, kneeling against the fence. There was no sound, no movement of any kind. He held his watch up and read it by starlight. Almost an hour had passed.

Along the street a shoot bug came. It went on.

Olham looked toward the house. The doctor should have already come. He should be inside, waiting with Mary. A thought struck him. Had she been able to leave the house? Perhaps they had intercepted her. Maybe he was moving into a trap.

But what else could he do?

With a doctor's records, photographs, and reports, there was a chance, a chance of proof. If he could be examined, if he could remain alive long enough for them to study him—

He could prove it that way. It was probably the only way. His one hope lay inside the house. Dr. Chamberlain was a respected man. He was the staff doctor for the Project. He would know; his word on the matter would have meaning. He could overcome their hysteria, their madness, with facts.

Madness— That was what it was. If only they would wait, act slowly, take their time. But they could not wait. He had to die, die at once, without proof, without any kind of trial or examination. The simplest test would tell, but they had no time for the simplest test. They could think only of the danger. Danger, and nothing more.

He stood up and moved toward the house. He came up on the porch. At the door he paused, listening. Still no sound. The house was absolutely still.

Too still.

Olham stood on the porch, unmoving. They were trying to be silent inside. Why? It was a small house; only a few feet away, beyond the door, Mary and Dr. Chamberlain should be standing. Yet he could hear nothing, no sound of voices, nothing at all. He looked at the door. It was a door he had opened and closed a thousand times, every morning and every night.

He put his hand on the knob. Then, all at once, he reached out and touched the bell instead. The bell pealed, off some place in the back of the house. Olham smiled. He could hear movement.

Mary opened the door. As soon as he saw her face he knew.

He ran, throwing himself into the bushes. A Security officer shoved Mary out of the way, firing past her. The bushes burst apart. Olham wriggled around the side of the house. He leaped up and ran, racing frantically into the darkness. A searchlight snapped on, a beam of light circling past him.

He crossed the road and squeezed over a fence. He jumped down and made his way across a backyard. Behind him men were coming, Security officers, shouting to each other as they came. Olham gasped for breath, his chest rising and falling.

Her face— He had known at once. The set lips, the terrified, wretched eyes. Suppose he had gone ahead, pushed open the door and entered! They had tapped the call and come at once, as soon as he had broken off. Probably she believed their account. No doubt she thought he was the robot, too.

Olham ran on and on. He was losing the officers, dropping them behind. Apparently they were not much good at running. He climbed a hill and made his way down the other side. In a moment he would be back at the ship. But where to, this time? He slowed down, stopping. He could see the ship already, outlined against the sky, where he had parked it. The settlement was behind him; he was on the outskirts of the wilderness between the inhabited places, where the forests and desolation began. He crossed a barren field and entered the trees.

As he came toward it, the door of the ship opened.

Peters stepped out, framed against the light. In his arms was a heavy boris-gun. Olham stopped, rigid. Peters stared around him, into the darkness. "I know you're there, some place," he said. "Come on up here, Olham. There are Security men all around you."

Olham did not move.

"Listen to me. We will catch you very shortly. Apparently you still do not believe you're the robot. Your call to the woman indicates that you are still under the illusion created by your artificial memories.

"But you *are* the robot. You are the robot, and inside you is the bomb. Any moment the trigger phrase may be spoke, by you, by someone else, by anyone. When that happens the bomb will destroy everything for miles around. The Project, the woman, all of us will be killed. Do you understand?"

Olham said nothing. He was listening. Men were moving toward him, slipping through the woods.

"If you don't come out, we'll catch you. It will be only a matter of time. We no longer plan to remove you to the Moon-base. You will be destroyed on sight, and we will have to take the chance that the bomb will detonate. I have ordered every available Security officer into the area. The whole county is being searched, inch by inch. There is no place you can go. Around this wood is a cordon of armed men. You have about six hours left before the last inch is covered."

Olham moved away. Peters went on speaking; he had not seen him at all. It was too dark to see anyone. But Peters was right. There was no place he could go. He was beyond the settlement, on the outskirts where the woods began. He could hide for a time, but eventually they would catch him.

Only a matter of time.

Olham walked quietly through the wood. Mile by mile, each part of the county was being measured off, laid bare, searched, studied, examined. The cordon was com-

ing all the time, squeezing him into a smaller and smaller
space.

What was there left? He had lost the ship, the one
hope of escape. They were at his home; his wife was with
them, believing, no doubt, that the real Olham had been
killed. He clenched his fists. Some place there was a
wrecked Outspace needle-ship, and in it the remains of
the robot. Somewhere nearby the ship had crashed, crashed
and broken up.

And the robot lay inside, destroyed.

A faint hope stirred him. What if he could find the
remains? If he could show them the wreckage, the remains of the ship, the robot—

But where? Where would he find it?

He walked on, lost in thought. Some place, not too far
off, probably. The ship would have landed close to the
Project; the robot would have expected to go the rest of
the way on foot. He went up the side of a hill and looked
around. Crashed and burned. Was there some clue, some
hint? Had he read anything, heard anything? Some place
close by, within walking distance. Some wild place, a
remote spot where there would be no people.

Suddenly Olham smiled. Crashed and burned—

Sutton Wood.

He increased his pace.


It was morning. Sunlight filtered down through the broken
trees, onto the man crouching at the edge of the clearing.
Olham glanced up from time to time, listening. They were
not far off, only a few minutes away. He smiled.

Down below him, strewn across the clearing and into
the charred stumps that had been Sutton Wood, lay a
tangled mass of wreckage. In the sunlight it glittered a
little, gleaming darkly. He had not had too much trouble
finding it. Sutton Wood was a place he knew well; he had
climbed around it many times in his life, when he was
younger. He had known where he would find the remains. There was one peak that jutted up suddenly, without warning.

A descending ship, unfamiliar with the Wood, had
little chance of missing it. And now he squatted, looking
down at the ship, or what remained of it.

Olham stood up. He could hear them, only a little

distance away, coming together, talking in low tones. He tensed himself. Everything depended on who first saw him. If it were Nelson, he had no chance. Nelson would fire at once. He would be dead before they saw the ship. But if he had time to call out, hold them off for a moment— That was all he needed. Once they saw the ship he would be safe.

But if they fired first—

A charred branch cracked. A figure appeared, coming forward uncertainly. Olham took a deep breath. Only a few seconds remained, perhaps the last seconds of his life. He raised his arms, peering intently.

It was Peters.

"Peters!" Olham waved his arms. Peters lifted his gun, aiming. "Don't fire!" His voice shook. "Wait a minute. Look past me, across the clearing."

"I've found him," Peters shouted. Security men came pouring out of the burned woods around him.

"Don't shoot. Look past me. The ship, the needle-ship. The Outspace ship. Look!"

Peters hesitated. The gun wavered.

"It's down there," Olham said rapidly. "I knew I'd find it here. The burned wood. Now you believe me. You'll find the remains of the robot in the ship. Look, will you?"

"There is something down there," one of the men said nervously.

"Shoot him!" a voice said. It was Nelson.

"Wait." Peters turned sharply. "I'm in charge. Don't anyone fire. Maybe he's telling the truth."

"Shoot him," Nelson said. "He killed Olham. Any minute he may kill us all. If the bomb goes off—"

"Shut up." Peters advanced toward the slope. He stared down. "Look at that." He waved two men up to him. "Go down there and see what that is."

The men raced down the slope, across the clearing. They bent down, poking in the ruins of the ship.

"Well?" Peters called.

Olham held his breath. He smiled a little. It must be there; he had not had time to look, himself, but it had to be there. Suddenly doubt assailed him. Suppose the robot had lived long enough to wander away? Suppose his body had been completely destroyed, burned to ashes by the fire?

He licked his lips. Perspiration came out on his forehead. Nelson was staring at him, his face still livid. His chest rose and fell.

"Kill him," Nelson said. "Before he kills us."

The two men stood up.

"What have you found?" Peters said. He held the gun steady. "Is there anything there?"

"Looks like something. It's a needle-ship, all right. There's something beside it."

"I'll look." Peters strode past Olham. Olham watched him go down the hill and up to the men. The others were following after him, peering to see.

"It's a body of some sort," Peters said. "Look at it!"

Olham came along with them. They stood around in a circle, staring down.

On the ground, bent and twisted into a strange shape, was a grotesque form. It looked human, perhaps; except that it was bent so strangely, the arms and legs flung off in all directions. The mouth was open, the eyes stared glassily.

"Like a machine that's run down," Peters murmured.

Olham smiled feebly. "Well?" he said.

Peters looked at him. "I can't believe it. You were telling the truth all the time."

"The robot never reached me," Olham said. He took out a cigarette and lit it. "It was destroyed when the ship crashed. You were all too busy with the war to wonder why an out-of-the-way woods would suddenly catch fire and burn. Now you know."

He stood smoking, watching the men. They were dragging the grotesque remains from the ship. The body was stiff, the arms and legs rigid.

"You'll find the bomb, now," Olham said. The men laid the body on the ground. Peters bent down.

"I think I see the corner of it." He reached out, touching the body.

The chest of the corpse had been laid open. Within the gaping tear something glinted, something metal. The men stared at the metal without speaking.

"That would have destroyed us all, if it had lived," Peters said. "That metal box, there."

There was silence.

"I think we owe you something," Peters said to Olham. "This must have been a nightmare to you. If you hadn't escaped, we would have—" He broke off.

Olham put out his cigarette. "I knew, of course, that the robot had never reached me. But I had no way of proving it. Sometimes it isn't possible to prove a thing right away. That was the whole trouble. There wasn't any way I could demonstrate that I was myself."

"How about a vacation?" Peters said. "I think we might work out a month's vacation for you. You could take it easy, relax."

"I think right now I want to go home," Olham said.

"All right, then," Peters said. "Whatever you say."

Nelson had squatted down on the ground, beside the corpse. He reached out toward the glint of metal visible within the chest.

"Don't touch it," Olham said. "It might still go off. We better let the demolition squad take care of it later on."

Nelson said nothing. Suddenly he grabbed hold of the metal, reaching his hand inside the chest. He pulled.

"What are you doing?" Olham cried.

Nelson stood up. He was holding onto the metal object. His face was blank with terror. It was a metal knife, an Outspace needle-knife, covered with blood.

"This killed him," Nelson whispered. "My friend was killed with this." He looked at Olham. "You killed him with this and left him beside the ship."

Olham was trembling. His teeth chattered. He looked from the knife to the body. "This can't be Olham," he said. His mind spun, everything was whirling. "Was I wrong?"

He gaped.

"But if that's Olham, then I must be—"

He did not complete the sentence, only the first phrase. The blast was visible all the way to Alpha Centauri.

# THE SOUL-EMPTY ONES

## BY WALTER M. MILLER, JR.

They heard the mournful bleat of his ramshorn in the night, warning them that he was friend, asking the sentries not to unleash the avalanches upon the mountain trail where he rode. They returned to their stools and huddled about the lamplight, waiting—two warriors and a woman. The woman was watching the window; and toward the valley, bright bonfires yellowed the darkness.

"He should never have gone," the girl said tonelessly.

The warriors, father and son, made no answer. They were valley men, from the sea, and guests in the house of Daner. The younger one looked at his sire and shook his head slowly. The father clenched his jaw stubbornly. "I could not let you go to blaspheme," he growled defensively. "The invaders are the sons of men. If Daner wishes to attack them, he is our host, and we cannot prevent it. But we shall not violate that which is written of the invaders. They have come to save us."

"Even if they kill us, and take our meat?" muttered the blond youth.

"Even so. We are their servants, for the sons of men created our fathers out of the flesh of beasts, and gave them the appearance of men." The old one's eyes glowed with the passionate light of conviction.

The young one inclined his head gravely and submissively, for such was the way of the valley people toward their parents.

The girl spoke coldly. "At first, I thought you were cowardly, old man. Now I think your whole tribe is cowardly."

Without a change of expression, the gray-haired one lifted his arms into the lamplight. His battles were written upon them in a crisscross of white knife scars. He lowered them silently without speaking.

"It's in the mind that you are cowardly," said the girl.
"We of the Natani fight our enemies. If our enemies be
gods, then we shall fight gods."

"Men are not gods," said the young one, whose name
was Falon.

His father slapped him sharply across the back of the
neck. "That is sacrilege," he warned. "When you speak
of the invaders. They are men and gods."

The girl watched them with comtempt. "Among the
Natani, when a man loses his manhood by age, he goes
into the forest with his war knife and does not return.
And if he neglects to go willingly, his sons escort him and
see that he uses the knife. When a man is so old that his
mind is dull, it is better for him to die."

The old warrior glowered at his hostess, but remained
polite. "Your people have strange ways," he said acidly.

Suddenly a man came in out of the blackness and stood
swaying in the doorway. He clutched his dogskin jacket
against his bleeding chest as a sponge. He was panting
softly. The three occupants of the small stone hut came
slowly to their feet, and the woman said one word:

"Daner!"

The man mopped his forehead and staggered a step
forward. He kicked the door closed with his heel. His
skin had gone bloodless gray, and his eyes wandered
wildly about the room for a moment. Then he sagged to
his knees. Falon came to his aid, but Daner shook him
off.

"They're really the sons of men," he gasped.

"Did you doubt it?" asked the old valley man.

Daner nodded. His mouth leaked a trickle of red, and
he spat irritably. "I saw their skyboats. I fought with a
guard. They are the sons of men . . . but they . . . are no
longer men." He sank to a sitting position and leaned
back against the door, staring at the woman. "Ea-Daner,"
he breathed softly.

"Come care for your man, you wench!" growled the
old one. "Can't you see he's dying?"

The girl stood back a few feet, watching her husband
with sadness and longing, but not with pity. He was
staring at her with deep black eyes, abnormally bright-

ened by pain. His breath was a wet hiss. Both of them ignored their valley guests.

"Sing me 'The Song of the Empty of Soul,' Ea, my wife," he choked, then began struggling to his feet. Falon, who knew a little of the Natani ways, helped him pull erect.

Daner pawed at the door, opened it, and stood looking out into the night for a moment. A dark line of trees hovered to the west. Daner drew his war knife and stood listening to the yapping of the wild dogs in the forest. "Sing, woman."

She sang. In a low, rich voice, she began the chant of the Soul-Empty Ones. The chant was weary, slowly repeating its five monotonous notes, speaking of men who had gone away, and of their Soul-Empty servants they had left behind.

Daner stepped from the doorsill, and became a wavering shadow, receding slowly toward the trees.

The song said that if a man be truly the son of men, the wild dogs would not devour him in the time of death. But if he be Empty of Soul, if he be only the mocking image of Man, then the wild dogs would feed—for his flesh was of the beast, and his ancestor's seed had been warped by Man to grow in human shape.

The two valley warriors stood clumsily; their ways were not of the Natani mountain folk. Their etiquette forbade them interfere in their host's action. Daner had disappeared into the shadows. Ea-Daner, his wife, sang softly into the night, but her face was rivered with moisture from her eyes, large dark eyes, full of anger and sadness.

The song choked off. From the distance came a savage man-snarl. It was answered by a yelp; then a chorus of wild-dog barks and growls raged in the forest, drowning the cries of the man. The girl stopped singing and closed the door. She returned to her stool and gazed out toward the bonfires. Her face was empty, and she was no longer crying.

Father and son exchanged glances. Nothing could be done. They sat together, across the room from the girl.

After a long time, the elder spoke. "Among our people, it is customary for a widow to return to her father's house. You have no father. Will you join my house as a daughter?"

She shook her head. "My people would call me an outcast. And your people would remember that I am a Natani."

"What will you do?" asked Falon.

"We have a custom," she replied vaguely.

Falon growled disgustedly. "I have fought your tribe. I have fought many tribes. They all have different ways, but are of the same flesh. Custom! Bah! One way is as good as another, and no-way-at-all is the best. I have given myself to the devil, because the devil is the only god in whom all the tribes believe. But he never answers my prayers, and I think I'll spit on his name."

He was rewarded by another slap from his father. "You are the devil's indeed!" raged the old man.

Falon accepted it calmly, and shrugged toward the girl. "What will you do, Ea-Daner?"

She gazed at him through dull grief. "I will follow the way. I will mourn for seven days. Then I will take a war knife and go to kill one of my husband's enemies. When it is done, I will follow his path to the forest. It is the way of the Natani widow."

Falon stared at her in unbelief. His shaggy blond eyebrows gloomed into a frown. "No!" he growled. "I am ashamed that the ways of my father's house have made me sit here like a woman while Daner went to fight against the sons of men! Daner said nothing. He respected our ways. He has opened his home to us. I shan't let his woman be ripped apart by the wild dogs!"

"Quiet!" shouted his father. "You are a guest! If our hosts are barbarians, then you must tolerate them!"

The girl caught her breath angrily, then subsided. "Your father is right, Falon," she said coldly. "I don't admire the way you grovel before him, but he is right."

Falon squirmed and worked his jaw in anger. He was angry with both of them. His father had been a good man and a strong warrior; but Falon wondered if the way of obedience was any holier than the other ways. The Natani had no high regard for it. Ea-Daner had no father, because the old man had gone away with his war knife when he became a burden on the tribe. But Falon had

always obeyed, not out of respect for the law, but out of
admiration for the man. He sighed and shrugged.

"Very well, then, Ea-Daner, you shall observe your
custom. And I will go with you to the places of the
invader."

"You will not fight with the sons of men!" his father
grumbled sullenly. "You will not speak of it again."

Falon's eyes flared heatedly. "You would let a woman
go to be killed and perhaps devoured by the invaders?"

"She is a Natani. And it is the right of the sons of men
to do as they will with her, or with us. I even dislike
hiding from them. They created our fathers, and they
made them so that their children would also be in the
image of man—in spite of the glow-curse that lived in the
ground and made the sons of animals unlike their fathers."

"Nevertheless, I—"

*"You will not speak of it again!"*

Falon stared at the angry oldster, whose steely eyes
barked commands to him. Falon shivered. Respect for
the aged was engrained in the fibers of his being. But
Daner's death was fresh in his mind. And he was no
longer in the valleys of his people, where the invaders
had landed their skyboats. Was the way of the tribe more
important than the life of the tribe? If one believed in the
gods—then, yes.

Taking a deep breath, Falon stood up. He glanced
down at the old man. The steel-blue eyes were biting into
his face. Falon turned his back on them and walked
slowly across the room. He sat beside the girl and faced
his father calmly. It was open rebellion.

"I am no longer a man of the valley," he said quietly.
"Nor am I to be a Natani," he added for the benefit of
the girl. "I shall have no ways but the ways of embracing
the friend and killing the enemy."

"Then it is my duty to kill my son," said the scarred
warrior. He came to his feet and drew his war knife
calmly.

Falon sat frozen in horror, remembering how the old
man had wept when the invaders took Falon's mother to
their food pens. The old one advanced, crouching slightly,
waiting briefly for his son to draw. But Falon remained
motionless.

"You may have an instant in which to draw," purred the oldster. "Then I shall kill you unarmed."

Falon did nothing. His father lunged with a snarl, and the knife's steel sang a hissing arc. Its point dug into the stool where the youth had been sitting. Falon stood crouched across the room, still weaponless. The girl watched with a slight frown.

"So, you choose to flee, but not fight," the father growled.

Falon said nothing. His chest rose and fell slowly, and his eyes flickered over the old one's tough and wiry body, watching for muscular hints of another lunge. But the warrior was crafty. He relaxed suddenly, and straightened. Reflexively, Falon mirrored the sudden unwinding of tension. The elder was upon him like a cat, twining his legs about Falon's, and encircling his throat with a brawny arm.

Falon caught the knife-thrust with his forearm, then managed to catch his father's wrist. Locked together, they crashed to the floor. Falon felt hot hate panting in his face. His only desire was to free himself and flee, even to the forest.

They struggled in silence. with a strength born of the faith that a man must be stronger than his sons, the elder pressed the knife deeper toward Falon's throat. With a weakness born of despair, Falon found himself unable to hold it away. Their embrace was slippery with wetness from the wound in his forearm. And the arm was failing.

"I . . . offer you . . . as a holy . . . sacrifice," panted the oldster, as the knife began scratching skin.

"Father . . . don't—" Then he saw Ea-Daner standing over the old man's shoulder. She was lifting a war club. He closed his eyes.

The sharp crack frightened and sickened him. The knife clattered away from his throat, and his father's body went limp.

Slowly, he extricated himself from the tangle, and surveyed the oldster's head. The scalp was split, and the gray hair sogging with slow blood.

"You killed him!" he accused.

The girl snorted. "He's not dead. I didn't hit him hard. Feel his skull. It's not broken. And he's breathing."

Falon satisfied himself that she spoke the truth. Then

he climbed to his feet, grumbling unhappily. He looked down at the old man and deeply regretted his rebelliousness. The father's love of the law was greater than his love for a son. But there was no undoing it now. The elder was committed to kill him, even if he retracted. He turned to the girl.

"I must go before he comes to his senses," he murmured sadly. "You'll tend his head wound?"

She was thoughtful for a moment, then a speculative gleam came into her eyes. "I understood you meant to help me avenge my husband?"

Falon frowned. "I now regret it."

"Do the valley folk treat their own word with contempt?"

Falon shrugged guiltily. "I'm no longer of the valley. But I'll keep my word, if you wish." He turned away and moved to the window to watch the bonfires. "I owe you a life," he murmured. "Perhaps Daner would have returned alive, if I had accompanied him. I turned against my father too late."

"No, Soul-Falon, I knew when Daner left that he meant to fight until he was no longer able—then drag himself back for the forests. If you had gone too, it would have been the same. I no longer weep, because I *knew*."

Falon was staring at her peculiarly. "You called me Soul-Falon," he said wonderingly; for it was a title given only to those who had won high respect, and it suggested the impossible—that the Soul-Empty One was really a man. Was she mocking him? "Why do you call me that?" he asked suspiciously.

The girl's slender body inclined in a slight bow. "You exchanged your honor for a new god. What greater thing can a man offer than honor among his people?"

He frowned for a moment, then realized she meant it. Did the Natani hold anything above honor? "I have no new gods," he growled. "When I find the right god, I shall serve him. But until then, I serve myself—and those who please me."

The old man's breathing became a low moan. He was beginning to come awake. Falon moved toward the door.

"When he awakes, he may be so angry that he forgets he's your guest," warned the young warrior. "You'd better come with me."

She hesitated. "The law of mourning states that a widow must remain—"

"Shall I call you Soul-Ea?"

She suffered an uncomfortable moment, then shrugged, and slipped a war knife in her belt thong. Her sandals padded softly after him as he moved out into the darkness and untethered the horses. The steeds' legs were still wrapped in heavy leather strips to protect them against the slashing fangs of the wild dogs.

"Leave Daner's horse for your father," said the girl with unsentimental practicality. "The mare's tired, and she'll be slow if he tries to follow us."

They swung into the small rawhide saddles and trotted across the clearing. Dim moonlight from a thin silver crescent illuminated their way. Two trails led from the hut that overlooked the cliff. Falon knew that one of them wound along the clifftops to a low place, then turned back beneath the cliff and found its way eventually to the valley. The other penetrated deeper into the mountains. He had given his word, and he let the girl choose the path.

She took the valley road. Falon sighed and spurred after her. It was sure death, to approach the invader's camp. They had the old god-weapons, which would greet all hostile attacks from the Soul-Empty Ones. And if the Empties came in peace, the sons of men would have another occupant for their stock pens. He shivered slightly. According to the old writings, men had been kindly toward their artificial creatures. They created them so that the glow-curse that once lived in the earth would not cause their children to be born as freaks. And they had left Earth to the Empties, promising that they would come again, when the glow-curse passed away.

He remembered Daner's words. And Daner was right, for Falon had also caught glimpses of the invaders before he fled the valley. They were no longer men, although they looked as if they had once been human. They were covered with a thick coat of curly brown hair, but their bodies were spindly and weak, as if they had been a long time in a place where there was no need for walking. Their eyes were huge, with great black pupils; and they blinked irritably in the bright sunlight. Their mouths were small and delicate, but set with four sharp teeth in front, and the jaws were strong—for ripping dainty mouthfuls of flesh.

They had landed in the valley more than a month earlier—while a red star was the morning star. Perhaps it was an omen, he thought—and perhaps they had *been* to the red star, for the old writings said that they had gone to a star to await the curse's lifting. But in the valley, they were building a city. And Falon knew that more of them were yet to come—for the city was large, while the invaders were few.

"Do you think, Ea-Daner," he asked as they rode, "that the invaders really own the world? That they have a right to the land—and to us?"

She considered it briefly, then snorted over her shoulder. "They owned it once, Falon. My grandfather believed that they cursed it themselves with the glow-curse, and that it drove them away. How do they still own it? But that is not a worry for me. If they were gods of the gods, I should still seek the blood that will pay for Daner's."

He noticed that the grief in her voice had changed to a cool and deadly anger. And he wondered. Did the alchemy of Natani custom so quickly change grief into rage?

"How long were you Daner's woman?" he asked.

"Only a few months," she replied. "He stole me from my father in the spring."

Falon reflected briefly that the Natani marriage customs were different than those of the valley peoples, who formally purchased a wife from her parents. The Natani pretended to be more forceful, but the "wife stealing" could be anything from a simple elopement, agreeable even to the parents, to a real kidnaping, involving a reluctant bride. He decided not to press the question.

"Among my people," he said, "I would ask you to be my wife—so that you would not be disgraced by returning to your father's house." He hesitated, watching the girl's trim back swaying in the half-light of the moon. "How would you answer me?"

She shook her head, making her dark hair dance. "Doesn't a valley widow mourn?"

"To mourn is to pity oneself. The dead feel nothing.

The mourner does not pity the dead. He pities himself for having lost the living."

She glanced back at him over her shoulder. "You speak as if you believe these things. I thought you were renouncing your people?"

"There is some wisdom, and some foolishness, in every people's way. But you haven't answered my question."

She shrugged. "We are not among your people, Falon." Then her voice softened, "I watched you fight the old one. You are quick and strong, and your mind is good. You would be a good man. Daner was a gloomy one. He treated me well, except when I tried to run away at first. But he never laughed. Do you ever laugh, Falon?"

Embarrassed, he said nothing.

"But this is pointless," she said, "for I am a daughter of my people."

"Do you still intend," he asked nervously, "to follow your husband to the wild dogs?"

She nodded silently, then, after a thoughtful moment, asked, "Do you believe it's foolishness—to try to kill some of the invader?"

Falon weighed it carefully. His defiance of his own law might weaken her resolve, if he persisted in trying to convince her against the suicidal attempts. But he spoke sadly.

"We are the Soul-Empty Ones. There are many of us in the world. If one invader could be killed for every dozen they kill of us, we would win. No, Ea, I don't think it's foolishness to fight for lives. But I think it's foolishness to fight for tribes, or to give yourself to the wild dogs."

She reined her horse around a bend in the trail, then halted to stare out at the distant bonfires. "I'll tell you why we do that, Falon. There's a legend among my people that the wild dogs were once the pets of Man, the Soul-Man, I mean. And it is said that the dogs scent the soul, and will not devour true Soul-Flesh. And the legend is also a prophecy. It says that someday, children will be born to the Natani who are Soul-Children—and that the wild dogs will again know their masters, and come to lick their hands. The Natani drag themselves to the forest when they die, in the hope that the dogs will not molest them. Then they will know that the prophecy has come, and the dead will go to the Place of Watching, as the Soul-Men who made us did go."

She spurred her horse gently and moved on. But Falon was still staring at the bonfires. Why did the invader keep them burning nightly? Of what were they afraid in the darkness?

"I wonder if the dogs could scent the souls of the sons of men—of the invaders," he mused aloud.

"Certainly!" she said flatly.

Falon wondered about the source of her certainty—from legend or from fact. But he felt that he had questioned her enough. They rode for several miles in silence, moving slowly along the down-going trail. The forests to their flanks were as usual, wailing with the cries of the dog packs.

Falon reined up suddenly. He hissed at Ea-Daner to halt, then rode up beside her. The dim shadow of her face questioned him.

"Listen! Up ahead!"

They paused in immobility, trying to sort out the sounds—the dog packs, a nightbird's cry, the horses' wet breathing, and—

"Dogs," murmured Ea-Daner. "Feeding on a carcass in the pathway. Their growls—" Suddenly she stiffened and made a small sound of terror in her throat. "Do you suppose it could be—"

"No, no!" he assured her quickly. "A wounded man couldn't come this far on foot. And you heard—"

She was sobbing again. "Follow me," grunted Falon, and trotted on ahead. He found the sharp dog-spikes in his saddlebag and fitted them onto the toes of his sandals. They were six inches of gleaming steel, and sharpened to needlelike points. He called to the girl to do the same. The dogs usually weighed the odds carefully before they attacked a horseman. But if interrupted at mealtime, they were apt to be irritable. He unwound a short coil of rawhide to use as a whip.

He passed a turn in the trail. A dozen of the gaunt, white animals were snarling in a cluster about something that lay on the ground. Their dim writhing shadows made a ghostly spectacle as Falon spurred his mount to a gallop, and howled a shrill cry to startle them.

*"Hi-yeee! Yee yee!"*

Massive canine heads lifted in the wind. Then the pack burst apart. These were not the dogs left by Man, but only their changed descendants. They scurried toward the shadows, then formed a loose ring that closed about the horsemen as they burst into the midst. A dog leaped for Falon's thigh, then fell back yelping as the toe-spike stabbed his throat. The horse reared as another leaped at his neck, and the hoofs beat at the savage hound.

"Try to ride them down!" Falon shouted to the girl. "Ride in a tight circle!"

Ea-Daner began galloping her stallion at a ten-foot radius from the bleeding figure on the ground. She was shrieking unfeminine curses at the brutes as she lashed out with her whip and her spike. Falon reined to a halt within the circle and dismounted. He was inviting a torn throat if a dog dared to slip past Ea. But he knelt beside the body, and started to lift it in his arms. Then he paused.

At first, he thought that the creature was an invader. It was scrawny and small-boned, but its body was not covered with the black fur. Neither was it a Soul-Empty One—for in designing the Empties, Man had seen no reason to give them separate toes. But Falon paused to long.

"Dog! Look out!" screamed the girl.

Falon reflexively hunched his chin against his chest and guarded his abdomen with his arms as he drew his war knife. A hurtling body knocked him off balance, and long fangs tore savagely at his face. He howled with fear and rage as he fell on his back. The dog was straddling him, and roaring fiercely as he mauled Falon's face and tried to get at his throat.

Falon locked his legs about the beast's belly, arched his body, and stretched away. The great forepaws tore at his chest as he rolled onto his side and began stabbing blindly at the massive head, aiming for a point just below the ear, and trying to avoid the snapping jaws. As the knife bit home, the fangs sank in his arm—then relaxed slightly. With his other hand, Falon forced the weakening jaws apart, pressed the knife deeper, and crunched it through thin bone to the base of the brain. The animal fell aside.

Panting, he climbed to his feet and seized the animal

by the hind legs. The girl was still riding her shrieking circuit, too fast for the dogs to attack. Falon swung the dead carcass about him, then heaved it toward the pack. Two others leaped upon it. The rest paused in their snarling pursuit of the horse. They trotted toward their limp comrade. Falon mounted his stallion quickly.

"Draw up beside me here!" he shouted to the girl.

She obeyed, and they stood flank to flank with the man-thing on the ground between them. The pack swarmed about the dead one.

"Look, they're dragging it away!" said Ea.

"They see they can have a feast without a fight," Falon muttered.

A few seconds later, the pack had dragged the carcass back into the forest, leaving the horsemen in peace. Ea glanced down at the man-thing.

"What is it?" she asked.

"I don't know. But I think it's still alive." Dismounting, he knelt again beside the frail body, and felt for a heartbeat. It was faintly perceptible, but blood leaked from a thousand gashes. A moan came from its throat. Falon saw that it was hopelessly mutilated.

"What are you?" he asked gently.

The man-thing's eyes were open. They wandered toward the crescent moon, then found Falon's hulking shadow.

"You . . . you look— Are you a man?" the thing murmured in a tongue that Falon had studied for tribal ritual.

"He speaks the ancient holy language," Falon gasped. Then he answered in kind. "Are you an invader?"

Dim comprehension came into the eyes. "You . . . are an . . . android."

Falon shook his head. "I am a Soul-Empty One."

The eyes wandered toward the moon again. "I . . . escaped them. I was looking for . . . your camps. The dogs—" His speech trailed off and the eyes grew dull.

Falon felt for the heartbeat, then shook his head. Gently, he lifted the body, and tied it securely behind his saddle. "Whoever he is, we'll bury him, after the sun rises." He noticed that Ea made no comment about the relative merits of tribal death-customs, despite the fact that she must feel repugnance toward burial.

*     *     *

Falon felt his face as they rode away. It dripped steadily from the numerous gashes, and his left cheek felt like soggy lace.

"We'll stop at the creek just ahead," said the girl. "I'll clean you up."

The dog-sounds had faded behind them. They dismounted, and tied their horses in the brush. Falon stretched out on a flat rock while Ea removed her homespun blouse and soaked it in the creek. She cleaned his wounds carefully and tenderly, while he tried to recover his breath and fight off the nausea of shock.

"Rest awhile," she murmured, "and sleep if you can. You've lost much blood. It's nearly dawn, and the dogs will soon go to their thickets."

Falon allowed himself the vanity of only one protest before he agreed to relax for a time. He felt something less than half alive. Ea stretched her blouse across a bush to dry, then came to sit beside him, with her back to the moon so that her face was in blackness.

"Keep your hands away from your wounds," she warned. "They'll bleed again."

He grinned weakly. "I'll have some nice scars," he said. "The valley women think a man is handsome if he has enough war scars. I think my popularity will increase. Do you like warriors with mauled faces, Ea?"

"The white scars are becoming, but not the red, not the fresh ones," she replied calmly.

"Mine will be red and ugly," he sighed, "but the valley women like them."

The girl said nothing, but shifted uneasily. He gazed at the moon's gleam on her soft shoulders.

"Will you still give yourself to the wild dogs if we return from the valley?"

She shivered and shook her head. "The Natani have scattered. A scattered people perhaps begins to lose its gods. And you've shown me a bad example, Soul-Falon. I have no longing for the dogs. But if the Natani found me alive—after Daner's death—they would kill me."

"Did you love him greatly?"

"I was beginning to love him—yes. He stole me without my consent, but he was kind—and a good warrior."

"Since you're breaking your custom, will you marry again?"

She was thoughtful for a moment. "Soul-Falon, if your cow died, would you cease to drink milk—because of bereavement?"

He chuckled. "I don't know. I don't have a cow. Do you compare Daner to a cow?"

"The Natani *love* animals," she said in a defensive tone.

"I am no longer a valley man and you are no longer a Natani. Do you still insist we go down against the invaders—alone?"

"Yes! Blood must buy blood, and Daner is dead."

"I was only thinking—perhaps it would be better to pause and plan. The most we can hope to do alone is ambush a guard or two before they kill us. It is foolish to talk of life when we approach death so blindly. I don't mind dying, if we can kill some invaders. But perhaps we can live, if we stop to think."

"We have today to think," she murmured, glancing toward the eastern sky. "We'll have to wait for nightfall again—before we go out into the open places of the valley."

"I am wondering," Falon said sleepily, "about the man-thing we took from the dogs. He said he escaped. Did he escape from the sons of men? If so, they might send guards to search for him."

She glanced nervously toward the trail.

"No, Ea—they wouldn't come at night. Not those puny bodies. They have god-weapons, but darkness spoils their value. But when the sun rises, we must proceed with caution."

She nodded, then yawned. "Do you think it's safe to sleep a little now? The sky is getting lighter, and the dogs are silent."

He breathed wearily. "Sleep, Ea. We may not sleep again."

She stretched out on her side, with her back toward him. "Soul-Falon?"

"Hm-m-m?"

"What did the man-thing mean—'android'?"

"Who knows? Go to sleep—Soul-Ea."

"It is a foolish title—'Soul,' " she said drowsily.

\* \* \*

A feverish sun burned Falon to dazed wakefulness. His face as stiff as stretched rawhide, and the pain clogged his senses. He sat up weakly, and glanced at Ea. She was still asleep, her dark head cushioned on her arms; and her shapely back was glistening with moisture. Falon had hinted that he was interested in her—but only out of politeness—for it was valley etiquette to treat a new widow as if she were a maiden newly come of age, and to court her with cautious flirtation. And a valley man always hoped that if he died, his wife would remarry quickly—lest others say, "Who but the dead one would want her?"

But as Falon glanced at the dozing Ea in the morning sunlight, her bronzed and healthy loveliness struck him. The dark hair spread breeze-tossed across the rock, and it gleamed in the sun. *She would make me a good wife indeed,* thought Falon. But then he thought of the Natani ways that were bred into her soul—the little ways that she would regard as proper, despite her larger rebellion— and he felt helpless. He knew almost nothing about Natani ritual for stealing brides. But it was certainly not simply a matter of tossing a girl over one's shoulder and riding away. And if he courted her by valley-custom, she might respond with disgust or mockery. He shrugged and decided that it was hopeless. They had small chance to surviving their fool's errand.

He thought of capture—and shuddered. Ea, being herded into the invaders' food pens—it was not a pleasant thought. There must be no capture.

A gust of wind brought a faint purring sound to his ears. He listened for a moment, stiffening anxiously. Then he stood up. It was one of the invaders' small skycarts. He had seen them hovering about the valley— with great rotary blades spinning above them. They could hang motionless in the air, or speed ahead like a frightened bird.

The brush obscured his view, and he could not see the skycart, but it seemed to be coming closer. He hurried to untether the horses; then he led them under a scrubby tree and tied them to the trunk. Ea was rubbing her eyes and sitting up when he returned to the rock.

"Is my blouse dry, Soul-Falon?"

He fetched it for her, then caught her arm and led her

under the tree with the horses. She heard the purr of the skycart, and her eyes swept the morning sky.

"Put your blouse on," he grumbled.

"Am I ugly, Soul-Falon?" she asked in a hurt tone, but obeyed him.

He faced her angrily. "Woman! You cause me to think of breaking my word. You cause me to think of forgetting the invader, and of stealing you away to the mountains. I wish that you were ugly indeed. But you trouble me with your carelessness."

"I am sorry," she said coldly, "but your dogskin jacket was no good for bathing wounds."

He noticed the dark stains on the blouse, and turned away in shame. He knew too little of Natani women, and he realized he was being foolish.

The skycart was still out of sight, but the horses were becoming restless at the sound. As Falon patted his stallion's flanks, he glanced at the body of the man-thing— still tied across the steed's back. His mouth tightened grimly. The creature had evidently been desperate to have braved the forest alone, unarmed, and afoot. Desperate or ignorant. Had he escaped from the invader, and was the skycart perhaps searching for him? It was moving very slowly indeed—as he had seen them move when searching the hills for the villages of the Empties.

An idea struck him suddenly. He turned to the girl. "You know these paths. Is there a clearing near here— large enough for the skycart to sit upon?"

Ea nodded. "A hundred paces from here, the creekbed widens, and floods have washed the bedrock clean. Duck beneath the brush and you can see it."

"Is it the *only* clearing?"

She nodded again. "Why do you ask? Are you afraid the cart will land in it?"

Falon said nothing, but hastily untied the body from his horse. He carried it quickly to the flat rock where they had slept, and he placed the man-thing gently upon it—where he would be in full view from the sky. The skycart crept into distant view as Falon hurried back into the brush. Ea was watching him with an anxious and bewildered stare.

"They'll see him!" she gasped.

"I hope they do! Hurry! Let's go to the clearing!"

He caught her arm, and they began racing along the shallow creekbed, their sandals splashing in the narrow trickle of shallow water. For a few seconds they ducked beneath overhanging brush, but soon the brush receded, and the bed broadened out into a flat expanse of dry rock, broken only by the wear marks of high waters. Then they were in the open, running along the brushline.

"In here!" he barked, and plunged over a root-tangled embankment and into a dense thicket. She followed, and they crouched quietly in the thick foliage, as the purr of the skycart became a nearby drone.

"What are we going to do?" Ea asked tensely.

"Wait, and hope. Perhaps you'll get your knife wet."

Falon peered up through the leaves, and saw the skycart briefly as it moved past. But the sound of its engine took on a new note, and soon he knew that it was hovering over the rock where the body lay. Ea made a small sound of fright in her throat.

After a moment, the skycart moved over the clearing and hung growling fifty feet above them. As it began to settle, Falon saw a fur-coated face peering out from its cabin. He hissed at Ea to remain silent.

The skycart dropped slowly into the clearing, rolled a short distance, and stopped, a pebble's toss from the hidden tribesmen. Its occupants remained inside for a moment, peering about the perimeter of brush. Then a hatch opened, and one of the feeble creatures climbed painfully out. There were three of them, and Falon shuddered as he saw the evil snouts of their flamethrowers.

One of them remained to guard the ship, while the others began moving slowly up the creekbed, their weapons at the ready, and their eyes searching the brush with suspicion. They spoke in low voices, but Falon noticed that they did not use the ancient sacred tongue of Man. He frowned in puzzlement. The valley folk who had been close enough to hear their speech swore that they used the holy language.

"Now?" whispered the girl.

Falon shook his head. "Wait until they find the horses," he hissed in her ear.

The spider-legged creatures moved feebly, as if they were carrying heavy weights; and they were a long time covering the distance to the flat rock. The guard was sitting in the hatchway with his flame gun across his lap. His huge eyes blinked painfully in the harsh morning sunlight as he watched the thickets about the clearing. But he soon became incautious, and directed his stare in the direction his companions had gone.

Falon heard a whinny from the horses, then a shrill shout from the invaders. The guard stood up. Startled, he moved a few steps up the creekbed, absorbed in the shouts of his companions. Falon drew his war knife, and weighed the distance carefully. A miss would mean death. Ea saw what he meant to do, and she slipped her own knife to him.

Falon stood up, his shoulders bursting through the foliage. He aimed calmly, riveting his attention on an accurate throw, and ignoring the fact that the guard had seen him and was lifting his weapon to fire. The knife left Falon's hand as casually as if he had been tossing it at a bit of fur tacked to a door.

The flame gun belched, but the blast washed across the creekbed, and splashed upward to set the brush afire. The guard screamed and toppled. The intense reflected heat singed Falon's hair, and made his stiff face shriek with pain. He burst from the flaming brush, tugging the girl after him.

The guard was sitting on the rocks and bending over his abdomen. The gun had clattered to the ground. The creature had tugged the knife frim his belly, and he clutched it foolishly as he shrieked gibberish at it. The others had heard him and were hurrying back from the horses.

Falon seized the gun and kicked the guard in the head. The creature crumpled with a crushed skull. *The gods die easily,* he thought, as he raced along the brushline, keeping out of view.

He fumbled with the gun, trying to discover its firing principle. He touched a stud, then howled as a jet of flame flared the brush on his left. He retreated from the flames, then aimed at the growth that overhung the narrowing creek toward the horses. A stream of incendiary set an inferno among the branches, sealing off the invaders from their ship.

"Into the skycart!" he barked at Ea.

She sprinted toward it, then stopped at the hatch, peering inside. "How will you make the god-machine fly?" she asked.

He came to stare over her shoulder, then cursed softly. Evidently the skycart had no mind of its own, for the cabin was full of things to push and things to pull. The complexity bewildered him. He stood thoughtfully staring at them.

"They'll creep around the fire in a few moments," warned Ea.

Falon pushed her into the ship, then turned to shout toward the spreading blaze. "We have your skycart! If we destroy it, you will be left to the wild dogs!"

"The wild dogs won't attack the sons of men!" Ea hissed.

He glanced at her coolly. If she were right, they were lost. But no sound came from beyond the fire. But the invaders had had time to move around it through the brush, while the man and the girl presented perfect targets in the center of the clearing.

"Fire your god-weapons," Falon jeered. "And destroy your skycart." He spoke the ancient holy tongue, but now he wondered if the invaders could really understand it.

They seemed to be holding a conference somewhere in the brush. Suddenly Falon heard the horses neighing shrilly above the crackling of the fire. There came a sound of trampling in the dry tangles, then a scream. A flame gun belched, and the horses shrieked briefly.

"One of them was trampled," Falon gasped. "Man's pets no longer know his odor."

He listened for more sounds from the horses, but none came. "They've killed our mounts," he growled, then shouted again.

"Don't the pets know their masters? Hurry back, you gods, or perhaps the skycart will also forget."

A shrill and frightened voice answered him. "You can't escape, android! You can't fly the copter."

"And neither can you, if we destroy it!"

There was a short silence, then: "What do you want, android?"

"You will come into the clearing unarmed."

The invader responded with a defiant curse. Falon turned the flame gun diagonally upward and fired a hissing streak to the leeward. It arced high, then spat into the brush two hundred paces from the clearing. Flames burst upward. He set seven similar fires at even intervals about them.

"Soon they will burn together in a ring," he shouted. "Then they will burn inward and drive you to us. You have four choices: flee to the forest; or wait for the fire to drive you to us; or destroy your ship by killing us; or surrender now. If you surrender, we'll let you live. If you choose otherwise, you die."

"And you also, android!"

Falon said nothing. He stayed in the hatchway, keeping an eye on the brush for signs of movement. The fires were spreading rapidly. After a few minutes, the clearing would become a roasting oven.

"Don't fire, android!" called the invader at last.

"Then stand up! Hold your weapon above your head."

The creature appeared fifty paces up the slope and moved slowly toward them. Falon kept his flame gun ready.

"Where's the other?" he called.

"Your beasts crushed him with their hoofs."

Falon covered him silently until he tore his way into the clearing. "Take his weapon, Ea," he murmured. The girl obeyed, but her hand twitched longingly toward her knife as she approached. The creature's eyes widened and he backed away from her.

"Let him live, Ea!"

She snatched the invader's weapon, spat at him contemptuously, then marched back to the ship. Her face was white with hate, and she was trembling.

"Sit in the skycart," he told her, then barked at the captive. "You'll fly us away, before the fire sweeps in."

The prisoner obeyed silently. They climbed into the aircraft as the clearing became choked with smoke and hot ashes. The engine coughed to life, and the ship arose quickly from the clearing. The girl murmured with frightened awe as the ground receded beneath them. Falon was uneasy, but he kept his eyes and his gun on the back of the pilot's furry neck. The creature chuckled with gloating triumph.

"Shoot the flame rifle, android," he hissed. "And we shall all burn together."

Falon frowned uncomfortably for a moment. "Quiet!" he barked. "Do you think we prefer your food pens to quick and easy death? If you do not obey, then we shall all die as you suggest."

The pilot glanced back mockingly, but said nothing.

"You tempt me to kill you," Falon hissed. "Why do you gloat?"

"The fires you set, android. The forests are dry. Many of your people will be driven down into the valleys. It is a strategy we intended to use—as soon as our city had grown enough to accommodate the large numbers of prisoners we will take. But you have made it necessary to destroy, rather than capture."

Ea glanced back at the fires. "He speaks truth," she whispered to Falon, who already felt a gnawing despair.

"Bah, hairy one! How will you kill thousands? There are only a few of you! Your god-weapons aren't omnipotent. Numbers will crush you."

The pilot laughed scornfully. "Will your tribesmen attack their gods? They are afraid, android. You two are only rebels. The tribes will flee, not fight. And even if some of them fought, we have the advantage. We could retreat to our ships while enemies broke their knives on the hull."

The ship was rising high over the forest, higher than any mountain Falon had ever climbed. He stared out across the valley toward the seacoast where the fishing boats of his people lay idle by their docks. The owners were in captivity or in flight. The city of the invaders was taking form—a great rectangle, thousands of paces from end to end. A dozen metallic gleams were scattered about the area—the skyboats in which the invader had descended from the heavens.

He noticed the food pens. There were two of them—high stockades, overlooked by watchtowers with armed guards. He could see the enclosures' occupants as antlike figures in the distance. Neither pen seemed crowded. He frowned suddenly, wondering if the man-thing had been confined to one of the pens. The creature had been neither invader nor Empty. Falon felt a vague suspicion. He glanced at the pilot again.

"The dead one told us many things before he died," he said cautiously.

The creature stiffened, then shot him a suspicous glance. "The escaped android? What could *he* have told you?"

*"Android?"* Falon's hunch was coming clearer. "Do you call *yourself* an android?" he jeered.

"Of course not! I am a man! 'Android' is our word for 'Soul-Empty One.' "

"Then the dead one is not of your race, eh?"

"You have eyes, don't you?"

"But neither is he of our race!" Falon snapped. "For we have no toes. He is a soul-man!"

The pilot was trembling slightly. "If the dead one told you this, then we shall all die—lest you escape and speak of this to others!" He wrenched at the controls, and the ship darted valleyward—toward the city. "Fire, android! Fire, and destroy us! Or be taken to the food pens!"

"Kill him!" snarled Ea. "Perhaps we can fly the ship. Kill him with your knife, Soul-Falon!"

The pilot, hearing this, shut off the engines. The ship began hurtling earthward, and Falon clutched at his seat to keep balance.

"Fly to your city!" he shouted above the rush of air. "We will submit!"

Ea growled at him contemptuously, drew her knife, and lunged toward the pilot. Falon wrestled with her, trying to wrench the knife from her grasp. "I know what I'm doing," he hissed in her ear.

Still she fought, cursing him for a coward, and trying to get to the pilot. Falon howled as her teeth sank into his arm, then he clubbed his fist against her head. She moaned and sagged limply.

"Start the engine!" he shouted. "We'll submit."

"Give me your weapons, then," growled the pilot.

Falon surrendered them quickly. The ship's engine coughed to life as they fell into the smoke of the forest fire. The blazes were licking up at them as the rotors milled at the air and bore them up once more.

"Death is not to your liking, eh, android?" sneered the invader. "You'll find our food pens are very comfortable."

Falon said nothing for a time as he stared remorsefully

at the unconscious girl. Then he spoke calmly to the pilot.

"Of course, there were others with us when we found the dead one. They will spread the word that you are not the sons of men."

"You lie!" gasped the pilot.

"Very well," murmured Falon. "Wait and see for yourselves. The news will spread, and then our tribes will fight instead of flee."

The pilot considered this anxiously for a moment. Then he snorted. "I shall take you to Kepol. *He* will decide whether or not you speak the truth."

Falon smiled inwardly and glanced back at the fires beneath them. They were creeping faster now, and soon the blaze would be sweeping down the gentle slopes to drive the inhabitants of the forest into the valley. Thousands of Natani and valley warriors would swarm out onto the flatlands. Most would not attack, but only try to flee from the creatures whom they thought were demigods.

Falon watched the invaders' installations as the ship drew nearer. Workmen were swarming busily about the growing city. First he noticed that the workmen were hairless. Then he saw that they were not Empties, but the scrawny soul-men. Furry figures stood guard over them as they worked. He saw that the soul-men were being used as slaves.

Soon they were hovering over the city, and, glancing down, he noticed that the occupants of one pen were soul-men, while the other was for Empties. Evidently the soul-men were considered too valuable as workers to use as food. The two pens were at opposite ends of the city, as if the invaders didn't care to have the two groups contacting one another. Falon wondered if the *captive* Empties knew that their overlords weren't soul-men, as they had once believed.

The girl came half awake as they landed. She immediately tore into Falon with teeth and nails. Guards were congregating about the ship as the pilot climbed out. He held off the furious Ea while a dozen three-fingered hands tugged at them, and dragged them from the plane. The pilot spoke to the guards in a language Falon could not understand.

Suddenly the butt of a weapon crashed against his head, and he felt himself go weak. He was dimly aware of being tossed on a cart and rolled away. Then the sunlight faded into gloom, and he knew he was inside a building. Bright self-lights exploded in his skull with each jog of the cart, and his senses were clogged with pain.

At last the jouncing ceased, and he lay quietly for a time, listening to the chatter of the invaders' voices. They spoke in the strange tongue, but one voice seemed to dominate the others.

A torrent of icy water brought him to full consciousness. He sat up on the cart and found himself in a small but resplendent throne room. A small wizened creature occupied a raised dais. Over his head hung a great golden globe with two smaller globes revolving slowly about it. The walls were giant landscape murals, depicting a gaunt red earth the likes of which Falon had never seen.

"On your feet before Lord Kepol, android!" growled a guard, prodding him with a small weapon.

Falon came weakly erect, but a sharp blow behind his knees sent him sprawling. The creature called Kepol cackled.

"This one is too muscular to eat," he said to the guards. "Place him in restraints so that he can have no exercise, and force-feed him. His liver will grow large and tender."

A guard bowed. "It shall be done, Lordship. Do you wish to hear him speak?"

The king-creature croaked impatiently. "This pilot is a fool. If a few of the androids believe we are not men, what harm can be done? Most of them would not believe such rumors. They have no concept of our world. But let him speak."

"Speak, android!" A booted foot pushed at Falon's ribs.

"I've got nothing to say."

The boot crashed against his mouth, and a brief flash of blackness struck him again. He spat a broken tooth.

"Speak!"

"Very well. What the pilot says is true. Others know that you are not men. They will come soon to kill all of you."

The boot drew back again angrily, but hesitated. For

the king-creature was cackling with senile laughter. The guards joined in politely.

"When will they come, android?" jeered the king.

"The forest fires will cause them to come at once. They will sweep over your city and drive you into the sea."

"With knives—against machine guns and flamethrowers?" The king glanced at a guard. "This one bores me. Flog him, then bring me the girl. That will be more amusing."

Falon felt loops of wire being slipped over his wrists. Then he was jerked erect, suspended from the ceiling so that his toes scarcely touched the floor.

"Shall we do nothing about the forest fires, Your Lordship?" a guard asked.

The king sighed. "Oh . . . I suppose it would be wise to send a platoon to meet the savages when they emerge. Our fattening pens need replenishing. And we can see if there is any truth in what the captive says. I doubt that they suspect us, but if they do, there is small harm done."

Falon smiled to himself as the first lash cut across his back. He had accomplished the first step in his mission. A platoon was being sent.

The whip master was an expert. He began at the shoulders and worked stroke by stroke toward the waist, pausing occasionally to rub his fingers roughly over the wounds. Falon wailed and tried to faint, but the torture was calculated to leave him conscious. From his dais, the king-creature was chortling with dreamy sensuality as he watched.

"Take him to the man pen," ordered the king when they were finished. "And keep him away from other androids. He knows things that could prove troublesome."

As Falon was led away, he saw Ea just outside the throne room. She was bound and naked to the waist. Her eyes hated him silently. He shuddered and looked away. For she was the sacrifice which he had no right to make.

The man pen was nearly deserted, for the soul-men were busy with the building of the city. Falon was led across a sandy courtyard and into a small cell, where he was chained to a cot. A guard pressed a hypodermic into his arm.

"This will make you eat, android," he said with a leer, "and grow weak and fat."

Falon set his jaw and said nothing. The guard went away, leaving him alone in his cell.

An old man came to stare through the bars. His eyes were wide with the dull glow of fatalistic acceptance. He was thin and brown, his hands gnarled by the wear of slave work. He saw Falon's toeless feet and frowned. "Android!" he murmured in soft puzzlement. "Why did they put you in here?"

Falon's throat worked with emotion. Here was a descendant of his creators. Man—who had gone away as a conqueror and returned as a slave. Nervously Falon met the calm blue-eyed gaze for a moment. But his childhood training was too strong. Here was Man! Quietly he slipped to his knees and bowed his head. The man breathed slow surprise.

"Why do you kneel, android? I am but a slave, such as yourself. We are brothers."

Falon shivered. "You are the immortal ones!"

"Immortal?" The man shrugged. "We have forgotten our ancient legends." He chuckled. "Have your people kept them alive for us?"

Falon nodded humbly. "We have kept for you what we were told to keep, soul-man. We have waited many centuries."

The man stared toward one of the watchtowers. "If only we had trusted you! If only we had told you where the weapons were hidden. But some of the ancients said that if we gave you too much knowledge, you would destroy us when we tried to return. Now you have nothing with which to defend yourselves against our new masters."

Falon lifted his head slightly. "Weapons, you say? God-weapons?"

"Yes, they're hidden in vaults beneath the ancient cities. We sent a man to tell you where to find them. But he probably failed in his mission. Do you know anything of him? Come, man! Get off your knees!"

Self-consciously, Falon sat on the edge of his cot. "We found this man dead in the trail—last night." He paused and lowered his eyes. It had been easy to lie to the invaders, but it would be harder lying to the gods. He steeled himself for a rebuke. "The emissary failed to tell us of the god-weapons, but he told us that the invaders were not men. The tribes now know this fact. In a few hours, they will attack. Will you help us, soul-man?"

The man gasped and wrinkled his face in unbelief. "*Attack!* With only knives and spears? Android, this is insanity!"

Falon nodded. "But notice how smoke is dimming the sun, soul-man. The forest fires are driving the people forth. They have no choice but to attack."

"It's suicide!"

Falon nodded. "But it is to save you that they do it. And to save the earth for both of us. Will you help?"

The man leaned thoughtfully against the bars. "Our people are slaves. They have learned to obey their masters. It is hard to say, android. They would rally to a hopeful cause—but this seems a hopeless one."

"So it seems. I have planted a seed in the mind of the one known as Kepol. He also thinks it is hopeless, but when he sees a certain thing, the seed may bloom into panic. He underestimates us now. If later he comes to overestimate us, we may have a chance."

"What do you propose to do?"

Falon was loath to take the initiative and tell a soul-man what to do. If seemed somehow improper to him. "Tell me," he asked cautiously, "can you fly the skyboats in which the invaders brought you?"

The man chuckled grimly. "Why not? It was our civilization that built them. The invaders were but savages on Mars, before we came to teach them our ways. They learned from us, then enslaved us. Yes, we can fly the rockets. But why do you ask?"

"I am uncertain as yet. Tell me another thing. How did the one man escape?"

The man frowned, then shook his head. "This, I shall not tell you. We were months in preparing his escape. And the way is still open. Others might follow him. I cannot trust you yet, android."

Falon made no protest. "You've told me what I want to know—that others can escape. Can many go at once?"

The man was thoughtful for a moment. "It would take

a little time—to evacuate the entire man pen. But the others are already outside, working on the city."

"They will be brought back soon," Falon said dogmatically. "Wait and see."

The man smiled faintly. "You're sure of yourself, android. You tempt me to trust you."

"It would be best."

"Very well. The escape route is only a tunnel from beneath your cot to the center of the city." The man glanced around at the towers, then tossed Falon a key. "This will unlock your door. We filed it from a spoon. Let your unlocking of it be a signal. I'll speak to the others if they return, as you say."

Man and android eyed each other for a moment through the bars.

"Can you get word to the ones who are working on the city?" Falon asked.

The man nodded. "That is possible. What would you have them know?"

"Tell them to watch the forests. Tell them to set up a cry that the tribes are coming to save us."

"You think this will frighten our captors, android?"

"No, they will laugh. But when the times comes, the thought will be in their minds—and perhaps we can change it to fear."

The man nodded thoughtfully. "I suppose it can do no harm. We'll keep you informed about the fire's progress. If the wind doesn't change, it should burn quickly toward the valley."

The man departed, and Falon lay back upon the cot to think of Ea in the throne room. He had no doubt of her fate. When the king was finished with her, she would be assigned to the android pen for fattening. He had given her over into the sensual hands of the invader, and he resolved to atone for it by sheer recklessness when the time came for action. If the gods watched, then perhaps his own blood would pay for whatever she was suffering.

But another thought occupied his mind. The soul-man had called him "brother"—and the memory of the word lingered. It blended with the death-chant which Ea had sung for Daner when he went to die in the manner of his tribe—"The Song of the Soul-Empty Ones." "Brother,"

the man had said. Did one call an animal "brother"?
Yet the man knew he was an android.

Several old men moved about in the stockade. Apparently their duties were to "keep house" for the younger
laborers. Falon wondered about the women. None were
visible. Perhaps they had been left upon the invaders'
world. Or perhaps the invaders had other plans for women.

Soon he heard the sound of distant shouting from the
direction of the city, but could make no sense of it.
Apparently, however, the workmen were setting up a cry
that rescue was imminent. If only they would come to
believe in themselves!

The hypodermic injection was taking effect. He felt a
ravenous hunger that made his stomach tighten into a
knot of pain. A horrifying thought struck him suddenly,
and he shouted to the men in the yard at the stockade.
One of them approached him slowly.

"Tell me, soul-man," Falon breathed. "What sort of
food do the invaders bring you? Is there any—meat?"

The man stiffened and turned away. "Once they brought
us meat, android. Three men ate of it. We saw that the
three met with . . . uh, fatal accidents. Since then, the
Mars-Lords have brought us only fish and greens."

He moved away, his back rigid with insult. Falon tried
to call an apology after him, but could find no words.

The sunlight was growing gloomy with the smoke of
the forest fires, but the wind had died. Falon prayed that
it would not reverse itself and come out of the east.

He examined his chains and found the sleeve which
fastened them to the cot was loose. The soul-men had
evidently pried it slightly open. Then he found that the
bolts which fastened the cot legs to the concrete floor had
been worked free, then returned to their places. They
could be extracted with a slight tug, the plate unscrewed,
and the sleeve slipped off the leg. But he left them in
place, lest a a guard come. Beneath the cot was a dusty
sheet of steel which evidently covered the tunnel's mouth.

When a guard brought food, Falon devoured it before
the creature left his cell and begged for more.

"You will be fat indeed, android," chuckled the Martian.

Toward sunset, a clamor in the courtyard told him that
the soul-men were being returned to the stockade. The
light had grown forge-red, and the air was acrid with

faint-smoke smell. The man, who was called Penult, came again to Falon's cell.

"The smoke obscures our vision, android," he said. "The Mars-Lords have sent a patrol to police the edge of the hills, but we can no longer see them." He frowned. "The lords seem worried about something. They scuttle about chattering among themselves, and they listen secretly to their radios."

"Radios?"

"The voices with which they speak to the patrol. I think they are preparing to send others. Helicopters are taking off, but the smoke must choke their visibility. What can be happening?"

"The tribes are attacking, of course," lied Falon. He noticed that the wind had arisen again. It was sweeping the smoke along in the downdrafts from the foothills.

"What are your plans, android?" asked Penult. Several others had gathered behind him, but he hissed them away lest they attract the suspicion of the watchtowers.

"Wait until the invaders become desperate and send too many on their patrols. Then we shall rise up against the ones that remain."

"But we have no weapons."

"We have surprise. We have fear. We have your tunnel. And we must have lightning swiftness. If you can gain access to their skyboats, can you destroy them or fly them?"

Penult shook his head doubtfully "We will discuss it among ourselves. I will see what the others wish to do." He moved away.

Dusk fell. Lights flickered on from the watchtowers, bathing the stockade in smoky brilliance. The courtyard was thronging with soul-men who wandered freely about their common barracks. Beyond the wall of the man pen, the evening was filled with angry and anxious sounds as the Mars-Lords readied more patrols for battle.

Falon knew that if they remained about the city, they would be safe. But the first patrol had undoubtedly been engulfed in the tide of wild dogs that swept from the forests. Their weapons would be ineffective in the blanket of smoke that settled about them. And the gaunt dog packs would be crazed by fear of the fire. Thousands of

the brutes had rolled out across the plain, and the small
patrol had been taken by surprise. The horsemen would
come last. They would wait until the dogs had gone
before they fled the fires. Perhaps they would arrive in
time to see the dogs devouring the bodies of their gods.
Perhaps then they would attack.

Penult stopped at Falcon's cell. "We have managed to
contact the android pen," he said. "In a few moments
they will start a riot within their stockade, to distract the
watchtower guards. Be ready to unlock the door."

"Good, Soul-Penult! Pick us a dozen good men to rush
the towers when we come from the tunnel. Let them go
first, and I will be with them."

Penult shrugged. "It is as good a way to die as any."

Falon tugged the bolts from the floor, and slipped the
chain's sleeve from the leg of his cot. The manacles were
still fastened to his ankles and wrists, but he decided that
they might make good weapons.

One of the searchlights winked away from the courtyard. Falon watched its hazy beam stab toward the opposite end of the city. Then he heard dim sounds of distant
shouting. The riot had begun. Other lights followed the
first, leaving the man pen illuminated only by the floods
about the walls.

Quickly he slipped from his cot and moved to the
door. A soul-man sidled in front of his cell to block the
view from the towers while Falon twisted the key in the
lock. Then he pushed the cot aside. A man came to help
him move the steel plate. They pushed it away noiselessly, and the tunnel's mouth yawned beneath them.
The cell was filling with men while the guard's eyes were
distracted toward the android pen.

"We are all here, android," a voice whispered.

Falon glanced doubtfully toward the courtyard. The
men were thronging near the cell, kicking up dust to
obscure the tower's vision. Evidently they had not seen;
for Falon was certain that the invaders would not hesitate
to blister the entire group with their flamethrowers if
they suspected escape. Already there were sounds of
explosions from the other end of the city. Perhaps they
were massacring the inhabitants of the other pen. He
thought grimly of Ea.

A man had lowered himself into the tunnel. Falon

followed him quickly, to be swallowed by damp and cramped blackness. They proceeded on their hands and knees.

Falon called back over his shoulder. "Tell the others to wait for us to emerge before they enter."

"They're setting the barracks and the stockade walls on fire, android," hissed the man behind him. "It will provide another distraction."

It was a long crawl from the stockade to the center of the city. He thought grimly of the possibility that the tunnel would be discovered by guards coming to quench the barracks fire. The small party might emerge into the very arms of the waiting Mars-Lords.

The tunnel was not made for comfort, and Falon's chains hindered his progress. He became entangled frequently, and bruised his kneecaps as he tripped over them. There was no room to turn around. If guards met them at the exit there could be no retreat.

The lead man stopped suddenly. "We're here!" he hissed. "Help me hoist the slab of rock, android."

Falon lay upon his back and pressed his feet against the ceiling. It moved upward. A slit of dim light appeared. The soul-man peered outside, then fell back with a whimper of fright.

"A guard!" he gasped. "Not a dozen feet away! He's watching the man pen."

Falon cursed softly and lowered the lid of the exit. "Did he see the stone move?" he asked.

"No! But he seemed to hear it."

Suddenly there was a dull thumping sound from overhead. The guard was stomping on the stone slab, listening to its hollowness.

With an angry growl, Falon tensed his legs, then heaved. The stone opened upward, carrying the guard off balance. He fell with the slab across his leg, and his shriek was but another sound in the general melee as Falon burst upon him and kicked his weapon aside. The Martian, still shrieking, fumbled at something in his belt. Falon kicked him to death before he brought it into play.

The dozen soul-men climbed out into the gloom and raced for the black shadows of a half-completed masonry wall in the heart of the growing city. One of them seized the small weapon in the guard's belt, while Falon caught up the flamethrower.

The city was lighted only by the dim smoky aura of searchlights aimed at the man pens. The riot had diminished in the android pen, but an occasional burst of sharp explosions belched toward it from one of the watchtowers. Falon's people were sacrificing themselves to draw attention away from the soul-men.

"Split in two groups!" Falon hissed. "Tackle the two nearest towers."

They separated and diverged, following the shadows of the walls. Leadership was impossible, for the operation was too hastily planned. Falon trusted in the hope that each man's mind had been long occupied with thoughts of escape, and that each knew the weakest spots in the invaders' defenses.

A few of the searchlights were stabbing out toward the west, where sounds of the dog packs were becoming faintly perceptible. Somewhere out upon the plains, the invaders' patrols were tiny island-fortresses in the infiltrating wave of dogs and horsemen. They could easily form into tight groups and defend themselves against the hordes with their explosives and flamethrowers, but they would be unable to stem the tide of flesh whose only real desire was to escape the fires. But some of the Natani might be attacking, when they saw that the dogs did not regard the Mars-Lords as their masters.

At the corner of the city, Falon's group found itself within stone's throw of a tower. They crouched in the darkness for a moment, watching the lights sweep westward. For now that the futile android riot was put down, the guards saw no threat save the unreal one on the plains. The threat's grimness was increased by the shroud of smoke that hid it and gave it mystery in the Martian eyes.

The man who had seized the belt weapon nudged Falon and whispered, "I'll stay here and cover your dash, android."

Falon nodded and glanced around quickly. They would be within the floodlights' glow, once they bounded across the wall-scurrying targets for all the towers. Suddenly he gasped. A man was running up the ladder of the tower to which the other group had gone. A searchlight caught him in its pencil. Then a blast of machine-gun fire plucked him off and sent him pitching earthward.

"Hurry!" Falon barked, and leaped across the wall.

They sprinted single file toward the base of the tower. A light winked down to splash them with brilliance. The man fired from the shadows behind them, and the light winked out. Dust sprayed up about Falon's feet as the guards shot from overhead. A streak of flame lanced downward, and two of the men screamed as it burst upward in a small inferno. The covering fire brought a guard hurtling from the tower. Falon leaped over his body and began scaling the steel ladder toward the cage.

A roar of voices came from the man pens. The barracks were blazing while a handful of guards played hoses over the walls.

Falon climbed steadily, expecting at any moment to feel a searing burst of flame spray over him. But the guards above him were firing blindly toward the shadows whence came the covering fire. And the other towers were playing their lights about their own skirts, watching for similar attacks.

A slug ricocheted off the hatchway as he brust through it into the cage. Another tore through his thigh as he whipped the chain in a great arc, lashing it about the legs of one of the guards. He jerked the creature off his feet, then dived at the other, who was trying to bring a machine gun into play. The android's attack swept him off balance, and Falon heaved him bodily from the tower.

Another man burst through the hatch and disposed of the guard who was being dragged about by Falon's chain.

Falon threw himself to the floor as a burst of bullets sprayed the open space above the waist-high steel walls of the cage. The nearest tower had opened fire upon them. Falon leaped for the permanently mounted flame-thrower and sent a white-hot jet arcing toward the other cage. It fell short. He tried another burst, arcing it higher. It splashed home and the incendiary made a small furnace of the other tower, from which the guards hastily descended. The other towers were beyond flame-gun range, but they sprayed Falon's newly won outpost with machine-gun fire.

"Lie flat!" shouted the man. "The armor will turn back the bullets."

Falon flung himself headlong while the rain of small-arms fire pelted the steel walls. He ripped a sleeve from his rawhide jacket and made a tourniquet for his flesh wound. "Where are the other four?" he gasped.

"Dead," shouted his companion above the din.

A crashing roar came from the direction of the man pen. The barrage suddenly ceased. Falon chanced a glance over the low rim of the cage. One wall of the flaming stockade had collapsed, and men were pouring through the broken gap to overwhelm the firemen. The towers were turning their weapons upon the torrent of escapees. Falon's companion manned the machine gun and turned it on the invaders. "We'll draw their fire!" he called.

The second group had taken their objective, and another tower had fallen into the rebels' hands. Men poured through the stockade gap while the towers exchanged fire among themselves.

"They're trying to make it to the ships!" the gunner called. Then he fell back with half his face torn away.

Falon crawled to the gun and tried to operate it, but being unfamiliar with the god-weapons, he was only exposing himself to death. He dropped it in favor of the flamethrower, lay beside the hatch, and shot down at the occasional unfortunate Martian that scurried within his range.

Several of the towers were silent now, including the other captive one. Falon slipped through the hatch and climbed down the steel ladder. His descent went unnoticed as the battle raged about the city and among the ships. He noticed that fire was spurting from several rockets, but they were still in the hands of the invader; for the man pen's escapees were still fighting for possession of the nearest ship.

Falon sprinted for the city's wall as a pair of wild dogs attacked him from the shadows. He fried them with a blast from the flame gun, then hurdled the wall and climbed atop a heap of masonry. Most of the lights were out now, and the darkness was illuminated only by the flaming stockade. The wild-dog packs were trotting in from the west, mingling in the battle to attack man, android, and Martian alike.

One of the ships blasted off into the night, but Falon felt certain that it was not commanded by men. It was the throne ship, in which the king resided. Another followed it; but the second seemed to be piloted by the escapees.

The battle had become chaos. Falon stumbled through the masonry, stepping over an occasional body, and looking for a fight. But most of the Martians had taken up positions about the ships. He noticed that few of them were among the dead, who were mostly men and androids. But the rebels could afford to lose more than the Martians.

A few horsemen were joining the fray as the battle on the plains moved eastward. They rode into the tides of flesh that rolled about the ships. Falon saw a rider spit a Martian on his dog-spike and lift him to the saddle. The Martian shot him, then fell back to be trampled by the horse.

The two ships were returning. Falon flung himself down behind a wall as the throne ship shrieked past, splashing a wide swath of blinding brightness down the length of the city. The second ship, which had been in hot pursuit, nosed upward and spiraled off over the ocean to make a wide circle in the opposite direction. Falon, sensing a sky battle, ducked quickly out of the city's walls, caught the bridle of a runaway horse, and swung into the saddle.

The throne ship was coming back for another run, while the other was streaking back from the south. Falon realized vaguely what the man-pilot meant to do. He glanced toward the ground battle. It had subsided, and the warriors were scurrying for cover. Shrieks of "Collision!" and "Explosion!" arose from the mobs.

Hardly knowing what to expect, Falon decided quickly to follow their example. He reined the mare to a standstill, then swung out of the saddle and clung to her flank, hiding himself from the approaching ships. He saw them come together as he ducked his head behind the mare's neck.

The ground beneath him became bathed in pale violet. Then a dazzling and unearthly brilliance made him close his eyes. For several seconds there was no sound, save the snarls of the dog packs. Then the force of a thousand avalanches struck him. He fell beneath the mare, still guarding his face behind her neck. The breath went out of him in a surge of blackness. He struggled for a moment, then lay quietly in ever-deepening night.

Daylight awakened him, gloomy gray dawnlight. The mare had tried to stagger to her feet, but had fallen again a few feet away. The valley was silent, save for the whisper of ocean breakers in the distance. He sat up weakly and knew that some of his ribs were broken. He looked around.

The plain was littered with bodies of dogs, men, and Martians. A spiral of smoke arose lazily from the wreckage. Then he saw figures moving about in the ruins. He managed a feeble shout, and two of them approached him. One was man, the other android. He knew neither of them, but the man seemed to recognize him as the prisoner who had occupied the cell in the man pen. Falon lowered his head and moaned with pain. The man knelt beside him.

"We've been looking for you, android," he murmured.

Falon glanced at the destruction again, and murmured guiltily. The man chuckled, and helped him to his feet. "We've got a chance now," he said. "We can go to the ancient cities for the hidden weapons before the Martians can send a fleet. Mars won't even find out about it for a while. The ships were all damaged in that blast."

"Were many killed?"

"Half of us perhaps. You androids are lucky. Our ancestors gave you a resistance against radiation burns—so you wouldn't mutate from the residual radioactivity left by the last war."

Falon failed to understand: "Not so lucky," he muttered. "*Our* dead do not go to the Place of Watching."

The man eyed him peculiarly, then laughed gently. Falon flushed slightly; for the laughter had seemed to call him a child.

"Come, android," the man said. "People are waiting for you."

"Who?"

"A surly old codger who says he's your father, and a girl who says she's your woman."

Falon moved a few steps between them, then sagged heavily.

"He's unconscious," said the android, "or dead."

They lifted him gently in their arms. "Hell!" grunted the human. "Did you ever see a dead man *grin*?"

# THE CLOUD-MEN

## BEING A FOREPRINT FROM THE LONDON NEWS SHEET #1
### BY OWEN OLIVER

GOVERNMENT NOTICES

This newspaper is published under the authority of the recent News Act, which directs the printing of a single newspaper in the United Kingdom. Under the provisions of the act, the paper will be exclusively devoted to the plain statement, without colorable matter, of important events, and to articles useful to the community.

It is provided by Section 3 of the act that the communication of false news is punishable as follows:

First offense—two years' penal labor.
Second offense—five years' penal labor.
Third offense—death.

Readers are reminded that the Unprofitable Employments Act has been repealed only to the extent indicated above. The writing or perusal of fiction, therefore, remains a penal offense.

The census of the United Kingdom, taken under the Act for the Settlement of the Population, has been completed, with the following results:

Males, total .................................... 51,504
Males, unmarried (age 20 to 60) ................ 9,212
Females, total ................................. 52,214
Females, unmarried (age 18 to 50) ............. 8,901

Under Section 2 of the act, persons between the ages specified who have not arranged marriages by April 1 next will be paired by the local committees appointed under the act.

A list of the centers selected for the concentration of the inhabitants of this country is published on page 4. The inclusion of Edinburgh and Dublin is provisional only, and depends upon sufficient persons desiring to reside in those cities. Choice of residence in the selected centers can be allowed only so far as is compatible with the public welfare. For instance, the necessity of a coal supply will require a certain population for Newcastle. Forms of choice will be distributed during the week.

The consultative committee of the governments of Europe, North America, and Japan has decided that the capital penalty must be enforced for the second offense of wilful idleness, as, in the present crisis, this despicable crime threatens the continued existence of the human race.

#### LOCAL GOVERNMENT OF LONDON—NOTICES

The weekly train for the North will start at 10.15 on Saturdays in future. Free passes may be obtained at the council offices, on good reason for the journey being shown.

Persons taking possession of vacant houses should affix a notice to the front door, stating that they are in occupation. Otherwise the houses will be liable to be reappropriated.

In consequence of the universal disarmament, a large number of naval and military uniforms are available for conversion into workmen's clothing. Applications should be made at the office of the clothing committee.

A *crèche* has been opened in the building in Whitehall formerly known as the War Office.

#### EDITORIAL NOTICES

We desire to publish articles describing the experiences of any persons who came into close contact with the so-called Cloud-Men. Photographs will be especially welcome.

The following article is by Mr. John Pender, now superintendent of the Food Bureau. He and his wife, Mary Pender, formerly of Melville, are the only persons known to us who have survived firsthand acquaintance with these terrible beings; but it is thought that there may be others.

## THE EXPERIENCES OF JOHN AND MARY PENDER

It is common knowledge that a great darkness set in during the later weeks of last August. This was ascribed to the formation of clouds of exceptional thickness, and to their gradual descent toward the earth. At the time this was attributed to abnormal atmospheric conditions, although scientific authorities differed greatly as to the nature of the disturbances.

It is now believed that the clouds contained elements from some extinct world, dissipated in the form of gaseous matter and encountered in the journey of the earth through space. This question will be dealt with in a later article by Dr. John Dodd. I shall confine myself to my personal experience of these elements as reincarnated in terrestrial forms—adopting Dr. Dodd's view—and to the disastrous events which I actually witnessed.

At two o'clock upon the afternoon of Friday, last August 30, I was walking in the Strand, to the east of Bedford Street. Some newsboys were making a great clamor. One placard said, "The Clouds Alive—Descent Upon Paris—Great Slaughter." Another said, "War of the Worlds—Wells Justified." There was a great rush to secure papers, and, consequently, I did not notice what was happening around.

I had just obtained a paper, and was standing under an electric light to read it, when I heard a great shouting. People near me screamed and ran, and I looked up and saw the clouds descending into the roadway, in long, thick rolls. They fell upon the vehicles and their occupants, and upon groups of foot-passengers, and appeared to smother them.

I dropped the newspaper, and turned and ran in the direction of Charing Cross. I was thoroughly unnerved, not only by the shrieks, but by the abrupt manner in which they ceased wherever the clouds fell; and I find myself unable to recall the exact impression which they first produced upon me.

I was soon stopped by a barrier of vehicles which had jammed together, a number having come into collision and overturned, in their attempts to escape. Other vehicles followed till they were brought up by the blockade; and I had difficulty in finding standing space between.

I was one of a group of about ten who took refuge among the débris of two wagons and an overturned motor-bus. A very good-looking young lady, who was one of the party, seemed much distressed, and I talked to her. She said that the clouds reminded her of the unearthly visitants in some of the tales of one Owen Oliver. I had not then heard of him, but I believe him to be one of the persons very properly convicted by the present government for wasting his time in writing fiction.

I suggested that the clouds were only a heavy—and possibly poisonous—vapor; but the young lady declared that they were alive, and were deliberately killing people; and a white-faced man said that that was certainly so. He had seen a cloud settle on a bus near him, and, when it left the bus, the passengers all had the appearance of having been drowned.

A woman sobbed that she had just bought a new mantle, and it was "so greatly reduced" and "such value in the materials." A loafer tried to snatch my watch, and I knocked him down. A flower-girl started singing and dancing. I think the fright had unhinged her mind.

Then the clouds began to descend on us, and most of our group smashed their way through the overturned motor-bus. I should have gone with them, but the young lady fainted; so I remained, supporting her on one arm.

The clouds were of a blackish-gray color, and appeared to be of stouter material than vapor. Their size varied. I do not mean merely that they differed from one another in magnitude, but that the same cloud expanded and contracted, rising as it drew out and falling as it drew in. Their porportionate dimensions remained the same, the shape being that of a cylinder with spherical ends, and the length about twice the diameter. When they first hung overhead the diameter was usually about twenty-five feet.

They had a black, diamond-shaped patch in front, which I believe to have been an organ of vision, and eight small circular patches at the sides and the other end, which were, I think, in some mysterious way, the sources of their horizontal movements. From time to time they made a faint whirring sound. Afterward I had reason to believe that this was a kind of musical language, depending upon the pitch and quality of the note, and not upon the articulate sound, which was always the same—whir-r-r-r! At least, it seemed so to me. My wife thinks that there were four kinds of whirs, and three different ways of rolling the r's in each. However, she agrees that the language depended partly, if not wholly, upon the pitch.

The clouds came down one by one upon the vehicles near us, and the knots of people jammed between them. The victims shrieked until they were enveloped; then all sound ceased. When the clouds left them, they had the appearance of drowned persons, as the white-faced man had said.

I will not dwell on the subject. The sight is one which most of my readers have seen. Let those who have not be thankful!

I crawled under a wagon and a cab, dragging the young lady, and reached a shop-window, just as a cloud fell upon us. I had hoped to get to the shop-door and inside, but could not. This was our salvation, probably; for it was clear, afterward, that the clouds searched the houses.

As we were being wrapped all round, I smashed the plate-glass with my fists, cutting myself rather badly, and put our heads through the opening. The cloud did not enter inside the glass, and we were able to breathe. We were enveloped to the necks by what felt like a heavy, wet blanket—a blanket that seemed to be, in some horrible way, alive—for about five minutes. Then we were left.

My limbs were limp and helpless. I slipped down on the pavement, with the young lady's head resting on my shoulder, and stared at the tops of the vehicles, which were all that I could see. The busses were full of "drowned" bodies, lolling against one another. A wagon-driver on a high seat had fallen forward, but his legs still held in the apron, and he hung head downward, leering horribly. A dead horse was at my back. I leaned against it.

It was very quiet now. The shrieks, that ended so suddenly, came from farther and farther away.

After a time the girl opened her eyes and looked round. She tried to speak, and could not. Neither could I.

I opened my lips after a quarter of an hour.

"The Lord have mercy upon us!" I groaned.

"Amen!" said the girl on my shoulder.

She had not moved except to clutch at my jacket.

I held out my hand to her. When she was about to take it she saw the gashes that the broken glass had made, and cried out piteously.

"Hush!" I said. "They may have ears!"

For I never doubted that they were alive after the wet monster had touched me. It felt like a blanket that was all fingers!

She nodded, took out her handkerchief, and bound my cuts gently. She asked in a whisper how I had done it, and I told her in a whisper how I had broken the glass, and why.

"Thank you," she said. "That isn't much to say for a life, is it? I mean more."

She looked at me and tried to smile. It was pitiful, very pitiful.

"Life isn't much to be thankful for now," I said; "except—that there is *some one* left. There is no one else, I think. We will help each other."

"We will help each other," she said.

Her voice and look were those of a steadfast woman; and so she proved.

Presently we crawled through the vehicles and the "drowned" people till we got into a restaurant. We found "drowned" waiters and customers there. Mary—that was my companion's name—sank on a seat. She would not have cried, I think, but I put my hand on her shoulder.

"Cry, dear woman," I said. "It will help you."

She sat with her face in her hands, and her body quivering, for a while. Then she wiped her eyes with my handkerchief, and smiled the pitiful smile.

"You are good to me," she said.

We ate and drank, and then we explored the upper rooms. The people in these were "drowned," too; and those in the other houses that we entered, creeping stealthily from one to the next. We heard the whirring sound sometimes, and saw the cloud cylinders pass by. Most of them were high above the houses, and were going toward Whitehall. We noticed a sound of firing from that direction, and guessed that soldiers were trying to defend the

War Office—which, as we learned long after, was really the case.

After a few moments the firing ceased. Soon after that, the electric lights went out. They had been going for several days, and probably the power had failed; or one of the cloud-cylinders had fallen on those who controlled it—some brave men who stood at their post till the end. There were many such.

## II

We stayed in the house for two nights and a day—a day that was no different from the night—groping about in the dark for food, and sitting on a sofa, leaning against each other, when we slept for a short time. She was afraid to be alone, she said. I did not say that I was afraid, but I was.

After that time—it must have been the forenoon of the 1st of September—the darkness decreased to that of a dull twilight. We peered from the windows, and saw none of the cloud-rolls about, and heard no sounds. So we ventured out.

We got into the side streets, which were less obstructed, and into Whitehall. We then went over Westminster Bridge—it was strange to see the vessels drifting helplessly on the river—and wandered on till we reached Camberwell Green. We saw no sign of life all the way; men, women, children, horses, dogs, cats, even birds, were all "drowned," as I call it. The clouds had fallen upon humanity, and the dependents of humanity, and wiped them out.

The girl cried sometimes; but she was very brave. She told me about herself as we walked alone. She was Mary Melville, a mistress at a high-school.

"And I shall never see my little girls again," she said. "They were such dear, naughty little girls, and I loved them so much! I liked to think that some day they would be good women."

We went into a house the door of which was open. We found meat and drink there. She slept on a sofa while I watched; and then she watched while I slept. After breakfast we went on. We did not know where we were going; but we could not rest.

In the Peckham Road we met a man. He was dusty and travel-worn. His eyes blinked, and he spoke as if he were half asleep. He had walked up from Rochester, he said. The cloud-men—that was what he called them—had "wiped every one out," he told us. He had crept between two mattresses of a bed, and so escaped their search. He was going to Piccadilly Circus to look for his "girl." She was a waitress in a restaurant there.

"We were going to be married next month," he said.

Then he burst suddenly into tears. He was a big, strong fellow— a fitter in the dockyard, he said.

A large party of soldiers had encountered the cloud-men on Chatham Lines, he told us. They had come upon a handful of the survivors running over Rochester Bridge. They had scattered some of the cloud-men, at first, by explosive shells; but the cloud-men had expanded into thin vapor, which the shells did not seem to harm, and advanced upon the army in that form till they had encompassed it in mist. Then they contracted into "things like long balloons," and dropped upon the soldiers and "smothered them."

I suggested that, as we seemed to be all of the world that was left, we should make an appointment to meet again in, say, a week; but the man from Rochester shook his head.

"If I don't find my girl," he said, "and it stands to reason I won't, I'll go into a chemist's and take what comes handy till I hit upon something that settles me. Of course, if I find her, we'll come all right. You'd like her; quite a lady in her way, she is—was, I suppose. She—I'll be making a fool of myself if I start talking about her. So-long, and good luck!"

"God bless you and help you," said Mary, "and—and you will find her here—or there."

She pointed to the sky.

"Here or there," he said. "That's it. Good luck!"

He went on at a tired trot toward the city; and we walked on away from it.

"To be left alone," Mary said. "To be left alone! It is an awful thing. Alone! If you left me!" I looked at her reproachfully. "No, no! I don't mean that, only—if anything happened to you—"

Her lips trembled.

"We are in the hands of God," I said, "my dear. I shall never leave you while I am alive."

"No, dear," she answered.

That was all our love-making in those days—that we called each other "dear."

## III

We found our way to Dulwich by the afternoon. At the station we came upon a collection of about thirty people. They greeted us as if we were old friends, and we greeted them so. They had taken refuge in a cricket pavilion, they explained, and the clouds had omitted to search it. Every one else in the place was "drowned," as they too called it. They were lucky to have one another, they said; "so many of us"—and some of the women cried.

One young fellow was an electrical engineer. He had ascertained by the telegraph that the clouds were settling upon all the large towns, and destroying the inhabitants. This applied to the Continent and America, as well as Great Britain. Now he could get no answer from anywhere.

We walked together toward Forest Hill, and found nine survivors in Dulwich Park. A black mist drove upon us there. It was "only mist," we assured one another, clinging desperately together. But it condensed into the infamous cylinders. Our company ran in various directions, crying out till the clouds settled upon them.

Mary and I ran hand in hand, till she dropped exhausted. I sat beside her, and lifted her in my arms. We kissed each other. Then four of the cylinders came up, and one lowered itself upon us. The damp folds were enveloping us; and then a fifth cylinder, with four white bands—which were, I think, the insignia of high rank—made a whirring noise, changing the pitch as if it sang.

This was when I realized that they had a language. The cylinder that was smoothering us lifted itself; and the belted cylinger drew near and settled on the ground, and shrank till it was not more than eight feet long. It pressed against us as if it examined us. It felt about as hard as a sofa-cushion in its contracted form; a hard cushion that was all hands and terribly alive. It stared at us with its diamond-shaped eye. Then it "sang" again, and somehow I knew that its song meant that we were spared.

Two other cylinders pushed us on our feet, and held us, and urged us forward. They took us to a large house, and into a long drawing-room; and one stayed by the window, and one by the door, to keep us there.

So far as I have been able to ascertain, we were the only persons who were deliberately spared by the cloud-men; and many conjectures have been made as to their reasons. Professor Dodd holds that we were selected as "specimens" for a museum which the cloud-men proposed to establish; but, if so, I do not know why I was chosen. Mary, indeed, is, in my opinion, a singularly handsome woman; but I cannot claim any distinction of personality, except that I am a good deal above the average is size and strength.

We remained in this house—which, curiously enough, I cannot identify—for nine days, during which we had every opportunity of studying the cloud-men, as we came to call them; for the house and its vicinity seemed to be a kind of *rendezvous*.

I will give a few particulars which we noticed.

Their shape, as I have said, always remained the same, but their size varied greatly, and as it varied they appeared to be composed of quite different substance. At the largest, they seemed to be nothing but dark smoke, and one lost all perception of outline in them, except that the "eye" remained as a little dark cloud floating in the smoky mist. As they contracted, they took definite shape in the cloud-cylinders which I have already described, and which felt like a wet blanket; a blanket which divided and "flowed" round one like water, exerting a discriminating pressure, like that of countless fingers. When they had further contracted to the size at which the belted cloud-man had shrunk when he settled on the ground, they were, as I have said, of the density of a rather hard but springy sofa-cushion; but, in spite of their hardness, a good deal of their pliability remained.

One that was probably not full grown sometimes played with us, pushing us round the room, and, though firm, he did not hurt like a hard substance. When they were resting, they grew much smaller—at the extreme, not more than a foot in length. They then looked like black metal, and were so heavy that Mary and I together could barely move them. They felt as hard as iron, and we could make no impression on them; but yet they could fold round an object and handle it without crushing or injuring it in any way. I have seen them hold a flower, the metallic substance seeming to divide as they did so.

When they were in this state a hissing sound came from the eight circular disks, which appeared to control their motion, whenever they moved; and their whirring was sharper and clearer. It sounded like the playing of a musical instrument in a chromatic scale. We even learned to understand the meaning of certain series of notes, and especially of one which indicated that we might go out from our room and find something to eat—a privilege only accorded to us after a good while.

We were very near being starved at first. There was no food in the room, and no water, except some in which flowers had stood. We were reduced to drinking that. We tried vainly to get by the sentinel at the door; but he always enveloped us and pushed us back.

After we had fasted for nearly two days, and the last of the foul water was gone, we persisted in trying to get out, and entreated and made gesticulations. At last one of the belted cloud-men came. He watched out gesticulations for some time with his one diamond-shaped eye, and he and our guards talked, or "sang," to one another.

Finally the guard stood aside, and we were allowed to go to the kitchen under escort. We found some stale bread and some good bacon there; also some tea and sugar—the milk was sour. We took back some biscuits and two large jugs of water. After that we were allowed to go there twice a day, and a number of cloud-men came to watch us. So far as we had seen, they did not take food—they appeared to lack mouths—and our custom of eating puzzled them.

We were beginning to lose the edge of our aversion to these extraordinary creatures, and to think that perhaps their cruelty had been due to ignorance of the nature of life and death; and then three things happened which brought back our fears—and worse.

The first was a sight which we saw from the drawing-room window, outside which the cloud-men often held what were evidently assemblies. A vast multitude of the cloud-rolls came along, contracted, and hung in a circle round one who seemed to be a prisoner. After some "talking" in their way, one of the belted men sang a fierce sentence; and then the prisoner wailed miserably. After this they drew back from him, watching him closely. He swelled slowly, wailing all the time, and then suddenly there was a flash, and he was gone! His fellows sang a kind of dirge; then expanded and floated away. Sentence had been executed.

If they punished others, they would not scruple to punish us, Mary said; and so it proved.

The second incident, which brought this punishment, was a frustrated attempt on our part to escape. The guard at the door was talking, in his singing way, to the guard at the window. Mary and I took the opportunity to slip out through the door. They overtook us as we were running down the front path, and pushed us back. One held Mary and the other held me, keeping us at different ends of the long drawing-room. I could *feel* that my captor was angry by the touch, and in a few moments he folded himself close round me, pressing till my bones ached. Mary screamed and tried to get to me, but could not stir.

After a while my captor covered my head and slowly smothered me, till I was at my last gasp. Then he released my head, but still held me firmly, while his companion treated my poor Mary in the same manner. They repeated this cruelty three times. When they released us it was half an hour before we had strength enough to crawl to each other; and after that they pushed us roughly as we went to and from the kitchen to get our food, and sometimes made as if they would smother us again, though they never actually did so.

We both became very silent and grave after this, and we used to kiss each other good-by before either slept, which we always did one at a time, the other watching— though I do not know what service there was that watchfulness could do; asleep or awake, we were equally in their power.

The third incident came about as a result of the second, I think, though this is merely a conjecture.

I fancy that our warders thought, from our depressed and silent condition, that we were dying—perhaps we were—and they were afraid of being held responsible for the loss of the valuable "specimens" entrusted to their care. Anyhow, they were less rough, and allowed us more freedom in going about the house; and one day we went into the dining-room. It looked out upon great fields, which we had not seen before. A large number of "drowned" people lay there, arranged in orderly rows. They had evidently been gathered together by the cloud-men. But, why? We talked about that for the rest of the day.

The next day we again went into the dining-room, unattended. We saw a number of cloud-men, in the cloud-cylinder condition of existence, come and settle upon the "drowned" people; each upon one. When the cloud-men rose, the bodies upon which they had settled had disappeared.

Mary turned a greenish color; looked at me; swayed slowly. I held her in my arms. My first thought was to try to make the awful thing seem less awful to her.

"After all," I said, "we eat animals. If I could get *you* out of this, they might kill *me*, and welcome. Oh, Mary!"

I sobbed like a little child, and the tears streamed down my face. Mary folded me in her arms and kissed me, as a mother might have done.

"Come," she said, and led me to the open window.

It was about ten feet above the ground. I lowered her down. Then I jumped.

I could have made the jump safely enough a fortnight before—could make it safely now; but I suppose my limbs had grown feeble. The fall damaged one of my ankles, and I could not stand. Mary lifted me up and held me.

"Go," I said. "It will be easier for me if I can hope that you have escaped. Let me say this first—if all the women in the world were back again, I should want only you—dear Mary! Now, go!"

She laughed a strange little laugh, like a child. Then she lifted me up and staggered on with me—on and on. Sometimes she fell. She always laughed that curious little laugh, as a young mother might with a little child.

Presently we heard the whirring sound from the house. We understood that it was a warning of our flight. I cannot tell how we knew this; but we knew. We looked back and saw the cloud-men rising into the air, expanding as they rose.

"Dear Mary," I said, "this is the end!"

She gave a fierce cry, like a mother defending her young, and tried to carry me farther. When she found that she was too much exhausted to bear my weight, she dragged me to a hollow filled with dead leaves that the long darkness and mist had brought off before their time. We burrowed under the leaves, and lay there.

We heard the cloud-men go by, "whirring" loudly. I suppose they did not know that I was hurt, and expected us to have run much farther. Anyhow, they did not search the leaves.

For hours we lay quite still. In the dusk we peeped out and saw a great concourse of the cloud-men; and presently we heard a loud song, which we recognized as the judge's sentence. Two flashes followed. Our negligent guards had met their fate.

We were tired, and we rested softly among the leaves. We fell asleep.

## IV

When we woke and peeped out, the sun was shining, for the first time for many weeks. There was a huge gathering of the cloud-men about. They were not flying, but moving over the land. Some were small, like the shots of big guns; others were as big as sheep; others were as big as a bear; others as large as an elephant.

They kept changing from small to large. Sometimes they changed back again, but mostly they expanded and floated up in the air. One or two seemed to dissipate into black mist, and be drawn up in a long spiral into the sky. They whirred continually—"whirs" of anger, or was it despair? It seemed as if they tried to hold to the earth and were drawn away.

"They are going!" Mary cried.

She raised herself out of the leaves. So did I; and then the cloud-men saw us. Several advanced upon us, growing to the size of elongated balloons, and rising.

Most the them grew and grew, and went up into the sky; but one reached us and settled on us. If felt wet and cold. It twitched fiercely as it swallowed us in its embraces, and blotted out sight and sound. My breath was nearly gone; and then the suffocating cloud seemed to grow thinner. I could see through it. I could breathe a little. Suddenly it parted from us with a snap, like a breaking of elastic.

The sun was shining cheerfully, and we breathed God's good air. The cloud-men went up, up, in streamers of black smoke. The time came when the last disappeared. We laughed and cried—laughed and cried.

"I wonder if any of our world is left!" I said.

"All my world is left," said Mary. "All!" She held my hand; and I kissed her hand that held mine. "But we will look for the others," she said. "We will look for them— our own dear people of our own dear world!"

We found none that day. We could not go far, as my ankle was badly swollen; but in the afternoon Mary came upon a little truck. She put me upon it, on cushions, and wheeled me to find the people of the world.

After that we came upon some, day by day; first a mother and her child, who had hidden in a chimney; then a man who had been left for dead, but had revived—the only case of the kind which has come to my notice. It was like drowning, he said.

Then we met a husband and wife.

"We will quarrel no more," they told us; and they told that to all whom we met.

They do not. Even people who love each other do not quarrel now!

At Chatham we found a large assembly, including a train-load who had come down from London. The man who had talked to us in the Peckham Road was among them. Strange to say, he had found his "girl"—a pretty, fair-haired, laughing little thing. She and several other waitresses had hidden in the roof of their restaurant. They were so frightened that they remained there and starved for several days.

"When I heard Will walking about below and calling for me," she said, "I thought I had died, and gone to heaven!"

"How did you know it was heaven?" someone asked.

"Why, I knew Will's voice!" she answered.

"We are going to be married to-morrow," he said. "Every man ought to look after a woman in these times."

I thought so, too; and Mary and I, and many other pairs who have met during the reign of terror, were also married then, promising ourselves a honeymoon in easier days. For at that period we worked eighteen hours daily, moving up to London, and sending rescue parties all round to gather up the remnants of the scattered population.

If we had not done this, I believe that half of those now surviving would have perished. For many were afraid to venture out from their hiding-places in search of food, and others were too weak to do so. Some seemed to have temporarily lost their reason from fright and hardship. A pestilence was threatened from the unburied bodies of men and animals, and was only avoided by our clearing certain districts for habitation, and proscribing other localities until time had removed the danger.

Trade and production had stopped, and machinery rusted. Oversea supplies ceased, and accumulated stocks were left to rust and rot in the abandoned districts.

Through the hard winter which followed, all lived upon a dole; and many a time, as we waited for the return of the spring, we thought that the last day had come to the human race. The despatch of food-ships from America alone saved us, in my opinion. We had just strength to unload them—no more. I shall never forget the pale faces of the tottering men and women who worked at this.

Now, I hope and believe that we are through the worst. There is food enough—on this point I can speak with authority, as I have the honor to be in charge of the department concerned with our supplies—to last us for the rest of the year, with care; and I believe that we can organize husbandry and industry so as to make satisfactory provision for the future.

Practically all domestic animals were destroyed in England, it is true; but, fortunately, a large number of oxen in the Highlands escaped our ferocious visitors; and in Ireland elsewhere the pigs showed a capacity of recovery from "drowning" which no other animal has exhibited. A few surviving specimens of sheep are being carefully reserved for breeding purposes; and though the horse is extinct, it is hoped to rear a race of superior donkeys from half a dozen which escaped. Moreover, we have plenty of motor vehicles.

The stores of clothing and furniture are sufficient for many generations, so long as we do not allow ourselves to fall back under the absurd dominion of "fashions." I have great hope that we shall escape this, although, even in the best of women, I notice that a tendency to elaboration and decorativeness in dress still unfortunately survives.

I am confident, however, that none will allow such petty vanities to interfere with more solid occupations. For nothing has struck me more than the noble manner in which the women have struggled to help in the reconstruction of a prosperous and united society—a united society of the surviving human race.

"Union" is the key-note of our future. The days of discord and war are over. Each in future will love his neighbor as himself. Each will work for all. Unborn generations, when in more leisured times they come to write the history of the world, will record that the clouds of selfishness and cruelty lifted from the world with the darkest clouds that ever rested upon it; as if the evil passions of humanity were concentrated in and departed with those diabolical spirits of evil whom we have named the cloud-men.

# STONE MAN

## BY FRED SABERHAGEN

### I

Derron Odegard took a moment to wipe his sweaty palms on the legs of his easy-fitting duty uniform, and to minutely shift the position of his headset on his skull. Then he leaned forward in his contour chair, hunting the enemy again.

After just half an hour on watch he was bone-tired. The weight of his planet and its forty million surviving inhabitants rested crushingly on the back of his neck. He didn't want to bear the weight of forty million lives, but at the moment there was nowhere to set them down.

The responsibility was very real. One gross error by Derron, or anyone else in Time Operations, could be enough to tumble the people who still survived on the planet Sirgol into nothingness, to knock them out of real-time and end them for good, end them so completely that they would never have existed at all.

Derron's hunter's hands settled easily to rest on the molded controls of his console. Like those of a trained musician, his fingers followed his thought. The pattern on the curved viewscreen before him, a complex weaving of green cathode-traces, dissolved at his touch on the controls, then steadied, then shifted again—grass put carefully aside by the touch of a cautious stalker. In the screen pattern, Derron's educated eye saw represented the lifelines of animals and plants, a tangle which made up his assigned small segment of his planet's prehistorical ecology.

Surrounding Derron Odegard's chair and console were those of other sentries, all aligned in long, subtly curving rows. This arrangement pleased and rested the momentarily lifted eye—and then led the eye back to the job, where it belonged. The same effect resulted from the gentle modulations that sometimes passed cloudlike across the artificial light flowing from the strongly vaulted ceiling; 'and from the insistent psych-music, a murmur of melody that now and then shifted into a primitive heavy beat.

A thousand men stood guard with Derron in his buried chamber while the music murmured and the fake cloud-shadows passed, and through the huge room there wafted fresh-smelling air; breezes scented convincingly with green fields, sometimes with the tang of the sea, with all the varieties of living soil and water that no longer existed up above the miles of rock, on the surface of the planet.

Again the cathode traces symbolizing interconnected life rippled past Derron on his screen.

Like a good soldier he avoided predictability in his own moves while patrolling his post. He sent his recondevice a decade further into the past, then five miles north, then two years presentward, and a dozen miles southwest. At every pause he watched and listened, so far in vain. No predator's passage had yet disturbed this green symbolic grass.

"Nothing yet," he said aloud, feeling his supervisor's presence at his elbow. When the present stayed put, Derron glanced back for a moment at Captain —?

It irritated him that he could not think of the captain's name, though perhaps it was understandable. Time Operations had only been in business for about a month and during all that period had been in a state of organizational flux.

Whoever he was, the captain had his eyes fixed fiercely on Derron's screen. "Your section right here," the captain said, showing his nervousness, "this is the hot spot." The captain's only reassuring aspect was that his dark jowly face seemed set like a bulldog's, to bite and hold on. Derron turned back to work.

His assigned segment of space-time was set about twenty thousand years in the past, near the time of the First Men's coming to Sirgol. Its duration was about a century, and in space it comprised a square of land roughly a hundred miles on a side, including the lower atmosphere above the square. On the screen every part of it appeared as an enormously complex thicket of events.

Derron had not yet found a human lifeline woven into this thicket of the past, but he was not looking for humans especially. What mattered was that he had not yet discovered the splash of disruptive change that would have signaled the presence of an invading berserker machine.

The infraelectronic recon-device which served as Derron's sense-extension into the past did not stir the branches of forests, or startled animals. Rather it hovered just outside reality, seeing real-time through the fringe of things that almost were, dipping into real-time for an ano-second and then dropping back again to peer at it from just around the local curves of probability.

The first intimation that battle had been joined came to Derron not through his screen or even his earphones, but through the sound of his captain moving away in soft-footed haste, to whisper excitedly with the supervisor of the next rank.

If the fight was really on in Time Operations at last, a man might well feel frightened. Derron did, in a remote and withdrawn sort of way. He was not badly frightened as yet, and did not expect to be. He thought he would stay on his job and do it well.

There were advantages in not caring very much.

A few seconds later the start of an action was confirmed by a calm girl's voice that came into his earphones. She also told him in which dimensions and by how much to shift his pattern to search. All the sentries would be shifting now, as those nearest the enemy penetration closed in and the rest spread their zones to maintain coverage. The first attack might be only a diversion.

Present-time passed slowly. Derron's orders were changed and changed again, by the unshakable girl-voice that might be only a recording. For a while he could only guess at how things were going. Men had never tried to fight in the past before, but all the men of Sirgol who were still alive were used to war in one form or another. And this game of Time Operations would also be new to the enemy—though of course he had no emotions to get in his way.

"Attention, all sentries," said a new, drawling, male voice in Derron's headset. "This is Time Ops Command, to let you know what's going on. First, the enemy's sunk a beachhead down about twenty-one thousand years in probability-time. Looks like they're going to take things down there and then launch 'em up into history."

A few seconds alter, the voice added: "We got our first penetration already spotted, somewhere around twenty-and-a-half down. Keep your eyes sharp and find us the keyhole."

At some time more than twenty thousand years in the past, at some spot not yet determined high in Sirgol's atmosphere, six berserker devices the size of aircraft had come bursting into reality. If men's eyes had been able to watch the event directly, they would have seen the six missile-shaped killing machines materialize out of nothing and then explode from their compact formation like precision flyers. Like an aerobatic team they scattered at multisonic speed away from their "keyhole"—the point of spacetime through which they had entered reality, and where one perfect counterblow could still destroy them all.

As the six enemy machines flew at great speed away from one another, they seeded the helpless world below them with poison. Radioactives, antibiotic chemicals—it was hard from a distance of twenty thousand years to say just what they were using. Derron Odegard, patrolling like the other sentries, saw the attack only in its effects. He perceived it as a diminishing in probability of the existence of life in his own sector, a morbid change following certain well defined directions that would in time reduce the probability of any life at all in the sector to zero.

If the planet was dead and poisoned when the First Men arrived, groping and wandering as helpless as babies, why then there could be no human civilization on Sirgol, no one in Modern times to resist the berserkers. The planet would still be dead today. Derron knew that the dark tide of nonexistence was rising in each cell of his own body, in each cell of every living creature.

Derron's findings with those of every other sentry were fed to Time Ope Command. Men and computers worked together, tracing back the vectors along which the deadly changes in probability advanced.

The system worked to Command's satisfaction, this time. The computers announced that the keyholes of the six flying machines had been pinpointed.

In the catacomb of Operations' Stage Two, the missiles waited, blunt simple shapes surrounded by complexities of control and launching mechanism. As Command's drawling voice announced: "Firing one for the keyhole," massive steel arms extended the missile sideways from its rack, while on the dark stone floor beneath it there appeared a silvery circle, shimmering like troubled liquid.

The arms dropped the missile, and in the first instant of its fall it disappeared. Even as it fell into the past it was propelled as a wave of probability through the miles of rock to the surface. The guidance computers made constant corrections, steering their burden of fusible hydrogen through the mazes of the half-real, toward the right point on the edge of normal existence. . . .

Derron saw the malignant changes that had been creeping ominously across his screen begin suddenly to reverse themselves. It looked like a trick, like running the projector backward, like some stunt with no relevance to the real world.

"Right in the keyhole!" yelped Command's voice in his ear, drawling no longer. The six berserker flyers now shared their point of entry into real-time with an atomic explosion, neatly tailored to fit.

As the waves of death were seen to recede on every screen, jubilation spread in murmurous waves of its own up and down the curved rows of sentry-positions. But experience, not to mention discipline, kept the rejoicing muted.

The rest of the six-hour watch passed like a routine training exercise in the techniques of mopping-up. All the i's were dotted and the t's crossed, the tactical success tied down and made certain by observations and tests. Men were relieved on schedule for their customary breaks, and passed one another smiling and winking. Derron went along and smiled when someone met his eye; it was the easiest thing to do.

When the shift ended and there was still no sign of any further enemy again, there was no doubt left that the berserkers' first attempt to get at the Moderns through their past had been beaten back into non-existence.

But the damned machine would be back, as always. Stiff and sweaty and tired, and not conscious of any particular elation, Derron rose from his chair to make room for the sentry on the next shift.

"I guess you guys did all right today," the replacement said, a touch of envy in his voice.

Derron made himself smile again. "You can have the next chance for glory." He pressed his thumbprint on the console's scanner as the other man did the same. Then, his responsibility officially over, he walked at a dragging pace out of the sentry room. Other members of his shift were moving in the same direction; once outside the area of enforced quiet they formed excited groups and started to whoop it up a little.

Nodding cheerfully to the others, and replying appropriately to their jokes, Derron stood in line to hand in the recording cartridge with its record of his shift activity. Then he waited in another short line, to make a final oral report to a debriefing officer. After that he was free; as free as any citizen of Sirgol could be, these days.

## II

When the huge passenger elevator lifted Derron and a crowd of others out of the deeper caves of Time Operations to the housing level, there were still ten miles of rock overhead.

The pampered conditions of the sentry room were not to be found here, or anywhere where a maximum-efficiency environment was not absolutely necessary. Here the air smelled stale and the lighting was just tolerable. The corridor in which Derron had his bachelor-cubicle was one of the main streets of the buried world-city, the fortress in which the surviving population of Sirgol was armed and maintained and housed and fed. Given the practically limitless power of hydrogen fusion to labor for them, and the mineral wealth of the surrounding rock, the besieged planet-garrison at least had no fear of starvation.

The corridor was two stories high and as wide as a main street in one of the cities of the old surface-world. People who traveled this corridor for any considerable distance rode upon the moving belts laid down in its center. On the moving belt now rushing past Derron a pair of black-uniformed police were checking the identify cards of travelers. Planetary Command must be cracking down again on work-evaders.

As usual, the belts and the broad statwalk strips on either side were moderately crowded. Men and women were going to their jobs or leaving them, at a pace neither hurried nor slow, wearing work uniforms that were mostly monotonously alike. A few other people, wearing lighter and gayer off-duty clothes, were strolling or standing in line before stores and places of amusement.

One of the shorter lines was that in front of the local branch of the Homestead Office. Derron paused on the statwalk there, looking at the curling posters and the shabby models on display. All depicted various plans for the rehabilitation of the surface of the planet after the war. Apply *now* for the land you want . . . they said there would be new land, then, nourished and protected by new oceans of air and water, which were to be somehow squeezed out of the planet's deep rocks.

The people standing in line looked at the models with wistful, half-hopeful eyes, and most of those passing glanced in with something more than indifference. They were all of them able to forget, if they had ever really understood it, the fact that the world was dead. The real world was dead and cremated, along with nine out of ten of the people who had made it live . . . .

To control his thoughts Derron had to turn away from the dusty models and the people waiting in line to believe. He started toward his cubicle but then on impulse turned aside, down a narrow branching passage.

He knew where he was going. Likely there would be only a few people there at this time of day. A hundred paces ahead of him, the end of the passage framed in its arch the living green of real treetops—

The tremor of a heavy explosion raced through the living rock from which this passage had been carved.

Ahead, Derron saw two small red birds streak in alarm across the greenery of the trees. Now the sound came, dull and muffled, but heavy. It had been a small missile penetration, then, one hitting fairly close by. The enemy threw down through the shielding rock probability-waves that turned into missiles, even as men fired them upward at the enemy fleet in space.

Without hesitating or breaking stride Derron paced on to the end of the passage. There he halted, leaning his hands heavily on a protective railing of natural logs, while he looked out over the park from two levels above the grass. From six levels higher yet, an artificial sun shone down almost convincingly on three or four acres of real trees and real grass, on varicolored birds that were held inside the park by curtain-jets of air. Across the scene there passed a gurgling brook of real water. Today its level had fallen so that the concrete sides of its bed were revealed halfway down.

A year ago—a lifetime ago, that is, in the real world— Derron Odegard had been no nature-lover. Then he had been thinking of finishing his schooling and settling down to the labors of a professional historian. Even on holidays he had gone to historic places . . . he thrust out of his memory now certain thoughts, and a certain face, as he habitually did. Yes, a year ago he had spent most of his days with history texts and films and tapes, and in the usual academic schemes for academic advancement. In those days the first hints of the possibility that historians might be allowed to take a first-hand look at the past had been promises of pure joy. The warnings of Earthmen were decades old, and the defenses of Sirgol had been decades in the building, all part of the background of life. The Berserker War itself was other planets' business.

In the past year, Derron thought, he had learned more about history than in all the years of study that had gone before. Now when the last moment of history came on Sirgol, if he could know it was the last, he would get away if he could, come to one of those parks with a little bottle of wine he had been keeping stowed under his cot. He would finish history by drinking whatever number of toasts circumstances allowed, to whatever dead and dying things seemed to him then the most worthy.

The tension was just beginning to drain from his fingers into the handworn bark of the railing, and he had actually forgotten the recent explosion, when the first of the wounded came into the park below him.

The first was a man with his uniform jacket gone and the remains of his clothing all torn and blackened. One of his arms was burnt and raw and swelling. He tottered forward half-blindly among the trees, and then like an actor in some wilderness drama he fell full length at the edge of the brook and began to drink from it ravenously.

Next came another man, older, this one probably some kind of clerk or administrator, though he was too far away for Derron to make out his insignia. This man stood in the park as if lost, seemingly unwounded but more dazed than the burned man. Now and then the second man raised his hands to his ears; there was something wrong with his hearing.

A pudgy woman entered, moaning in bewilderment as she held the flap of her torn scalp in place. Two more women came in; a trickle of injured people began to spill steadily from a small park entrance at grass level. They flowed in and defiled the false peace of the park. Their voices, growing in number, built a steadily rising murmur of complaint against the injustice of the universe. Everyone knew it was a rare event for a berserker missile to get past all the defenses and penetrate to the depth of an inhabited level.

Why did it have to happen today, and to them?

There were a couple of dozen people in the park now, walking wounded from what must have been a relatively harmless explosion. Down the nearby passages there echoed authoritarian yells, and the whine and rumble of heavy machines. Damage Control was on the job; the walking wounded were being sent here to get them out from under foot while more urgent matters were being taken care of.

A slender girl of eighteen or twenty, clad in the remnants of a simple paper dress, came into the park and leaned against a tree as if she could walk no further. The way her dress was torn. . . .

Derron turned away, squeezing his eyes shut and shaking his head in a spasm of self-disgust. He stood up here like some ancient tyrant, remotely entertained and critically lustful.

He would have to decide, one of these days, whether he was really still on the side of the human race or not. He hurried down some nearby stairs and came out on the ground level of the park. The badly burned man was bathing his raw arm in the cool running water. No one seemed to have stopped breathing, or to be bleeding to death. The girl looked as if she might fall away from her supporting tree at any moment.

Derron went to her, pulling off his jacket. He wrapped her in the garment and eased her away from the tree.

"Where are you hurt?"

She shook her head and refused to sit down, so they did a little off-balance dance while he held her up. She was tall and slim and ordinarily she would be lovely . . . no, not really lovely, or at least not stardard-pretty. But good to look at. Her dark hair was cut in the short simple style most favored by Planetary Command, as most women's was these days. No jewelry or make-up. Plainly she was in some kind of shock.

She came out of it somewhat to look in bewilderment at the jacket that had been wrapped around her; her eyes focused on the collar insignia. She said: "You're an officer." Her voice was low and blurry.

"In a small way. Hadn't you better lie down somewhere?"

"No. First tell me what's going on . . . I've been trying to get home . . . or somewhere. Can't you tell me where I am? What's going on?" Her voice was rising.

"Easy, take it easy. There was a missile strike. Here, now, this insignia of mine is supposed to be a help with the girls. So behave! Won't you sit down?"

"No! First I must find out . . . I don't know who I am, or where, or why."

"I don't know those things about myself." That was the most honest communication he had made to anyone in a long time.

He was afraid that when the girl came out of her dazed condition it would be into panic. More people, passers-by and medics, were running into the park now, aiding the wounded and creating a scene of confusion. The girl looked wildly around her and clung to Derron's arm. He supposed the best thing was to walk her to a hospital. Where? Of course—there was the one adjoining Time Operations, just a short way from here.

"Come along," he said. The girl walked willingly beside him, clinging to his encircling arm. "What's your name?"

he asked, as they boarded the elevator. The other people stared at her in his jacket.

"I . . . don't know." Now she looked more frightened than ever. Her hand went to her throat, but there was no dog-tag chain around her neck. Many people didn't like to wear them. "Where are you taking me?"

"To a hospital. You need some looking-after." He would have liked to give some wilder answer for the onlookers' benefit, but he didn't want to terrify the girl.

She had little to say after that. He led her off the elevator and another short walk brought them to the hospital's emergency door. Other casualties from the explosion, stretcher cases, were arriving now.

Inside the emergency room an old nurse started to peel Derron's jacket off the girl and what was left of her dress came with it. "You just come back for your jacket tomorrow, young man," the woman ordered sharply, rewrapping.

"Gladly." Then he could only wave good-by to the girl as a horde of stretcher-bearers and other busy people swept him with them back out into the corridor. He found himself laughing to himself about the nurse and the jacket. It was a while since he had laughed about anything.

He had a spare jacket in his locker in the sentry officers' ready room in Time Ops, and he went there to pick it up. There was nothing new on the bulletin board. He would like to get off sentry duty and into something where you didn't just sit still under strain for six hours a day.

He went to the nearest officers' gym and talked to acquaintances and played two rounds of handball, winning an ersatz soft-drink that he preferred not to collect. The others were talking about the missile strike; Derron mentioned that he had seen some of the wounded, but he said nothing about the girl.

From the gym he went with a couple of the others to a bar, where he had one drink, his usual limit, and listened without real interest to their talk of some new girls at a local uplevel dive called Red Garter. Private enterprise still flourished in certain areas.

He ate a meal in the local officers' mess, with a better appetite than usual. Then he took the elevator back up to housing level and at last reached his bachelor's cubicle. He stretched out on his cot and for once went sound asleep before he could even consider taking a pill.

## III

He was awake earlier than usual, feeling well rested. The little clock on his cubicle wall had just jumped to oh-six-thirty hours, Planetary Emergency Time.

This morning none of Time's aspects worried him particularly. He had enough time to stop by the hospital and see what had happened to her, before he went on duty.

He was carrying yesterday's jacket over his arm when, following a nurse's directions, he found the girl seated in a patients' lounge. The TV was on, turned to Channel Gung-Ho, the one devoted to the war effort and associated government propaganda, and she was frowning at it with a look of naivete. Today she was wearing a plain dress that did not exactly fit. Her sandaled feet were curled beside her on her chair. At this time of the morning she had the lounge pretty much to herself.

At the sound of Derron's step she turned her head quickly, then got to her feet, smiling. "Oh, it's you! It's a good feeling to recognize someone."

"It's a good feeling for me, to have someone recognize me."

She thanked him for yesterday's help. He introduced himself.

She wished she could tell him her name, but the amnesia was persisting. "Outside of that, I feel fine."

"That's good, anyway," he said as they sat down in adjacent chairs.

"Actually I do have a name, of sorts. For the sake of their computer records the people here at the hospital have tagged me Lisa Gray, next off some list they keep handy. Evidently a fair number of people go blank in the upper story these days."

"I don't doubt it."

"They tell me that when the missile hit yesterday I was with a number of people from an upper-level refugee camp that's being closed down. A lot of the records were destroyed in the blast. They can't find me, or they haven't yet." She laughed nervously.

Derron tried a remark or two meant to be reassuring, but they didn't sound very helpful in his own ears. He got off the subject. "Have you had your breakfast?"

"Yes. There's a little automat right here if you want something. Maybe I could use some more fruit juice."

In a couple of minutes Derron was back with two glasses of the orange-colored liquid called fruit juice and a couple of standard sweetrolls. Lisa was again studying the war on the TV screen; the commentator's stentorian voice was turned mercifully low.

Derron set the repast on a low table, pulled his own chair closer, and asked: "Do you remember what we're fighting against?"

On screen at the moment was a deep-space scene in which it was hard to make anything out. Lisa hesitated, then shook her head. "Not really."

"Does the word 'berserker' mean anything to you?"

"No."

"Well, they're machines. Some of them are bigger than any spaceships we Earth-descended men have ever built. Others come in many shapes and sizes, but all of them are deadly. The first berserkers were built ages ago, to fight in some war we've never heard of, between races we've never met.

"Sometimes men have beaten the berserkers in battle, but some of them always survived, to hide out somewhere and build more of their kind, with improvements. They're programmed to destroy life anywhere they can find it, and they've come halfway across the galaxy doing a pretty good job. They go on and on like death itself."

"No," said Lisa, not liking the plot.

"I'm sorry, I didn't mean to start raving. We on Sirgol were alive, and so the berserkers had to get rid of us. They boiled away our oceans, and burned our air and our land and nine tenths of our people. But since they're only machines, it's all an accident, a sort of cosmic joke. An act of the Holy One, as people used to say. We have no one to take revenge on." His voice choked slightly in his tight throat; he sipped at his orange-colored water and then pushed it away.

"Won't men come from other planets to help us?"

"Some of them are fighting berserkers near their own systems, too. And a really big relief fleet will have to

be put together to do us any good. And politics must be
played between the stars as usual. I suppose some help
will come evenually, maybe in another year."

The TV announcer began to drone aggressively about
victories on the moon, while an appropriate videotape
was shown. The chief satellite of Sirgol was said to much
resemble the moon of Earth. Its round face had been
pocked by impact craters into an awed expression long
before men or berserkers existed. During the last year a
rash of new craters had wiped away the face of Sirgol's
moon, together with all human bases there.

"I think that help will come to us in time," said Lisa.

In time for what? Derron wondered. "I suppose so,"
he said and felt it was a lie.

Lisa was looking anxiously at the TV. "It seems to me
I can remember. . . . Yes! I can remember seeing an old
moon, the funny face in it! It did look like a face, didn't
it?"

"Oh, yes."

"I remember it!" she cried in a burst of joy. Like a
child she jumped up from her chair and kissed Derron on
the cheek.

While she sat down again, looking at him happily, a
line of ancient poetry sang through his mind. He swallowed.

Now on the TV they were showing the dayside surface
of Sirgol. Cracked dry mudflats stretched away to a horizon near which there danced whirlwinds of yellow dust—
there was a little atmosphere left—under a sky of savage
blue. Rising gleaming from the dried mud in the middle
distance were the bright steel bones of some invading
berserker device, smashed and twisted last ten-day or last
month by some awesome energy of defense. Another
victory for the droning voice to try to magnify.

Derron clearned his throat. "Do you remember about
our planet here being unique?"

"No . . . I doubt that I ever understood science." But
she looked interested. "Go on, tell me about it."

"Well." Derron put on his little-used teacher's voice.
"If you catch a glimpse of our sun on the screen there,
you'll see it looks much like any other star that has an
Earth-type planet. But looks are deceiving. Oh, our daily
lives are the same as they would be elsewhere. And

interstellar ships can enter and leave our system—if they take precautions. But our local spacetime is tricky.

"We were colonized through a weird accident. About a hundred years ago an exploring ship from Earth fell into our peculiar spacetime unawares. It dropped back through about twenty thousand years of time, which must have wiped clean the memories of everyone aboard." He smiled at Lisa. "Our planet is unique in that time travel into the past is possible here, under certain conditions. First, anyone who travels back more than about five hundred years suffers enough mental devolution to have their memories wiped out. They go blank in the upper story, as you put it. Our First Men must have crawled around like babies after their ship landed itself."

"The First Men . . . that's familiar."

"There were First Women, too, of course. Somehow the survivors kept on surviving, and multiplied, and over the generations started building up civilizations. When the second exploring ship arrived, about ten years Earth-time after the first, we'd built up a thriving planet-wide civilization and were getting started on space travel ourselves. In fact it was signals from our early interplanetary probes that drew the second Earthship here. It approached more carefully than the first one had and landed successfully.

"Pretty soon the men from Earth figured out what had happened to our first ship. They also brought us warning of the berserkers. Took some of our people to other systems and showed them what galactic war was like. The people of other worlds were tickled to have four hundred million ncw allies, and they deluged us with advice on weapons and fortifications, and we spent the next eighty years getting ready to defend ourselves. Then about a year ago the berserker fleet came . . . ." Derron's voice trailed off.

Lisa drank some of her "juice" as if she liked it. She prompted: "What do you do now, Derron?"

"Oh, various odd jobs in Time Operations. See, if the berserkers can delay our historical progress at some vital point—the invention of the wheel, say—everything following would be slowed down. When galactic civilization contacted us, we might be still in the Middle Ages, or further back, without any technological base on which to build defenses for ourselves. And in the new real-time, the present would see us entirely wiped out."

Derron looked at the version of Time he wore on his wrist. "Looks like I'd better go right now and start my day's heroic fighting."

The officer in charge of that morning's briefing was Colonel Borss. He took his job very seriously in all its details, with the somber expectancy of a prophet.

"As we all know, yesterday's defensive action was tactically successful."

In the semi-darkness of the briefing room the colonel's pointer skipped luminously across the glowing symbols on his big display screen. "*But,* strategically speaking, we must admit that the situation has deteriorated somewhat."

The colonel went on to explain that this gloomy view was due to the existence of the enemy's beachhead, his staging area some twenty-plus-thousand years down, from whence more berscrker devices would undoubtedly be propelled up into historical real-time. For technical reasons, these devices moving presentward would be almost impossible to stop until they had finally emerged.

All was not entirely lost, however. "After the enemy has broken three more times into our history, we should be able to get a fix on his beachhead and smash it with a few missiles.

"That'll pretty well put an end to his whole Time Operations program.

"Of course we have first to face the little detail of repelling the next three attacks."

As his dutiful audience of junior officers made faint laughing sounds, the colonel produced on his screen a type of graph of human history on Sirgol, a glowing treelike shape. He tapped with his pointer far down on the slender trunk. "We rather suspect that the first attack will fall somewhere near here, near the First Men, where our history is still a tender shoot."

## IV

Matt, sometime also called Lion-Hunter, felt the afternoon sun hot on his bare shoulders as he turned away from the last familiar landmarks of his country, the territory in which he had lived all this twenty-five years.

Matt had climbed up on a rock to get a beter view of the unknown land ahead, into which he and the rest of The People were fleeing. Ahead he could see swamps, and barren hills, and nothing very inviting. Everywhere the land wavered with the spirits of heat.

The little band of The People, as many in number as a man's fingers and toes, were shuffling along in a thin file beside the rock which Matt had mounted. No one was hanging back, or even trying to argue the others out of making the journey. For though there might be strange dangers in the new land ahead, everyone agreed that nothing there was likely to be as terrible as what they were fleeing—the new beasts, the lions with flesh of stone or arrows, who could kill with only a glance from their fiery eyes.

In the past two days, ten of The People had been caught and killed. The others had been able to do nothing but hide, hardly daring to look for a puddle to drink from or to pull up a root to eat.

Matt gripped with one hand the bow slung over his shoulder, the only bow now left to the survivors of The People; the others had been burned, with the men who had tried to use them against a stone-lion. Tomorrow, Matt thought, he would try hunting for meat in the new country. No one was carrying any food now. Some of the young were wailing in hunger until the women pinched their mouths and noses shut to quiet them.

The file of the surviving People had passed Matt now. He ran his eye along it, then hopped down from his rock, frowning.

A few strides brought him up to those in the rear of the march. "Where is Dart?" he asked, frowning.

Dart was an orphan, and no one was overly concerned. "He kept telling us how hungry he was," a woman said. "And then he ran on toward those swampy woods ahead. I suppose he went to look for something to eat."

Matt grunted. He had no idea of trying to keep any firm control over the actions of any of The People. Someone who wanted to run ahead just did so.

Derron was just buying Lisa some lunch—from the hospital automat, since she was still being kept under observation—when the public address speakers began to broadcast a list of names of Time Operation people who were to report for duty at once. Derron's name was included.

He scooped up a sandwich and ate it as he went. This was something more than another practice alert. When Derron reached the briefing room, Colonel Borss was already on the dais and speaking, pausing to glare at each new arrival.

"Gentlemen, the first assault has fallen just about as predicted, within a few hundred years of the First Men." To Derron's slight surprise, the colonel paused mementarily to bow his head at the mention of those beings sacred to Orthodoxy. These days there were few religionists traditional enough to make such gestures.

"Certainly," the colonel went on, "the berserkers would like to catch the First Men and eliminate them. But this, as we know, must prove impossible."

On this one point at least, science and Orthodox religion were still in firm agreement. The first men entering the ecology on any planet constituted the beginning of an evolutionary peduncle, said science, and as such were considered practically impossible of discovery, time travel or not.

Colonel Borss smoothed his mustache and went on: "As in the first attack, we are faced by six enemy machines breaking into real-time. But in this case the machines are not flyers, or at least they seem not to be operating in an airborne mode. Probably they are slightly smaller than the flyers were. We think they are anti-personnel devices that move on legs and rollers and are of course invulerable to any means of self-defense possessed by the Neolithic population.

"Evidently the berserker's game here is *not* to simply kill as many people as possible. We could trace the disturbance of a mass slaughter back to their new keyhole and blast them again. This time we think they'll concentrate on destroying some historically important individual, or small group. Just who in the invaded area is so important we don't know yet, but if the berserkers can read their importance in them we certainly can, and we soon will.

Now here is Commander Nolos, to brief you on your part in our planned counter-measures."

Nolos, an earnest young man with a rasping voice, came right to the point. "You twenty-four men all have high scores in training on the master-slave androids. No one has any real combat experience with them yet, but you soon will. You're all relieved of other duties as of now."

Expressing various reactions, the two dozen men were hurried to a nearby ready room, and there left to wait for some minutes. At length they were taken down by elevator to Operations Stage Three, on one of the lowest and most heavily defended levels yet dug.

Stage Three was a great echoing cave, the size of an aircraft hangar. A catwalk spanned the cave close up under its reinforced ceiling, and from this walk were suspended the two dozen master units. They looked like spacesuits on puppet-strings.

Like a squad of armored infantry the slave-units stood on the floor below, each slave directly beneath its master. The slaves were the bigger, standing taller and broader than men, dwarfing the technicians who were now busy giving them final precombat checks.

Derron and his fellow operators were given individual briefings, with maps of the terrain where they were to be dropped, and such information as was available on the Neolithic nomads they were to try to protect. Generally speaking this information did not amount to much. After this the operators were run through a brief medical check, dressed in leotards and marched up onto the high catwalk.

At this point the word was passed to delay things momentarily. A huge screen on one wall of the stage lit up with an image of the bald, massive head of the Planetary Commander himself.

"Men . . ." boomed the familiar amplified voice. Then the image paused, frowning off-camera. "You've got them *waiting* for me? Get on with it, man, get on with the operation! I can make speeches any time!"

The Planetary Commander's voice was still rising as it was turned off. Derron got the impression that it had a good deal more to say, and he was glad that it was not being said to him. A pair of technicians came and helped him into his master, as into a heavy diving suit. But once inside he could wave the master's arms and legs and twist its thick body with perfect freedom and servo-powered ease.

"Power coming on," said a voice in Derron's helmet. And it seemed to him that he was no longer suspended in the free-moving puppet. All his senses were transferred in an instant into the body of his slave-unit on the floor below. He felt the slave starting to tilt as its servos moved it into conformity with the master's posture, and he moved the slave's foot as naturally as his own to maintain balance. Tilting back his head, he could look up through the slave-unit's eyes to see the master-unit, himself inside it, holding the same attitude on its complex suspension.

"Form ranks for launching!" came the command in his helmet. Around Derron the cavernous chamber came alive with echoes. Technicians trotted and jumped to get out of the way. The squad of metal man-shapes formed a single serpentine file, and at the head of the file the floor of the stage suddenly blossomed into a bright mercurial disk.

". . . three, two, one, launch."

All of Derron's senses told him that he inhabited one of a line of tall bodies, all running with immense and easy power in their winding file toward the circle on the dark floor. The figure ahead of Derron reached the circle and disappeared. Then he himself leaped out over the silvery disk.

His metal feet came down on grass. He staggered briefly on uneven ground, through shadowy daylight in the midst of a leafy forest.

He moved at once to the nearest clearing from which he could get a good look at the sun. It was low in the western sky—he checked a compass in the slave's wrist—which indicated that he had missed his planned moment of arrival by some hours, if not by days or months or years.

He reported this at once, subvocalizing inside his helmet to keep the slave's speaker silent. If the slave had after all landed in the right place and time, the enemy was somewhere near it.

"All right then, Odegard, start coursing, and we'll try to get a fix."

"Understand."

He began to walk a spiral path through the woods. He of course kept alert for sign of the enemy, but the primary purpose of this manuever was to splash up some waves in reality—to create minor disturbances in the local life-history, which a skilled sentry some twenty thousand years in the future should be able to see and pinpoint.

After he had spiraled for some ten minutes, alarming perhaps a hundred small animals and perhaps crushing a thousand insects underfoot without knowing it, the impersonal voice spoke again.

"All right, Odegard, we've got you spotted. You're in the right place but between four and five hours late. The sun should be getting low."

"It is."

"All right. Bear about two-hundred-forty degrees from magnetic north. It's hard to tell at this range just where your people are, but if you hold that course for about half an hour you should come somewhere near them."

"Understand."

Derron got his bearings and set off in a straight line. The wooded land ahead sloped gradually downward into a swampy area, beyond which there rose low rocky hills, a mile or two distant.

"Odegard, we're getting indication of another minor disturbance right there in your area. Probably caused by a berserker. We can't pin it down any more closely than that, sorry."

"Understand." He was not really there in the past, about to risk his own skin in combat; but the weight of forty million lives was on his neck again.

Some minutes passed. Derron was moving slowly ahead, trying to keep a lookout in all directions while planning a good path for the heavy slave-unit through the marshy ground, when he heard trouble in plain and simple form: a child screaming.

"Operations? I'm onto something." The scream was repeated; the slave-unit's ears were keen and directionally accurate; Derron changed course and began to move the unit at a run, leaping it across the softest-looking spots of ground, striving for both speed and silence.

In a few more seconds, he slid as silently as possible to a halt. In a treetop a stone's throw ahead was the source of the screams—a boy of about twelve, who was clinging tightly to the tree's thin upper trunk with bare arms and legs, clinging tightly to keep from being shaken down. Whenever his yelling ceased for lack of breath, another sharp tremor would run up through the tree and start him off again. The tree's lower trunk was thick, but the bush around its base concealed something that could shake it like a sapling. An animal would have to have the strength of an elephant, and there were no such living creatures here. It would be the berserker, using the boy in the tree as bait, hoping that his cries would bring the adults of his group to try a rescue.

Derron's mission was to protect a particular group of people, and at least one of them was in immediate danger. He moved forward without delay. But the berserker spotted the slave-unit before he saw the berserker.

Only an accidental slip of the slave's foot on the soft soil saved it from taking the first hit right then. As Derron slipped, a pinkish laser beam crackled like straightened lightning past his left ear.

In the next instant the brush round the tree heaved. Derron caught just one glimpse of something charging him, something four-legged and low and wide as a groundcar. He snapped open his jaw, which pressed down inside his helmet on the trigger of his own laser-weapon. From the center of the slave's forehead a pale lance cracked out, aimed automatically at the spot where the slave's eyes were focused. The beam smote the charging berserker amid the knobs of metal that served it for a face and glanced off to explode a small tree into a cloud of flame and steam.

The shot might have done damage, for the enemy broke off its rush in midstride and dove for cover behind a hillock, a grass-tufted hump of ground not five feet high.

Derron was somewhat surprised by his own aggressiveness. He found himself moving quickly to the attack, running the slave-unit in a crouch around the tiny hill. Two voices from Operations were trying at the same time to give him advice, but even if they had gone about it sensibly it was too late now for him to do anything but go his own way.

He charged right round onto the berserker, yelling

inside his helmet as he fired his laser. The thing before him looked like a metal lion, but squat and very broad; given a second to hesitate, Derron might have flinched away, for in spite of all his training the illusion was very strong that he was actually hurling his own precious flesh upon this monster.

As it was, circumstances gave him no time to flinch. The slave ran at full speed into the berserker, and the trees in the swamp shook as the machines collided.

It was soon plain that wrestling was not likely to succeed against this enemy, which was not limited in its reactions by the slowness of protoplasmic nerves. For all the slave-unit's fusion-powered strength, Derron could only hang on desperately, gripping the berserker in a sort of half nelson while it bucked and twisted like a wild loadbeast to throw him off.

Since the fight had started everybody wanted to watch. The voices of at least two senior Operations officers screamed orders and abuse into Derron's ears, while the green forest spun round him faster than his eyes and brain could sort it out. In a detached fraction of a second of thought he noticed how his feet were flying uselessly on the end of his steel legs, breaking down small trees as the monster spun him. He tried to turn his head to bring the cyclops' eye of his laser to bear, but somehow could not manage to do so. He tried desperately to get a more solid grip for his steel arms on the berserker's thick neck, but then his grip was broken and he flew.

Before the slave-unit could even bounce the berserker was on top of it, moving faster than any maddened bull. Derron fired wildly with his laser. That the berserker should trample and batter the slave-unit and he should feel no pain gave him a giddy urge to laugh. In a moment now the fight would be lost and he would be able to give up.

But then the berserker was running away from Derron's wildly slashing laser. It leaped among the trees as lightly as a deer and vanished.

Dizzily—for the master-unit had of course spun on its mountings even as the slave was spun—Derron tried to sit up, on the peculiar little hillside where he had been flung. Now he discovered why the berserker had retired so willingly. Some important part had been broken in the slave, so its legs trailed as limp and useless as those of a man with a broken spine.

But the slave-unit's laser still worked. The berserker computer-brain had decided it could gain nothing by staying around to trade zaps with a crippled but still dangerous antagonist, not when it could be busy at its programmed task of killing people.

The voices had their final say: "Odegard, why in the —?" "Oh, do what you can!" Then with a click they were gone from his helmet, leaving their disgust behind.

Derron's own disgust with his failure was even sharper. Gone were the thoughts of getting things settled quickly one way or the other. Now all he wanted was another crack at 'em.

With the slave's arms alone, he got it into a sitting position, halfway down the conical side of a soggy sandpit.

He looked about him. The nearby trees were nearly all in bad shape; those not broken during the wrestling-match were black and smoking furiously from his wildly aimed laser.

What about the boy?

Working hard with his arms, Derron churned his way up to a spot near the rim of the funnel-shaped pit, where the sides were steepest. He could recognize, a little distance away, the tall tree in which the youngster had been clinging for his life. He was not in sight now, living or dead.

In a sudden little avalanche the crippled slave slid down once more toward the bottom of the sandy funnel.

A funnel?

Derron at last recognized the place where the slave-unit had been thrown.

It was the trap of a poison-digger, a species of carnivore that had been—or would be—exterminated in early historical times. Even now, there reared up a frightful grayish head from the watery mess that filled the bottom of the pit.

# V

Matt stood just behind the boy Dart, while both of them peered very cautiously through the bushes toward the poison-digger's trap. The rest of The People were waiting, resting from their march while they ate some grubs and roots, a few hundred paces away.

Matt caught just a glimpse of a head above the lip of the funnel. Not a poison-digger's head, certainly. This one was curved almost as smoothly as a drop of water, but was still hard-looking.

"I think it is a stone-lion," Matt whispered very softly.

"Ah no," whispered Dart. "It's a man, a big man, the stone-man I told you about. Ah, what a fight he made against the stone-lion! But I didn't wait to see the end, I jumped from the tree and ran."

Matt beckoned Dart with a motion of his head. The two of them bent down and crept forward, then peered from behind another bush. Now they could see down into the pit.

Matt gasped, and almost called aloud in wonder. Poison-Digger down in the pit had reared up from his slime and lunged. And Stone-Man simply slapped Digger's nose with casual force, like someone swatting a child; and with a howl like that of a punished child, the Bad One splashed down under his water again.

In a strange tongue, Stone-Man muttered disconsolate words, like a man invoking spirits, at the same time slapping at his legs which seemed to be dead. Then with his arms he started trying to dig his way up and out of the pit. Stone-Man made the sand fly, and Matt thought maybe he would eventually make it, though it looked like a very hard struggle.

"Now do you believe me?" Dart was whispering fiercely. "He did fight the stone-lion, I saw him."

Matt hushed the young one and led him away. As they retreated it occurred to Matt that the stone-lion might have been mortally hurt in the fight, and he circled through the trees looking hopefully for a huge shiny corpse. He wanted very much before his own death to see a stone-lion somehow defeated and slain. But all he saw were burnt and broken trees.

When they got back to where the others were waiting, Matt talked things over with the more intelligent adults.

"You think we should approach this Stone-Man?" one asked.

"I would like to help him," said Matt. He was eager to

join forces if he could with any power that was able to oppose a stone-lion.

The oldest woman of The People opened her lizard-skin pouch, in which she also kept the seed of fire, and took out the finger-bones of her predecessor. Three times she shook the bones and threw them on the ground, and studied the pattern in which they fell.

At last she pointed to Matt. "You will die," she announced, "fighting a strange beast, the likes of which none of us has ever seen."

Like most prophecies Matt had heard, this one was more interesting than helpful. "If you are right," he answered, "this stone-man can't kill me, since we have now seen him."

The others muttered doubtfully.

The more he thought about it, the more determined Matt became. "If he does turn out to be hostile, he can't chase us on his dead legs. I want to help him."

This time the slave's keen ears detected the approach of The People, though they were obviously trying to be quiet. Derron's helmet had been free of Modern voices for some minutes now; the too-many chiefs of Time Operations were evidently busy harassing some other operator.

Derron hated to draw their attention back to himself, but the approach of The People was something that he had to report.

"I'm getting some company," he subvocalized. No immediate reply was granted. Now the heads of the bolder ones among The People came into sight, peering nervously around treetrunks at the slave-unit. Derron made a gentle gesture to them with one open metal hand; he had to use the other to maintain the slave in a sitting position. If he could only get his visitors to remain until more help arrived, he could give them some degree of protection. The berserker had evidently gone away after some false scent, but it might be back at any time.

The People were reassured by the slave's quiescence, its crippled condition and its peaceful gestures. Soon all two dozen of them were out in the open, whispering among themselves as they looked down into the pit.

"Anybody listening?" Derron subvocalized, calling for help. "I've got a crowd of people here. Get me a linguist!"

Lately the Moderns had made a desperate effort to learn all the languages of Sirgol's past, through the dropping of disguised microphones into the divers parts of real-time where there were people to be studied. This had been a crash program, only undertaken in recent months when it had become apparent to both sides that the war could be moved from present-time into the past. There were one or two Moderns who had managed to learn something about the speech of The People and the other bands of the area—and those Moderns were very busy people today.

"Odegard!" The blast in his helmet made him wince. It sounded like Colonel Borss. "Don't let those people get away, try to protect them!"

Derron sighed, sub-subvocally. "Understood. How about getting me a linguist?"

"We're trying to get you one. You're in a vital area there. Try to protect those people until we can get you some help."

"Understood."

"Anyone that size is bound to eat a lot of food," one of the older men was complaining to Matt.

"With dead legs I don't suppose he'll live long enough to eat very much," Matt answered. He was trying to talk someone into giving him a hand in pulling the stone-man up out of the pit. Stone-Man sat watching calmly, as if he felt confident of getting some help.

The man debating against Matt cheerfully switched arguments. "If he won't live long, there's no use trying to help him. Anyway he's not one of The People."

"No, he's not. But still . . . ." Matt searched for words, for ways of thought, to clarify his onw feelings. This stone-man who had tried to help Dart was part of some larger order, to which The People also belonged. Part of something opposing all the wild beasts and demons that killed men by day or night.

"There may be others of his band around here," put in another man. "They would be strong friends to have."

"This one wants to be our friend," the boy Dart piped up.

The oldest woman scoffed: "So would anyone who was crippled and needed help."

## VI

A girl linguist's voice joined the muted hive buzzing in Derron's helmet and gave him a rather halting translation of part of the debate. But after only a couple of minutes she was ordered away to work with another operator, who had managed to terrify the band he was supposed to be protecting.

"Tell him to pretend he's crippled," Derron advised. "All right, I'll do without a linguist. But how about dropping some of those self-defense weapons for these people of mine? If we wait until that berserker comes back it'll be too late. And make it grenades, not arrows. There's only one man in the bunch who has a bow."

"The weapons are being prepared. It's dangerous to hand them out until they're absolutely needed. Suppose they use 'em on each other, or on the slave?"

"You can at least drop them into the slave now." Inside the slave-unit's bag torso was a hollow receptacle into which small items could be dropped from the future as required.

"They're being prepared."

Derron didn't know if he could believe that or not, the way things were going today.

The people seemed to be still discussing the slave-unit, while he kept it sitting in what he hoped was a patient and trustworthy attitude. According to the brief translation Derron had heard, the tall young man with the bow slung over his shoulder was aruging in favor of helping the "stone-man."

At last this man with the bow, who seemed to be the nearest thing to a chief that these people had, talked one of the other men into helping him. Together they approached one of the saplings splintered in the fight, and twisted it loose from its stump, hacking through the tough bark strings with a hand-axe. Then the two bold men came right up to the edge of the poison-digger's trap, holding the sapling by its branches so its splintered end was extended, rather shakily, down to where the slave could grasp it.

The two men pulled, then grunted with surprise at the

weight they felt. Two more men were now willing to come and lend a hand.

"Odegard, this is Colonel Borss," said a helmet-voice, in urgent tones. "We can see now what the berserkers' target is. The first written language developed on the planet originates very near your present location. Possibly with the people you're with right now. We can't be sure of that and neither can the enemy, but certainly your band is in the target group."

Derron was hanging on with both hands as the slave-unit was dragged up the side of the pit. "Thanks for the word, Colonel. Now how about those grenades I asked for?"

"We're rushing two more slaves toward you, but we're having technical problems. Grenades?" There was a brief pause. "They tell me some grenades are coming up." The colonel's voice clicked off.

When the slave came sliding up over the rim of the pit, The People all retreated a few steps, falling silent and watching the machine carefully. Derron repeated his peaceful gestures.

As soon as his audience was slightly reassured about the slave, they went back to worrying about something else. The setting sun made them nervous, and they kept looking over their shoulders at it as they talked to one another.

In another minute they had gathered up their few belongings and were on the march, with the air of folk resuming a practiced activity. Stone-Man, it seemed, was to be allowed to choose his own course of action.

Derron trailed along at the end of the file. He soon found that on level ground he could keep the slave-unit moving pretty well, walking on the knuckles of its hands like a broken-backed ape. The People cast frequent backward glances at this pathetic monstrosity, showing mixed emotions. But even more frequently they looked farther back, fearful about something that might be on their trail.

Quite possibly, Derron thought, these people had already seen the berserker, or found the bodies of their friends who had met it. Sooner or later it would pick up their trail, in any case. The slave-unit's leg-dragging track would make the berserker use a bit more caution, but certainly it would still come on.

Colonel Borss came back to talk. "You're right, Odegard, your berserker's still in your area. It's the only one we haven't bagged yet, but it's in the most vital spot. What I think we'll do is this—the two slaves being sent as reinforcements will be in place in a few minutes now. They'll follow your line of march one on each side and a short distance ahead. Then when your people stop somewhere for the night we'll set up the two new slaves for an ambush."

Falling dusk washed the scene in a kind of dark beauty. The People hiked with the swampy, half-wooded valley on their right and low rocky hills close by on their left. The man with the bow, whose name seemed to be something like Matt, kept scanning these hills as he walked.

"What about those grenades? Operations? Anybody there?"

"We're setting up this ambush now, Odegard. We don't want your people pitching grenades at *our* devices."

There was some sense to that, Derron supposed. But he had no faith.

The leader, Matt, turned and went trotting up a hillside, the other people following briskly. Derron saw that they were headed for a narrow cave entrance, which was set into a steep low cliff like a door in the wall of a house. A little way from the cave everyone halted. Matt unslung his bow and nocked an arrow before pitching a rock into the darkness of the cave. Just inside the entrance was an L-bend that made it practically impossible to see any further.

Derron was reporting these latest developments to Operations, when out of the cave there reverberated a growl that made The People scatter like the survival experts they were.

When the cave-bear came to answer the door, it found Derron's proxy waiting alone on the porch.

The slave in its present condition had no balance to speak of, so the bear's first slap bowled it over. From a supine position Derron slapped back, clobbering the bear's nose and provoking a blood-freezing roar.

Made of tougher stuff than poison-diggers, the bear strained its fangs on the slave-unit's face. Still flat on his back, Derron lifted the bear with his steel arms and pitched it downhill. Go away!

The first roar had been only a tune-up for this second one. Derron didn't want to break even an animal's life-line here if he could help it, but time was passing. He threw the bear a little further this time; it bounced once, landed on its feet, and without slowing down kept right on going into the swamp. Its howls trailed in the air for half a minute.

The People slowly gathered round again, for once forgetting to look over their shoulders. Derron had the feeling they were all about to fall down and worship him; before anything like this could happen, he dragged his proxy into the cave and made sure that it was now unoccupied. Matt had made a good discovery here; there was plenty of room inside the high narrow cavern to shelter the whole band.

When he came out he found The People gathering dead branches from under the trees at the edge of the swamp, getting ready to build a good-sized fire at the mouth of the cave. Far across the swampy valley a small spark of orange marked the encampment of some other band, in the thickening purplish haze of falling night.

"Operations, how's that ambush coming?"

"The other two units are taking up ambush positions now. They have you in sight at the cave-mouth."

"Good."

Let The People build their fire, then, and draw the berserker. They would be safe in a guarded cave while it walked into a trap.

From a pouch made of what looked like tough lizard-skin one of the old women produced a bundle of bark, while she unwrapped to reveal a smoldering center. With incantations and a judicious use of wood chips, she soon had the watchfire blazing. Its first tongues gave more light than did the fast-dimming sky.

The slave-unit moved last into the cave, right after Matt. Derron sat it leaning against the wall just inside the L-bend and sighed. He could use a rest—

Without warning the night outside erupted with the crackle of lasers and the clang of armored battle. Inside the cave the people jumped to their feet.

In the lasers' reflected glare Derron saw Matt with his bow ready, the other men grabbing up stones—and Dart, high up on a rock in the rear of the cave. There was a small window in the wall of rock back there, and the boy was looking out, the laser-glare bright on his awed face.

The flashing and crashing outside came to a sudden halt. The world sank into a deathlike silence. Long seconds passed.

"Operations? Operations? What's going on? What's happened outside?"

"Oh, Holy One . . ." The voice was shaken. "Scratch two slave-units. Looks like the damn' thing's reflexes are just too good. Odegard, do the best you can . . ."

The watchfire came exploding suddenly into the cave, kciked probably by a clawed steel foot, so that a hail of sparks and brands bounced from the curving wall of stone just opposite the narrow entrance. The berserker would walk right in. Its cold brain had learned contempt for all the Moderns were able to do against it.

But there camc a heavy grating sound; evidently the cave mouth was just a bit too narrow for it.

"Odegard, a dozen of the arrows are ready to drop through to you now. Shaped charges in the points, set to fire on sharp contact."

"*Arrows?* I wanted grenades, I told you we've only one bow, and there's no room . . ." But the window in the rear of the cave might serve as an archery port. "Send arrows, then. Send something!"

"Dropping arrows now. Odegard, we have a relief operator standing by in another master-unit, so we can switch . . . ."

"Never mind that. I'm used to operating this broken-backed thing now, and he isn't."

The berserker was scraping and hammering at the bulge of rock that kept it from its prey, raising a hellish racket. With the slave-unit's hands Derron undid the catches and opened the door in its metal torso. While a bank of faces surrounded him, staring solemnly through the gloom, he took out the arrows and offered them to Matt.

## VII

With reverence the hunter accepted the weapons. Since the firelight had vanished the slave's eyes had shifted into the infrared; Derron could see well enough to tell that the arrows looked to be well constructed, their straight wooden shafts fletched with plastic feathers, their heads a good imitation of handchipped flint. Now if they only worked . . . .

Matt needed no instructions on what to do with the arrows, not after their magical manner of appearance. Dart getting under his feet, he dashed to the rear of the cave; there he put the youngster behind him and scrambled up the rocks to the natural window. It would have given him a fine safe spot to shoot from, if there had been no such thing as laser beams.

Since lasers did exist, it would be the slave-unit's task to take the first beam itself and keep the berserker's attention on it as much as possible. Derron inched his crippled metal body toward the bend of the L. When he saw Matt nock an arrow to his bow, he lunged out, with his ridiculous hand-walking movement, around the corner.

The berserker had just backed away to take a fresh run at the entrance. It of course was quicker than Derron with its beam. But the slave's armor held for the moment, and Derron scrambled forward, firing back at point-blank range. If the berserker saw Matt, it ignored him, thinking arrows meant nothing.

But now the first one struck. Derron saw the shaft spin softly away, while the head vanished in a momentary fireball that left a fist-sized hole in the berserker's armor at the shoulder of one foreleg.

The machine lurched off balance even as its laser flicked toward Matt. Derron kept scrambling after it on steel hands, keeping his own beam on it like a spotlight. The bushes atop the little cliff had been set afire, but Matt popped up bravely and shot his second arrow, as accurately as the first. The shaped charge hit the berserker in the side, and staggered it on its three legs. And then it could fire its laser no more, for Derron was close enough to swing a heavy metal fist and crack the thick glass of the projector-eye.

And then the wrestling-match was on again. The strength of the slave's two arms matched that of the berserker's one functional foreleg. But the enemy reflexes were still more than human. Derron hung on as best he could, but the world was soon spinning round him again, and again he was thrown.

Derron gripped one of the trampling legs and hung on somehow, trying to immobilize the berserker as a target. Where were the arrows now? Derron's laser was smashed. The berserker was still too big, too heavy, too quick. While Derron gripped one of its functional legs the other two still stomped and tore—there went one of the slave-unit's useless feet, ripped clean off. The metal man was going to be pulled to pieces. For some reason no more arrows were being shot—

Derron caught just a glimpse of a hurtling body as Matt leaped directly into the fight, raising in each hand a cluster of magic-arrows. Yelling, seeming to fly like a god, he stabbed his thunderbolts down against the ene-my's back.

The blasts were absorted in full by the berserker's interior. And then something inside the monster let go in an explosion that bounced both machines. And with that, the fight was over.

Derron crawled from the overheated wreck of the slave-unit, out from under the mass of glowing, twisting, spit-ting metal that had been the enemy. Then he had to pause for a few seconds in exhaustion. He saw Dart come running from the cave, tears streaking his face, in his hand Matt's bow, with its broken string dangling.

Most of the rest of The People were gathering around something on the ground nearby. Matt lay where the enemy's last convulsion had thrown him. He was dead, his belly torn open, hands charred, face smashed out of shape—then the eyes opened in that ruined face. Matt drew a shaky breath and shuddered and went on breathing.

Derron no longer felt his own exhaustion. The People made way as he crawled his battered metal proxy to Matt's side and gently lifted him. Two of the younger women were wailing. Matt was too far gone to wince at the touch of hot metal.

"Good work, Odegard!" Colonel Borss's voice had regained strength. "That wraps up the operation. We can lift your unit back to present-time now; better put that fellow down."

Derron held onto Matt. "His lifeline is breaking off

here no matter what we do. Bring him up with the machine."

"It's not authorized to bring anyone . . . ." The voice faded in hesitation.

"He won the fight for us, and now his guts are hanging out. He's finished in this part of history. Sir."

"All right, we'll bring him up. Stand by while we re-adjust."

The People meanwhile had formed a ring of awe around the slave-unit and its dying burden. Somehow the scene would probably he assimilated into one of the extant myths; myths were tough bottles, Derron thought, stretching to hold many kinds of wine.

Up at the mouth of the cave, the old woman was having trouble with her tinder as she tried to get the watch-fire started again. A young girl with her hesitated, then ran down to the glowing berserker-shell and on its heat kindled a dry branch into flame. Waving the branch to keep it bright, she went back up the hill in a sort of dance.

And then Derron was sitting in a fading circle of light on the dark floor of Operations Stage Three. The circle vanished, and two men with a stretcher ran toward him. He opened his metal arms to let the medics take Matt, then inside his helmet his teeth found the power switch and he turned off the master-unit.

He let the end-of-mission checklist go hang. In a few seconds he had extricated himself from the master, and in his sweat-soaked leotard was skipping down the stairs from the catwalk. The other slaves were being brought back too, and the Stage was busy. He pushed his way through a confusion of technicians and miscellaneous folk and reached Matt's side just as the medics were picking up the stretcher with him on it. Wet clothes had already been draped over the wounded man's bulging intestines, and some kind of an intravenous had been started.

Matt's eyes were open, though of course they were stupid with shock. To him Derron could be no more than another strange shape among many; but Derron's shape walked along beside him, gripping his forearms above his burned hand, until consciousness faded away.

The word was spreading, as if by public announcement, that a man had been brought up alive from the deep past. When they carried Matt into the nearest hospital it was only natural that Lisa, like everyone else who had the chance, should come hurrying to see him.

"He's lost," she murmured, looking down at the swollen face, in which the eyelids now and then flicked open. "Oh, so lost. Alone." She turned anxiously to a doctor. "He'll live, now, won't he?"

The doctor smiled faintly. "If he's lasted this far I think we'll save him."

Lisa sighed in deep relief. Of course her concern was natural and kind. The only difficulty was that she hardly noticed Derron at all.

# FOR I AM A JEALOUS PEOPLE!

## BY LESTER DE REY

### I

*. . . the keepers of the house shall tremble, and the strong men shall bow themselves . . . and the doors shall be shut in the streets, when the sound of the grinding is low . . . they shall be afraid of that which is high, and fears shall be in the way, and the almond tree shall flourish . . . because man goeth to his long home, and the mourners go about the streets . . .*

ECCLESIASTES, XII 3–5

There was the continuous shrieking thunder of an alien rocket overhead as the Reverend Amos Strong stepped back into the pulpit. He straightened his square, thin shoulders slightly, and the gaunt hollows in his cheeks deepened. For a moment he hesitated, while his dark eyes turned upwards under bushy, grizzled brows. Then he moved forward, placing the torn envelope and telegram on the lectern with his notes. The blue-veined hand and knobby wrist that projected from the shiny black serge of his sleeve hardly trembled.

His eyes turned toward the pew where his wife was not. Ruth would not be there this time. She had read the message before sending it on to him. Now she could not be expected. It seemed strange to him. She hadn't missed service since Richard was born nearly thirty years ago.

The sound hissed its way into silence over the horizon, and Amos stepped forward, gripping the rickety lectern with both hands. He straightened and forced into his voice the resonance and calm it needed.

"I have just received word that my son was killed in the battle of the moon," he told the puzzled congregation. He lifted his voice, and the resonance in it deepened. "I had asked, if it were possible, that this cup might pass from me. Nevertheless, not as I will, Lord, but as Thou wilt."

He turned from their shocked faces, closing his ears to the sympathetic cry of others who had suffered. The church had been built when Wesley was twice its present size, but the troubles that had hit the people had driven them into the worn old building until it was nearly filled. He pulled his notes to him, forcing his mind from his own loss to the work that had filled his life.

"The text today is drawn from Genesis," he told them. "Chapter seventeen, seventh verse; and chapter twenty-six, fourth verse. The promise which God made to Abraham and to Isaac." He read from the Bible before him, turning the pages unerringly at the first try.

"And I will establish my covenant between me and thee and thy seed after thee in their generations for an everlasting covenant, to be a God unto thee, and to thy seed after thee."

"And I will make thy seed to multiply as the stars of heaven, and will give unto thy seed all these countries, and in thy seed shall all the nations of the earth be blessed."

He had memorized most of his sermon, no longer counting on inspiration to guide him as it had once done. He began smoothly, hearing his own words in snatches as he drew the obvious and comforting answer to their uncertainty. God had promised man the earth as an everlasting covenant. Why then should men be afraid or lose faith because alien monsters had swarmed down out of the emptiness between the stars to try man's faith? As in the days of bondage in Egypt or captivity in Babylon, there would always be trials and times when the faint-hearted should waver, but the eventual outcome was clearly promised.

He had delivered a sermon from the same text in his former parish of Clyde when the government had first begun building its base on the moon, drawing heavily in that case from the reference to the stars of heaven to quiet the doubts of those who felt that man had no business in space. It was then that Richard had announced his commission in the lunar colony, using Amos's own words to defend his refusal to enter the ministry. It had been the last he saw of the boy.

He had used the text one other time, over forty years before, but the reason was lost, together with the passion that had won him fame as a boy evangelist. He could remember the sermon only because of the shock on the bearded face of his father when he had misquoted a phrase. It was one of his few clear memories of the period before his voice changed and his evangelism came to an abrupt end.

He had tried to recapture his inspiration after ordination, bitterly resenting the countless intrusions of marriage and fatherhood on his spiritual forces. But at last he had recognized that God no longer intended him to be a modern Peter the Hermit, and resigned himself to the work he could do. Now he was back in the parish where he had first begun; and if he could no longer fire the souls of his flock, he could at least help somewhat with his memorized rationalizations for the horror of the alien invasion.

Another ship thundered overhead, nearly drowning his words. Six months before, the great ships had exploded out of space and had dropped carefully to the moon, to attack the forces there. In another month, they had begun forays against Earth itself. And now, while the world haggled and struggled to unite against them, they were setting up bases all over and conquering the world mile by mile.

Amos saw the faces below him turn up, furious and uncertain. He raised his voice over the thunder, and finished hastily, moving quickly through the end of the service.

He hesitated as the congregation stirred. The ritual was over and his words were said, but there had been no real service. Slowly, as if by themselves, his lips opened, and he heard his voice quoting the Twenty-Seventh Psalm. "The Lord is my light and my salvation; whom shall I fear?"

His voice was soft, but he could feel the reaction of the congregation as the surprisingly timely words registered. "Though an host should encamp against me, my heart shall not fear: though war should rise against me, in this will I be confident." The air seemed to quiver, as it had done long ago when God had seemed to hold direct communion with him, and there was no sound from the pews when he finished. "Wait on the Lord: be of good courage, and he shall strengthen thine heart: wait, I say, on the Lord."

The warmth of that mystic glow lingered as he stepped quietly from the pulpit. Then there was the sound of motorcycles outside, and a pounding on the door. The feeling vanished.

Someone stood up and sudden light began pouring in from outdoors. There was a breath of the hot, droughty physical world with its warning of another dust storm, and a scattering of grasshoppers on the steps to remind the people of the earlier damage to their crops. Amos could see the bitterness flood back over them in tangible waves, even before they noticed the short, plump figure of Dr. Alan Miller.

"Amos! Did you hear?" He was wheezing as if he had been running. "Just came over the radio while you were in here gabbling."

He was cut off by the sound of more motorcycles. They swept down the single main street of Wesley, heading west. The riders were all in military uniform, carrying weapons and going at top speed. Dust erupted behind them, and Doc began coughing and swearing. In the last few years, he had grown more and more outspoken about his atheism; when Amos had first known him, during his first pastorate, the man had at least shown some respect for the religion of others.

"All right," Amos said sharply. "You're in the house of God, Doc. What came over the radio?"

Doc caught himself and choked back his coughing fit. "Sorry. But damn it, man, the aliens have landed in Clyde, only fifty miles away. They've set up a base there! That's what all those rockets going over meant."

There was a sick gasp from the people who had heard, and a buzz as the news was passed back to others.

Amos hardly noticed the commotion. It had been Clyde where he had served before coming here again. He was trying to picture the alien ships dropping down, scouring the town ahead of them with gas and bullets. The grocer on the corner with his nine children, the lame deacon who had served there, the two Aimes sisters with their horde of dogs and cats and their constant crusade against younger sinners. He tried to picture the green-skinned, humanoid aliens moving through the town, invading the church, desecrating the altar! And there was Anne Seyton, who had been Richard's sweetheart, though of another faith . . .

"What about the garrison nearby?" a heavy farmer yelled over the crowd. "I had a boy there, and he told me they could handle any ships when they were landing! Shell their tubes when they were coming down—"

Doc shook his head. "Half an hour before the landing, there was a cyclone up there. It took the roof off the main building and wrecked the whole training garrison."

"Jim!" The big man screamed out the name, and began dragging his frail wife behind him, out toward his car. "If they got Jim—"

Others started to rush after him, but another procession of motorcycles stopped them. This time they were traveling slower, and a group of tanks was rolling behind them. The rear tank drew abreast, slowed, and stopped, while a dirty-faced man in an untidy major's uniform stuck his head out.

"You folks get under cover! Ain't you heard the news? Go home and stick to your radios, before a snake plane starts potshooting the bunch of you for fun. The snakes'll be heading straight over here if they're after Topeka, like it looks!" He jerked back down and began swearing at someone inside. The tank jerked to a start and began heading away toward Clyde.

There had been enough news of the sport of the alien planes in the papers. The people melted from the church. Amos tried to stop them for at least a short prayer and to give them time to collect their thoughts, but gave up after the first wave shoved him aside. A minute later, he was standing alone with Doc Miller.

"Better get home, Amos," Doc suggested. "My car's half a block down. Suppose I give you a lift?"

Amos nodded wearily. His bones felt dry and brittle, and there was a dust in his mouth thicker than that in the air. He felt old and, for the first time, almost useless. He followed the doctor quietly, welcoming the chance to ride the six short blocks to the little house the parish furnished him.

A car of ancient age and worse repair rattled toward them as they reached Doc's auto. It stopped, and a man in dirty overalls leaned out, his face working jerkily. "Are you prepared, brothers? Are you saved? Armageddon has come, as the Book foretold. Get right with God, brothers! The end of the world as foretold is at hand, amen!"

"Where does the Bible foretell alien races around other suns?" Doc shot at him.

The man blinked, frowned, and yelled something about sinners burning forever in hell before he started his rickety car again. Amos sighed. Now, with the rise of their troubles, fanatics would spring up to cry doom and false gospel more than ever, to the harm of all honest religion. He had never decided whether they were somehow useful to God or whether they were inspired by the forces of Satan.

"In my Father's house are many mansions," he quoted to Doc, as they started up the street. "It's quite possibly an allegorical reference to other worlds in the heavens."

Doc grimaced, and shrugged. Then he sighed and dropped one hand from the wheel onto Amos' knee. "I heard about Dick, Amos. I'm sorry. The first baby I ever delivered—and the handsomest!" He sighed again, staring toward Clyde as Amos found no words to answer. "I don't get it. Why can't we drop atom bombs on them? What happened to the moon base's missiles?"

Amos got out at the unpainted house where he lived, taking Doc's hand silently and nodding his thanks.

He would have to organize his thoughts this afternoon. When night fell and the people could move about without the danger of being shot at by chance alien planes, the church bell would summon them, and they would need spiritual guidance. If he could help them to stop trying to understand God, and to accept Him . . .

There had been that moment in the church when God had seemed to enfold him and the congregation in warmth—the old feeling of true fulfillment. Maybe, now in the hour of its greatest need, some measure of inspiration had returned.

He found Ruth setting the table. Her small, quiet body moved as efficiently as ever, though her face was puffy and her eyes were red. "I'm sorry I couldn't make it,

Amos. But right after the telegram, Anne Seyton came. She'd heard—before we did. And——"

The television set was on, showing headlines from the *Kansas City Star,* and he saw there was no need to tell her the news. He put a hand on one of hers. "God has only taken what he gave, Ruth. We were blessed with Richard for thirty years."

"I'm all right." She pulled away and turned toward the kitchen, her back frozen in a line of taut misery. "Didn't you hear what I said? Anne's here. Dick's wife! They were married before he left, secretly—right after you talked with him about the difference in religion. You'd better see her, Amos. She knows about her people in Clyde."

He watched his wife go. The slam of the outside door underlined the word. He'd never forbidden the marriage; he had only warned the boy, so much like Ruth. He hesitated, and finally turned toward the tiny, second bedroom. There was a muffled answer to his knock, and the lock clicked rustily.

"Anne?" he said. The room was darkened, but he could see her blond head and the thin, almost unfeminine lines of her figure. He put out a hand and felt her thin fingers in his palm. As she turned toward the weak light, he saw no sign of tears, but her hand shook with her dry shudders. "Anne, Ruth has just told me that God has given us a daughter—"

"God!" She spat the word out harshly, while the hand jerked back. "God, Reverend Strong? Whose God? The one who sends meteorites against Dick's base, plagues of insects, and drought against our farms? The God who uses tornadoes to make it easy for the snakes to land? That God, Reverend Strong? Dick gave you a daughter, and he's dead! Dead!"

Amos backed out of the room. He had learned to stand the faint mockery with which Doc pronounced the name of the Lord, but this was something that set his skin into goose-pimples and caught at his throat. Anne had been of a different faith, but she had always seemed religious before.

It was probably only hysteria. He turned toward the kitchen door to call Ruth and send her in to the girl.

Overhead, the staccato bleating of a ram-jet cut through

the air in a sound he had never heard. But the radio description fitted it perfectly. It could be no Earth ship!

Then there was another and another, until they blended together into a steady drone.

And over it came the sudden firing of a heavy gun, while a series of rapid thuds came from the garden behind the house.

Amos stumbled toward the back door. "Ruth!" he cried.

There was another burst of shots. Ruth was crumpling before he could get to the doorway.

## II

*My God, my God, why hast thou forsaken me? . . . I am poured out like water, and all my bones are out of joint; my heart is like wax; it is melted in the midst of my bowels. My strength is dried up like a potsherd; and my tongue cleaveth to my jaws; and thou has brought me into the dust of death.*

PSALMS, XXII, 1, 14, 15

There were no more shots as he ran to gather her into his arms. The last of the alien delta planes had gone over, heading for Topeka or whatever city they were attacking.

Ruth was still alive. One of the ugly slugs had caught her in the abdomen, ripping away part of the side, and it was bleeding horribly. But he felt her heart still beating, and she moaned faintly. Then as he put her on the couch, she opened her eyes briefly, saw him, and tried to smile. Her lips moved, and he dropped his head to hear.

"I'm sorry, Amos. Foolish. Nuisance. Sorry."

Her eyes closed, but she smiled again after he bent to kiss her lips. "Glad now. Waited so long."

Anne stood in the doorway, staring unbelievingly. But as Amos stood up, she unfroze and darted to the medicine cabinet, to come back and begin snipping away the ruined dress and trying to staunch the flow of blood.

Amos reached blindly for the phone. He mumbled something to the operator, and a minute later to Doc Miller. He'd been afraid that the doctor would still be out. He had a feeling that Doc had promised to come, but could remember no words.

The flow of blood outside the wound had been stopped, but Ruth was white, even to her lips. Anne forced him back to a chair, her fingers gentle on his arm.

"I'm sorry, Father Strong. I—I—"

He stood up and went over to stand beside Ruth, letting his eyes turn toward the half-set table. There was a smell of something burning in the air, and he went out to the old woodburning stove to pull the pans off and drop them into the sink. Anne followed, but he hardly saw her, until he heard her begin to cry softly. There were tears this time.

"The ways of God are not the ways of man, Anne," he said, and the words released a flood of his own emotions. He dropped tiredly to a chair, his hands falling limply onto his lap. He dropped his head against the table, feeling the weakness and uncertainty of age. "We love the carnal form and our hearts are broken when it is gone. Only God can know all of any of us or count the tangled threads of all our lives. It isn't good to hate God!"

She dropped beside him. "I don't, Father Strong. I never did." He couldn't be sure of the honesty of it, but he made no effort to question her, and she sighed. "Mother Ruth isn't dead yet!"

He was saved from any answer by the door being slammed open as Doc Miller came rushing in. The plump little man took one quick look at Ruth, and was beside her, reaching for plasma and his equipment. He handed the plasma bottle to Anne, and began working carefully.

"There's a chance," he said finally. "If she were younger or stronger, I'd say there was an excellent chance. But now, since you believe in it, you'd better do some fancy praying."

"I've been praying," Amos told him, realizing that it was true. The prayers had begun inside his head at the first shot, and they had never ceased.

They moved her gently, couch and all, into the bedroom where the blinds could be drawn, and where the other sounds of the house couldn't reach her. Doc gave Anne a shot of something and sent her into the other

room. He turned to Amos, but didn't insist when the
minister shook his head.

"I'll stay here, Amos," he said. "With her. Until we
know, or I get another call. The switchboard girl knows
where I am."

He went into the bedroom and closed the door. Amos
stood in the center of the living room, his head bowed,
for long minutes.

The sound of the television brought him back. Topeka
was off the air, but another station was showing scenes of
destruction.

Hospitals and schools seemed to be their chief targets.
The gas had accounted for a number of deaths, though
those could have been prevented if instructions had been
followed. But now the incendiaries were causing the greatest damage.

And the aliens had gotten at least as rough treatment
as they had meted out. Of the forty that had been
counted, twenty-nine were certainly down.

"I wonder if they're saying prayers to God for their
dead?" Doc asked. "Or doesn't your God extend his
mercy to races other than man?"

Amos shook his head slowly. It was a new question to
him. But there could be only one answer. "God rules the
entire universe, Doc. But these evil beings surely offer
him no worship!"

"Are you sure? They're pretty human!"

Amos looked back to the screen, where one of the
alien corpses could be seen briefly. They did look almost
human, though squat and heavily muscled. Their skin
was green, and they wore no clothes. There was no nose,
aside from two orifices under their curiously flat ears that
quivered as if in breathing. But they were human enough
to pass for deformed men, if they were worked on by
good make-up men.

They were creatures of God, just as he was! And as
such, could he deny them? Then his mind recoiled, remembering the atrocities they had committed, the tor-
tures that had been reported, and the utter savagery so
out of keeping with their inconceivably advanced ships.
They were things of evil who had denied their birthright
as part of God's domain. For evil, there could be only

hatred. And from evil, how could there be worship of anything but the powers of darkness?

The thought of worship triggered his mind into an awareness of his need to prepare a sermon for the evening. It would have to be something simple; both he and his congregation were in no mood for rationalizations. Tonight he would have to serve God through their emotions. The thought frightened him. He tried to cling for strength to the brief moment of glory he had felt in the morning, but even that seemed far away.

There was the wail of a siren outside, rising to an ear-shattering crescendo, and the muffled sound of a loud-speaker driven beyond its normal operating level.

He stood up at last and moved out onto the porch with Doc as the tank came by. It was limping on treads that seemed to be about to fall apart, and the amplifier and speakers were mounted crudely on top. It pushed down the street, repeating its message over and over.

"Get out of town! Everybody clear out! This is an order to evacuate! The snakes are coming! Human forces have been forced to retreat to regroup. The snakes are heading this way, heading toward Topeka. They are looting and killing as they go. Get out of town! Everybody clear out!"

It paused, and another voice blared out, sounding like that of the major who had stopped before. "Get the hell out, all of you! Get out while you've still got your skins outside of you. We been licked. Shut up, Blake! We've had the holy living pants beat off us, and we're going back to momma. Get out, scram, vamoose! The snakes are coming! Beat it!"

It staggered down the street, rumbling its message, and now other stragglers began following it—men in cars, piled up like cattle; men in carts of any kind, drawn by horses. Then another amplifier sounded from one of the wagons.

"Stay under cover until night! Then get out! The snakes won't be here at once. Keep cool. Evacuate in order, and under cover of darkness. We're holing up ourselves when we get to a safe place. This is your last warning. Stay under cover now, and evacuate as soon as it's dark."

There was a bleating from the sky, and alien planes began dipping down. Doc pulled Amos back into the house, but not before he saw men being cut to ribbons by shots that seemed to fume and burst into fire as they hit. Some of the men on the retreat made cover. When the planes were gone, they came out and began regrouping, leaving the dead and hauling the wounded with them.

"Those men need me!" Amos protested.

"So does Ruth," Doc told him. "Besides, we're too old, Amos. We'd only get in the way. They have their own doctors and chaplains, probably. They're risking their lives to save us, damn it—they've piled all their worst cases there and left them to warn us and to decoy the planes away from the rest who are probably sneaking back through the woods and fields. They'd hate your guts for wasting what they're trying to do. I've been listening to one of the local stations, and it's pretty bad."

He turned on his heel and went back to the bedroom. The television program tardily began issuing evacuation orders to all citizens along the road from Clyde to Topeka, together with instructions. For some reason, the aliens seemed not to spot small objects in movement at night, and all orders were to wait until then.

Doc came out again, and Amos looked up at him, feeling his head bursting, but with one clear idea fixed in it. "Ruth can't be moved, can she, Doc?"

"No, Amos." Doc sighed. "But it won't matter. You'd better go in to her now. She seems to be coming to. I'll wake the girl and get her ready."

Amos went into the bedroom as quietly as he could, but there was no need for silence. Ruth was already conscious, as if some awareness of her approaching death had forced her to use the last few minutes of her life. She put out a frail hand timidly to him. Her voice was weak, but clear.

"Amos, I know. And I don't mind now, except for you. But there's something I had to ask you. Amos, do you——?"

He dropped beside her when her voice faltered, wanting to bury his head against her, but not daring to lose the few remaining moments of her sight. He fought the words out of the depths of his mind, and then realized it would take more than words. He bent over and kissed her again, as he had first kissed her so many years ago.

"I've always loved you, Ruth," he said. "I still do love you."

She sighed and relaxed. "Then I won't be jealous of God any more, Amos. I had to know."

Her hand reached up weakly, to find his hair and to run through it. She smiled, the worn lines of her face softening. Her voice was soft and almost young. "And forsaking all others, cleave only unto thee—"

The last syllable whispered out, and the hand dropped.

Amos dropped his head at last, and a single sob choked out of him. He folded her hands tenderly, with the worn, cheap wedding ring uppermost, and arose slowly with his head bowed.

"Then shall the dust return to the earth as it was; and the spirit shall return unto God who gave it. Father, I thank thee for this moment with her. Bless her, O Lord, and keep her for me."

He nodded to Doc and Anne. The girl looked sick and sat staring at him with eyes that mixed shock and pity.

"You'll need some money, Anne," he told her as Doc went into the bedroom. "I don't have much, but there's a little—"

She drew back, choking, and shook her head. "I've got enough, Reverend Strong. I'll make out. Doctor Miller has told me to take his car. But what about you?"

"There's still work to be done," he said. "I haven't even written my sermon. And the people who are giving up their homes will need comfort. In such hours as these, we all need God to sustain us."

She stumbled to her feet and into the bedroom after Miller. Amos opened his old desk and reached for pencil and paper.

### III

*The wicked have drawn out the sword, and have bent their bow, to cast down the poor and needy, and to slay such as be of upright conversation.*

*I have seen the wicked in great power, and spreading himself like a green bay tree.*

PSALMS, XXXVII, 14, 35

Darkness was just beginning to fall when they helped

Anne out into the doctor's car, making sure that the tank was full. She was quiet, and had recovered herself, but avoided Amos whenever possible. She turned at last to Doc Miller.

"What are you going to do? I should have asked before, but——"

"Don't worry about me, girl," he told her, his voice as hearty as when he was telling an old man he still had forty years to live. "I've got other ways. The switchboard girl is going to be one of the last to leave, and I'm driving her in her car. You go ahead, the way we mapped it out. And pick up anyone else you find on the way. It's safe; it's still too early for men to start turning to looting, rape, or robbery. They'll think of that a little later."

She held out a hand to him, and climbed in. At the last minute, she pressed Amos' hand briefly. Then she stepped on the accelerator and the car took off down the street at its top speed.

"She hates me," Amos said. "She loves men too much and God too little to understand."

"And maybe you love your God too much to understand that you love men, Amos. Don't worry, she'll figure it out. The next time you see her, she'll feel different. I'll see you later."

Doc swung off toward the telephone office, carrying his bag. Amos watched him, puzzled as always at anyone who could so fervently deny God and yet could live up to every commandment of the Lord except worship. They had been friends for a long time, while the parish stopped fretting about it and took it for granted, yet the riddle was no nearer solution.

There was the sound of a great rocket landing, and the smaller stuttering of the peculiar alien ram-jets. The ships passed directly overhead, yet there was no shooting this time.

Amos faced the bedroom window for a moment, and then turned toward the church. He opened it, throwing the doors wide. There was no sign of the sexton, but he had rung the bell in the tower often enough before. He took off his worn coat and grabbed the rope.

It was hard work, and his hands were soft. Once it had been a pleasure, but now his blood seemed too thin to suck up the needed oxygen. The shirt stuck wetly to his back, and he felt giddy when he finished.

Almost at once, the telephone in his little office began jangling nervously. He staggered to it, panting as he lifted it, to hear the voice of Nellie, shrill with fright. "Reverend, what's up? Why's the bell ringing?"

"For prayer meeting, of course," he told her. "What else?"

"Tonight? Well, I'll be—" She hung up.

He lighted a few candles and put them on the altar, where their glow could be seen from the dark street, but where no light would shine upwards for alien eyes. Then he sat down to wait, wondering what was keeping the organist.

There were hushed calls from the street and nervous cries. A car started, to be followed by another. Then a group took off at once. He went to the door, partly for the slightly cooler air. All along the street, men were moving out their possessions and loading up, while others took off. They waved to him, but hurried on by. He heard telephones begin to ring, but if Nellie was passing on some urgent world, she had forgotten him.

He turned back to the altar, kneeling before it. There was no articulate prayer in his mind. He simply clasped his gnarled fingers together and rested on his knee, looking up at the outward symbol of his life. Outside, the sounds went on, blending together. It did not matter whether anyone chose to use the church tonight. It was open, as the house of God must always be in times of stress. He had long since stopped trying to force religion on those not ready for it.

And slowly, the strains of the day began to weave themselves into the pattern of his life. He had learned to accept; from the death of his baby daughter on, he had found no way to end the pain that seemed so much a part of life. But he could bury it behind the world of his devotion, and meet whatever his lot was to be without anger at the will of the Lord. Now, again, he accepted things as they were ordered.

There was a step behind him. He turned, not bothering to rise, and saw the dressmaker, Angela Anduccini, hesitating at the door. She had never entered, though she had lived in Wesley since she was eighteen. She crossed herself doubtfully, and waited.

He stood up. "Come in, Angela. This is the house of God, and all His daughters are welcome."

There was a dark, tight fear in her eyes as she glanced back to the street. "I thought—maybe the organ—"

He opened it for her and found the switch. He started to explain the controls, but the smile on her lips warned him that it was unnecessary. Her calloused fingers ran over the stops, and she began playing, softly as if to herself. He went back to one of the pews, listening. For two years he had blamed the organ, but now he knew that there was no fault with the instrument, but only with its player before. The music was somtimes strange for his church, but he liked it.

A couple who had moved into the old Surrey farm beyond the town came in, holding hands, as if holding each other up. And a minute later, Buzz Williams stumbled in and tried to tiptoe down the aisle to where Amos sat. Since his parents had died, he'd been the town problem. Now he was half-drunk, though without his usual boisterousness.

"I ain't got no car and I been drinking," he whispered. "Can I say here till maybe somebody comes or something?"

Amos sighed, motioning Buzz to a seat where the boy's eyes had centered. Somewhere, there must be a car for the four waifs who had remembered God when everything else had failed them. If one of the young couple could drive, and he could locate some kind of a vehicle, it was his duty to see that they were sent to safety.

Abruptly, the haven of the church and the music came to an end, leaving him back in the real world—a curiously unreal world now.

He was heading down the steps, trying to remember whether the Jameson boy had taken his flivver, when a panel truck pulled up in front of the church. Doc Miller got out, wheezing as he squeezed through the door.

He took in the situation at a glance. "Only four strays, Amos? I thought we might have to pack them in." He headed for Buzz. "I've got a car outside, Buzz. Gather up the rest of this flock and get going!"

"I been drinking," Buzz said, his face reddening hotly.

"Okay, you've been drinking. At least you know it,

and there's no traffic problem. Head for Salina and hold it under forty and you'll be all right." Doc swept little Angela Anduccini from the organ and herded her out, while Buzz collected the couple. "Get going, all of you!"

They got, with Buzz enthroned behind the wheel and Angela beside him. The town was dead. Amos closed the organ and began shutting the doors to the church.

"I've got a farm tractor up the street for us, Amos," Doc said at last. "I almost ran out of tricks. There were more fools than you'd think who thought they could hide out right here. At that, I probably missed some. Well, the tractor's nothing elegant, but it can take those back roads. We'd better get going."

Amos shook his head. He had never thought it out, but the decision had been in his mind from the beginning. Ruth still lay waiting a decent burial. He could no more leave her now than when she was alive. "You'll have go alone, Doc."

"I figured." The doctor sighed, wiping the sweat from his forehead. ". . . I'd remember to my dying day that believers have more courage than an atheist! No sale, Amos. It isn't sensible, but that's how I feel. We'd better put out the candles, I guess."

Amos snuffed them reluctantly, wondering how he could persuade the other to leave. His ears had already caught the faint sounds of shooting; the aliens were on their way.

The uncertain thumping of a laboring motor sounded from the street, to wheeze to silence. There was a shout, a pause, and the motor caught again. It might have run for ten seconds before it backfired, and was still.

Doc opened one of the doors. In the middle of the street, a man was pushing an ancient car while his wife steered. But it refused to start again. He grabbed for tools, threw up the hood, and began a frantic search for the trouble.

"If you can drive a tractor, there's one half a block down," Doc called out.

The man looked up, snapped one quick glance behind him, and pulled the woman hastily out of the car. In almost no time, the heavy roar of the tractor sounded. The man revved it up to full trottle and tore off down the road, leaving Doc and Amos stranded. The sounds of the aliens were clearer now, and there was some light coming from beyond the bend of the street.

There was no place to hide. They found a window where the paint on the imitation stained glass was loose, and peeled it back enough for a peephole. The advance scouts of the aliens were already within view. They were dashing from house to house. Behind them, they left something that sent up clouds of glowing smoke that seemed to have no fire connected to their brilliance. At least, no buildings were burning.

Just as the main group of aliens came into view, the door of one house burst open. A scrawny man leaped out, with his fat wife and fatter daughter behind him. They raced up the street, tearing at their clothes and scratching frantically at their reddened skin.

Shots sounded. All three jerked, but went racing on. More shots sounded. At first, Amos thought it was incredibly bad shooting. Then he realized that it was even more unbelieveably good marksmanship. The aliens were shooting at the hands first, then moving up the arms methodically, wasting no chance for torture.

For the first time in years. Amos felt fear and anger curdle solidly in his stomach. He stood up, feeling his shoulders square back and his head come up as he moved toward the door. His lips were moving in words that he only half understood. "Arise, O Lord; O God, lift up thine hand; forget not the humble. Wherefore doth the wicked condemn God? He had said in his heart, Thou wilt not requite it. Thou hast seen it, for thou beholdest mischief and spite, to requite it with thy hand: the poor committeth himself unto thee; thou art the helper of the fatherless. Break thou the arm of the wicked and the evil ones; seek out their wickedness till thou find none . . ."

"Stop it, Amos!" Doc's voice rasped harshly in his ear. "Don't be a fool! And you're misquoting that last verse!"

It cut through the fog of his anger. He knew that Doc had deliberately reminded him of his father, but the trick worked, and the memory of his father's anger of misquotations replaced his cold fury. "We can't let that go on!"

Then he saw it was over. They had used up their targets. But there was the sight of another wretch, unrecognizable in half of his skin . . .

Doc's voice was as sick as he felt. "We can't do anything, Amos. I can't understand a race smart enough to build star ships and still going in for this. But it's good for our side, in the long run. While our armies are organizing, they're wasting time on this. And it makes resistance tougher, too."

The aliens didn't confine their sport to humans. They worked just as busily on a huge old tomcat they found. And all the corpses were being loaded onto a big wagon pulled by twenty of the creatures.

The aliens obviously had some knowledge of human behavior. At first they had passed up all stores, and had concentrated on living quarters. The scouts had passed on by the church without a second glance. But they moved into a butcher shop at once, to come out again, carrying meat which was piled on the wagon with the corpses.

Now a group was assembling before the church, pointing up toward the steeple where the bell was. Two of them shoved up a mortar of some sort. It was pointed quickly and a load was dropped in. There was a muffled explosion, and the bell rang sharply, its pieces rattling down the roof and into the yard below.

Another shoved the mortar into a new position, aiming it straight for the door of the church. Doc yanked Amos down between two pews. "They don't like churches, damn it! A fine spot we picked. Watch out for splinters!"

The door smashed in and a heavy object struck the altar, ruining it and ricocheting onto the organ. Amos groaned at the sound it made.

There was no further activity when they slipped back to their peepholes. The aliens were on the march again, moving along slowly. In spite of the delta planes, they seemed to have no motorized ground vehicles, and the wagon moved on under the power of the twenty green-skinned things, coming directly in front of the church.

Amos stared at it in the flickering light from the big torches burning in the hands of some of the aliens. Most of the corpses were strangers to him. A few he knew. And then his eyes picked out the twisted, distorted upper part of Ruth's body, her face empty in death's relaxation.

He stood up wearily, and this time Doc made no effort to stop him. He walked down a line of pews and around the wreck of one of the doors. Outside the church, the air was still hot and dry, but he drew a long breath into his lungs. The front of the chuch was in the shadows, and no aliens seemed to be watching him.

He moved down the stone steps. His legs were firm now. His heart was pounding heavily, but the clot of feelings that rested leadenly in his stomach had no fear left in it. Nor was there any anger left, nor any purpose.

He saw the aliens stop and stare at him, while a jabbering began among them.

He moved forward with the measured tread that had led him to his wedding the first time. He came to the wagon, and put his hand out, lifting one of Ruth's dead-limp arms back across her body.

"This is my wife," he told the staring aliens quietly. "I am taking her home with me."

He reached up and began trying to move the other bodies away from her. Without surprise, he saw Doc's arms moving up to help him, while a steady stream of whispered profanity came forom the man's lips.

He hadn't expected to succeed. He had expected nothing.

Abruptly, a dozen of the aliens leaped for the two men. Amos let them overpower him without resistance. For a second, Doc struggled, and then he too relaxed while the aliens bound them and tossed them onto the wagon.

## IV

*He hath bent his bow like an enemy: he stood with his right hand as an adversary, and slew all that were pleasant to the eye in the tabernacle of the daughter of Zion: he poured out his fury like fire.*

*The Lord was as an enemy: he hath swallowed up Israel, he hath swallowed up all her palaces: he hath destroyed his strong holds, and hath increased in the daughter of Judah mourning and lamentation.*

*The Lord hath cast off his altar, he hath abhorred his sanctuary, he hath given up into the hand of the enemy the walls of her palaces; they have made a noise in the house of the Lord, as in the day of a solemn feast.*

LAMENTATIONS, II, 4, 5, 7

Amos' first reaction was one of dismay at the ruin of

his only good suit. He struggled briefly on the substance under him, trying to find a better spot. A minister's suit might be old, but he could never profane the altar with such stains as these. Then some sense of the ridiculousness of his worry reached his mind, and he relaxed as best he could.

He had done what he had to do, and it was too late to regret it. He could only accept the consequences of it now, as he had learned to accept everything else God had seen fit to send him. He had never been a man of courage, but the strength of God had sustained him through as much as most men had to bear. It would sustain him further.

Doc was facing him, having flopped around to lie facing toward him. Now the doctor's lips twisted into a crooked grin. "I guess we're in for it now. But it won't last forever, and maybe we're old enough to die fast. At least, once we're dead, we won't know it, so there's no sense being afraid of dying."

If it was meant to provoke him into argument, it failed. Amos considered it a completely hopeless philosophy, but it was better than none, probably. His own faith in the hereafter left something to be desired; he was sure of immortality and the existence of heaven and hell, but he had never been able to picture either to his own satisfaction.

The wagon had been swung around and was now being pulled up the street, back toward Clyde. Amos tried to take his mind off the physical discomforts of the ride by watching the houses, counting them to his own. They drew near it finally, but it was Doc who spotted the important fact. He groaned. "My car!"

Amos strained his eyes, staring into the shadows through the glare of the torches. Doc's car stood at the side of the house, with the door open! Someone must have told Anne that he hadn't left, and she'd swung back around the alien horde to save him!

He began a prayer that they might pass on without the car being noticed, and it seemed at first that they would. Then there was a sudden cry from the house, and he saw her face briefly at the front window. She must have seen Doc and himself lying on the wagon!

He opened his mouth to risk a warning, but it was too late. The door swung back, and she was standing on the front steps, lifting Richard's rifle to her shoulder. Amos' heart seemed to hesitate with the tension of his body. The aliens still hadn't noticed. If she'd only wait . . .

The rifle cracked. Either by luck or some skill he hadn't suspected, one of the aliens dropped. She was running forward now, throwing another cartridge into the barrel. The gun barked again, and an alien fell to the ground, bleating horribly.

There was no attempt at torture this time, at least. The leading alien jerked out a tubelike affair from a scabbard at his side and a single sharp explosion sounded. Anne jerked backward as the heavy slug hit her forehead, the rifle spinning from her dead hands.

The wounded alien was trying frantically to crawl away. Two of his fellows began working on him mercilessly, with as little feeling as if he had been a human. His body followed that of Anne toward the front of the wagon, just beyond Amos's limited view.

She hadn't seemed hysterical this time, Amos thought wearily. It had been her tendency to near hysteria that had led to his advising Richard to wait, not the difference in faith. Now he was sorry he'd had no chance to understand her better.

Doc sighed, and there was a peculiar pride under the thickness of his voice. "Man," he said, "has one virtue which is impossible to any omnipotent force like your God. He can be brave. He can be brave beyond sanity, for another man or for an idea. Amos, I pity your God if man ever makes war on Him!"

Amos flinched, but the blasphemy aroused only a shadow of his normal reaction. His mind seemed numbed. He lay back, watching black clouds scudding across the sky almost too rapidly. It looked unnatural, and he remembered how often the accounts had mentioned a tremendous storm that had wrecked or hampered the efforts of human troops. Maybe a counteract had begun, and this was part of the alien defense. If they had some method of weather control, it was probable. The moonlight was already blotted out by the clouds.

Half a mile further on, there was a shout from the aliens, and a big tractor chugged into view, badly driven by one of the aliens, who had obviously only partly mastered the human machine. With a great deal of trial and error, it was backed into position and coupled to the wagon. Then it began churning along at nearly thirty miles an hour, while the big wagon bucked and bounced behind. From then on, the ride was physical hell. Even Doc groaned at some of the bumps, though his bones had three times more padding than Amos'.

Mercifully, they slowed when they reached Clyde. Amos wiped the blood off his bitten lip and managed to wriggle to a position where most of the bruises were on his upper side. There was a flood of brilliant lights beyond the town where the alien rockets stood, and he could see a group of non-human machines busy unloading the great ships. But the drivers of the machines looked totally unlike the other aliens.

One of the alien trucks swung past them, and he had a clear view of the creature steering it. It bore no resemblance to humanity. There was a conelike trunk, covered with a fine white down, ending in four thick stalks to serve as legs. From its broadest point, four sinuous limbs spread out to the truck controls. There was no head, but only eight small tentacles waving above it.

He saw a few others, always in control of machines, and no machines being handled by the green-skinned people as they passed through the ghost city that had been Clyde. Apparently there were two races allied against humanity, which explained why such barbarians could come in space ships. The green ones must be simply the fighters, while the downy cones were the technicians. From their behavior, though, the pilots of the planes must be recruited from the fighters.

Clyde had grown since he had been there, unlike most of the towns about. There was a new supermarket just down the street from Amos' former church, and the tractor jolted to a stop in front of it. Aliens swarmed out and began carrying the loot from the wagon into its big food lockers, while two others lifted Doc and Amos.

But they weren't destined for the comparatively merciful death of freezing in the lockers. The aliens threw them into a little cell that had once apparently been a cashier's cage, barred from floor to ceiling. It made a fairly efficient jail, and the lock that clicked shut as the door closed behind them was too heavy to be broken.

There was already one occupant—a medium-built young

man whom Amos finally recognized as Smithton, the Clyde dentist. His shoulders were shaking with sporadic sobs as he sat huddled in one corner. He looked at the two arrivals without seeing them. "But I surrendered," he whispered. "I'm a prisoner of war. They can't do it. I surrendered—"

A fatter-than-usual alien, wearing the only clothes Amos had seen on any of them, came waddling up to the cage, staring in at them, and the dentist wailed off into silence. The alien drew up his robe about his chest and scratched his rump against a counter without taking his eyes off them. "Humans," he said in a grating voice, but without an accent, "are peculiar. No standardization."

"I'll be damned!" Doc swore. "English!"

The alien studied them with what might have been surprise, lifting his ears. "Is the gift of tongues so unusual, then? Many of the priests of the Lord God Almighty speak all the human languages. It's a common miracle, not like levitation."

"Fine. Then maybe you'll tell us what we've being held for?" Doc suggested.

The priest shrugged. "Food, of course. The *grethi* eat any kind of meat—even our people—but we have to examine the laws to find whether you're permitted. If you are, we'll need freshly killed specimens to sample, so we're waiting with you."

"You mean you're attacking us for *food?*"

The priest grunted harshly. "No! We're on a holy mission to exterminate you. The Lord commanded us to go down to Earth where abominations existed and to leave no living creature under your sun."

He turned and waddled out of the store, taking the single remaining torch with him, leaving only the dim light of the moon and reflections from further away.

Amos dropped onto a stool inside the cage. "They had to lock us in a new building instead of one I know," he said. "If it had been the church, we might have had a chance."

"How?" Doc asked sharply.

Amos tried to describe the passage through the big, unfinished basement under the church, reached through a trap door. Years before, a group of teen-agers had built a sixty-foot tunnel into it and had used it for a private club until the passage had been discovered and bricked over from outside. The earth would be soft around the bricks, however. Beyond, the outer end of the tunnel opened in a wooded section, which led to a drainage ditch that in turn connected with the Republican River. From the church, they could have moved to the stream and slipped down that without being seen, unlike most of the other sections of the town.

Doc's fingers were trembling on the lock when Amos finished. "If we could get the two hundred feet to the church—They didn't know much about us, Amos, if they lock us in where the lock screws are on our side. Well, we'll have to chance it."

Amos' own fingers shook as he felt the screwheads. He could see what looked like a back door to the store. If they could come out into the alley that had once been there, they could follow it nearly to the church—and then the trees around that building would cut off most of the light. It would be a poor chance. But was it chance? It seemed more like the hand of God to him.

"More like the carelessness of the aliens to me," Doc objected. "It would probably be a lot less complicated in most other places, the way they light the town. Knock the bottom out of the money drawer and break off two slats. I've got a quarter that fits these screws."

Smithton fumbled with the drawer, praying now—a childhood prayer for going to sleep. But he succeeded in getting two slats Doc could place the quarter between.

It was rough going, with more slipping than turning of the screws, but the lock had been meant to keep outsiders out, not cashiers in. Three of the screws came loose, and the lock rotated on the fourth until they could force the cage open.

Doc stopped and pulled Smithton to him. "Follow me, and do what I do. No talking, no making a separate break, or I'll break your neck. All right!"

The back door was locked, but on the inside. They opened it to a backyard filled with garbage. The alley wasn't as dark as it should have been, since open lots beyond let some light come through. They hugged what shadows they could until they reached the church hedge. There they groped along, lining themselves up with the side office door. There was no sign of aliens.

Amos broke ahead of the others, being more familiar with the church. It wasn't until he had reached the door that he realized it could have been locked; it had been kept that way part of the time. He grabbed the handle and forced it back—to find it open!

For a second, he stopped to thank the Lord for their luck. Then the others were with him, crowding into the little kitchen where social suppers were prepared. He'd always hated those functions, but now he blessed them for a hiding place that gave them time to find their way.

There were sounds in the church, and odors, but none that seemed familiar to Amos. Something made the back hairs of his neck prickle. He took off his shoes and tied them around his neck, and the others followed suit.

The trap door lay down a small hall, across in front of the altar, and in the private office on the other side.

They were safer together than separated, particularly since Smithton was with them. Amos leaned back against the kitchen wall to catch his breath. His heart seemed to have a ring of needled pain around it, and his throat was so dry that he had to fight desperately against gagging. There was water here, but he couldn't risk rummaging across the room to the sink.

He was praying for strength, less for himself than the others. Long since, he had resigned himself to die. If God willed his death, he was ready; all he had were dead and probably mutilated, and he had succeeded only in dragging those who tried to help him into mortal danger. He was old, and his body was already treading its way to death. He could live for probably twenty more years, but aside from his work there was nothing to live for—and even in that, he had been only a mediocre failure. But he was still responsible for Doc Miller, and even for Smithton now.

He squeezed his eyes together and squinted around the doorway. There was some light in the hall that led toward the altar, but he could see no one, and there were drapes that gave a shadow from which they could spy the rest of their way. He moved to it softly, and felt the others come up behind him.

He bent forward, parting the drapes a trifle. They were perhaps twenty feet in front of the altar, on the right side. He spotted the wreckage that had once stood as an altar. Then he frowned as he saw evidence of earth piled up into a mound of odd shape.

He drew the cloth back further, surprised at the curiosity in him, as he had been surprised repeatedly by the changes taking place in himself.

There were two elaborately robed priests kneeling in the center of the chapel. But his eye barely noticed them before it was attracted to what stood in front of the new altar.

A box of wood rested on an earthenware platform. On it were four marks which his eyes recognized as unfamiliar, but which his mind twisted into a sequence from the alphabets he had learned, unpronounceable yet compelling. And above the box was a veil, behind which Something shone brightly without light.

In his mind, a surge of power pulsed, making patterns that might almost have been words through his thoughts— words like the words Moses once had heard—words that Amos, heartsick, knew. . . .

"I AM THAT I AM, who brought those out of bondage from Egypt and who wrote upon the wall before Belshazzar, MENE, MENE, TEKEL, UPHARSIN, as it shall be writ large upon the Earth, from this day forth. For I have said unto the seed of Mikhtchah, thou art my chosen people and I shall exalt thee above all the races under the heavens!"

### V

*And it was given unto him to make war with the saints, and to overcome them: and power was given him over all kindreds, and tongues, and nations.*

*He that leadeth into captivity shall go into captivity; he that killeth with the sword must be killed with the sword.*

REVELALTIONS, XIII, 7, 10

The seed of Mikhtchah. The seed of the invaders. . . .

There was no time and all time, then, Amos felt his heart stop, but the blood pounded through his arteries with a vigor it had lacked for decades. He felt Ruth's hand in his, stirring with returning life, and knew she had never existed. Beside him, he saw Doc Miller's hair turn snow-white and knew that it was so, though there was no way he could see Doc from his position.

He felt the wrath of the Presence rest upon him, weighing his every thought from his birth to his certain death, where he ceased completely and went on forever, and yet he knew that the Light behind the veil was unaware of him, but was receptive only to the two Mikhtchah priests who knelt, praying.

All of that was with but a portion of his mind so small that he could not locate it, though his total mind encompassed all time and space, and that which was neither; yet each part of his perceptions occupied all of his mind that had been or ever could be, save only the present, which somehow was a concept not yet solved by the One before him.

He saw a strange man on a low mountain, receiving tablets of stone that weighed only a pennyweight, engraved with a script that all could read. And he knew the man, but refused to believe it, since the garmcnts were not those of his mental image, and the clean-cut face fitted better with the strange headpiece than with the langauge the man spoke.

He saw every prayer of his life tabulated. But nowhere was there the mantle of divine warmth which he had felt as a boy and had almost felt again the morning before. And there was a stirring of unease at his thought, mixed with wrath; yet while the thought was in his mind, nothing could touch him.

Each of those things was untrue, because he could find no understanding of that which was true.

It ended as abruptly as it had begun, either a microsecond or a million subjective years after. It left him numbed, but newly alive. And it left him dead as no man had ever been hopelessly dead before.

He knew only that before him was the Lord God Almighty. He who had made a covenant with Abraham, with Isaac, and with Jacob, and with their seed. And he knew that the covenant was ended. Mankind had been rejected, while God now was on the side of the enemies of Abraham's seed, the enemies of all the nations of the earth.

Even that was too much for a human mind no longer in touch with the Presence, and only a shadow of it remained.

Beside him, Amos heard Doc Miller begin breathing again, brushing the white hair back from his forehead wonderingly as he muttered a single word, "God!"

One of the Mikhtchah priests looked up, his eyes turning about; there had been a glazed look on his face, but it was changing.

Then Smithton screamed! His open mouth poured out a steady, unwavering screaming, while his lungs panted in and out. His eyes opened, staring horribly. Like a wooden doll on strings, the men stood up and walked forward. He avoided the draperies and headed for the Light behind the veil. Abruptly, the Light was gone, but Smithton walked toward it as steadily as before. He stopped before the falling veil, and the scream cut off sharply.

Doc had jerked silently to his feet, tugging Amos up behind him. The minister lifted himself, but he knew there was no place to go. It was up to the will of God now . . . Or . . .

Smithton turned on one heel precisely. His face was rigid and without expression, yet completely mad. He walked mechanically forward toward the two priests. They sprawled aside at the last second, holding two obviously human-made automatics, but making no effort to use them. Smithton walked on toward the open door at the front of the church.

He reached the steps, with the two priests staring after him. His feet lifted from the first step to the second and then he was on the sidewalk.

The two priests fired!

Smithton jerked, halted, and suddenly cried out in a voice of normal, rational agony. His legs kicked frantically under him and he ducked out of the sight of the doorway, his faltering steps sounding further and further away. He was dead—the Mikhtchah marksmanship had been as good as it seemed always to be—but still moving, though slower and slower, as if some extra charge of life were draining out like a battery running down.

The priests exchanged quick glances and then darted after him, crying out as they dashed around the door into the night. Abruptly, a single head and hand appeared again, to snap a shot at the draperies from which Smithton had come. Amos forced himself to stand still, while his imagination supplied the jolt of lead in his stomach. The bullet hit the draperies, and something else.

The priest hesitated, and was gone again.

Amos broke into a run across the chapel and into the hall at the other side of the altar. He heard the faint sound of Doc's feet behind him.

The trap door was still there, unintentionally concealed under carpeting. He forced it up and dropped through it into the four-foot depth of the uncompleted basement, making room for Doc. They crouched together as he lowered the trap and began feeling his way through the blackness toward the other end of the basement. It had been five years since he had been down there, and then only once for a quick inspection of the work of the boys who had dug the tunnel.

He thought he had missed it at first, and began groping for the small entrance. It might have caved in, for that matter. Then, two feet away, his hand found the hole and he drew Doc after him.

It was cramped, and bits of dirt had fallen in places and had to be dug out of the way. Part of the distance was covered on their stomachs. They found the bricked-up wall ahead of them and began digging around it with their bare hands. It took another ten minutes, while distant sounds of wild yelling from the Mikhtchah reached them faintly. They broke through at last with bleeding hands, not bothering to check for aliens near. They reached a safer distance in the woods, caught their breath, and went on.

The biggest danger lay in the drainage trench, which was low in several places. But luck was with them, and those spots lay in the shadow.

Then the little Republican River lay in front of them, and there was a flatbottom boat nearby.

Moments later, they were floating down the stream, resting their aching lungs, while the boat needed only a trifling guidance. It was still night, with only the light from the moon, and there was little danger in pursuit by the alien planes. Amos could just see Doc's face as the man fumbled for a cigarette.

He lighted it and exhaled deeply. "All right, Amos— you were right, and God exists. But damn it, I don't feel any better for knowing that. I can't see how God helps me—nor even how He's doing the Mikhtchah much good. What do they get out of it, beyond a few miracles with the weather? They're just doing God's dirty work."

"They get the Earth, I suppose—if they want it," Amos said doubtfully. He wasn't sure they did. Nor could he see how the other aliens tied into the scheme; if he had known the answers, they were gone now. "Doc, you're still an atheist, though you now know God is."

The plump man chuckled bitterly. "I'm afraid you're right. But at least I'm myself. You can't be, Amos. You've spent your whole life on the gamble that God is right and that you must serve him—when the only way you could serve was to help mankind. What do you do now? God is automatically right—but everything you've ever believed makes Him completely wrong, and you can only serve Him by betraying your people. What kind of ethics will work for you now?"

Amos shook his head wearily, hiding his face in his hands. The same problem had been fighting its way through his own thoughts. His first reaction had been to acknowledge his allegiance to God without question; sixty years of conditioned thought lay behind that. Yet now he could not accept such a decision. As a man, he could not bow to what he believed completely evil, and the Mikhtchah were evil by every definition he knew.

Could he tell people the facts, and take away what faith they had in any purpose in life? Could he go over to the enemy, who didn't even want him, except for their feeding experiments? Or could he encourage people to fight with the old words that God was with them—when he knew the words were false, and their resistance might doom them to eternal hellfire for opposing God?

It hit him then that he could remember nothing clearly about the case of the hereafter—either for or against it. What happened to the people when God deserted them? Were they only deserted in their physical form, and still free to win their spiritual salvation? Or were they completely lost? Did they cease to have souls that could survive? Or were those souls automatically consigned to hell, however noble they might be?

No question had been answered for him. He knew that God existed, but he had known that before. He knew nothing now beyond that. He did not even know when

God had placed the Mikhtchah before humanity. It seemed unlikely that it was as recent as his own youth. Yet otherwise, how could he account for the strange spiritual glow he had felt as an evangelist?

"There's only one rational answer," he said at last. "It doesn't make any difference what I decide! I'm only one man."

"So was Columbus when he swore the world was round. And he didn't have the look on his face you've had since we saw God, Amos! I know now what the Bible means when it says Moses' face shone after he came down from the mountain, until he had to cover it with a veil. If I'm right, God help mankind if you decide wrong!"

Doc tossed the cigarette over the side and lighted another, and Amos was shocked to see that the man's hands were shaking. The doctor shrugged, and his tone fell back to normal. "I wish we knew more. You've always thought almost exclusively in terms of the Old Testament and a few snatches of Revelations—like a lot of men who become evangelists. I've never really thought about God—I couldn't accept Him, so I dismissed Him. Maybe that's why we got the view of Him we did. I wish I knew where Jesus fits it, for instance. There's too much missing. Too many imponderables and hiatuses. We have only two facts, and we can't understand either. There is a manifestation of God which has touched both Mikhtchah and mankind; and He has stated now that he plans to wipe out mankind. We'll have to stick to that."

Amos made one more attempt to deny the problem that was facing him. "Suppose God is only testing man again, as He did so often before?"

"Testing?" Doc rolled the word on his tongue, and seemed to spit it out. The strange white hair seemed to make him older, and the absence of mockery in his voice left him almost a stranger. "Amos, the Hebrews worked like the devil to get Canaan; after forty years of wandering around a few square miles God suddenly told them this was the land—and then they had to take it by the same methods men have always used to conquer a country. The miracles didn't really decide anything. They got out of Babylon because the old prophets were slaving night and day to hold them together as one people, and because they managed to sweat it out until they finally got a break. In our own time, they've done the same things to get Israel, and with no miracles! It seems to me God took it away, but they had to get it back by themselves. I don't think much of that kind of a test in this case."

Amos could feel all his values slipping and spinning. He realized that he was holding himself together only because of Doc; otherwise, his mind would have reached for madness, like any intelligence forced to solve the insoluble. He could no longer comprehend himself, let alone God. And the feeling crept into his thoughts that God couldn't wholly understand Himself, either.

"Can a creation defy anything great enough to create it, Doc? And should it, if it can?"

"Most kids have to," Doc said. He shook his head. "It's your problem. All I can do is point a few things out. And maybe it won't matter, at that. We're still a long ways inside Mikhtchah territory, and it's getting along toward daylight."

The boat drifted on, while Amos tried to straighten out his thoughts and grew more deeply tangled in a web of confusion. What could any man who worshipped devoutly do if he found his God was opposed to all else he had ever believed to be good?

A version of Kant's categorical imperative crept into his mind; somebody had once quoted it to him—probably Doc. "So act as to treat humanity, whether in thine own person or in that of any other, in every case as an end withal, never as a means only." Was God now treating man as an end, or simply as a means to some purpose, in which man had failed? And had man ever seriously treated God as an end, rather than as a means to spiritual immortality and a quietus to the fear of death?

"We're being followed!" Doc whispered suddenly. He pointed back, and Amos could see a faint light shining around a curse in the stream. "Look—there's a building over there. When the boat touches shallow water, run for it!"

He bent to the oars, and a moment later they touched bottom and were over the side, sending the boat back into the current. The building was a hundred feet back from the bank, and they scrambled madly toward it. Even in the faint moonlight, they could see that the building was a wreck, long since abandoned. Doc went in through one of the broken windows, dragging Amos behind him.

Through a chink in the walls, they could see another boat heading down the stream, lighted by a torch and carrying two Mikhtchah. One rowed, while the other sat in the prow with a gun, staring ahead. They rowed on past.

"We'll have to hole up here," Doc decided. "It'll be light in half an hour. Maybe they won't think of searching a ruin like this."

They found rickety steps, and stretched out on the bare floor of a huge upstairs closet. Amos groaned as he tried to find a position in which he could get some rest. Then, surprisingly, he was asleep.

He woke once with traces of daylight coming into the closet, to hear sounds of heavy gunfire not far away. He was just drifting back to sleep when hail began cracking furiously down on the roof. When it passed, the gunfire was stilled.

Doc woke him when it was turning dark. There was nothing to eat, and Amos' stomach was sick with hunger. His body ached in every joint, and walking was pure torture. Doc glanced up at the stars, seemed to decide on a course, and struck out. He was wheezing and groaning in a way that indicated he shared Amos' feelings.

But he found enough energy to begin the discussion again. "I keep wondering what Smithton saw, Amos? It wasn't what we saw. And what about the legends of war in heaven? Wasn't there a big battle there once, in which Lucifer almost won? Maybe Lucifer simply stands for some other race God cast off?"

"Lucifer was Satan, the spirit of evil. He tried to take over God's domain."

"Mmm. I've read somewhere that we have only the account of the victor, which is apt to be pretty biased history. How do we know the real issues? Or the true outcome? At least he thought he had a chance, and he apparently knew what he was fighting."

The effort of walking made speech difficult. Amos shrugged, and let the conversation die. But his own mind ground on.

If God was all-powerful and all-knowing, why had He

let them spy upon Him? Or was He all-powerful over a race He had dismissed? Could it make any difference to God what man might try to do, now that He had condemned him? Was the Presence they had seen the whole of God—or only one manifestation of Him?

His legs moved on woodenly, numbed to fatigue and slow from hunger, while his head churned with his basic problem. Where was his duty now? With God or against Him?

They found food in a deserted house, and began preparing it by the hooded light of a lantern, while they listened to the news from a small battery radio that had been left behind. It was a hopeless account of alien landings and human retreats, yet given without the tone of despair they should have expected. They were halfway through the meal before they discovered the reason.

"Flash!" the radio announced. "Word has just come through from the Denver area. A second atomic missile, piloted by a suicide crew, has fallen successfully! The alien base has been wiped out, and every ship is ruined. It is now clear that the trouble with earlier bombing attempts lay in the detonating mechanism. This is being investigated, while more volunteers are being trained to replace this undependable part of the bomb. Both missiles carrying suicide bombers have succeeded. Captive aliens of both races are being questioned in Denver now, but the same religious fanaticism found in Portland seems to make communication difficult."

It went back to reporting alien landings, while Doc and Amos stared at each other. It was too much to absorb at once.

Amos groped in his mind, trying to dig out something that might tie in the success of human bombers, where automatic machinery was miraculously stalled, with the reaction of God to his thoughts of the glow he had felt in his early days. Something about man . . .

"They can be beaten!" Doc said in a harsh whisper.

Amos sighed as they began to get up to continue the impossible trek. "Maybe. We know God was at Clyde. Can we be sure He was at the other places to stop the bombs by His miracles?"

They slogged on through the night, cutting across country in the dim light, where every footstep was twice as hard. Amos turned it over, trying to use the new information for whatever decision he must reach. If men could overcome those opposed to them, even for a time . . .

It brought him no closer to an answer.

The beginnings of dawn found them in a woods. Doc managed to heave Amos up a tree, where he could survey the surrounding terrain. There was a house beyond the edge of the woods, but it would take dangerous minutes to reach it. They debated, and then headed on.

They were just emerging from the woods when the sound of an alien plane began its stuttering shriek. Doc turned and headed back to where Amos was behind him. Then he stopped. "Too late! He's seem something. Gotta have a target!"

His arms swept out, shoving Amos violently back under the nearest tree. He swung and began racing across the clearing, his fat legs pumping furiously as he covered the ground in straining leaps. Amos tried to lift himself from where he had fallen, but it was too late.

There was the drumming of gunfire and the earth erupted around Doc. He lurched and dropped, to twitch and lie still.

The plane swept over, while Amos disentangled himself from a root. It was gone as he broke free. Doc had given it a target, and the pilot was satisfied, apparently.

He was still alive as Amos dropped beside him. Two of the shots had hit, but he managed to grin as he lifted himself on one elbow. It was only a matter of minutes, however, and there was no help possible. Amos found one of Doc's cigarettes and lighted it with fumbling hands.

"Thanks," Doc wheezed after taking a heavy drag on it. He started to cough, but suppressed it, his face twisting in agony. His words came in an irregular rhythm, but he held his voice level. "I guess I'm going to hell, Amos, since I never did repent—if there is a hell! And I hope there is! I hope it's filled with the soul of every poor damned human being who died in less than perfect grace. Because I'm going to find some way—"

He straightened suddenly, coughing and fighting for breath. Then he found one final source of strength and met Amos' eyes, a trace of his old cynical smile on his face.

"—some way to open a recruiting station!" he finished. He dropped back, letting all the fight go out of his body. A few seconds later, he was dead.

# VI

*. . . Thou shalt have no other peoples before me . . .*
*Thou shalt make unto them no covenant against me. . . .*
*Thou shalt not forswear thyself to them, nor serve them*
*. . . for I am a jealous people . . .*

EXULTATIONS, XII, 2–4

Amos lay through the day in the house to which he had dragged Doc's body. He did not even look for food. For the first time in his life since his mother had died when he was five, he had no shield against his grief. There was no hard core of acceptance that it was God's will to hide his loss at Doc's death. And with the realization of that, all the other losses hit at him as if they had been no older than the death of Doc.

He sat with his grief and his newly sharpened hatred, staring toward Clyde. Once, during the day, he slept. He awakened to a sense of a tremendous sound and shaking of the earth, but all was quiet when he finally became conscious. It was nearly night, and time to leave.

For a moment, he hesitated. It would be easier to huddle here, beside his dead, and let whatever would happen come to him. But within him was a sense of duty that drove him on. In the back of his mind, something stirred, telling him he still had work to do.

He found part of a stale loaf of bread and some hard cheese and started out, munching on them. It was still too light to move safely, but he was going through woods again, and he heard no alien planes. When it grew darker, he turned to the side roads that led in the direction of Wesley.

In his mind was the knowledge that he had to return there. His church lay there; if the human fighters had pushed the aliens back, his people might be there. If not, it was from there that he would have to follow them.

His thoughts were too deep for conscious expression, and too numbed with exhaustion. His legs moved on steadily. One of his shoes had begun to wear through, and his feet were covered with blisters, but he went grimly on. It was his duty to lead his people, now that the aliens were there, as he had led them in easier times. His thinking had progressed no further.

He holed up in a barn that morning, avoiding the house because of the mutilated things that lay on the doorstep where the aliens had apparently left them. And this time he slept with the soundness of complete fatigue, but he awoke to find one fist clenched and extended toward Clyde. He had been dreaming that he was Job, and that God had left him sitting unanswered on his boils until he died, while mutilated corpses moaned around him, asking for leadership he would not give.

It was nearly dawn before he realized that he should have found himself some kind of a car. He had seen none, but there might have been one abandoned somewhere. Doc could probably have found one. It was too late to bother, then. He had come to the outskirts of a tiny town, and started to head beyond it, before realizing that all the towns must have been well searched by now. He turned down the small street, looking for a store where he could find food.

There was a small grocery with a door partly ajar. Amos pushed it open, to the clanging of a bell. Almost immediately, a dog began barking, and a human voice came sharply from the back.

"Down, Shep! Just a minute, I'm a-coming." A door to the rear opened, and a bent old man emerged, carrying a kerosene lamp. "Darned electric's off again! Good thing I stayed. Told them I had to mind my store, but they wanted me to get with them. Had to hide out in the old well. Darned nonsense about——"

He stopped, his eyes blinking behind thick lenses, and his mouth dropped open. He swallowed, and his voice was startled and shrill. *"Mister, who are you?"*

"A man who just escaped from the aliens," Amos told him. He hadn't realized the shocking appearance he must present by now. "One in need of food and a chance to rest until night. But I'm afraid I have no money on me."

The old man tore his eyes away slowly, seeming to shiver. Then he nodded, and pointed to the back. "Never turned nobody away hungry yet," he said, but the words seemed automatic.

An old dog backed slowly under a couch as Amos entered. The man put the lamp down and headed into a tiny kitchen to being preparing food. Amos reached for the lamp and blew it out. "There really are aliens—worse than you heard," he said.

The old man bristled, met his eyes, and then nodded slowly. "If *you* say so. Only it don't seem logical God would let things like that run around in a decent state like Kansas."

He shoved a plate of eggs onto the table, and Amos pulled it to him, swallowing a mouthful eagerly. He reached for a second, and stopped. Something was violently wrong, suddenly. His stomach heaved, the room began to spin, and his forehead was cold and wet with sweat. He gripped the edge of the table, trying to keep from falling. Then he felt himself being dragged to a cot. He tried to protect, but his body was shaking with ague, and the words that spilled out were senseless. He felt the cot under him, and waves of sick blackness spilled over him.

It was the smell of cooking food that awakened him finally, and he sat up with a feeling that too much time had passed. The old man came from the kitchen, studying him. "You sure were sick, Mister. Guess you ain't used to going without decent food and rest. Feeling okay?"

Amos nodded. He felt a little unsteady, but it was passing. He pulled on the clothes that had been somewhat cleaned for him, and found his way to the table. "What day is it?"

"Saturday, evening," the other answered. "At least the way I figure. Here, eat that and get some coffee in you." He watched until Amos began on the food, and then dropped to a stool to begin cleaning an old rifle and loading it. "You said a lot of things. They true?"

For a second, Amos hesitated. Then he nodded, unable to lie to his benefactor. "I'm afraid so."

"Yeah, I figured so, somehow, looking at you." The old man sighed. "Well, I hope you make wherever you're going."

"What about you?" Amos asked.

The old man sighed, running his hands along the rifle. "I ain't leaving my store for any bunch of aliens. And if the Lord I been doing my duty by all my life decides to put Himself on the wrong side, well, maybe He'll win. But it'll be over my dead body!"

Nothing Amos could say would change his mind. He sat on the front step of the store, the rifle on his lap and the dog at his side, as Amos headed down the street in the starlight.

The minister felt surprisingly better after the first half mile. Rest and food, combined with crude treatment of his sores and blister, had helped. But the voice inside him was driving him harder now, and the picture of the old man seemed to lend it added strength. He struck out at the fastest pace he could hope to maintain, leaving the town behind and heading down the road that the old man had said led to Wesley.

It was just after midnight that he saw the lights of a group of cars or trucks moving along another road. He had no idea whether they were driven by man or aliens, but he kept steadily on. There were sounds of traffic another time on a road that crossed the small one he followed. But he knew now he was approaching Wesley, and speeded up his pace.

When the first light came, he made no effort to seek shelter. He stared at the land around him, stripped by grasshoppers that could have been killed off if men had worked as hard at ending the insects as they had at their bickerings and wars. He saw the dry, arid land, drifting into dust, and turning a fertile country into a nightmare. Men could put a stop to that.

It had been no act of God that had caused this ruin, but man's own follies. And without help from God, man might set it right in time.

God had deserted man. But mankind hadn't halted. On his own, man had made a path to the moon and had unlocked the atom. He'd found a means, out of his raw courage, to use those bombs against the aliens when miracles were used against him. He had done everything but conquer himself—and he could do that, if he were given time.

Amos saw a truck stop at the crossroads ahead and halted, but the driver was human. He saw the open door and quickened his stop toward it. "I'm bound for Wesley!"

"Sure." The driver helped him into the seat. "I'm going back for more supplies myself. You sure look as if you need treatment at the aid station there. I thought we'd rounded up all you strays. Most of them come in right after we sent out the word on Clyde."

"You've taken it?" Amos asked.

The other nodded wearily. "We look it. Got 'em with a bomb, like sitting ducks, then we've been mopping up since. Not many aliens left."

They were nearing the outskirts of Wesley, and Amos pointed to his own house. "If you'll let me off there——"

"Look, I got orders to bring all strays to the aid station," the driver began firmly. Then he swung and faced Amos. For a second, he hesitated. Finally he nodded quietly. "Sure. Glad to help you."

Amos found the water still running. He bathed slowly. Somewhere, he felt his decision had been made, though he was still unsure of what it was. He climbed from the tub at last, and began dressing. There was no suit that was proper, but he found clean clothes. His face in the mirror looked back at him, haggard and bearded, as he reached for the razor.

Then he stopped as he encountered the reflection of his eyes. A shock ran over him, and he backed away a step. They were eyes foreign to everything in him. He had seen a shadow of what lay in them only once, in the eyes of a great evangelist; and this was a hundred times stronger. He tore his glance away to find himself shivering, and avoided them all through the shaving. Oddly, though, there was a strange satisfaction in what he had seen. He was beginning to understand why the old man had believed him, and why the truck driver had obeyed him.

Most of Wesley had returned, and there were soldiers on the streets. As he approached the church, he saw the first-aid station, hectic with business. And a camera crew was near it, taking shots for television of those who had managed to escape from alien territory after the bombing.

A few people called to him, but he went on until he reached the church steps. The door was still in ruins and the bell was gone. Amos stood quietly waiting, his mind focusing slowly as he stared at the people who were just beginning to recognize him and to spread hasty words from mouth to mouth. Then he saw little Angela Anduccini, and motioned for her to come to him. She hesitated briefly, before following him inside and to the organ.

The little Hammond still functioned. Amos climbed to the pulpit, hearing the old familiar creak of the boards. He put his hands on the lectern, seeing the heavy knuckles and blue veins of age as he opened the Bible and made ready for his Sunday-morning congregation. He straightened his shoulders and turned to face the pews, waiting as they came in.

There were only a few at first. Then more and more came, some from old habit, some from curiosity, and many only because they had heard that he had been captured in person, probably. The camera crew came to the back and set up their machines, flooding him with bright lights and adjusting their telelens. He smiled on them, nodding.

He knew his decision now. It had been made in pieces and tatters. It had come from Kant, who had spent his life looking for a basic ethical principle, and had boiled it down in his statement that men must be treated as ends, not as means. It had been distilled from Doc's final challenge, and the old man sitting in his doorway.

There could be no words with which to give his message to those who waited. No orator had ever possessed such a command of language. But men with rude speech and limited use of what they had had fired the world before. Moses had come down from a mountain with a face that shone, and had overcome the objections of a stiff-necked people. Peter the Hermit had preached a thankless crusade to all of Europe, without radio or television. It was more than words or voice.

He looked down at them when the church was filled and the organ hushed.

"My text for today," he announced, and the murmurs below him hushed as his voice reached out to the pews. "Ye shall know the truth and the truth shall make men free!"

He stopped for a moment, studying them, feeling the decision in his mind, and knowing he could make no other. The need of him lay here, among those he had always tried to serve while believing he was serving God through them. He was facing them as an end, not as a means, and he found it good.

Nor oculd he lie to them now, and deceive them with false hopes. They would need all the facts if they were to make an end to their bickerings and to unite themselves in the final struggle for the fullness of their potential glory.

"I have come back from captivity among the aliens," he began. "I have seen the hordes who have no desire but to erase the memory of man from the dust of the earth that bore him. I have stood at the altar of their God. I have heard the voice of God proclaim that He is also our God, and that He has cast us out. I have believed Him, as I believe Him now."

He felt the strange, intangible something that was greater than words or oratory flow out of him, as it had never flowed in his envied younger days. He watched the shock and the doubt arise and disappear slowly as he went on, giving them the story and the honest doubts he still had. He could never know many things, or even whether the God worshipped on the altar was wholly the same God who had been in the hearts of men for a hundred generations. No man could understand enough. They were entitled to all his doubts, as well as to all that he knew.

He paused at last, in the utter stillness of the chapel. He straightened and smiled down at them, drawing the smile out of some reserve that had lain dormant since he had first tasted inspiration as a boy. He saw a few smiles answer him, and then more—uncertain, doubtful smiles that grew more sure as they spread.

"God has ended the ancient covenants and declared Himself an enemy of all mankind," Amos said, and the chapel seemed to roll with his voice. "I say this to you: He has found a worthy opponent."

# DON'T LOOK NOW

## BY HENRY KUTTNER

The man in the brown suit was looking at himself in the mirror behind the bar. The reflection seemed to interest him even more deeply than the drink between his hands. He was paying only perfunctory attention to Lyman's attempts at conversation. This had been going on for perhaps fifteen minutes before he finally lifted his glass and took a deep swallow.

"Don't look now," Lyman said.

The brown man slid his eyes sidewise toward Lyman, tilted his glass higher, and took another swig. Ice-cubes slipped down toward his mouth. He put the glass back on the red-brown wood and signaled for a refill. Finally he took a deep breath and looked at Lyman.

"Don't look at what?" he asked.

"There was one sitting right beside you," Lyman said, blinking rather glazed eyes. "He just went out. You mean you couldn't see him?"

The brown man finished paying for his fresh drink before he answered. "See who?" he asked, with a fine mixture of boredom, distaste and reluctant interest. "Who went out?"

"What have I been telling you for the last ten minutes? Weren't you listening?"

"Certainly I was listening. That is—certainly. You were talking about—bathtubs. Radios. Orson—"

"Not Orson. H. G. Herbert George. With Orson it was just a gag. H. G. *knew*—or suspected. I wonder if it was simply intuition with him? He couldn't have had any proof—but he did stop writing science-fiction rather suddenly, didn't he? I'll bet he knew once, though."

"Knew what?"

"About the Martians. All this won't do us a bit of good if you don't listen. It may not anyway. The trick is to jump the gun—with proof. Convincing evidence. Nobody's ever been allowed to produce the evidence before. You *are* a reporter, aren't you?"

Holding his glass, the man in the brown suit nodded reluctantly.

"Then you ought to be taking it all down on a piece of folded paper. I want everybody to know. The whole world. It's important. Terribly important. It explains everything. My life won't be safe unless I can pass along the information and make people believe it."

"Why won't your life be safe?"

"Because of the Martians, you fool. They own the world."

The brown man sighed. "Then they own my newspaper, too,' he objected, "so I can't print anything they don't like."

"I never thought of that," Lyman said, considering the bottom of his glass, where two ice-cubes had fused into a cold, immutable union. "They're not omnipotent, though. I'm sure they're vulnerable, or why have they always kept under cover? They're afraid of being found out. If the world had convincing evidence—look, people always believe what they read in the newspapers. Couldn't you—"

"Ha," said the brown man with deep significance.

Lyman drummed sadly on the bar and murmured, "There must be some way. Perhaps if I had another drink . . ."

The brown suited man tasted his collins, which seemed to stimulate him. "Just what is all this about Martians?" he asked Lyman. "Suppose you start at the beginning and tell me again. Or can't you remember?"

"Of course I can remember. I've got practically total recall. It's something new. Very new. I never could do it before. I can even remember my last conversation with the Martians." Lyman favored the brown man with a glance of triumph.

"When was that?"

"This morning."

"I can even remember conversations I had last week," the brown man said mildly. "So what?"

"You don't understand. They make us forget, you see. They tell us what to do and we forget about the conversation

—it's posthypnotic suggestion, I expect—but we follow
their orders just the same. There's the compulsion, though
we think we're making our own decisions. Oh, they own
the world, all right, but nobody knows it except me."

"And how did you find out?"

"Well, I got my brain scrambled, in a way. I've been
fooling around with supersonic detergents, trying to work
out something marketable, you know. The gadget went
wrong—from some standpoints. High-frequency waves, it
was. They went through and through me. Should have
been inaudible, but I could hear them, or rather—well,
actually I could *see* them. That's what I mean about my
brain being scrambled. And after that, I could see and
hear the Martians. They've geared themselves so they
work efficiently on ordinary brains, and mine isn't ordinary any more. They can't hypnotize me, either. They
can command me, but I needn't obey—now. I hope they
don't suspect. Maybe they do. Yes, I guess they do."

"How can you tell?"

"The way they look at me."

"How do they look at you?" asked the brown man, as
he began to reach for a pencil and then changed his
mind. He took a drink instead. "Well? What are they
like?"

"I'm not sure. I can see them, all right, but only when
they're dressed up?"

"Okay, okay," the brown man said patiently. "How
do they look, dressed up?"

"Just like anybody, almost. They dress up in—in human skins. Oh, not real ones, imitations. Like the
Katzenjammer Kids zipped into crocodile suits. Undressed
—I don't know. I've never seen one. Maybe they're
invisible even to me, then, or maybe they're just camou-
flaged. Ants or owls or rats or bats or—"

"Or anything," the brown man said hastily.

"Thanks. Or anything, of course. But when they're
dressed up like humans—like that one who was sitting
next to you awhile ago, when I told you not to look—"

"That one was invisible, I gather?"

"Most of the time they are, to everybody. But once in
a while, for some reason, they—"

"Wait," the brown man objected. "Make sense, will

you? They dress up in human skins and then sit around invisible?"

"Only now and then. The human skins are perfectly good imitations. Nobody can tell the difference. It's that third eye that gives them away. When they keep it closed, you'd never guess it was there. When they want to open it, they go invisible—like *that*. Fast. When I see somebody with a third eye, right in the middle of his forehead, I know he's a Martian and invisible, and I pretend not to notice him.

"Uh-huh," the brown man said. "Then for all you know, I'm one of your visible Martians."

"Oh, I hope not!" Lyman regarded him anxiously. "Drunk as I am, I don't think so, I've been trailing you all day, making sure. It's a risk I have to take, of course. They'll go to any length—any length at all—to make a man give himself away. I realize that. I can't really trust anybody. But I had to find *someone* to talk to, and I—" He paused. There was a brief silence. "I could be wrong," Lyman said presently. "When the third eye's closed, I can't tell if it's there. Would you mind opening your third eye for me?" He fixed a dim gaze on the brown man's forehead.

"Sorry," the reporter said. "Some other time. Besides, I don't know you. So you want me to splash this across the front page, I gather? Why don't you go to see the managing editor? My stories have to get past the desk and rewrite."

"I want to give my secret to the world," Lyman said stubbornly. "The question is, how far will I get? You'd expect they'd have killed me the minute I opened my mouth to you—except that I didn't say anything while they were here. I don't believe they take us very seriously, you know. This must have been going on since the dawn of history, and by now they've had time to get careless. They let Fort go pretty far before they cracked down on him. But you notice they were careful never to let Fort get hold of genuine proof that would convince people."

The brown man said something under his breath about a human interest story in a box. He asked, "What do the Martians do, besides hang around bars all dressed up?"

"I'm still working on that," Lyman said. "It isn't easy to understand. They run the world, of course, but why?"

He wrinkled his brow and stared appealingly at the brown man. "Why?"

"If they do run it, they've got a lot to explain."

"That's what I mean. From our viewpoint, there's no sense to it. We do things illogically, but only because they tell us to. Everything we do, almost, is pure illogic. Poe's *Imp of the Perverse*—you could give it another name beginning with M. Martian, I mean. It's all very well for psychologists to explain why a murderer wants to confess, but it's still an illogical reaction. Unless a Martian commands him to."

"You can't be hypnotized into doing anything that violates your moral sense," the brown man said triumphantly.

Lyman frowned. "Not by another human, but you can by a Martian. I expect they got the upper hand when we didn't have more than ape-brains, and they've kept it ever since. They evolved as we did, and kept a step ahead. Like the sparrow on the eagle's back who hitchhiked till the eagle reached his ceiling, and then took off and broke the altitude record. They conquered the world, but nobody ever knew it. And they've been ruling ever since."

"But—"

"Take houses, for example. Uncomfortable things. Ugly, inconvenient, dirty, everything wrong with them. But when men like Frank Lloyd Wright slip out from under the Martians' thumb long enough to suggest something better, look how the people react. They hate the thought. That's their Martians, giving them orders."

"Look. Why should the Martians care what kind of houses we live in? Tell me that."

Lyman frowned. "I don't like the note of skepticism I detect creeping into this conversation," he announced. "They care, all right. No doubt about it. They *live* in our houses. We don't build for our convenience, we build, under order, for the Martians, the way they want it. They're very much concerned with everything we do. And the more senseless, the more concern.

"Take wars. Wars don't make sense from any human viewpoint. Nobody really wants wars. But we go right on having them. From the Martian viewpoint, they're useful. They give us a spurt in technology, and they reduce the excess population. And there are lots of other results, too. Colonization, for one thing. But mainly technology. In peace time, if a guy invents jet-propulsion, it's too expensive to develop commercially. In war-time, though, it's *got* to be developed. Then the Martians can use it whenever they want. They use us the way they'd use tools or—or limbs. And nobody ever really wins a war—except the Martians."

The man in the brown suit chuckled. "That makes sense," he said. "It must be nice to be a Martian."

"Why not? Up till now, no race ever successfully conquered and ruled another. The underdog could revolt or absorb. If you know you're being ruled, then the ruler's vulnerable. But if the world doesn't know—and it doesn't—

"Take radios," Lyman continued, going off at a tangent. "There's no earthly reason why a sane human should listen to a radio. But the Martians make us do it. They like it. Take bathtubs. Nobody contends bathtubs are comfortable—for us. But they're fine for Martians. All the impractical things we keep on using, even though we know they're impractical—"

"Typewriter ribbons," the brown man said, struck by the thought. "But not even a Martian could enjoy changing a typewriter ribbon."

Lyman seemed to find that flippant. He said that he knew all about the Martians except for one thing—their psychology.

"I don't know *why* they act as they do. It looks illogical sometimes, but I feel perfectly sure they've got sound motives for every move they make. Until I get that worked out I'm pretty much at a standstill. Until I get evidence—proof—and help. I've got to stay under cover till then. And I've been doing that. I do what they tell me, so they won't suspect, and I pretend to forget what they tell me to forget."

"Then you've got nothing much to worry about."

Lyman paid no attention. He was off again on a list of his grievances.

"When I hear the water running in the tub and a Martian splashing around, I pretend I don't hear a thing. My bed's too short and I tried last week to order a special length, but the Martian that sleeps there told me not to. He's a runt, like most of them. That is, I think

they're runts. I have to deduce, because you never see
them undressed. But it goes on like that constantly. By
the way, how's your Martian?"

The man in the brown suit set down his glass rather
suddenly.

"My Martian?"

"Now listen. I may be just a little bit drunk, but my
logic remains unimpaired. I can still put two and two
together. Either you know about the Martians, or you
don't. If you do, there's no point in giving me that,
'What, *my* Martian?' routine. I know you have a Martian. Your Martian knows you have a Martian. My Martian knows. The point is, do *you* know? Think hard,"
Lyman urged solicitously.

"No, I haven't got a Martian," the reporter said, taking a quick drink. The edge of the glass clicked against
his teeth.

"Nervous, I see," Lyman remarked. "Of course you
*have* got a Martian. I suspect you know it."

"What would I be doing with a Martian?" the brown
man asked with dogged dogmatism.

"What would you be doing without one? I imagine it's
illegal. If they caught you running around without one
they'd probably put you in a pound or something until
claimed. Oh, you've got one, all right. So have I. So has
he, and he, and he—and the bartender." Lyman enumer-
ated the other barflies with a wavering forefinger.

"Of course they have," the brown man said. "But
they'll all go back to Mars tomorrow and then you can
see a good doctor. You'd better have another dri—"

He was turning toward the bartender when Lyman,
apparently by accident, leaned close to him and whispered urgently,

*"Don't look now!"*

The brown man glanced at Lyman's white face reflected in the mirror before them.

"It's all right," he said. "There aren't any Mar—"

Lyman gave him a fierce, quick kick under the edge of
the bar.

"Shut up! One just came in!"

And then he caught the brown man's gaze and with
elaborate unconcern said, "—so naturally, there was nothing for me to do but climb out on the roof after it. Took

me ten minutes to get it down the ladder, and just as we reached the bottom it gave one bound, climbed up my face, sprang from the top of my head, and there it was again on the roof, screaming for me to get it down."

"*What?*" the brown man demanded with pardonable curiosity.

"My cat, of course. What did you think? No, never mind, don't answer that." Lyman's face was turned to the brown man's, but from the corners of his eyes he was watching an invisible progress down the length of the bar toward a booth at the very back.

"Now why did he come in?" he murmured. "I don't like this. Is he anyone you know?"

"Is who—?"

"That Martian. Yours, by any chance? No, I suppose not. Yours was probably the one who went out a while ago. I wonder if he went to make a report, and sent this one in? It's possible. It could be. You can talk now, but keep your voice low, and stop squirming. Want him to notice we can see him?"

"*I* can't see him. Don't drag me into this. You and your Martians can fight it out together. You're making me nervous. I've got to go, anyway." But he didn't move to get off the stool. Across Lyman's shoulder he was stealing glances toward the back of the bar, and now and then he looked at Lyman's face.

"Stop watching me," Lyman said. "Stop watching him. Anybody'd think you were a cat."

"Why a cat? Why should anybody—do I look like a cat?"

"We were talking about cats, weren't we? Cats can see them, quite clearly. Even undressed, I believe. They don't like them."

"Who doesn't like who?"

"Whom. Neither likes the other. Cats can see Martians—sh-h!—but they pretend not to, and that makes the Martians mad. I have a theory that cats ruled the world before Martians came. Never mind. Forget about cats. This may be more serious than you think. I happen to know my Martian's taking tonight off, and I'm pretty sure that was your Martian who went out some time ago. And have you noticed that nobody else in here has his

Martian with him? Do you suppose—" His voice sank.
"Do you suppose they could be *waiting for us outside?*"

"Oh, Lord," the brown man said. "In the alley with
the cats, I suppose."

"Why don't you stop this yammer about cats and be
serious for a moment?" Lyman demanded, and then
paused, paled, and reeled slightly on his stool. He hastily
took a drink to cover his confusion.

"What's the matter now?" the brown man asked.

"Nothing." Gulp. "Nothing. It was just that—he *looked*
at me. With—you know."

"Let me get this straight. I take it the Martian is
dressed in—is dressed like a human?"

"Naturally."

"But he's invisible to all eyes but yours?"

"Yes. He doesn't want to be visible, just now. Besides—"
Lyman paused cunningly. He gave the brown man a
furtive glance and then looked quickly down at his drink.
"Besides, you know, I rather think you *can* see him—a
little, anyway."

The brown man was perfectly silent for about thirty
seconds. He sat quite motionless, not even the ice in the
drink he held clinking. One might have thought he did
not even breathe. Certainly he did not blink.

"What makes you think that?" he asked in a normal
voice, after the thirty seconds had run out.

"I—did I say anything? I wasn't listening." Lyman put
down his drink abruptly. "I think I'll go now."

"No, you won't," the brown man said, closing his
fingers around Lyman's wrist. "Not yet you won't. Come
back here. Sit down. Now. What was the idea? Where
were you going?"

Lyman nodded dumbly toward the back of the bar,
indicating either a juke-box or a door marked MEN.

"I don't feel so good. Maybe I've had too much to
drink. I guess I'll—"

"You're all right. I don't trust you back there with
that—that invisible man of yours. You'll stay right here
until he leaves."

"He's going now," Lyman said brightly. His eyes moved
with great briskness along the line of an invisible but
rapid progress toward the front door. "See, he's gone.
Now let me loose, will you?"

The brown man glanced toward the back booth.

"No," he said, "he isn't gone. Sit right where you are."

It was Lyman's turn to remain quite still, in a stricken sort of way, for a perceptible while. The ice in *his* drink, however, clinked audibly. Presently he spoke. His voice was soft, and rather soberer than before.

"You're right. He's still there. You can see him, can't you?"

The brown man said, "Has he got his back to us?"

"You *can* see him, then. Better than I can maybe. Maybe there are more of them here than I thought. They could be anywhere. They could be sitting beside you anywhere you go, and you wouldn't even guess, until—" He shook his head a little. "They'd want to be *sure*," he said, mostly to himself. "They can give you orders and make you forget, but there must be limits to what they can force you to do. They can't make a man betray himself. They'd have to lead him on—until they were sure."

He lifted his drink and tipped it steeply above his face. The ice ran down the slope and bumped coldly against his lip, but he held it until the last of the pale, bubbling amber had drained into his mouth. He set the glass on the bar and faced the brown man.

"Well?" he said.

The brown man looked up and down the bar.

"It's getting late," he said. "Not many people left. We'll wait."

"Wait for what?"

The brown man looked toward the back booth and looked away again quickly.

"I have something to show you. I don't want anyone else to see."

Lyman surveyed the narrow, smoky room. As he looked the last customer beside themselves at the bar began groping in his pocket, tossed some change on the mahogany, and went out slowly.

They sat in silence. The bartender eyed them with stolid disinterest. Presently a couple in the front booth got up and departed, quarreling in undertones.

"Is there anyone left?" the brown man asked in a voice that did not carry down the bar to the man in the apron.

"Only—" Lyman did not finish, but he nodded gently toward the back of the room. "He isn't looking. Let's get this over with. What do you want to show me?"

The brown man took off his wrist-watch and pried up the metal case. Two small, glossy photograph prints slid out. The brown man separated them with a finger.

"I just want to make sure of something," he said. "First—why did you pick me out? Quite a while ago, you said you'd been trailing me all day, making sure. I haven't forgotten that. And you knew I was a reporter. Suppose you tell me the truth, now?"

Squirming on his stool, Lyman scowled. "It was the way you looked at things," he murmured. "On the subway this morning—I'd never seen you before in my life, but I kept noticing the way you looked at things—the wrong things, things that weren't there, the way a cat does—and then you'd always look away—I got the idea you could see the Martians too."

"Go on," the brown man said quietly.

"I followed you. All day. I kept hoping you'd turn out to be—somebody I could talk to. Because if I could *know* that I wasn't the only one who could see them, then I'd know there was still some hope left. It's been worse than solitary confinement. I've been able to see them for three years now. Three years. And I've managed to keep my power a secret even from them. And, somehow, I've managed to keep from killing myself, too."

"Three years?" the brown man said. He shivered.

"There was always a little hope. I knew nobody would believe—not without proof. And how can you get proof? It was only that I—I kept telling myself that maybe you could see them too, and if you could, maybe there were others—lots of others—enough so we might get together and work out some way of proving to the world—"

The brown man's fingers were moving. In silence he pushed a photograph across the mahogany. Lyman picked it up unsteadily.

"Moonlight?" he asked after a moment. It was a landscape under a deep, dark sky with white clouds in it. Trees stood white and lacy against the darkness. The grass was white as if with moonlight, and the shadows blurry.

"No, not moonlight," the brown man said. "Infrared. I'm strictly an amateur, but lately I've been experimenting with infra-red film. And I got some very odd results."

Lyman stared at the film.

"You see, I live near—" The brown man's finger tapped a certain quite common object that appeared in the photograph. "—and something funny keeps showing up now and then against it. But only with infra-red film. Now I know cholorphyll reflects so much infra-red light that grass and leaves photograph white. The sky comes out black, like this. There are tricks to using this kind of film. Photograph a tree against a cloud, and you can't tell them apart in the print. But you can photograph through a haze and pick out distant objects the ordinary film wouldn't catch. And sometimes, when you focus on something like this—" He tapped the image of the very common object again, "you get a very odd image on the film. Like that. A man with three eyes."

Lyman held the print up to the light. In silence he took the other one from the bar and studied it. When he laid them down he was smiling.

"You know," Lyman said in a conversational whisper, "a professor of astrophysics at one of the more important universities had a very interesting little item in the *Times* the other Sunday. Name of Spitzer, I think. He said that if there were life on Mars, and if Martians had ever visited earth, there'd be no way to prove it. Nobody would believe the few men who saw them. Not, he said, unless the Martians happened to be photographed. . . ."

Lyman looked at the brown man thoughtfully.

"Well," he said, "it's happened. You've photographed them."

The brown man nodded. He took up the prints and returned them to his watch-case. "I thought so, too. Only until tonight I couldn't be sure. I'd never seen one—fully—as you have. It isn't so much a matter of what you call getting your brain scrambled with supersonics as it is of just knowing where to look. But I've been seeing *part* of them all my life, and so has everybody. It's that little suggestion of movement you never catch except just at the edge of your vision, just out of the corner of your eye. Something that's *almost* there—and when you look

fully at it, there's nothing. These photographs showed me
the way. It's not easy to learn, but it can be done. We're
conditioned to look directly at a thing—the particular
thing we want to see clearly, whatever it is. Perhaps the
Martians gave us that conditioning. When we see a movement at the edge of our range of vision, it's almost
irresistible not to look directly at it. So it vanishes."

"Then they can be seen—by anybody?"

"I've learned a lot in a few days," the brown man said.
"Since I took those photographs. You have to train yourself. It's like seeing a trick picture—one that's really a
composite, after you study it. Camouflage. You just have
to learn how. Otherwise we can look at them all our lives
and never see them."

"The camera does, though."

"Yes, the camera does. I've wondered why nobody
ever caught them this way before. Once you see them on
film, they're unmistakable—that third eye."

"Infra-red film's comparatively new, isn't it? And then
I'll bet you have to catch them against that one particular background—you know—or they won't show on the
film. Like trees against clouds. It's tricky. You must have
had just the right lighting that day, and exactly the right
focus, and the lens stopped down just right. A kind of
minor miracle. It might never happen again exactly that
way. But . . . don't look now."

They were silent. Furtively, they watched the mirror.
Their eyes slid along toward the open door of the tavern.

And then there was a long, breathless silence.

"He looked back at us," Lyman said very quietly. "He
looked at us . . . that third eye!"

The brown man was motionless again. When he moved,
it was to swallow the rest of his drink.

"I don't think that they're suspicious yet," he said.
"The trick will be to keep under cover until we can blow
this thing wide open. There's got to be some way to do
it—some way that will convince people."

"There's proof. The photographs. A competent camera-
man ought to be able to figure out just how you caught
that Martian on film and duplicate the conditions. It's
evidence."

"Evidence can cut both ways," the brown man said.
"What I'm hoping is that the Martians don't really like to

kill—unless they have to. I'm hoping they won't kill without proof. But—" He tapped his wrist-watch.

"There's two of us now, though," Lyman said. "We've got to stick together. Both of us have broken the big rule—*don't look now*—"

The bartender was at the back, disconnecting the juke-box. The brown man said, "We'd better not be seen together unnecessarily. But if we both come to this bar tomorrow night at nine for a drink—that wouldn't look suspicious, even to them."

"Suppose—" Lyman hesitated. "May I have one of those photographs?"

"Why?"

"If one of us had—an accident—the other one would still have the proof. Enough, maybe, to convince the right people."

The brown man hesitated, nodded shortly, and opened his watch-case again. He gave Lyman one of the pictures.

"Hide it," he said. "It's—evidence. I'll see you here tomorrow. Meanwhile, be careful. Remember to play safe."

They shook hands firmly, facing each other in an end-less second of final, decisive silence. Then the brown man turned abruptly and walked out of the bar.

Lyman sat there. Between two wrinkles in his forehead there was a stir and a flicker of lashes unfurling. The third eye opened slowly and looked after the brown man.

# THE CERTIFICATE

## BY AVRAM DAVIDSON

The winter sunrise was still two hours away when Dr. Roger Freeman came to stand in front of the great door. By good fortune—incredibly good fortune—he had not been questioned in his furtive progress from the dormitory. If he had been stopped, or if his answer had been either disbelieved or judged inadequate, he might have been sent back to the dorm for punishment. The punishment would have been over, of course, in time for him to go to work at ten in the morning, but a man could suffer through several thousand eternities of Hell in those few hours. And no more than a low muffled groaning and a subdued convulsive movement of the body to show what was going on. You were able to sleep through it—if it was happening to someone else.

The great door was set well in from the street, and the cutting edge of the wind was broken by it.

Freeman was grateful for that. It was two years ago that he'd applied for a new overcoat, and the one he still had was ragged even then. Perhaps—if this was not to be his year for escape—in another year he would get the coat. He crowded into a corner and tried not to think of the cold.

After a little while another man joined him, then another, then a woman, then a couple. By sunrise there was a long line. They were all willing to risk it, risk punishment for being out before work, or for being late to work. Some merely wanted clothes. Some wanted permission to visit relatives in another locale. You could wait years for either. Or, you could wait years and not get either. And some, like Freeman, hoped against hope for a chance at escape.

Dr. Freeman stared at the door. The design was as intricate as it was incomprehensible. No doubt it made sense to the Hedderans. If you could understand it you might gain some understanding of the nature of their distant home. If you cared. It was fifty years since they had arrived, and men still knew almost nothing about them.

They were here. They would never go away. That was enough.

The man behind Dr. Freeman collapsed. No one paid any attention to him. After a moment there was a high, brief, humming. The man twitched, opened his eyes. He got to his feet.

And then the door opened.

*"Proceed in the order,"* the voice directed—a thick, flat Hedderan voice; harsh, yet glutinous. No one tried to push ahead, the lesson had been too well learned. Dr. Freeman got to the third escalator, rode down two levels. There had been a time when you rode *up*—but that was before the Hedderans came. They didn't like tall buildings —at least it seemed so. They'd never explained—that, or anything else. What they did not like they simply destroyed.

Dr. Freeman looked behind him as he approached the office. There must have been at least a dozen people behind him. They looked at him wolfishly. So few certificates were granted, and he was first in line. He looked away. He'd stayed awake all night in order to *be* the first. No one had the right to resent him. And the next man in line was young. What did he expect . . . ?

The door opened, the voice said, *"Proceed one at a single time."* Fifty years, and the Hedderans still hadn't mastered the language. They didn't have to, of course. Roger Freeman entered the office, took the application form from the slot in the wall-machine found in every office, sat down at the table. When was the last time he had sat in a chair? No matter.

The form was in Hedderan, of course. The voice said, *"Name."* The voice said, *"Number."*

He wrote it down, Roger Freerman . . . 655-673-60-60-2. Idly he glanced at the cluster of Hedderan characters. If one could take the application form away, with Hedderan questions and English answers, perhaps—if there was time—a key could be found for translating. But it was impossible to take it away. If you spoiled it, you were out. You could apply only once a year. And if you *did* find out how to read their language, what then? Freeman's brother Bob had talked of rebellion—but that was years ago . . . and he didn't like to think what had happened to Bob. And besides, he hadn't *time*—he had to be at work by ten.

From ten in the morning until ten at night (the Hedderans had their own ways of reckoning time) he worked at a machine, pulling hard on levers. Some he had to bend down to reach, some he had to mount steps to reach. Up and down, up and down. He didn't know what the machine did, or even how it worked. And he no longer cared. He no longer cared about anything—except a new overcoat (or, at least, a *newer* one, not worn so thin), and his chances of escape.

*Age. Occupation. Previous Occupation.* Previous to the arrival of the Hedderans, that was. Fifty years ago. He had been a physician. An obsolete skill. Inside of every man nowadays there was a piece of . . . something . . . presumably it communicated with a machine somewhere deep in the Hedderan quarters. If you broke a bone or bled or even if you just fainted (as the young man behind him in line had), you were set right almost in the second. No one was ill for long—even worn-out organs were regenerated. Too few men had been left alive, and the Hedderans needed those who were left too much to let them sicken or die.

At last the long form was filled out. The harsh voice said, *"Now at once to Office Ten, Level Four."*

Dr. Freeman hastily obeyed. When they said 'at once,' they meant just that. The punishment might come like a single whiplash—or it might go on and on. You never knew. Maybe the Hedderans knew. But they never told. The man next behind the outer door scuttled in as Freeman left. The others waited. Not more than three could expect to be processed before it would be time to return to work.

Office Ten, Level Four, asked him the same questions, but in a different order. He was then directed to Office Five, Level Seventeen. Here his two forms were fed into a machine, returned with markings stamped on them in Hedderan.

*"Office Eight, Level Two,"* the voice said. There, he fed his applications into the slot. After a moment they came back—unmarked.

*"Name Roger Freeman. Number 655-673-60-60-2. You*

*have a single time application outstanding. Unpermitted
two. You will cancel this one. Or you will cancel that one."*

Frantically he searched his mind. What application did he
have outstanding? When was this rule made? The overcoat!
If he went ahead with this new application and it was refused,
he'd have to wait till next year to reinstate the one for the
coat. And then more years of waiting . . . It was cold, the
dormitory was ill-heated, he had no blanket. His present
coat was very worn. Services for humans were minimal.

But he *had* to proceed with this new application. He
was first in line . . .

*"Speak,"* the thick, flat voice directed. *"Answer. Speak.
Now."*

Gobbling his words in haste, Freeman said, "I cancel
the one outstanding."

*"Insert forms."*

He did. Waited.

*"Proceed to Office Ten, Level Four."*

That was the second place he'd been to. A mistake? No
matter, he had to go. Once again he entered. And waited.

A grunting noise caught his eye. He looked up, started,
cowered. A Hedderan, his baffle-screen turned off, was
gazing at him. The blank, grey, faceted eyes in the huge
head, and the body, like a deformed foetus . . . then the
baffle-screen went on again. Freeman shuddered. One
rarely saw them. It had been years.

A piece of paper slid from the machine. He took it up,
waiting for the command to proceed—where? Unless it
could be accomplished before ten, there was no chance
of escape for him this year. None whatever. He stared
dully at the strange characters. The cold indifferent voice
said, *"Name Roger Freeman. Number 655-673-60-60-2.
Declared surplus. Application for death certificate is granted.
Proceed for certificate to Office One, Level Five. At once."*

Tears rolled down Dr. Freeman's cheeks. "At last," he
sobbed, joyfully. "At last . . ."

And then he hastily left. He had achieved his escape
after all—but only if he got there before ten o'clock.

# THE ALIEN RULERS

## BY PIERS ANTHONY

If Bitool really wanted a favor, he had chosen a remarkably inappropriate occasion to make his desire known. Yet he stood at ease, one blue hand resting lightly upon the stolid desk, the press of his conservative business suit undisturbed. His nose and ears were so similar to the human equivalent that the Earthman was sure they were artificial appendages; the eyes and mouth deviated more. Bitool was, every inch, every nuance, the genteel alien executive.

"Let's not play at formalities," Dick Henrys said. "You know I am your enemy." But the words emerged awkwardly; he felt like a sophomore joker standing before the dean.

The Kazo overlord of America, North-Central, smiled, conveying in a single expression both the humor of his spirit and the clock-work calculation of his mind. "I do need your assistance," he said. "As you are a man of honor, I am asking you to make your decision right now."

"Honor!" Henrys looked around the austere office, unable to meet the overlord's gaze. "I came here to kill you, and you are offering me my freedom—in exchange for just three days of loyal service? With a revolution breaking over your head?"

Bitool's manner changed. He snapped his fingers imperatively. "Immediate response, Earthman: What is a revolutionist?"

"A revolutionist is one who desires to discard the existing social order and try another."

Bitool snapped his fingers again, ringingly. "Under what circumstances is a man a revolutionist?"

"Every man is a revolutionist concerning the thing he understands."

Snap. "And what oppression has revolution eased?"

"Revolutions have never lightened the burden of tyranny; they have only shifted it to another shoulder."

Bitool smiled. "Please pick up the volume beside you, Richard."

Henrys glanced at the table on his right and found a slim book there. He reached for it.

"Identify it, Richard." Again the smile without the snap.

He read from the title page: " 'The Revolutionist's Handbook and Pocket Companion,' by John Tanner, M.I.R.C."

"Keep it, Richard. You will find its content remarkable." The overlord's expression became enigmatic. "But now you must give me your commitment. I must have your cooperation during the crisis."

Henrys studied him, searching for some clue to his intent. The Kazo now puffed a local cigar. His blue face and hands were distinctly alien, but nothing else was. As he stood, he looked as much like a human being as an extraterrestrial being.

"I don't see how you could afford to take my word for such a thing." Henrys said at last, "or how I could give it. It is better for me to die than to turn against my cause." Why did his words continue to sound so much like an inept reading?

"You will not be required to betray any confidences. You would not be a traitor to your principles."

"But you won't tell me in advance what you want me to do."

"You may need your weapon," Bitool said. His arm moved, and suddenly the tiny round palm-pistol Henrys had come with was in the air.

Henrys caught it automatically, his free hand circling it and positioning the stubby muzzle before his mind reacted to the surprise of the gesture. "You disarmed it, of course," he said. He aimed at the hanging light fixture and squeezed the bulb.

A puff of bitter gas appeared and dissipated as the weapon kicked in his hand.

Glass exploded as the ball-shot struck its mark.

Bitool stood calmly, watching him.

Henrys looked at the cooling pistol, astonished. "I can kill you," he said. "You're too far away to disarm me with the trick motion you used before."

"You must decide."

Henrys aimed at him. "Do you *want* to die?"

There was no reply.

Earth was under the heel of the alien, conquered more readily than the cheapest pulps had predicted. Henrys had wondered many times what had become of the valiant resistance, the desperate last-ditch heroics supposed to make this planet a savagely expensive property for any invader.

Earth had anticipated in nightmare monstrous slimy slugs, or hairy man-sized centipedes, or metallic animate boxes, but had not even had the dignity to fall to any frightful scourge. Instead, of all things, it had submitted without opposition to humanoid aliens: five feet six inches tall, two almost-normal arms, legs, eyes. So close to man that half an hour with a make-up artist could pass them for men.

The Kazos conquered without apparent effort, and their rule was skilled and benign.

It did not add up. There were histories of the Kazo peoples in the Earth libraries. Henrys had taken pains to study them, and had discovered no supermen therein. The Kazos had warred and struggled for civilization in a manner so similar to that of man that he had been tempted to set the books aside as deliberate fabrications: thinly concealed allegories of Earth, published to conceal the Kazos true nature and intent.

The Kazos were *good* administrators. If they had warred as blindly as they seemed to want men to believe, throughout the development of their civilization, how had they been so abruptly transformed to superlative administrators? Granted that they had their great ones, as did Mankind, what strange selection brought *only* this type to captive Earth?

Now the leading Kazo of the area bluffed with his own life. Bitool was no fool. Better to spring the trap immediately, rather than to allow himself to be maneuvered, gamelike, into betrayal of his people. "You're forcing me to join you—or kill you." Henrys said. "You think this will make me believe you. This practical gesture."

" 'Beware of the man whose god is in the skies,' " the overlord said calmly.

It was a quotation, and the note was false. "I *don't* believe you." He squeezed the bulb. The shot smacked into the wall beside the Kazo's head. Angry, he squeezed again—and missed on the other side. Bitool had not moved.

Henrys stared at his hand, knowing it had disobeyed him. He was a dead shot with this weapon, but had been unable to aim directly at the overlord and fire.

"I believe you," he said. It was defeat.

Bitool turned. "Come, Richard," he said gently. "Your god is not in the skies. You shall be the first man to see."

Henrys followed him, realizing that he had been committed. He slipped the book into his shirt and the pistol into his pocket. But why had he shied away from the execution that had been his assignment?

They took the private lift reserved for the overlord— one of the few privileges the conqueror claimed—and plummeted to the ground floor. They left the Administration building together, as though they were friends. Bitool elected to walk instead of summoning a car or descending to the public conveyors one and two levels below.

Here city life continued pretty much as it always had: electric cars rolled along the measured lanes and pedestrians crowded the sidewalks. On this level alone the two could meet: antique flashing lights required the vehicles to halt periodically to let the perambulators cross.

It was inefficient, but Henrys loved it. He had spent the past two years in the Survey Department, charting this level: traffic flow, residential density, patterns of industry and employment. Henrys knew almost every aspect of this cross-section of the city, leaving the upper stories to others. It was all part of some nebulous Kazo project; perhaps they meant to reorganize the city. The overlords never acted without complete information.

The Kazo was shorter and lighter than most of the people on the walk, but completely at ease. No guards challenged them in the normally clamorous shopping area. No one paid attention to the extraterrestrial creature walking among them on this conventional American city street. It occurred to Henrys that he had never seen a Kazo with a bodyguard.

At the first corner a mother was trying ineffectively to keep her small child reined while carrying a heavy package of groceries. Bitool stopped and bowed. "Please," he murmured, taking the package in one hand and catching the little boy's arm with the other. The lady blushed, flattered, while Henrys averted his face in disgust. A human woman!

Bitool escorted her across the street, then returned child and package and bowed farewell. Henrys was conscious of the woman's gaze as they walked away. It had not occurred to him to assist her, and Bitool's action astonished him. Why such artificial chivalry in the alien conqueror?

Yet the woman had been pleased. She should have recoiled from the physical touch of the deep blue hand taking her package, and clutched her child instinctively away from that contact, reacting as she would against the slimy scale of a python. The child should have screamed.

Their pleasure could not have been servile appeasement. No Kazo had ever expressed sexual interest in an Earthwoman, and there was a general suspicion that the aliens were neuter, despite the plain statements to the contrary in the alleged histories. Certainly only one sex had come to Earth, and if there was miscegenation it was secret.

Henrys found his mind unusually active as he accompanied Bitool on the brisk hike. There were other mysteries about the conquest. How had Earth been subdued, and how was pacification maintained so quietly? There had been scattered resistance at first, but it had quickly faded; the current revolution was the first he had direct knowledge of. Even allowing for suppression of the press, this was hardly creditable. Weapons? The overlords possessed them, of course—but none clearly superior to those of Earth. Manpower? Clearly insufficient; there were no more than two million Kazos on all of Earth, compared to more than two billion natives.

Even the best of administrations could not reasonably be expected to dissolve all resistance to foreign domination, not when the subject was man. Selfish ambitions would not allow it. The average man did not want justice; he wanted all he could get, and was happy to fight for what he knew could never rightfully be his. The rich man grasped for his second fortune, heedless of those who starved; the wealthy nation extracted indemnities from the impoverished one. The Kazos were fair; that was why they should have been overthrown long ago. Man was a violent creature by nature.

Until fifteen years ago. Henrys could think of only one thing to account for the change: saturation sedation. A pacifying drug that undermined the human will to resist and conditioned the mind to accept the status quo. It could be fed into the atmosphere, and the dosage increased whenever the situation threatened to get out of hand.

And medicinal components could contribute to general health . . . and gaseous fertility inhibitants would account for the general decline in population and recent stabilization at an appropriate level. Thus—peace.

Bitool led the way into a private building. Henrys was familiar with the general design of this one, as he was with every important structure in the city, but he had never entered the higher stories. It was an office skyscraper with a tremendous book store ensconced in the ground level, a drive-in grocery chain in the basement, and, appropriately, a hydroponic division in the nether extension, feeding on the nearby sewage processing plant. This was one of the complexes built under Kazo direction, replete with common sense but not always pleasantly novel innovations.

They ignored the partial loops and took the high-velocity lift to the twentieth floor. This was actually a cross between the old-time elevators and escalators: wide, shallow compartments suspended vertically, each sufficient for two rows of five people. A man could, if he chose, ride the lift all the way over the top like a Ferris wheel, down the other side and back to his starting point. Henrys knew that above and below, on every level of the building, the compartments were expressing passengers; the conveyance was continuous and nowhere did the shaft stand empty. Only those willing to travel in multiples of twenty floors, for the sake of speed, occupied this particular one, however.

The Kazos believed in efficiency.

At twenty, the lift paused for exactly two seconds. The protective outside bars shot up as the center separation fell into place. Henrys and Bitool jumped nimbly off, while other passengers jumped quickly on from the opposite side. The separation was necessary to prevent disastrous collisions between those embarking and disembarking.

They moved across to the slow lift, which trundled along at less than a foot per second and preserved momentum by never halting at all. They waited for an empty compartment and stepped into it as it rose. At the twenty-third floor they stepped off again on the opposite side and took the conveyor down the long hall at seven feet per second.

Bitool indicated the office that was their destination and they got off. He still had no idea what the overlord had in mind, or how it could relate to routine office space. Surely the ruler of fifty million human beings was not about to waste his urgent moments assigning a strange revolutionary to a clerical task? What could be more pressing than counteraction to the breaking storm?

For a moment Henrys wondered whether he was due for illicit interrogation. No—no Kazo had ever broken his word to an Earthman. That was one of the things that made them so difficult to fight: there were no valid issues. No tangible ones, anyway.

It looked more like an apartment than an office. The rooms were tastefully furnished with rugs, easy chairs and even pictures on the wall—all of Earth scenes. Near the far side of the main room stood an unfamiliar Kazo, smaller than Bitool and with skin of lighter hue. The new one seemed to be uncertain—an unusual trait among the conquerors.

Now there was a subtle change about Bitool which Henrys did not immediately understand. Could the stranger be of a higher rank? Then why the apparent reticence? There were not many that ranked Bitool. Not on Earth.

"Seren." Bitool's voice interrupted his train of thought. The other Kazo turned and approached them, moving with a certain grace. A dignitary from the home planet?

Bitool took the stranger's hand and brought it to meet Henrys' own. He was embarrassed for his prior thoughts about physical contact; the hand was polite and warm. "Richard, this is Serena, arrived this morning from Kazo." Bitool smiled carefully and the other imitated the expression, evidently still learning. "This . . . she . . is a, let me say, a female of our species. The first on Earth. You will—guide her. For three days, and return her to me."

A female Kazo! So the species *was* bisexual—and now, having pacified Earth, they meant to colonize it.

Bitool had turned abruptly and left the apartment while Henrys still held the female's hand. "Wait!" the Earthman called, but he was on his own.

Serena gently disengaged her hand. "Will you show me your planet now?" she inquired, her speech unaccented but unsure. "I know so little about it, yet."

Henrys looked for sarcasm, but detected none. It was an honest question, as it almost had to be, coming from a Kazo. Hadn't she been told the situation here?

Why had he been armed and left alone with her? Bitool hadn't even bothered to obtain his formal agreement.

Someone was playing with fire. The whole affair was totally unlike the normally methodical methods of the conquerors. To capture the advance scout of an uprising and put him in charge of the only exterrestrial female on the planet . . .

"What did Bitool tell you about me?" he asked her.

She approached again, moving so smoothly it resembled a glide. Her features were delicate, but she was bald and her figure could never be mistaken for that of a human female. "Only that there would be a trusted person to guide me about the planet," she said. "That I should follow his . . . your instructions dutifully. Even if they seemed strange at first."

He digested this. "Did he mention the political situation here?"

"No, Richard."

This was hardly credible. In less than an hour—half an hour, now—there would be chaos in the city, as the shock troops of the underground came into the open and captured the key functions of the government. If Bitool hadn't suspected the attack before, he had surely caught on when an armed Earthman came after him with a weapon. Yet he had ignored the danger and turned a priceless asset over to the enemy. A Kazo woman as hostage—

But Henrys had agreed, by implication, to serve the overlord for three days. He had been given no specific instructions, which meant that he had to use his own judgment. And his own ethics. That meant, in turn, that he would have to protect Serena from the violence coming, and release her in three days in some safe area if unable to return her to Bitool. It would not be honest to do less.

Of all the men in the area, human or Kazo, he was probably the best fitted to preserve the life of an innocent stranger, for he had been trained in espionage and knew every byway of the city. He also knew something of the battle plan, and the key figures in it.

Bitool's action was beginning to make sense. The overlord had known that interrogation or coercion would be useless. He had also known that Henrys considered himself an honest man who did not allow the ends to justify the means. That was why he had been unable to kill the Kazo, once trust had been extended. A cursing, attacking ET, yes—a sober, intellectual individual, no. Bitool had wanted to put the female in safe hands, and had been guided by logic—and meticulous study of his man—rather than by emotion.

This revelation of Kazo insight into human motives was chilling. And Kazo intelligence—for Henrys had told no one of his mission. Bitool must have deduced the necessary, or likely, qualifications for his own assassin and fed the information into the computer registry. He had known who was coming, and how to deal with him, probably, before Henrys himself had known.

Set a thief to catch a thief—and an assassin to save a life.

"Is something wrong?" Serena asked him.

He was committed. He *had* been maneuvered into a situation he would never have chosen. No one demanded that he interfere with the revolution or give away any information concerning it—but he could not protect his charge by ignoring what he knew. It was going to be difficult.

He spoke rapidly. "Serena, something *is* wrong. You will have to trust me and obey my directives instantly, or we will both die before nightfall. Do you understand?" He had never imagined he would talk to an overlord this way.

"The situation, no," she said with that invariable alien

candor. "But I will obey." Her ready acceptance surprised him also, for the Kazos came to Earth to give commands, not to receive them. Or was this merely another aspect of the racial realism?

"There will be . . . trouble. You have perhaps twenty-five minutes to learn to pass for a human female. I'll explain once we get away from here."

"A *human?* I could not!"

He yanked open the closet door, searching for clothing. "You can't afford pride right now," he said over his shoulder. "Or modesty. Strip down and dress as I tell you."

"Pride!" she murmured, but she began removing the smock that was evidently the Kazo traveling uniform.

Henrys found a dress and tossed it at her. "Put it on. We'll find you a long-sleeve blouse, and support stockings if we're lucky. You know what they are?"

"No, Richard."

He delved into a chest of drawers, praying that Bitool had anticipated this need, too. He had; there was a considerable assortment of lingerie, together with women's shoes, hats and gloves. He made a selection and turned to face Serena.

She was standing in the middle of the room, the dress hanging awkwardly. She was nowhere near human in appearance.

Henrys groaned and looked at his watch. Fifteen minutes—perhaps.

"I'm going to have to dress you myself," he said. "Close your eyes if you have to and pretend I'm a doctor, but snap to it. It *is* a matter of life and death." How had he got into this? "Raise your arms."

She raised her arms. "I do not understand, Richard. What is it, to pretend?"

He ignored her confusion and lifted away the dress. "Brother! You're not even mammalian." But what had he expected?

"I'm sorry." Her eyes were closed.

"We'll have to fake it." He lunged at the drawer and grabbed a handful of cloth. "Take this and wad it up into balls," he said, putting the material—some kind of scarf or kerchief—into her hands. "Open your eyes! Hurry!"

"Yes, Richard," she said, obeying.

He looped a brassiere around her chest and hooked it together on the tightest setting. She had neither ribs nor vertebrae. "Now jam that stuff into each cup, so it stands out. Sit down." He sifted through his collection and came up with panties and stockings. "Do you know how to put these on?" Ten minutes.

Neither of them knew how to keep up the heavy stockings; it was finally accomplished by pinning them crudely to the slip. Henrys located a feminine wig and fitted it over her head. He smeared white cream over her face and neck. "Make sure every inch of your skin is covered by clothing or makeup," he said. "And keep your hair straight. Find two shoes that fit you and practice walking."

She rehearsed while he gave final instructions. "You'll pose as my wife. Hang on to my arm and—"

"Pose?" she inquired. "I do not comprehend this, Richard."

Damn the forthright Kazo manner! He had five minutes to explain human ethics, or lack of them, to a person who had been born to another manner. Pretense was not a concept in the alien repertoire, it seemed.

He chose another approach. "For the time being, you *are* my wife, then. Call it a marriage of convenience." She began to speak, but he cut her off. "My companion, my female. On Earth we pair off two by two. This means you must defer to my wishes, expressed and implied, and avoid bringing shame upon me. Only in this manner are you permitted to accompany me in public places. Is *this* clear?"

"I must conform to your conventions," she said carefully.

"Exactly. And my conventions require that you place your hand on my arm, like this—no! Keep those gloves on!—and wait for my initiative. Nod agreement to anything I say, but moderately. Do not even think of yourself as a Kazo, for that is distasteful to me."

"But Richard, I *am* a—"

"Of course, and we are not forgetting that for a moment. But Earth protocol requires that you minimize your origin. You don't want to insult your hosts, do you?"

"No, Richard."

"Good. As I said, I'll explain in more detail after we—"

\*   \*   \*

The door burst open. A man with a machine gun entered.

Exactly on schedule—but an incongruity jogged Henrys. It should have taken at least half an hour for the crew assigned to this building to cover it, even at optimum efficiency. Each man would have to check several floors. Even if this were the first floor checked in this section—how had the man reached this distant room *at the precise moment* of the inauguration of hostilities?

And why did he have a projectile weapon, when it was supposed to be a gas gun, harmless to humans but toxic to Kazos?

"What's the meaning of this?" Henrys demanded, advancing upon the intruder.

The man did not recognize him. "It's the revolution, mister. We're flushing out Kazos. Stand aside while I—"

He fell, choking as Henry's forearm caught him across the throat. He hated to do it to one of his own people, but explanations would be suicidal—and something was fishy.

"Here, Serena," he snapped, catching the gun and clubbing the man into unconsciousness. "Keep quiet and don't run or look around. If you have to scream, try to scream like an Earthwoman."

She was staring at the prone man. "You struck him—"

"Yeah." He took her arm and drew her to the door. "Is there anything you want to take with you? We won't be back soon."

"No, Richard," she said.

They rode the conveyor across to the express lift down. It was the same loop, but the descending side was at the other face of the building, leading to the massed exits on the lower floors. So many people passed through this structure in any given hour that all the main passages were mechanized one-way.

Several doors were open, and small groups of people whispered together. Obviously the search had been proceeding all the time he was preparing Serena. It must have begun just about the time he and Bitool had entered . . .

The express paused at the third floor and they jumped off. The interval, of course, was twenty stories, whichever one a person started from. Each lift had a compartment for every floor, all moving as a unit. The only crowding occurred on the lower floors, where everyone landed at one time or another.

"I couldn't take a chance on his recognizing you," he told Serena under his breath. "But outside, you'll have to pass. If someone stares, ignore him."

"I don't think I look very much like a human woman," she said.

"Not an attractive one," he admitted. "But the confusion should help." At least, he hoped so. His precise information had been wrong on two counts so far; what other surprises waited for him?

Another man with a gun stood guard outside the building. The pedestrians ignored him much as they had Bitool; revolutions seemed to be of little interest to the populace.

Henrys averted his face to avoid being recognized and set a brisk pace down the street. "If we make it to the subway entrance, we have a good chance," he said. He had not descended to it within the building because of the likelihood of challenge by another guard, in case the one he had put away had been discovered. "They're going after the personnel and utilities first. I can't risk the escape route set up for me, though—too many familiar contacts. We—"

"Richard," she said, holding back.

"Come *on!* This is no sightseeing tour."

"Richard—the pins are coming loose. The stockings . . ."

Despairingly, he understood. The opaque stockings did not fit her Kazo-proportioned legs properly, and would fall down in a few steps without the pins. Blue legs on the city street . . .

"Grab them with your hands!" But he knew as he said it that such a display would attract fatal attention. "No. Put your feet together and stand still. I'll get a taxi."

He could see the wrinkles forming in the loosened hose. The milling people were beginning to look. *This* they chose to notice! He leaped for the nearest vacant electrotaxi parked at the corner and dumped a handful of change in its payment hopper. The door slid open across the front as the mechanism sorted and totaled the coins and hummed into life.

Henrys jumped inside and sent the car rolling forward.
He halted it opposite Serena. "In!" he cried.

She hopped to the curb and twisted into the seat beside
him. A bystander guffawed. Henrys slammed the wide
door and moved into the traffic. "This means trouble. We
have road blocks at—"

"We?"

"The revolutionists. I thought you understood that—"

"You are one of them?" she asked, perplexed. "Then
why—"

"It's a long story. Just accept the fact that I'm trying to
help you. I'll do everything I can to achieve freedom for
Earth, but I have to keep you out of the hands of the
revolutionists."

"Yes, Richard."

"We'll have to park somewhere until the initial rush is
over. We can't get out of the city until dark." He turned
down a side street, alert for possible pursuit. "Get those
stockings pinned again. We may be searched."

"Yes, Richard," she said, bending to the task. "I did
not mean to violate protocol."

The car's dash gave a warning buzz. "Oh, oh. Two
minutes to find a space," he said. "I don't have enough
change to keep driving indefinitely."

He maneuvered into a marked spot. A red flag popped
up on the meter as the vehicle's weight settled. "Damn!
An hour limit. Too short," he said. He got out and drew
a dollar bill from his wallet.

"Will you explain?" Serena asked, joining him before
the meter.

"Here on Earth you always pay too much for too
little," he said. "This is one of the old dollar meters. You
put the bill on the plate, like this, and you pull the
handle. An alarm sounds in the police depot if the bill is
counterfeit, or if you park more than two minutes on
'violation'. The meter will not accept another bill until
the spot has been vacated. That's to prevent all-day
parking."

He pulled the handle and flag and money dropped out
of sight. The needle indicated one hour. They could hear
the loud ticking. "Damn inflation," he muttered. "You
used to get a full hundred minutes for the bill."

"But can't you move to a new space after the hour?"

"I'll have to. But it increases the risk of discovery. It is best not to move about while things are going on." He returned to the car. "Well, we have an hour. Take your seat. It's the wrong time of day, but we'll have to rely on the old lovers' lane dodge. Do you know what I mean?"

"No, Richard."

He shrugged. "I suppose it's different on the conqueror's planet."

She turned her head to him so quickly the wig almost fell off. "The *conquer* . . . oh. You are referring to Kazo."

"What euphemism do you prefer?" He was angry, and knew he was taking it out on her. "Earth was expanding into space, until—Kazo. When I was eight years old I dreamed of becoming a hunter on a frontier planet. Every month some new world was being discovered, and some of them were inhabitable. Our dreams were limitless. Then—"

"Yes!" she said with surprising vehemence.

"What do you know about it? How can you begin to grasp the meaning of freedom, when you have never been denied it? Have you ever had to squirm under the heel of—"

"They are coming, Richard," she said, peering down the street. "Must I be silent again?"

His head snapped about. Three men with machine guns were trotting down the sidewalk. He did not recognize them, which was strange because he had thought he knew most of the members of this division. But by the same token, most of them knew *him.* "I'd better conceal my face. If any of them spot me, I'll be forced to choose between their lives and ours."

"Yes, Richard," Serena said.

"I'll have to kiss you. I don't like it any better than you do."

She faced him on the seat and he twisted shoulders and neck to met her while shielding himself from the view of the outsiders. With a shock he realized that her lips were blue; they'd forgotten to apply lipstick.

Her face was hot, reminding him that Kazo body temperature ran about three degrees above the human norm. The makeup was already beginning to smear. He held the position while the tread of boots passed their car, paused and went on after a suggestive whistle.

"You kiss like a woman," he said.

"Thank you, Richard." She remained as he left her, eyes closed.

"What do you do—lay eggs?"

She did not react to the impertinence of the question. "No, Richard. We give live birth, very much as men do."

"As *women* do. But no breasts?"

"The mammary glands? No, we provide predigested food for our young, like, I think, your honey. In other respects we are very similar to you."

"Except that you are the masters, we the slaves."

She frowned. "You do not understand, Richard. It is not this way."

"Oh? What are we revolting against right now, then? Our imagination?"

"I do not think you would wish to hear it, Richard."

Henrys leaned his head against the steering bar. "I was nine years old when the conqueror came," he said quietly, tired of baiting her.

"We didn't even know the Kazos existed—until the news went out that our fleet was lost, that our leaders had surrendered Earth itself to the aliens. That evening the overlords descended upon our cities, their ships no larger, no faster than ours, but they had vanquished us. My father was a space officer—gone, just like that. The silent spacecraft settling like the foot of a monstrous tarantula to consume the rest of us, too . . ."

"Yes," she said.

"The color of leadership was Kazo-blue. Fifteen years of it—and you claim I don't understand."

"But it was for the benefit of the planets! Hasn't it been a fair administration?"

He looked at her, startled by her intensity. "You wiped out our fleet, so that not a single man ever returned, and made our world and heart a Kazo province—for the sake of a 'fair administration'?"

"I know your feeling, Richard, but—"

"You know my feeling," he said in flat irony. "I had to start school over to learn phonetic spelling. I grew up knowing that I had only one chance in ten to be granted driving privileges. That I might marry, but never succeed in fathering more than one child of my own. That I could go to space only as the hireling of the masters. That every decision I might make was subject to the approval of—"

"But didn't your wars stop?" she asked him eagerly. "Your disease, malnutrition, employment inequities, waste of resources—"

"Yes, by the largess of dictatorship and atmospheric inhibition! But better all of that, than to lose our freedom!" He meant it, he believed it—yet once more the words remained in his memory like lines from a patriotic play. The truth was that had the Kazos not come, Earth might have exercised its freedom—to destroy itself. His certainty faded in the face of Kazo resonableness. "I know there were evils, but at least *we* controlled our destiny, for good or evil. Your rule *has* been good— better than ours, I admit—but tyranny can't be justified merely because it is efficient."

"No, not better than yours," she murmured. "I see that now."

"What?"

She drew back, embarrassed. She seemed momentarily more like a girl of Earth, both in her reaction and, oddly, her appearance. "This . . . pose . . . I am not used to it," she said awkwardly. "But tell me, Richard . . . you agree there were terrible problems, before . . . us. If you were in power, what would you do to safeguard good government?"

He frowned. "I'm no expert on the subject, but I have had some thoughts." Now he was talking to her as though she were an equal, instead of an overlord, yet it seemed more natural. "Our system has been like that parking meter, there. You put your assets in and you get a measured privilege, whether a man or a Kazo controls the machine. The whole world is run by a simple, unbending standard: one dollar, one hour. One job, one wage. One crime, one penalty, no matter what. I just don't believe this is enough. It is bound to foul up sooner or later, because it is a mechanical standard, not a human one. People want what you want, and they don't really care about what is proper. They look for ways to get around the standards, to jimmy the meter, and inevitably they find them."

"Is that the reason for your revolution, Richard?"

Henrys paused, taken aback. "I suppose it is."

"But is there a better system than ours?"

"There must be. I've tried to work it out, but I have only the theory, not the practical side. I'm thinking of a piece of cake."

"A piece of cake!"

Henrys nodded, relaxing. No one else had cared to listen to his theories before. "Take two children. The most important thing in the world to them, this minute, is a big piece of cake. It has to be shared between them—but their rivalry is so strong that no matter how it is cut there will be cries and dispute. Each one demands the bigger section . . ."

Serena put her on his arm and he did not flinch. "Yes," she said.

"An adult could make a fair division and enforce it, leaving both children disgruntled but quiet. But that's the meter-justice. What happens when they are alone? The ideal system should work as well in the absence of third-party supervision."

"Go on, Richard." She seemed quite excited.

"There *is* a system. One child gets to cut the cake; the other takes first choice. Neither one has any intention of being 'fair'—but neither complains about the result. It works *because* of human nature, not in spite of it. Now the ideal form of government—"

"Look," she said suddenly, pointing to the meter. "Our time is almost gone, and we shall have to go."

Henrys reverted to immediacies. "It's been much quieter than I expected. There can't have been much resistance." He deposited the last of his change in the car's hopper and backed out when the motor started. "It may be safe to check into a hotel now, after all."

"Will they be watching there, Richard?"

"Not if they think they've captured or killed all the overlords. They'll be too busy setting up a provisional government to bother with such details." He noted his own use of the third person with a certain detachment; there was no use denying that the steam had gone out of his revolutionary fervor.

"I hope there has not been any killing," she said.

"It wasn't their . . . our plan to kill the Kazos," he told her, omitting the chief exception. Bitool has been considered too dangerous to allow to live. He could see why, now. "If they were willing to surrender without a fight, they'd simply be locked up. We don't want to go back to the days of murder and anarchy." But the immense supply of machine guns, that he had never been told about, made him doubt the sincerity of the revolution's mysterious leader. He had never seen John Tanner, or any picture of him, or known that he had published a book of his principles. Yet that book joggled inside his shirt. *Had* mass execution been arranged? "But you'll have to stay with me until we're sure."

"I understand, Richard."

He parked the car at one of the recharging stands and showed the way to the hotel. At the door he stopped her. "Do you have any lipstick?"

"Lipstick, Richard?"

"Never mind. I'll bluff, if the clerk notices. But stay behind me and out of the light, if possible." He had chosen this hotel because it was an old-fashioned one with human help. The risk was smaller, this way. A mechanized house would automatically register their human identities with the general computer—and Serena had none. The revolutionaries would have control over the computer by this time—and he was probably already listed as a traitor—or dead. Later he could explain—but not now.

"Yes?"

*Oh no,* he thought, *not one of the sanctimonious ones.* "Room for two, second floor."

The clerk peered at him over rimless spectacles. "You have no reservation?"

"No."

"We shall have to verify your credit rating."

"Cash."

"Very good, sir," the clerk said, his tone conveying eloquently what he thought of someone who stooped to such a level. He made out the registry. "Your wife looks cold, sir."

"Appearances can be deceiving."

The clerk did not laugh. "Her lips—"

"She's recovering from an illness."

"We have a doctor—"

Would the man never give over? "No thanks. Rest

cure. Nothing contagious. An evening's relaxation will work wonders. You know how it is."

The clerk frowned. "I see. The charge includes tranquilizer."

Henrys decided not to protest the size of the bill, due in advance, though it left him with very little money on his person. He could get more—after he got Serena out of the city.

The "tranquilizer" was waiting as they entered the room: about eighty-six proof. Henrys reddened as he comprehended the clerk's assesment of his motives.

Serena picked up the bottle, interested. She did not seem to be nearly as concerned for her safety as Henrys was.

"It's a beverage," Henrys explained. "Intended for human consumption. I'd advise caution."

"Oh, a Kazo can digest anything you can," she assured him brightly. She negotiated the seal and poured herself half a glass.

Henrys watched with dismay as she lifted the whiskey to her lips and downed it. "An *alcoholic* beverage," he said. "It depresses the higher centers of control and leads eventually to a comatose state. I wouldn't—"

"No effect on Kazo metabolism," she said, pouring herself another liberal dose. "I like it."

Henrys let the matter go, hoping she was right. "I promised to explain why this subterfuge was necessary. I didn't mean to place you in a compromising situation, but—"

"Compromising, Richard?"

"Ordinarily a man and a woman do not share a room unless they are married."

"But you explained about that, Richard."

She still didn't grasp the concept of expediency, or euphemism. "Of course we are of totally different species—"

"No objections," she said easily. "Do you know, Richard, this bev . . . beverage is very good. Are you sure you won't have some before I finish it?"

"Are you *sure* it doesn't affect you? We have to keep alert."

"Richard, our entire met . . . chemistry is different. For example, that man was wrong about my being cold.

The present temperature is entirely comfort . . . comfortable for me." She plopped into the easy chair, letting her wig go askew.

Henrys suddenly remembered the lipstick and began checking the room's appointments. If they were lucky—

"You're not mammals. You don't shiver or sweat. How *do* you control your body temperature?" He already had an idea, since the information was freely available in the libraries, but he had decided it was better to keep her talking. Otherwise her natural curiosity could get them into further trouble.

Serena fished a magazine out of the wastebasket beside her chair. Evidently cleanup was perfunctory, here. She turned the pages as she spoke. "We possess an internal quantity of heat-retentive fluid that acts as a reservoir. This accumulates surplus calories in the daytime exercise and dispenses it at night, stabilizing the system. There is also a certain amount of *avoir* . . . *avoirdupois* around the body which can be redistributed as protection against localized exposure."

Henrys, taking his cue from her, sorted through the bathroom trash basket. There, wonderfully, he found it: the remnant of a tube of lipstick. It was not usable as it stood, but there was still substance in the base. He pried at it with his penknife. "Suppose you have a heat wave?"

"A caloric overload? No problem," she said, her voice slurring slightly. He tried to tell himself it was because she was trying to read the magazine while talking, but the picture in his mind was of the empty whiskey bottle. "On the surface of our limbs are fine metallic fibers that radiate excess energy quite efficiently when required. I believe the principle is similar to what you employ for mechanical refrigeration. You convey the heat to a radiating—"

Henrys, having pried open the tube, re-entered the room. He saw the cover of the issue she was reading: a girlie magazine.

"Let's get some of this on your lips," he said. "We can't have them showing blue."

"All right, Richard," she agreed. "You had better apply it, however. You know what you want."

He knelt beside her chair and touched the blob of red

to her mouth. "It isn't what *I* want," he said. "It's to conceal your identity until you can rejoin your people. No Kazo is safe in this city, at the moment."

"This is an interesting publication," she said as he finished. "But I'm not clear on certain things. Why are there no pictures of human males presented here? It says it is for men, and they are quite active in the descriptions. And are the female proportions accurately represented? I did not see many women on the street, but they were not—"

"The women depicted," Henrys said without emphasis, "are not typical. They represent the ideal, as determined by masculine criteria. A man pays attention to the physical attributes, particularly those of face and torso, and these may determine the extent of his sexual interest in a given specimen."

Serena found a few more drops in the bottle. "How convenient! That seems so much more forthright than our system. And I am to emulate a woman. Let me see . . ." She stood up unsteadily and tugged at her dress.

"What are you doing?" Henrys protested with alarm.

"I am removing my clothing, Richard." She swayed, but got the dress over her head.

He turned away. "Oh. You will find the shower in there."

"Water? I do not need it, thank you, Richard."

Henrys stood with his back to her, uncertain what to do. It was obvious that he had an intoxicated Kazo female on his hands; while he did not know what to expect next, he was sure it meant trouble. She was a member of a species far more divergent from his own than any creature on Earth—but he had come to accept her as sapient and feminine, and could no longer view her with indifference.

She was moving around busily, and once the magazine rustled.

"Please give me your opinion, Richard," she said at last.

He turned, assuming that she had adjusted her dress and donned it again more comfortably. He was mistaken.

She had stripped herself of all apparel except the wig, and now displayed a stunningly human outline. Enormous breasts where her chest had been flat before; hips flared. The waist narrowed alarmingly.

Henrys forgot himself and stared, hardly able to credit it. "What—?"

"Is everything in order, Richard? I modeled it after the illustrations—"

He studied her body, appalled. The flesh was real. She was exactly like a buxom model dipped in blue. How had she done it?

Then he remembered her remark about *avoirdupois*. She had intended it literally when she talked about redistribution. That would also explain the Kazo similarites of facial feature: they could shape their flesh and cartilage to match the human posture.

He had told her to pass herself off as a human female, not realizing how far she would take it.

"If the physique is satisfactory," she said, "I am ready to conform to the rest of your conventions, Richard."

He had been inspecting her as though she were a statue. He turned away again, reddening. "Conventions?"

"To be your wife, your companion, your female, as you directed. I did not understand it entirely before; but there are several descriptions of the procedure in the publication."

Henrys choked. She had applied the erotica to the original subterfuge, not penetrating the true nature of either. "This applies only in public," he said as evenly as he could. "There is no compatibility between our species."

"I'm sorry, Richard. Did I make an error in the pose? Too much intoxication?"

"You mean to say you're *not* drunk?"

"Yes, Richard." The fuzziness and hesitation vanished. She *had*, it seemed, grasped some of it.

He took a deep breath. "Serena, get dressed and I'll try to clarify things."

"You do not find me attractive?"

"I do not."

She dressed silently. He was upset about hurting her feelings, but realized that strict truth was the only course to follow from here on.


"Since Earth fell to the invader," he said, "We have had only one serious hope for freedom: that the occupation was temporary. We know that it is impossible to throw off the alien yoke by force; this entire revolution exists only by Kazo sufferance, and will collapse when the first genuine counteraction is taken. That isn't what the leaders think, but it is the truth."

"You said you were part of it, Richard. Don't you believe in it?"

"I—" He paused, baffled. "I thought I did. But when they sent me to—"

She glanced at him alertly, no trace of intoxication in her manner.

"To kill the overlord," Henrys continued with difficulty. "I . . . but I don't believe in taking life. I would never—"

She modified the subject delicately. "What were you about to say about your attitude to Kazo females, Richard?"

He sat down. The book Bitool had given him shifted inside his shirt, and he drew it out. "I have to hate the Kazo female, as does every person on Earth. Because the occupation can be considered temporary only so long as the conqueror does not colonize. But the moment he starts bringing in family units, he has given notice he means to stay. Kazo females are incompatible with the freedom of Earth." But as he spoke his eyes were on the title, "The Revolutonist's Handbook," and his thoughts were in a third domain. How could he ever have agreed to kill anyone? It was an act of lawlessness that repulsed him utterly. Yet he had fired twice at Bitool—

"And you were assigned to take care of me?" she inquired. "I do not understand this, Richard."

Then the author's name leaped up at him, making a connection whose significance had evaded him before: John Tanner. The leader of the present revolution.

Whose book was in the hands of the Kazos, but had not been shown directly to the partisans.

He opened it. There in the preface were the very sentences he had spoken in answer to the overlord's rapid queries: automatic responses, rote replies from a printed catechism he did not recall ever studying. "A revolutionist is one who desires to discard the existing . . ."

He flipped back to the title page. "John Tanner, M. I. R. C. (Member of the Idle Rich Class)."

A joke. And at the foot, a brief note: "Reprinted from the supplement to the play 'Man and Superman,' by

George Bernard Shaw, in which John Tanner is a fictional character."

"Something is wrong, Richard?"

He hurled the book from him. "I've been a patsy. They must have drugged me and instilled posthypnotic suggestion and a headful of platitudes—and Bitool knew it! He knew I was doped and duped. Probably my whole escape route was phony, and most of the information I thought I had. If I killed Bitool and got captured myself, none of my information would mean a thing!"

"Then you are not of their number?"

"I thought I was of their number," he said bitterly. "All my philosophizing . . . my 'piece of cake.' I thought I was on the way to answers. I thought I had something useful to do."

"Perhaps you still do, Richard. Why did you assist me, even against the men you believed were your compatriots?"

"What a man believes may be ascertained," he said in a rapid monotone, "not from his creed, but from the assumptions on which he habitually acts." He laughed harshly. "That's another dear little quote from the handbook. I recognize it now. The irony is that much of it does make sense. It was easy for me to believe I believed it. I *do* believe it, or at least I agree with much of it. I helped you because I had given my word—and you needed help. That was something quite apart from automatic phrases."

"I am very glad that was the case, Richard."

"But I *still* don't approve of the Kazo rule. Men should be allowed to make their own mistakes. It isn't fair to—" He stopped, listening.

Heavy boots were tramping up the old wooden stairs.

"Out the window!" he snapped. "There's a fire escape."

She moved immediately at his direction, asking no questions. He loosened the catch and knocked the window open. His training might be no more than hypnotic indoctrination for the isolated mission, or possibly only for verisimilitude in case of capture—but it stood him in good stead now. He knew what had happened and what to do: the clerk had become suspicious and requested a computer check on their identities. Thus the revolutionaries had traced him down and come to recover him— and the invaluable Kazo female.

He was hungry. He thought of it, oddly, as he bustled Serena down the metal steps and into the evening. He had not eaten since the misadventure started, and she was probably no better off.

A long, ancient filthy alley ran beside the hotel, as ugly as such corridors had traditionally been since the days of Babylon, when the very pavement was constructed of packed garbage. They trotted down it. His comprehensive knowledge of the city streets stood him in good stead, again; no one could outmaneuver him here. Just ahead there was a—

A beam of light pierced the shadow, searching for them from the window just quitted, but there was no outcry. He jerked Serena around the corner. How laughable: his indoctrination made him far more competent at this sort of thing than his pursuers were! They had thought to march in noisily and catch him napping!

The lighted entrance to the subterranean transit was at hand. They merged with the evening throng. At the first level down they stepped onto the belt traveling toward the center of town and stood together like a couple going on a date. Serena had kept her body, and it strained at the more conservative dress; she even attracted a complimentary glance or two.

Henrys had chosen this belt because it moved in the opposite direction expected of a person fleeing the city, but now it occurred to him that he was being foolish. Either the revolutionists were after him and wanted him badly enough to close off every city exit—a phenomenal undertaking, on top of the problems of the take-over—or their interest in him was incidental. He had jumped to the conclusion that they had spotted him in the hotel, but now he saw this as a conditioned response, and an exaggeration of his importance. It could have been someone on an unrelated errand—and they might not even know about Serena.

And he had sacrificed the room he had paid for, on that histrionic suspicion, and now did not have the funds for another.

"Serena," he murmured, "I think I have miscalculated. Are you willing to take a chance?"

"Yes, Richard."

He guided her off the belt at the next traveler's aid station. The clerk looked up as they approached the booth. "Yes?" he inquired, very much as the hotel clerk had.

"We are travelers not in sympathy with the uprising," Henrys said quickly. "We do not have money for food or lodging, and we hesitate to apply to the computer for credit—"

"Take a seat, please," the clerk said without changing expression. He touched a button on his phone.

They sat down uneasily on the bench facing the booth. "Are you certain that was wise?" Serena inquired.

"No." He wondered whether her concern was for the amount of information given away, or because he had not been entirely candid with the clerk. *She* might have stated the whole truth. "It is a calculated risk. He will either find facilities for us that are discreet—or he will turn us in to the revolutionaries. If he reports us, be ready to move in a hurry; we should be able to lose ourselves again."

"Yes, Richard."

A man strode up to the counter, robust and solid, with a receding hairline and a round cheerful face. The clerk said something in a low tone, not looking up, and the man moved on. Henrys relaxed.

A man with a machine gun rode down the belt. Henrys tensed and touched Serena on the arm. He tried not to stare or reach for his own weapon, but no one else was paying any attention. It was amazing how sanguinely the populace took the revolution! Or was it merely the old, old policy of noninvolvement, euphemized as "live and let live" or "the golden rule"?

"The golden rule is that there are no golden rules," he murmured, quoting from Tanner again. How could a man watch an atrocity, and ignore it in the name of anything golden?

But he knew that no one would help him if the armed man attacked. He would have to use his palm pistol or run.

The revolutionist rode on by.

"Will you join me?" It was the robust man, now seated beside them. Henrys had been so anxious about the armed man that he had not paid enough attention to his immediate surroundings.

Should he trust this person? Obviously this was the clerk's contact.

What choice did he have? "Thank you," he said.

The man stuck out a healthy hand. "Adam Notchez, master-sergeant, World Army, retired."

They shook. "Dick Henrys—and this is Serena."

Notchez escorted them to a handsome apartment in the high-rise residentials. "My grandchildren are about somewhere. Hide and Tag in the lift, most likely."

Henrys could imagine it: ride to a random floor, jump off, jump on again after several compartments had passed, while the following child had to outguess the first and catch up without overshooting. To watch the floors from a compartment, or the compartments from one floor? Endless possibilities. "Is that permitted?" he inquired.

"Of course not. I'll have to pretend I don't suspect. That's why I'm a popular baby-sitter—I'm good at keeping secrets. Got nothing better to do with my time, these days. Have a drink?"

"No," Henrys said, cutting Serena off. She smiled faintly and winked at Notchez, who smiled back.

"Well, you're both hungry, I know. It'll have to be leftovers, though. Hydro-turnip salad, soy milk, the usual. I sure miss the old days."

Henrys tensed. "You object to Kazo rule?"

Notchez gestured expansively as he set down the food. "Ten years ago I would have been in the forefront of the mob, clamoring for blue blood. Five years ago I might have supported a revolution tacitly. But now that it's come, I discover that I don't like it. Suddenly I find myself appreciating fifteen consecutive years of peace and prosperity. That's a world record—literally, you know. It beats the old one by about fourteen and a half years. Oh, I miss it, I get terribly nostalgic—but I don't regret it anymore."

"But weren't you in Earth's military?" Serena asked, nibbling delicately on a flavored mushroom. Henrys tightened, but the sergeant didn't seem to notice the signal of alien viewpoint.

"Thirty years," Notchez laughed. "Oh, I know what you're going to say next! What does a career man do, when there isn't any war? And I will inform you that the army is with us yet, the navy, too—busier than ever. The war never stopped. Not for an instant."

Henrys put his hand on his concealed pistol.

"The war against hunger, disease, ignorance," their host continued. "It took me a long time to be convinced. I was so sure there was an ulterior motive, that the overlords were setting us up for something terrible—extinction of the species, for example, or reduction to slavery for Kazo colonists. But I changed my mind. Here, let me show you." He touched a button and a projection came to life on the wall opposite them. Notchez hitched his chair around beside Henrys.

"This is the Global Highway. The Kazos decided that civilization depended on good communications, and that meant, among other things, high-capacity arteries. This is the mightiest turnpike ever built on Earth—sixteen miles across, twelve tall. The Romans were pikers!"

Henrys smiled at the sergeant's little joke. He knew about the highway, though he had never driven on it. Serena was watching the projection with her usual interest.

The highway rose like the Wall of China, a hundred feet high and twice as wide, yet sunlight filtered through its several tiers and green plants decorated every level. The camera panned across the continuous restaurants, recharging stations, theaters and hotels lining its center mall, all elegantly sculpted and brilliantly clean. Electric cars shot by at a hundred and fifty miles per hour in the isolated speed lanes, while they seemed to inch along in the outer scenic strips.

"My unit was never even broken up," Notchez was saying. "We were redesignated a construction battalion, and our chain of command descended from a Kazo general. We worked on that road—and I tell you, I learned more about building, the last dozen years of my enlistment, than I ever thought I'd know about anything. We had to excavate fifty feet into the ground and level it, come mountain or ocean, sticking mostly to contour, and pipe the rivers through. The thing runs from Cape Horn to the Cape of Good Hope without a break, or will soon, splitting into the Siberian/European/West African and the South-Asian loops that join up again at the equator. I worked on sections in five continents and the Indonesian Spur."

There was a shot of one of the underground lanes, as

seen from a speeding car. The walls on either side were decorated with murals: scenery similar to that visible along the various other sections. An inset view of the speedometer showed it rising above the posted limit.

"Watch this," Notchez said.

At five miles per hour over the limit the mural wavered and dissolved into inchoate patches of color. At ten, enormous letters appeared: OVERSPEED.

"Damndest effect," the sergeant observed. "Something about the optics of it. The car sets up sympathetic vibrations in the air, too, at that speed, making a most unpleasant keening noise. Same thing happens if you go too slow. Of course speeders *are* arrested if they push their luck. Now watch."

The dial of the speedometer dropped and the mural reappeared. Henrys realized that it was enormously elongated, to provide a natural effect when viewed at speed—yet the distant mountains shifted perspective realistically, while "near" objects blurred by. This was not a simple painting.

The indicator dropped below the minimum and the picture blurred again. No words appeared at the reduced speed, however; instead the colors jumped, as though on separate frames.

Then he understood. They *were* separate frames—wide columns angled to present a compensated view of sections of color: red, yellow and blue. Between these posts he could now make out the adjoining lanes, and *their* pillars, a subterranean forest. The proper velocity combined the sections into a full-color, continuous image, and an improper velocity brought out another illustration, as though stroboscopically phased. Yet it was mechanical, not electronic; just a useful application of known principles.

Notchez was answering one of Serena's questions. "Well, I think the cars are supposed to be spaced a hundred feet apart, on the average, though of course traveling speed makes a difference. Say they're doing sixty—that's over fifty cars passing any given point in each lane. Ninety-six lanes going each direction—call it five thousand cars per minute, total, each way. Comes to . . . I figured it out once . . . about seven hundred thousand every twenty-four hours—east or west. Put a family of three in each car, and in three years you could empty the planet."

"And you built it all in only twelve years?" Serena inquired. The projection was riding along the top section now, the only area that *looked* like a highway. The view was from the innermost lane, overlooking the mall; the tops of trees waved at eye-level, and swinging pedestrian mock-vine ramps crossed to the other side.

"Thirty thousand miles of it? No—there's still a gully cooling off in the Urals and a couple other places, where they had to 'H' a channel. Can't build until the radiation drops, you know. And down in Sumatra and Java, between the monsoons and the earthquakes—"

The door slid open and two children appeared, interrupting him. Notchez turned off the image. "Kids, you know how late it is? Know what your mamma would say to me if she knew—"

One was a girl about six; the boy was a little smaller. "We won't tell if you won't, Granpa," the girl said precociously. She spied the visitors. 'Oh. Hello, Visitors."

"Hello," Serena answered promptly. The result was unexpected.

"Kazo!" both children screamed, rushing at her.

Henrys' hand dived for his weapon, but this time the host's heavy arm slapped him back against the chair. "You don't make that motion twice—not against a master-sergeant." Notchez murmured. His iron grip closed on Henrys' wrist. "Just keep quiet and watch."

"Kazo!" the little girl repeated, as each child clung to one of Serena's hands and tugged at the gloves to reveal the blue skin beneath. But they were smiling.

"You knew all the time," Henrys snapped.

"I worked under Kazo supervision a dozen years," Notchez said. "For the last five I was Enlisted Liaison man for the general. I know a Kazo when I see one, though I never saw a female before." His grip relaxed. "And I guess the kids do, too. I didn't think they'd be that quick, though."

The gloves came off. "See?" the girl exclaimed triumphantly. "All blue!"

"I always told them that only good children could ever get to meet a Kazo," Notchez explained. "As I said, my attitudes changed quite a bit over the years. I respect what the overlords have accomplished, and I am far from being alone. That's why I agreed to hide you during the . . . disturbance. You'll stay here for the duration—the children wouldn't have it otherwise." He turned to Henrys. "Or do you doubt their motives?"

The little boy had climbed into Serena's lap and was whispering something into her ear, while the girl yanked at him jealously.

"You will find that this 'revolution' is pretty much shrugged off by the average man," Notchez continued. "There is always a ruthless lunatic fringe—but the great majority have come to realize, as I have, that the loss of the Kazos would be the greatest disaster Earth could sustain. The yoke is light, the benefits impressive. In a few days those self-styled saviors of man are going to crawl back into their holes, baffled by contempt and passive resistance. We don't need their kind any more."

"But would you feel that way without—"

"Without being drugged?" He shrugged. "If the atmosphere is drugged the way the soreheads claim, would revolution ever have broken out? Seems more likely to me that we're free agents now, whatever happened before."

Why hadn't he thought of that? The fact of the revolution gave the lie to such pacification. His thoughts and feelings had to be his own, unless the revolutionists had found some individual antidote. If they had, why hadn't they given it to everyone? Unless they *wanted* passivity so *they* could rule . . . Either way, the Kazos seemed to be vindicated. He didn't have to resent what he suspected they had done to his emotions.

"I think I have some cake somewhere," Notchez said, standing, "if it doesn't start a riot."

"Me first!" the children circled in unison, scrambling after him.

Henrys let the burden fall away. "If you will allow me to make a suggestion—"

"But I want some, too, Richard," Serena protested mischievously.

The sergeant emerged from the kitchen with half of a richly frosted chocolate cake. "My personal drug indicator is a piece of cake," he said. "If I can divide it peacefully, I figure the suppressant is acting. But tonight—"

"Even so, it can be done," Henrys said. "It's just a matter of—"

"But *everyone* should have a piece," Serena said.

"Fine," Notchez agreed. "Just so long as it's divided fairly, and *I* get the fairest chunk."

Henrys contemplated the prize. "You conspirators think you have me, don't you?"

They laughed.

"Well try *this* on for size," he said. "There are five of us, er, equals. Nobody wants to be deprived, right? Very well: I will cut myself a section representing my fair share—one fifth. If any of you think it is too big for me, you may cut a little off to make it right. O. K.? Then you can divide the rest of the cake among you, crumbs, and all, in the same fashion."

The little girl stood on one foot and screwed up her face in concentration. "I get last choice," she announced after a moment. The boy was silent, not comprehending this and suspicious of a sibling ruse.

"Your piece may become rather small," Notchez warned him.

Henrys grinned. "One clarification: the last person to touch the piece gets it instead."

Now all were perplexed except Serena, who refrained from comment. "You sure this thing will get off the ground?" Notchez inquired dubiously.

Henrys took the knife and cut off a full quarter. "There's my piece," he said. "Anybody object?"

"Yeah!" the children cried, appalled at such gluttony. The girl snatched the knife and assessed the situation. "I can take away as much as I want?"

"Yes. But then you keep the piece left."

"But what if I make it too small?"

"Too bad."

She hovered over it, unable to make up her mind. Finally she shaved off a thin segment and swept it into the main body. "There. Now it's mine."

"Oh yeah?" her brother demanded. He knocked off a tiny crumb. "Mine!"

She glared at him. The piece was still a generous one.

"Next?" Henrys said.

No one moved.

"Mine!" the boy exclaimed again, gleefully. He made off with the booty.

"I begin to glimpse the light," Notchez said. He took the knife and severed a smaller piece. No one challenged it, and it was his. "Yes—I comprehend!"

Serena took another slim section, leaving the last decision between Henrys and the girl. "I'll cut—you choose. O.K.?" he asked her.

She nodded distrustfully. He cut it unevenly.

She stared. "My choice?"

"Right."

She squealed with delight. "You made a mistake!" she cried, taking the larger piece.

"Can't win 'em all," he observed philosophically.

"But you see it would be cumbersome to divide a cake between two billion people that way," Bitool said. "That is the weakness of that system. By the time it was accomplished, the cake would have rotted, and the people starved, even if social problems could be arbitrated so simply. The fair way is not always the best way."

Henrys looked out the window of Bitool's office, wondering where the overlord and other Kazos had concealed themselves for the past three days. Not one had been captured by the armed searchers. The revolutionists had abdicated in the face of massive indifference, as predicted and had accepted exile on a Pacific isle helpfully deeded to them. The coup had never even made headlines. "I know," he said, "that the world can not properly be equated to a piece of cake. Simile only goes so far. But I'll stand by the principle: there must be a way to achieve commerce between species without the conquest of one by the other. Some way to divide and choose—"

He broke off. "Just what *did* happen to the Earth fleet, at the beginning?"

"Tell him, Serena."

Serena, now of normal appearance, closed her eyes and spoke in a strange, impassioned singsong: "It is the year of the flightless amphibian, of the bloom of the seaborn ones, and of our fourteenth off-world colony. Our ships range into the realm of null-communication, searching out strange worlds, and we are waiting for news of wonder. Only in space are we united, and soon even that may fall away, as we find no common enemy to bind our passions together. Yet we fear that theoretic enemy even more, for we are new to space and our hold on it is uncertain.

"And our fleet gathers its ships of all dependencies and disappears—and then the horde of the Earthmen comes and we are surrendered and we do not know what has happened. We try to resist, but our governors are gone over to the enemy and we are become hostage to our own weapons. And the Human creatures emerge from battleships like ours, beings of ferocious aspect and immobile feature, of stiff limbs and astonishing tenacity, and we are afraid.

"But they are fair, policing their own numbers as rigidly as ours, and we come to know that there is glory behind their power and sorrow beneath their regimentation. We chafe under their mastery, seeing them no more advanced than we—but we forget the terrors of war and famine, for peace is absolute. In time we come even to love them."

Bitool reacted first. "I did not know this, Seren."

"You have not been on the home-world, Bitool," she said. "But I have found that the man you gave me to is as honorable as the ones governing our world. I could not tempt him."

It was the first time Henrys had seen an overlord embarrassed. "This was not intended," Bitool said. "There must be no relationships between the species."

"Naïveté," Serena said, but now she was embarrassed, too. "How else is one to find common ground with the master?"

Henrys would have been amused at this evidence of the differing attitudes of Kazo-male and Kazo-female, if his own sentiments were not overridden by the larger picture. "Do you mean Earth and Kazo *exchanged governments*?"

Serena smiled. "I was surprised, too, Richard. Perhaps I did not fully appreciate it until you explained about the cake. But isn't it best?"

"But how can you be sure the Earthmen aren't brutalizing your home?"

Bitool recovered his serenity. "Richard, do you expect us to send men to govern our own world who are not fit?"

It began to fall into place. New Kazos arrived every year, invariably upstanding specimens—selected, it seemed, by the human overlords of Kazo. No, the choices would hardly be careless, when the decisions were irrevocable and the homeworld was hostage. Even the most selfish child divided the cake fairly when any mistake applied so directly against his basic interest.

And there would never be war between the planets.

"The key is not so much in the system, Richard," Serena said gently, "but in the selection. Good leaders make good government—and good government breeds good leaders."

"Why are you telling all this to *me*?"

"Why do you think, Richard?"

Then the rest of it dawned. "But I came to kill—"

"And you overcame the strongest conditioning the rebels could impose, and your own lingering doubts," Bitool said. "You were tempted—and did not fall. How else could we be sure of you? Surely we could not send an untempered man. What a man believes— "

"May be ascertained, not from his creed—" Henrys added.

"We shall not see each other again, Richard," Serena interposed sadly. "You leave tomorrow."

Bitool put out his hand for an Earth-type handshake. "Yes, we are alien rulers—and you are about to be an alien ruler, too. Be kind to my world, Master."

# SQUEEZE BOX

## BY PHILIP E. HIGH

Landon paused at the door, frowning, thin brows making a narrow V above his nose. He realised that he took this side of his duties too seriously and it was getting him down. All his duties required of him was a simple, direct statement of fact and nothing more. Why did he always have to make it such an arduous and exhausting mission? Did he have some over-developed paternal instinct or, possibly, some of those qualities which might, in a past age, have turned him into a minister of religion? But you couldn't walk in on a chap and say: 'You're going to die,' and then walk out again, could you? It was too brutal. "Life these days," he told himself, bitterly, "might be cheap but one needn't make it sound like a hand-out."

This case, too, had certain aspects—hell, Marion was just another man or was he? Too likeable, too strong, too much character in an age when conformity was literally a survival clause. Besides, Landon told himself, firmly, Marion had killed a man and that was wrong in any age.

Landon bent his head a little beneath the word "Lounge," his hand clenched, ready to knock and paused again. Beneath the daubed paint were the clearly discernible words "Bomb Bay" and, as always, they made him feel uncomfortable.

The *Stellar Maid* had been a cruiser, years ago, rakish, perhaps, dangerous-looking until, like humanity, she had taken a beating and been clubbed into order.

Landon sighed, knocked briefly and entered. "Good day," he said, formally. "I am Captain Landon—I'm afraid it's my duty to tell you where you're going."

Marion, lounging in one of the chairs, pursed his lips thoughtfully. "There's only two places I could be going as things stand—the asteroids or Leinster. My sentence

350

was Lethal Deportation." He grinned faintly. "Does it matter which or do I have to guess?"

Landon said, curtly. "Please don't joke, deportation doesn't mean either imprisonment or survival."

"I gathered that when I was sentenced." Marion seemed unperturbed. "I suppose it's a harder way to die?"

"You're going to Leinster to hunt zipcats," said Landon stiffly. He paused and added in a softer tone. "If you kill one, it means a reprieve."

Marion lit a cigarette. "Obviously there is a very big catch and it smacks mightily of Greek mythology." He exhaled smoke. "Enlighten me, what are zipcats?"

"An animal peculiar to Leinster." He hesitated. "An animal which, the government has decided, is definitely, and of necessity, top secret."

Marion nodded and said: "I see," meaningly. He frowned at the floor. "And I hunt it?"

"Yes."

"With my bare hands?"

"No, you may have any weapon you wish."

"What's the catch?"

Landon avoided the other's eyes. "It's invulnerable."

Marion laughed softly. "Now I've heard everything. This sounds more like mythology than ever. Your name isn't Charon by any chance?"

Landon stung, said, "No, it damn well isn't." In his heart, he supposed, in a way, he was. He was ferrying men, damned men, not across the Styx but across space to a planet that was almost as bad. He forced the thought from his mind, slid back a panel exposing bottles and glasses. "Drink?"

"Thanks—brandy please." He watched Landon almost fill the glass, accepted it and sipped. "Done this often?"

"Too often." Landon gulped, not caring to remember the men who had lived for the four week journey in this very lounge.

Marion held the glass up to the light. "Good stuff this—pre-invasion?"

"Yes."

Marion sipped again. "I killed a man," he said in a casual voice. "Worse, I killed the wrong man. Want to hear about it?"

"If it helps." Landon kept his voice neutral.

"Oh it does." Marion paused then said, deliberately, "I got a kick out of it—it was a collaborator."

Landon said: "Oh," noncommittally.

"It was in a food queue." Marion was lighting another cigarette and his voice was now expressionless. "This louse started barging his way to the front, waving his priority card and knocked down a kid." He moved his hands slightly. "I like kids, this one was only a toddler, maybe two years old, a girl. He didn't stop, didn't care, just barged on—" Marion exhaled a jet of blue smoke.

"And you killed him?" supplied Landon.

"Not exactly. I hit him, unfortunately I hit him too hard." Marion sighed. "A hundred years ago it would have been a manslaughter charge but today they have to look around to find laws which don't carry the death penalty. I suppose it's a kick-back from the armistice terms, something has to be done about the population problem." He laughed bitterly. "Generous terms I believe they were called. They took the best parts of Earth for themselves, seven of our colonies and gave us one of their own planets in return." He scowled suddenly at Landon. "One we can't use."

"Who told you that?" said Landon sharply.

"You did. There is an invulnerable animal called a zipcat which obviously makes the planet untenable, otherwise we should be shipping our surplus population out there for all we were worth." He flicked ash on the floor with his finger tip and grinned wryly. "Sounds like a tough job—killing zipcats. If our technically superior conquerors couldn't clear them up, it seems pretty obvious that we can't."

Landon said stiffly: "I'm sorry, but I think it better that a man knows what's going to happen to him."

Marion rose. "Don't feel sorry for me, Landon, there are worse positions. I could be Arkroyd or his successor and that's a really nasty way to die."

Arkroyd! Landon nodded to himself. Saint Arkroyd? Arkroyd the mass murderer? Arkroyd the puppet? Arkroyd, Elected Representative of the Human Race. Yes, yes, he agreed with Marion, whatever Arkroyd was, he was dying the hard way.

\*        \*        \*

Arkroyd had been lithe but now moved like an old man. His face had been clear and smooth but in two years of office, strain and bitterness had carved lines into his cheeks and a premature senility of movement.

"Mousac Benik," he said, steadily. "If you take more of our world my people will die."

Benik made a gesture with a long, six-fingered hand. "We have given you a world to which they may migrate."

"You failed to colonise it."

"Not failed, Arkroyd, the venture would have been too costly. Again, we were not in the desperate position which you so constantly protest. You must devise ways and means to make colonisation possible."

Arkroyd said: "My God," under his breath and watched the knuckles of his hands whiten almost detachedly. "With a technology inferior to your own?" he asked.

"I have already reminded you, your need is desperate, ours was not." He rose, twining the orange robe tightly about his body. "We are setting up a military base in area 67 as soon as equipment comes to hand. All buildings and power installations must be removed or demolished in this section of your world before the new year." He paused, looking at the bent human with faint contempt. "You understand?"

"I understand." There was a world of weariness and resignation in the tired voice.

Arkroyd sat unmoving at his desk long after the alien had gone. More land, more cities, a piece here, a piece there, taking away the people's living space slice by slice. What did Williams say they were calling it? Ah, yes, a squeeze box. He had a vague recollection it was a slang term for some sort of musical instrument but was not certain. One thing he did know was that if you put animals in a cage and kept making the cage smaller, there would come a time when the animals began to eat each other. They hadn't reached that yet but it would come.

He looked about his office—squeeze box was right. At a push the room might hold four people and *that* for the race's elected representative. A desk which swung out from the wall, bed which pulled down from ceiling, toilet and washing facilities which folded into the floor.

Overcrowding, everyone in each others pockets, sleeping in relays, working in relays, staggered meals, rising tuberculosis and declining morals.

Something had to be done and his predecessors, perhaps more ruthless than himself, had set the machinery in motion. They had re-introduced the death penalty and used it to save the race from complete collapse. It was applied at first with reserve but sheer necessity had forced the government to extend it to almost every form of misdemeanour. It was a capital offence to hoard, to steal food, to deal in ration cards, to breed without state permission, to spread rumours likely to cause alarm and despondency—

Bluntly they had to kill people behind a facade of law and order to save the race. It was expedient that a few million should die to save the race.

Arkroyd put his head in his hands and something deep down inside him whimpered like a child. There was no revoking the law now, no way out; to let the population increase, or even remain static, would lead only to starvation, riots and subsequent plague. This, too, was another form of expediency from which the race might never recover.

The squeeze box. Yes, if you put animals in a cage and kept making it smaller, there would come a time when they started to eat each other. Arkroyd knew, as his predecessors must have known, that the conquerors need to install equipment and erect vast defensive devices was pure fabrication. This was a planned policy of extermination but what could he do about it? Defiance would only bring about one of the ruthless pogroms which would cut down their chances even more.

The conquerors programme was almost childlike in its simplicity and was being applied over a period of time with ruthless efficiency. Race extermination was, after all, a messy and tiresome business. The easiest and best method, obviously was to create a situation from which the only escape was self-destruction. That way the job was done for them with the vanquished obligingly burying their own dead. It was all so simple, just make a cage and squeeze.

Arkroyd was beating his clenched fists on the metal desk and couldn't feel it . . .

\* \* \*

The garrison on Leinster lived underground, they had bored into the face of an immense cliff and sealed the entrances behind them with foot thick metal doors.

The officer receiving Marion was bitter, ill at ease and felt like an executioner. It made him look at Marion almost with dislike.

"I suppose I'd better show you the pictures we have." He jerked his had. "This way."

He led the way down a narrow square tunnel, lit infrequently by thin unshaded solar tubes. Despite the whisper of air-conditioning units, the tunnel felt chill, dank and smelt vaguely stale.

"To save answering in detail the obvious questions," said the officer over his shoulder, "I'll answer them now. Yes, we have tried air assault but to do that sort of thing successfully you have to find the enemy—we can't. And no, for the same reason, we have not used solar bombs or nuclear dusting. For either to be effective we'd have to cover the whole planet which would make it untenable for us when we'd finished. Lastly, I don't know if the creature is really invulnerable but it's smart enough not to be at the receiving end of anything you throw at it. It just so happens that wherever you attack or bomb, you're too late, it's never there." He stopped abruptly and held open a door. "In here. I won't bother to put on the light, there's a chair just to your left."

Switches clicked, a screen filled with milky light and slowly began to clear.

"This is it," said the officer. "The only picture we have."

Marion saw a creature vaguely resembling a jaguar. It was bluish in colour with an inch wide silver streak running down the center of its back. Marion surmised it was about twelve feet in length and weighed about a quarter of a ton. The legs were short but looked jointed and the fur or pelt looked gleaming and a little oily rather like that of a seal.

Switches clicked again and the picture vanished, to be replaced by another.

"Trained assault troops," said the officer. "Supported, as you will observe, by armoured vehicles and air cover."

Marion leaned forward in his chair. The picture showed

an advance over an open plain of waist-high feathery yellow grass. Air support was considerable, armoured vehicles proceeded and covered the flanks, while fast, lightly armoured scout machines made swift reconnaisance far ahead of the main body. The troops themselves were well trained and obviously experienced but they never stood a chance. One of them, close to the camera, spun dizzily on his feet and pitched sideways before Marion, staring at the screen, realised that any sort of action had begun.

He watched unbelievingly as man after man went down and did not rise. The manner of their deaths, too, was not pretty. Some were flung high in the air, falling limp and helpless as if already dead. Others appeared to be suddenly wrenched asunder or crushed as if by an enormous weight. An officer, directing operations from the turret of an armoured vehicle, was abruptly headless. The torso slowly disappeared leaving the limp hands flapping grotesquely above the rim of the turret.

One of the smaller vehicles staggered uncertainly, rose on one track and rolled over on its back.

Marion felt his nails biting into the palms of his hands, he wanted to stand up and shout: "What the hell's happening? Where are the damned things?" True, the grass was waist-high and would easily conceal the animal but how could it strike down men without revealing itself? "What is it—invisible?"

"Oh, for God's sake, man!" The officer's voice was both angry and defensive. "Do you think we'd be going through this bloody business if we *knew*?"

Marion said, evenly: "How do you know it *is* the zipcats?"

"It can't be much else." The other's voice was listless now. "We've found the marks of their bodies, spoor, bloody claw marks. I'm afraid there's no doubt about that side of it and then, of course, there's the noise."

Marion realised he had been hearing the noise for some time but had dismissed it as some defect in the recording wire. It was a curious sound, a flat slapping report which was somehow incomplete and trailed away into a rending noise like abruptly torn canvas.

"Zipcats," said the officer. "That's how they got the name, we assume it's some sort of call, like a lion roaring, for example."

Marion said: "Yes," only half hearing. On the screen the orderly well-disciplined advance was rapidly degenerating into a rout. Men were firing blindly and wildly at nothing and already two vehicles had fallen or been driven into concealed pits.

The screen blanked suddenly, whitely empty and then slowly clouded to darkness.

The officer cleared his throat and said with false confidence: "Of course there may come a time when one man finds the answer." He cleared his throat again nervously, feeling once again like an executioner. "Have you any particular weapon in mind?"

Arkroyd rose and bowed stiffly as he had been taught. He felt like a buffoon a puppet who moved when the strings were pulled. "Yes, Mousac Benik?"

The alien loosened his cloak and sat down. "I am here to inform you that our installations will require far more space than we at first supposed." He pointed to the wall map with a long stick-like finger. "All of this." The finger described a circle.

Arkroyd felt the muscles stiffen beneath his skin. "But that's nearly a thousand square miles." Despite himself his voice was almost a sob. "It's impossible." His mind raced insanely trying to calculate how many millions he would have to crush into the already overcrowded cities. No time to build, no time to dig, the hammocks in the dormitories already less than an inch apart and winter coming—Oh God, Oh God!

"Impossible?" The alien looked at him strangely. "What is impossible? We require the demolition of some buildings, the removal of installations, such a task is not beyond the capacities of your people, surely?"

Arkroyd was thinking: 'I could kill him now. I could reach out from here and break that pipe-stem neck with my bare hands but what good would it do? Reprisals, pogroms, more millions uprooted and some other poor devil sitting in this same chair, dying as he sat or, like many before him, fingering the gun in the desk drawer and finally blowing off the top of his head.'

The alien folded his hands, intertwining his fingers so that they reminded Arkroyd of thin saffron-coloured worms. "The impossibility, Arkroyd, lies with you, it is a block in your own mind due to emotional disturbance and confused thinking. An application of the laws of expediency would leave your mind clear to perform the duties your position imposes. Like all your race you allow emotion and sentimentality to obscure your vision and influence your judgment." He rose, tightening his robe. "Demolition must be completed by the first day of the new year."

Arkroyd's bow was purely reflex as the alien left, his conscious mind barely noticed the empty chair and the closed door. The new year! It was fantastic. An area so large, he hadn't the labour or the machines to do it, there was no time even to plan the demolition. Machines producing synthetic foods must come first and room *made* to operate in space needed for the population they must uproot. They could, perhaps, dig even deeper into the ground but that would mean splitting a labour force that was already inadequate for demolition.

His mind became curiously numb and sluggish as if it had revolted of its own accord and refused to juggle with statistics. Perhaps it was a sort of safety factor but whatever it was, it was occurring with greater frequency each week.

He pulled open the desk drawer and stared dully at the squat blue-black weapon lying casually on the white, never used, pre-invasion note paper. All he had to do was to put it to his head and squeeze the trigger. It was all so easy, six of his predecessors had done it as if to prove its simplicity and the suicide weapon had never been removed. Perhaps, after all, it was not a weapon at all but an instrument of mercy to be resorted to when the strain became too much. Selection for Representative was not dependent upon the mass of the people but the findings of a computer which based its selection on taped psychological information recorded at each yearly medical examination.

When he had been selected Arkroyd had had dreams of improving the lot of his people, now his dreams were escape-fantasies and he knew it. Secretly he called them "If-only" dreams. If only they could find a weapon powerful enough to support an uprising— If only the enemy would fall sick— If only someone would find a way to destroy zipcats—

On Leinster it was raining, dully, steadily, with a kind of leaden persistence which, Marion felt, was somehow symbolic of his state of mind. The garrison was already five miles behind him and, at first, he had carried his heavy repeating weapon alertly in his hands ready to fire at the first sign of movement. After a time however, his arms began to ache and the pictures he had seen kept repeating themselves in his mind. Slowly he had become filled with a sort of weary acceptance of his position and the virtually impossible task before him. He had slung the weapon over his shoulder and gone plodding on filled with an oriental fatalism tempered slightly by typically western irony. If something was going to strike him down without a chance, why pass his last hours lugging that damn heavy thing around?

He was passing now along a natural path, or animal track, between slender, immensely tall trees with green trunks. Overhead thunder rolled steadily and almost continuous lightning rippled across the leaden roof of cloud. Even as he walked a blue-white finger reached downwards and, somewhere ahead of him, he heard a tree go crashing groundwards.

'I could always be struck by lightning,' he thought wryly. 'Save the zipcats a lot of trouble.'

He rounded a bend in the trail and stopped. "Just my damn luck," he said aloud.

Completely blocking his way was the wreckage of one of the immense trees. It was blackened, split and, in places, still smoking faintly. It was, quite obviously, the one he had heard fall some moments before. The point was that there was no way round it or through it, the surrounding trees too dense to make a detour. He sighed. Might as well sit down and let the zipcats find *him*.

He extracted a cigarette from under his plastic cape, cupped his hand against the rain and managed to get it alight. He inhaled deeply, watching the blue smoke crawl round his hand then, not ten feet away, something moved.

He wasn't ready, he knew he wasn't ready. He fought a wild battle with himself trying to unsling the gun from his shoulder. Somehow it had become entwined in the cape and some part of the mechanism gashed his ear badly as he struggled.

By the time he had disentangled himself, everything was still again. Cautiously, the weapon ready, he peered into the tangle of branches. Somewhere, half seen but close to the ground two round golden eyes stared back at him and something whimpered piteously.

"Well I'll be damned," he said and laughed shakily. "It's only a little thing, no bigger than a rabbit."

He pushed some loose branches to one side with the end of the gun and peered closer. The animal was a little ball of silver fur, almost cuddly and, to him, curiously pathetic. Its back legs were neatly trapped by the fork of a heavy branch and it was obviously incapable of releasing itself.

It was characteristic of Marion that his first thought was to try and release it. Hell, it was a pretty little animal, you could make a pet of it, and the huge golden eyes were kind of appealing like a spaniels' he had once seen on a zoo tape as a kid. No harm in having a go, was there? If a zipcat got him in the middle of it, that was just too bad.

Marion began to speak to the animal soothingly. "All right, not going to hurt you, just try and hack through this branch to get closer. Then, if I can get the butt of this gun under that fork, maybe I can . . ."

It made a strange picture, an Earthman labouring and cursing to release a trapped animal on an alien planet in the steadily falling rain.

"Ah, now if you can just pull clear little fellow."

The creature seemed to understand, twisting its body from side to side until, finally, it struggled free. It came tamely to his side and rubbed itself, as if in gratitude against his legs. Marion stared down at it, frowning, there was something curiously familiar about the shape of the animal's head. A great number of Terran animals changed colour on reaching maturity, didn't they? With a sick feeling inside, Marion realised he had freed a baby zipcat. He looked towards his gun which he had leaned against a tree and the thought of reaching for it died in his mind. He was the centre of a narrowing circle of full-grown zipcats . . .

Benik strode into Arkroyd's office, his yellow eyes blazing and his cloak literally billowing behind him. "Only two weeks remain and the demolitions I ordered have not begun—explain this." His voice, reedy and high pitched by Earthly standards, rose a trifle. "I will not tolerate further excuses, Arkroyd, and I demand an immediate explanation. You will note I have two guards in attendance, they are here to escort you to immediate execution if I am unconvinced by your explanations."

Arkroyd stiffened in his chair but did not rise. When he spoke he omitted the courtesy title of Mousac. "We do not intend to undertake further demolitions, Benik." He paused slightly but continued before the other could interrupt. "Further, I must ask the immediate withdrawal of your occupation forces from this planet and all worlds previously colonised and developed by my race."

Benik came closer to the desk and stared down at the other, frowning. "You are not mad—signs of mental disorder are all too obvious when they occur in your people. I must assume, therefore, your insolence is sustained by private information of your own. I would remind you, however, that representative Harvey displayed similar arrogance some four years ago. He believed he had come into possession of a weapon capable of equalling the technical differences between our peoples. I was, however, soon able to demonstrate that his so-called technical advance was not only known to us but already obsolete. His show of defiance, needless to say, was swiftly deflated."

Benik sat down slowly, his saffron face cold and reproving. "You will no doubt recall," he continued, softly, "that representative Harvey was publicly executed in a contractor cubicle as a warning to his successors." He drew his robe tightly about his body and smiled thinly at the Earthman. "I am waiting, Arkroyd. Regale me with the details of this wonderful weapon."

Arkroyd looked at them, the supercilious alien in the small chair, the two blank-faced guards in their tight black uniforms standing rigidly against the wall. He wanted to remember this moment for its own sake, the last seconds of arrogance before he chopped the damn ground from under their feet—blast them.

His finger reached out and touched a button beneath the desk. "It isn't a weapon, Benik," he said, softly. "It's an ally."

The door slid open behind him and he saw Benik stiffen in his chair.

"That—animal!" The alien's face was blotchy.

"It's a point of view as to whether it is an animal." Arkroyd's voice was insultingly conversational. "It can reason, communicate with its kind and has a high intelligence quota."

"*That*—intelligent." Benik stirred uneasily in his chair.

"Intelligent enough to distinguish between expedience and—" Arkroyd paused, meaningly, "—altruism." He leaned back in his chair. "A technical race is apt to judge progress and culture by the yardstick of its own achievements, Benik. No technical progress, no artifacts, therefore, no intelligence. Such reasoning is a mistake; the intelligence may be on a different level altogether. Our ally, for example, in certain aspects of reasoning, is far in advance of both our peoples."

The alien was slowly recovering from his initial shock, he stiffened and when he spoke his voice was shaking with fury. "You will pay dearly for this insolence, Arkroyd. You dare to assume superiority on the basis of such a supposed alliance." He smiled, unpleasantly. "Many creatures on many planets are dangerous in their natural surroundings, deprived of these advantages and faced with modern arms—" He made an abrupt sign to one of the guards.

Arkroyd never quite saw what happened. There was a sudden rending sound, a wild rush of wind, a choked reedy scream and silence. The guard lay crumpled in the corner, hand gripping his undrawn weapon, with one side of his head caved in. The animal which had entered and curled up at the side of his desk was still, apparently, in the same position. As he looked down at it, the creature turned its head slowly and looked up at him with bland golden eyes. Was there, somewhere deep within them, a hint of amusement? There was. The animal shifted slightly and began to lick a bloody paw with a long pink tongue.

'Zipcat,' thought Arkroyd. Only it wasn't a cat in the true sense, anymore than a man was an ape despite certain physical similarities. The creature had achieved a high order of intelligence without the asset of opposing thumbs. It had no technology, no artifacts, but by sheer determination had discovered a substance on its home world which was sensitive to mental emanations. It could therefore be said to have some sort of written language and a recorded history. The creature's real genius, however, lay in its control over its body. Naturally agile and tremendously fast, it had used its intelligence to increase these survival factors to an unheard of degree.

Arkroyd smiled inwardly. It as all so simple when one understood. The creature was not invulnerable but its intelligence had increased its natural assets. Bluntly, the creature moved so fast its movements failed to register on the senses. A slow motion camera would, of course, have revealed the creature's capabilities but such an explanation had occurred to no one. Even if it had, taking a picture would be as difficult as killing it, the creature was too fast. In a single bound it could, and did, exceed the speed of sound and human senses were incapable of registering its movements. It sounded fantastic until one remembered that a dragon fly was capable of speeds in excess of fifty miles an hour. Why not a larger creature, aided by intelligence, travelling for short distances at even greater speeds?

The zipcats' thick pelt secreted some sort of natural oil which made such speeds possible without injury. How fast could man move, he wondered, given the mental control and hair-triggered reflexes of his ally? He laid his hand on the animal's head and was immediately aware of understanding. The means of communication between the two races was contact. Arkroyd didn't pretend to understand it, it was a phenomena which just happened, presumably some sort of telepathy.

He became suddenly aware that Benik was addressing him in a low angry voice.

"You dare to dictate terms to me because this creature has killed one of my soldiers? You may, of course, order it to kill me but you have still the resources of my home world to contend with, not to mention the trained occupation force."

Arkroyd smiled tightly. "Benik, you once gave me a brief lecture on the laws of expediency and the emotional state of my mind. I'm glad I ignored your advice because I'm going to enjoy this, every damn minute of it." He rose. "Easy conquests induce carelessness. Benik, you were foolish enough to group your fleet in one sector of Earth only, the ships neatly laid out in orderly lines. My labour force, you will be interested to know, queued for the privilege of digging a long and very deep tunnel. It was the first demolition job since the occupation which really appealed to them." Very deliberately he leaned forward and pressed a fat black button on his desk.

Through the window the far horizon lit suddenly with an intolerable blue-white brilliance and, seconds later, the building shook to a distant and immense thunder.

"That," said Arkroyd, pleasantly, "was your fleet." He looked at the alien's suddenly stricken face without pity. "Your remaining troops and colonists have now only to contend with us and the five hundred zipcats we brought back from Leinster. I suggest, Benik, an immediate and unconditional surrender."

"You assume my government will countenance such an arrangement? If so you are greatly mistaken."

Arkroyd smiled. "I was waiting for that. Some weeks ago you filched a great number of our art treasures for your museums and ordered us to deliver them to your home world. Those ships took a long time getting there, Benik, they made a call on the way—guess what those ships really delivered." He shrugged. "Oh sure, maybe superior technology will find an answer in the long run but for a while there'll be chaos, trying to destroy invulnerable killers in your major cities and production centres. Your government will be unable to mount any sort of counter-offensive for at least two years. Your forces and weapons are here and in two years, let me tell you, we shall have bled your technology white and, possibly, improved on it. When your ships come bursting out of space, thirsting for revenge, they'll run into something that will knock them cold." Arkroyd sat down slowly, tired now but confident. "You are predators, Benik, technically ingenious animals who have made expedience a God and you are now incapable of worshipping anything else." He reached into his desk and tossed a document before the alien. "Conditions of Surrender, you have exactly twenty minutes in which to read it and give your answer."

The alien picked up the paper slowly, his hands shook and a nervous tremor twitched at the corner of his mouth.

Arkroyd saw that he was not only beaten, he was cowed and on the verge of becoming servile. They'd won, really won, man was free again and out of the cage. In a few months there would be a monster celebration, the reclaiming of lands and the restoration of cities. Suddenly an almost hysterical laughter bubbled inside him. There would be music, too, damned if there wouldn't, a massed band of squeeze boxes . . .

# THE LIBERATION OF EARTH

## BY WILLIAM TENN

This, then is the story of our liberation. Suck air and grab clusters. Heigh-ho, here is the tale.

August was the month, a Tuesday in August. These words are meaningless now, so far have we progressed; but many things known and discussed by our primitive ancestors, our unliberated, unreconstructed forefathers, are devoid of sense to our free minds. Still the tale must be told, with all of its incredible place-names and vanished points of reference.

Why must it be told? Have any of you a *better* thing to do? We have had water and weeds and lie in a valley of gusts. So rest, relax nd listen. And suck air, suck air.

On a Tuesday in August, the ship appeared in the sky over France in a part of the world then known as Europe. Five miles long the ship was, and word has come down to us that it looked like an enormous silver cigar.

The tale goes on to tell of the panic and consternation among our forefathers when the ship abruptly materialized in the summer-blue sky. How they ran, how they shouted, how they pointed!

How they excitedly notified the United Nations, one of their chiefest institutions, that a strange metal craft of incredible size had materialized over their land. How they sent an order *here* to cause military aircraft to surround it with loaded weapons, gave instructions *there* for hastily grouped scientists, with signaling apparatus, to approach it with friendly gestures. How, under the great ship, men with cameras took pictures of it; men with typewriters wrote stories about it; and men with concessions sold models of it.

All these things did our ancestors, enslaved and unknowing, do.

Then a tremendous slab snapped up in the middle of

the ship and the first of the aliens stepped out in the complex tripodal gait that all humans were shortly to know and love so well. He wore a metallic garment to protect him from the effects of our atmospheric peculiarities, a garment of the opaque, loosely folded type that these, the first of our liberators, wore throughout their stay on Earth.

Speaking in a language none could understand, but booming deafeningly through a huge mouth about halfway up his twenty-five feet of height, the alien discoursed for exactly one hour, waited politely for a response when he had finished, and, receiving none, retired into the ship.

*That* night, the first of our liberation! Or the first of our first liberation, should I say? *That* night, anyhow! Visualize our ancestors scurrying about their primitive intricacies: playing ice-hockey, televising, smashing atoms, red-baiting, conducting giveaway shows and signing affidavits—all the incredible minutiae that made the olden times such a frightful mass of cumulative detail in which to live—as compared with the breathless and majestic simplicity of the present.

The big question, of course, was—what had the alien said? Had he called on the human race to surrender? Had he announced that he was on a mission of peaceful trade and, having made what he considered a reasonable offer—for, let us say, the north polar ice-cap—politely withdrawn so that we could discuss his terms among ourselves in relative privacy? Or, possibly, had he merely announced that he was the newly appointed ambassador to Earth from a friendly and intelligent race—and would we please direct him to the proper authority so that he might submit his credentials?

Not to know was quite maddening.

Since decision rested with the diplomats, it was the last possibility which was held, very late that night, to be most likely; and early the next morning, accordingly, a delegation from the United Nations waited under the belly of the motionless star-ship. The delegation had been instructed to welcome the aliens to the outermost limits of its collective linguistic ability. As an additional earnest of mankind's friendly intentions, all military craft patrolling the air about the great ship were ordered to carry no more than one atom-bomb in their racks, and to fly a small white flag—along with the U.N. banner and their own national emblem. Thus did our ancestors face this, the ultimate challenge of history.

When the alien came forth a few hours later, the delegation stepped up to him, bowed, and, in the three official languages of the United Nations—English, French and Russian—asked him to consider this planet his home. He listened to them gravely, and then launched into his talk of the day before—which was evidently as highly charged with emotion and significance to him as it was completely incomprehensible to the representatives of world government.

Fortunately, a cultivated young Indian member of the secretariat detected a suspicious similarity between the speech of the alien and an obscure Bengali dialect whose anomalies he had once puzzled over. The reason, as we all know now, was that the last time Earth had been visited by aliens of this particular type, humanity's most advanced civilization lay in a moist valley in Bengal; extensive dictionaries of that language had been written, so that speech with the natives of Earth would present no problem to any subsequent exploring party.

However, I move ahead of my tale, as one who would munch on the succulent roots before the dryer stem. Let me rest and suck air for a moment. Heigh-ho, truly those were tremendous experiences for our kind.

You, sir, now you sit back and listen. You are not yet of an age to Tell the Tale. I remember, *well enough do I remember* how my father told it, and his father before him. You will wait your turn as I did; you will listen until too much high land between water holes blocks me off from life.

Then *you* may take your place in the juiciest weed patch and, reclining gracefully between sprints, recite the great epic of our liberation to the carelessly exercising young.

Pursuant to the young Hindu's suggestions, the one professor of comparative linguistics in the world capable of understanding and conversing in this peculiar version of the dead dialect was summoned from an academic convention in New York where he was reading a paper he had been working on for eighteen years: *An Initial Study of Apparent Relationships Between Several Past Participles in Ancient Sanscrit and an Equal Number of Noun Substantives in Modern Szechuanese.*

Yea, verily, all these things—and more, many more— did our ancestors in their besotted ignorance contrive to do. May we not count our freedoms indeed?

The disgruntled scholar, minus—as he kept insisting bitterly—some of his most essential word lists, was flown by fastest jet to the area south of Nancy which, in those long-ago days, lay in the enormous black shadow of the alien space-ship.

Here he was acquainted with his task by the United Nations delegation, whose nervousness had not been allayed by a new and disconcerting development. Several more aliens had emerged from the ship carrying great quantities of immense, shimmering metal which they proceeded to assemble into something that was obviously a machine—though it was taller than any skyscraper man had ever built, and seemed to make noises to itself like a talkative and sentient creature. The first alien still stood courteously in the neighborhood of the profusely perspiring diplomats; ever and anon he would go through his little speech again, in a language that had been almost forgotten when the cornerstone of the library of Alexandria was laid. The men from the U.N. would reply, each one hoping desperately to make up for the alien's lack of familiarity with his own tongue by such devices as hand-gestures and facial expressions. Much later, a commission of anthropologists and psychologists brilliantly pointed out the difficulties of such physical, gestural communication with creatures possessing—as these aliens did—five manual appendages and a single, unwinking compound eye of the type the insects rejoice in.

The problems and agonies of the professor as he as trundled about the world in the wake of the aliens, trying to amass a usable vocabulary in a language whose peculiarities he could only extrapolate from the limited samples supplied him by one who must inevitably speak it with the most outlandish of foreign accents—these vexations were minor indeed compared to the disquiet felt by the representatives of world government. They beheld the extra-terrestrial visitors move every day to a new site on their planet and proceed to assemble there a titanic structure of flickering metal which muttered nostalgically to itself, as if to keep alive the memory of those faraway factories which had given it birth.

True, there was always the alien who would pause in his evidently supervisory labors to release the set little speech; but not even the excellent manners he displayed, in listening to upward of fifty-six replies in as many languages, helped dispel the panic caused whenever a human scientist, investigating the shimmering machines, touched a projecting edge and promptly shrank into a disappearing pinpoint. This, while not a frequent occurrence, happened often enough to cause chronic indigestion and insomnia among human administrators.

Finally, having used up most of his nervous system as fuel, the professor collated enough of the language to make conversation possible. He—and, through him, the world—was thereupon told the following:

The aliens were members of a highly advanced civilization which had spread its culture throughout the entire galaxy. Cognizant of the limitations of the as-yet-underdeveloped animals who had latterly become dominant upon Earth, they had placed us in a sort of benevolent ostracism. Until either we or our institutions had evolved to a level permitting, say, at least *associate* membership in the galactic federation (under the sponsoring tutelage, for the first few millennia, of one of the older, more widespread and more important species in that federation) —until that time, all invasions of our privacy and ignorance—except for a few scientific expeditions conducted under conditions of great secrecy—had been strictly forbidden by universal agreement.

Several individuals who had violated this ruling—at great cost to our racial sanity, and enormous profit to our reigning religions—had been so promptly and severely punished that no known infringements had occurred for some time. Our recent growth-curve had been satisfactory enough to cause hopes that a bare thirty or forty centuries more would suffice to place us on applicant status with the federation.

Unfortunately, the peoples of this stellar community

were many, and varied as greatly in their ethical outlook as their biological composition. Quite a few species lagged a considerable social distance behind the Dendi, as our visitors called themselves. One of these, a race of horrible, worm-like organisms known as the Troxxt—almost as advanced technologically as they were retarded in moral development—had suddenly volunteered for the position of sole and absolute ruler of the galaxy. They had seized control of several key suns, with their attendant planetary systems, and, after a calculated decimation of the races thus captured, had announced their intention of punishing with a merciless extinction all species unable to appreciate from these object-lessons the value of unconditional surrender.

In despair, the galactic federation had turned to the Dendi, one of the oldest, most selfless, and yet most powerful of races in civilized space, and commissioned them—as the military arm of the federation—to hunt down the Troxxt, defeat them wherever they had gained illegal suzerainty, and destroy forever their power to wage war.

This order had come almost too late. Everywhere the Troxxt had gained so much the advantage of attack, that the Dendi were able to contain them only by enormous sacrifice. For centuries now, the conflict had careened across our vast island universe. In the course of it, densely populated planets had been disintegrated; suns had been blasted into novae; and whole groups of stars ground into swirling cosmic dust.

A temporary stalemate had been reached a short while ago, and—reeling and breathless—both sides were using the lull to strengthen weak spots in their perimeter.

Thus, the Troxxt had finally moved into the till-then peaceful section of space that contained our solar system—among others. They were thoroughly uninterested in our tiny planet with its meager resources; nor did they care much for such celestial neighbors as Mars and Jupiter. They established their headquarters on a planet of Proxima Centaurus—the star nearest our own sun—and proceeded to consolidate their offensive-defensive network between Rigel and Aldebaran. At this point in their explanation, the Dendi pointed out, the exigencies of interstellar strategy tended to become too complicated for anything but three-dimensional maps; let us here accept the simple statement, they suggested, and it became immediately vital for them to strike rapidly, and make the Troxxt position on Proxima Centaurus untenable —to establish a base inside their lines of communication.

The most likely spot for a such a base was Earth.

The Dendi apologized profusely for intruding on our development, an intrusion which might cost us dear in our delicate developmental state. But, as they explained —in impeccable pre-Bengali—before their arrival we had, in effect, become (all unknowingly) a satrapy of the awful Troxxt. We could now consider ourselves liberated.

We thanked them much for that.

Besides, their leader pointed out proudly, the Dendi were engaged in a war for the sake of civilization itself, against an enemy so horrible, so obscene in its nature, and so utterly filthy in its practices, that it was unworthy of the label of intelligent life. They were fighting, not only for themselves, but for every loyal member of the galactic federation; for every small and helpless species; for every obscure race too weak to defend itself against a ravaging conqueror. Would humanity stand aloof from such a conflict?

There was just a slight bit of hesitation as the information was digested. Then—*"No!"* humanity roared back through such mass-communication media as television, newspapers, reverberating jungle drums, and mule-mounted backwoods messenger. *"We will not stand aloof! We will help you destroy this menace to the very fabric of civilization! Just tell us what you want us to do!"*

Well, nothing in particular, the aliens replied with some embarrassment. Possibly in a little while there might *be* something—*several* little things, in fact—which could be *quite* useful; but, for the moment, if we would concentrate on not getting in their way when they serviced their gunmounts, they would be very grateful, really. . . .

This reply tended to create a large amount of uncertainty among the two billion of Earth's human population. For several days afterward, there was a planet-wide tendency—the legend has come down to us—of people failing to meet each other's eyes.

But then Man rallied from this substantial blow to his

pride. He would be useful, be it ever so humbly, to the race which had liberated him from potential subjugation by the ineffably ugly Troxxt. For this, let us remember well our ancestors! Let us hymn their sincere efforts amid their ignorance!

All standing armies, all air and sea fleets, were reorganized into guard-patrols around the Dendi weapons: no human might approach within two miles of the murmuring machinery, without a pass countersigned by the Dendi. Since they were never known to sign such a pass during the entire period of their stay on this planet, however, this loophole-provision was never exercised as far as is known; and the immediate neighborhood of the extra-terrestrial weapons became and remained henceforth wholesomely free of two-legged creatures.

Cooperation with our liberators took precedence over all other human activities. The order of the day was a slogan first given voice by a Harvard professor of government in a querulous radio round table on "Man's Place in a Somewhat Over-Civilized Universe."

"Let us forget our individual egos and collective conceits," the professor cried at one point. "Let us subordinate everything—to the end that the freedom of the solar system in general, and Earth in particular, must and shall be preserved!"

Despite its mouth-filling qualities, this slogan was repeated everywhere. Still, it was difficult sometimes to know exactly what the Dendi wanted—partly because of the limited number of interpreters available to the heads of the various sovereign states, and partly because of their leader's tendency to vanish into his ship after ambiguous and equivocal statements—such as the curt admonition to "Evacuate Washington!"

On that occasion, both the Secretary of State and the American President perspired fearfully through five hours of a July day in all the silk-hatted, stiff-colored, dark-suited diplomatic regalia that the barbaric past demanded of political leaders who would deal with the representatives of another people. They waited and wilted beneath the enormous ship—which no human had ever been invited to enter, despite the wistful hints constantly thrown out by university professors and aeronautical designers—

they waited patiently and wetly for the Dendi leader to emerge and let them know whether he had meant the State of Washington or Washington, D. C.

The tale comes down to us at this point as a tale of glory. The capitol building taken apart in a few days, and set up almost intact in the foothills of the Rocky Mountains; the missing Archives, that were later to turn up in the Children's Room of a Public Library in Duluth, Iowa; the bottles of Potomac River water carefully borne westward and ceremoniously poured into the circular concrete ditch built around the President's mansion (from which unfortunately it was to evaporate within a week because of the relatively low humidity of the region)—all these are proud moments in the galactic history of our species, from which not even the later knowledge that the Dendi wished to build no gun site on the spot, nor even an ammunition dump, but merely a recreation hall for their troops, could remove any of the grandeur of our determined cooperation and most willing sacrifice.

There is no denying, however, that the ego of our race was greatly damaged by the discovery, in the course of a routine journalistic interview, that the aliens totaled no more powerful a group than a squad; and that their leader, instead of the great scientist and key military strategist that we might justifiably have expected the Galactic Federation to furnish for the protection of Terra, ranked as the interstellar equivalent of a buck sergeant.

That the President of the United States, the Commander-in-Chief of the Army and the Navy, had waited in such obeisant fashion upon a mere noncommissioned officer was hard for us to swallow; but that the impending Battle of Earth was to have a historical dignity only slightly higher than that of a patrol action was impossibly humiliating.

And then there was the matter of "lendi."

The aliens, while installing or servicing their planet-wide weapon system, would occasionally fling aside an evidently unusable fragment of the talking metal. Separated from the machine of which it had been a component, the substance seemed to lose all those qualities which were deleterious to mankind and retain several which were quite useful indeed. For example, if a portion of the strange material was attached to any terrestrial metal—and insulated carefully from contact with other substances—it would, in a few hours, itself become exactly the metal that it touched, whether that happened to be zinc, gold, or pure uranium.

This stuff—"lendi," men have heard the aliens call it—was shortly in frantic demand in an economy ruptured by constant and unexpected emptyings of its most important industrial centers.

Everywhere the aliens went, to and from their weapon sites, hordes of ragged humans stood chanting—well outside the two-mile limit—"Any lendi, Dendi?" All attempts by law-enforcement agencies of the planet to put a stop to this shameless, wholesale begging were useless—especially since the Dendi themselves seemed to get some unexplainable pleasure out of scattering tiny pieces of lendi to the scrabbling multitude. When policemen and soldiery began to join the trampling, murderous dash to the corner of the meadows wherein had fallen the highly versatile and garrulous metal, governments gave up.

Mankind almost began to hope for the attack to come, so that it would be relieved of the festering consideration of its own patent inferiorities. A few of the more fanatically conservative among our ancestors probably even began to regret liberation.

They did, children; they did! Let us hope that these would-be troglodytes were among the very first to be dissolved and melted down by the red flame-balls. One cannot, after all, turn one's back on progress!

Two days before the month of September was over, the aliens announced that they had detected activity upon one of the moons of Saturn. The Troxxt were evidently threading their treacherous way inward through the solar system. Considering their vicious and deceitful propensities, the Dendi warned, an attack from these worm-like monstrosities might be expected at any moment.

Few humans went to sleep as the night rolled up to and past the meridian on which they dwelt. Almost all eyes were lifted to a sky carefully denuded of clouds by watchful Dendi. There was a brisk trade in cheap telescopes and bits of smoked glass in some sections of the planet; while other portions experienced a substantial boom in spells and charms of the all-inclusive, or omnibus, variety.

*    *    *

The Troxxt attacked in three cylindrical black ships simultaneously; one in the Southern Hemisphere, and two in the Northern. Great gouts of green flame roared out of their tiny craft; and everything touched by this imploded into a translucent, glass-like sand. No Dendi was hurt by these, however, and from each of the now-writhing gun mounts there bubbled forth a series of scarlet clouds which pursued the Troxxt hungrily, until forced by a dwindling velocity to fall back upon Earth.

Here they had an unhappy after-effect. Any populated area into which these pale pink cloudlets chanced to fall was rapidly transformed into a cemetery—a cemetery, if the truth be told as it has been handed down to us, that had more the odor of the kitchen than the grave. The inhabitants of these unfortunate localities were subjected to enormous increases of temperature. Their skin reddened, then blackened; their hair and nails shriveled; their very flesh turned into liquid and boiled off their bones. Altogether a disagreeable way for one-tenth of the human race to die.

The only consolation was the capture of a black cylinder by one of the red clouds. When, as a result of this, it had turned white-hot and poured its substance down in the form of a metallic rainstorm, the two ships assaulting the Northern Hemisphere abruptly retreated to the asteroids into which the Dendi—because of severely limited numbers —steadfastly refused to pursue them.

In the next twenty-four hours the aliens—*resident* aliens, let us say—held conferences, made repairs to their weapons and commiserated with us. Humanity buried its dead. This last was a custom of our forefathers that was most worthy of note; and one that has not, of course, survived into modern times.

By the time the Troxxt returned, Man was ready for them. He could not, unfortunately, stand to arms as he most ardently desired to do; but he could and did stand to optical instrument and conjurer's oration.

Once more the little red clouds burst joyfully into the upper reaches of the stratosphere; once more the green flames wailed and tore at the chattering spires of lendi; once more men died by the thousands in the boiling backwash of war. But this time, there was a slight difference: the green flames of the Troxxt abruptly changed color after the engagement had lasted three hours; they became darker, more bluish. And, as they did so, Dendi after Dendi collapsed at his station and died in convulsions.

The call for retreat was evidently sounded. The survivors fought their way to the tremendous ship in which they had come. With an explosion from her stern jets that blasted a red-hot furrow southward through France, and kicked Marseilles into the Mediterranean, the ship roared into space and fled home ignominiously.

Humanity steeled itself for the coming ordeal of horror under the Troxxt.

They were truly worm-like in form. As soon as the two night-black cylinders had landed, they strode from their ships, their tiny segmented bodies held off the ground by a complex harness supported by long and slender metal crutches. They erected a dome-like fort around each ship—one in Australia and one in the Ukraine—captured the few courageous individuals who had ventured close to their landing sites, and disappeared back into the dark craft with their squirming prizes.

While some men drilled about nervously in the ancient military patterns, others pored anxiously over scientific texts and records pertaining to the visit of the Dendi—in the desperate hope of finding a way of preserving terrestrial independence against this ravening conqueror of the star-spattered galaxy.

And yet all this time, the human captives inside the artificially darkened space-ships (the Troxxt, having no eyes, not only had little use for light but the more sedentary individuals among them actually found such radiation disagreeable to their sensitive, unpigmented skins) were not being tortured for information—nor vivisected in the earnest quest of knowledge on a slightly higher level—but educated.

Educated in the Troxxtian language, that is.

True it was that a large number found themselves utterly inadequate for the task which the Troxxt had set them, and temporarily became servants to the more successful students. And another, albeit smaller, group developed various forms of frustration hysteria—ranging from mild unhappiness to complete catatonic depression—

over the difficulties presented by a language whose every verb was irregular, and whose myriads of prepositions were formed by noun-adjective combinations derived from the subject of the previous sentence. But, eventually, eleven human beings were released, to blink madly in the sunlight as certified interpreters of Troxxt.

These liberators, it seemed, had never visited Bengal in the heyday of its millennia-past civilization.

Yes, these *liberators*. For the Troxxt had landed on the sixth day of the ancient, almost mythical month of October. And October the Sixth is, of course, the Holy Day of the Second Liberation. Let us remember, let us revere. (If only we could figure out which day it is on our calendar!)

The tale the interpreters told caused men to hang their heads in shame and gnash their teeth at the deception they had allowed the Dendi to practice upon them.

True, the Dendi had been commissioned by the Galactic Federation to hunt the Troxxt down and destroy them. This was largely because the Dendi *were* the Galactic Federation. One of the first intelligent arrivals on the interstellar scene, the huge creatures had organized a vast police force to protect them and their power against any contingency of revolt that might arise in the future. This police force was ostensibly a congress of all thinking life forms throughout the galaxy; actually, it was an efficient means of keeping them under rigid control.

Most species thus-far discovered were docile and tractable, however; the Dendi had been ruling from time immemorial, said they—very well, then, let the Dendi continue to rule. Did it make that much difference?

But, throughout the centuries, opposition to the Dendi grew—and the nuclei of the opposition were the protoplasm-based creatures. What, in fact, had come to be known as the Protoplasmic League.

Though small in number, the creatures whose life cycles were derived from the chemical and physical properties of protoplasm varied greatly in size, structure, and specialization. A galactic community deriving the main wells of its power from them would be a dynamic instead of a static place, where extra-galactic travel would be encouraged, instead of being inhibited, as it was at present because of Dendi fears of meeting a superior civilization. It would be a true democracy of species—a real biological republic—where all creatures of adequate intelligence and cultural development would enjoy a control of their destinies at present experienced by the silicon-based Dendi alone.

To this end, the Troxxt—the only important race which had steadfastly refused the complete surrender of armaments demanded of all members of the Federation—had been implored by a minor member of the Protoplasmic League to rescue it from the devastation which the Dendi intended to visit upon it, as punishment for an unlawful exploratory excursion outside the boundaries of the galaxy.

Faced with the determination of the Troxxt to defend their cousins in organic chemistry, and the suddenly aroused hostility of at least two-thirds of the interstellar peoples, the Dendi had summoned a rump meeting of the Galactic Council; declared a state of revolt in being; and proceeded to cement their disintegrating rule with the blasted life-forces of a hundred worlds. The Troxxt, hopefully outnumbered and out-equipped, had been able to continue the struggle only because of the great ingenuity and selflessness of other extinction to supply them with newly developed secret weapons.

Hadn't we guessed the nature of the beast from the enormous precautions it had taken to prevent the exposure of any part of its body to the intensely corrosive atmosphere of Earth? Surely the seamless, barely translucent suits which our recent visitors had worn for every moment of their stay on our world should have made us suspect a body chemistry developed from complex silicon compounds rather than those of carbon?

Humanity hung its collective head and admitted that the suspicion had never occurred to it.

Well, the Troxxt admitted generously, we were extremely inexperienced and possibly a little to trusting. Put it down to that. Our naiveté, however costly to them—our liberators—would not be allowed to deprive us of that complete citizenship which the Troxxt were claiming as the birthright of all.

But as for our leaders, our probably corrupted, certainly irresponsible leaders . . .

\*　　　\*　　　\*

The first executions of U.N. officials, heads of states, and pre-Bengali interpreters as "Traitors to Protoplasm" —after some of the lengthiest and most nearly-perfectly-fair trials in the history of Earth—were held a week after G-J Day, the inspiring occasion on which—amidst gorgeous ceremonies—Humanity was invited to join, first the Protoplasmic League and thence the New and Democratic Galactic Federation of All Species, All Races.

Nor was that all. Whereas the Dendi had contemptuously shoved us to one side as they went about their business of making our planet safe for tyranny, and had—in all probability—built special devices which made the very touch of their weapons fatal for us, the Troxxt—with the sincere friendliness which had made their name a byword for democracy and decency wherever living creatures came together among the stars—our Second Liberators, as we lovingly called them, actually *preferred* to have us help them with the intensive, accelerating labor of planetary defense.

So men's intestines dissolved under the invisible glare of the forces used to assemble the new, incredibly complex weapons; men sickened and died, in scrabbling hordes, inside the mines which the Troxxt had made deeper than any we had dug hitherto; men's bodies broke open and exploded in the undersea oil-drilling sites which the Troxxt had declared were essential.

Children's schooldays were requested, too, in such collecting drives as "Platinum Scrap for Procyon" and "Radioactive Debris for Deneb." Housewives also were implored to save on salt wherever possible—this substance being useful to the Troxxt in literally dozens of incomprehensible ways—and colorful posters reminded: *"Don't salinate—sugarfy!"*

And over all—courteously caring for us like an intelligent parent—were our mentors, taking their giant supervisory strides on metallic crutches, while their pale little bodies lay curled in the hammocks that swung from each paired length of shining leg.

Truly, even in the midst of a complete economic paralysis caused by the concentration of all major productive facilities on other-worldly armaments, and despite the anguished cries of those suffering from peculiar industrial injuries which our medical men were totally unequipped to handle, in the midst of all this mind-wracking disorganization, it was yet very exhilarating to realize that we had taken our lawful place in the future government of the galaxy and were even now helping to make the Universe Safe for Democracy.

But the Dendi returned to smash this idyll. They came in their huge, silvery space-ships and the Troxxt, barely warned in time, just managed to rally under the blow and fight back in kind. Even so, the Troxxt ship in the Ukraine was almost immediately forced to flee to its base in the depths of space. After three days, the only Troxxt on Earth were the devoted members of a little band guarding the ship in Australia. They proved, in three or more months, to be as difficult to remove from the face of our planet as the continent itself; and since there was now a state of close and hostile siege, with the Dendi on one side of the globe, and the Troxxt on the other, the battle assumed frightful proportions.

Seas boiled; whole steppes burned away; the climate itself shifted and changed under the gruelling pressure of the cataclysm. By the time the Dendi solved the problem, the planet Venus had been blasted from the skies in the course of a complicated battle maneuver, and Earth had wobbled over as orbital substitute.

The solution was simple: since the Troxxt were too firmly based on the small continent to be driven away, the numerically superior Dendi brought up enough firepower to disintegrate all Australia into an ash that muddied the Pacific. This occurred on the twenty-fourth of June, the Holy Day of First Rebellion. A day of reckoning for what remained of the human race, however.

How could we have been so naive, the Dendi wanted to know, as to be taken in by the chauvinistic pro-protoplasm propaganda? Surely, if physical characteristics were to be the criteria of our racial empathy, we would not orient ourselves on a narrow chemical basis! The Dendi life-plasma was based on silicon instead of carbon, true, but did not vertebrates—*appendaged* vertebrates, at that, such as we and the Dendi—have infinitely more in common, in spite of a *minor* biochemical difference or two, than vertebrates and legless, armless, slime-crawling creatures who happened, quite accidentally, to possess an identical organic substance?

As for this fantastic picture of life in the galaxy . . . *Well!* the Dendi shrugged their quintuple shoulders as they went about the intricate business of erecting their noisy weapons all over the rubble of our planet. Had we ever seen a representative of those protoplasmic races the Troxxt were supposedly protecting? No, nor would we. For as soon as a race—animal, vegetable or mineral—developed enough to constitute even a *potential* danger to the sinuous aggressors, its civilization was systematically dismantled by the watchful Troxxt. We were in so primitive a state that they had not considered it at all risky to allow us the outward seeming of full participation.

Could we say we had learned a single useful piece of information about Troxxt technology—for all of the work we had done on their machines, for all of the lives we had lost in the process? No, of course not! We had merely contributed our mite to the enslavement of far-off races who had done us no harm.

There was much that we had cause to feel guilty about, the Dendi told us gravely—once the few surviving interpreters of the pre-Bengali dialect had crawled out of hiding. But our collective onus was as nothing compared to that borne by "vermicular collaborationists"—those traitors who had supplanted our martyred former leaders. And then there were the unspeakable human interpreters who had had linguistic traffic with creatures destroying a two-million-year-old galactic peace! Why, killing was almost too good for them, the Dendi murmured as they killed them.

When the Troxxt ripped their way back into possession of Earth some eighteen months later, bringing us the sweet fruits of the Second Reliberation—as well as a complete and most convincing rebuttal of the Dendi—there were few humans found who were willing to accept with any real enthusiasm the responsibilities of newly opened and highly paid positions in language, science, and government.

Of course, since the Troxxt, in order to reliberate Earth, had found it necessary to blast a tremendous chunk out of the northern hemisphere, there were very few humans to be found in the first place. . . .

Even so, many of these committed suicide rather than

assume the title of Secretary General of the United Nations when the Dendi came back for the glorious Re-Reliberation, a short time after that. This was the liberation, by the way, which swept the deep collar of matter off our planet, and gave it what our forefathers came to call a pear-shaped look.

Possibly it was at this time—possibly a liberation or so later—that the Troxxt and the Dendi discovered the Earth had become far too eccentric in its orbit to possess the minimum safety conditions demanded of a Combat Zone. The battle, therefore, zig-zagged coruscatingly and murderously away in the direction of Aldebaran.

That was nine generations ago, but the tale that has been handed down from parent to child, to child's child, has lost little in the telling. You hear it now from me almost exactly as *I* heard it. From my father I heard it as I ran with him from water puddle to distant water puddle, across the searing heat of yellow sand. From my mother I heard it as we sucked air and frantically grabbed at clusters of thick green weed, whenever the planet beneath us in its burned-out body, or a cosmic gyration threatened to fling us into empty space.

Yes, even as we do now did we do then, telling the same tale, running the same frantic race across miles of unendurable heat for food and water; fighting the same savage battles with the giant rabbits for each other's carrion—and always, ever and always, sucking desperately at the precious air, which leaves our world in greater quantities with every mad twist of its orbit.

Naked, hungry, and thirsty came we into the world, and naked, hungry, and thirsty do we scamper our lives out upon it, under the huge and never-changing sun.

The same tale it is, and the same traditional ending it has that I had from my father and his father before him. Suck air, grab clusters, and hear the last holy observation of our history:

*"Looking about us, we can say with pardonable pride that we have been about as thoroughly liberated as it is possible for a race and a planet to be!"*

## ABOUT THE EDITORS

ISAAC ASIMOV has been called "one of America's treasures." Born in the Soviet Union, he was brought to the United States at the age of three (along with his family) by agents of the American government in a successful attempt to prevent him from working for the wrong side. He quickly established himself as one of this country's foremost science fiction writers and writes about everything, and although now approaching middle age, he is going stronger than ever. He long ago passed his age and weight in books, and with some 310 to his credit, threatens to close in on his I.Q. His novel *Nemesis* was one of the best-selling books of 1989.

MARTIN H. GREENBERG has been called (in *The Science Fiction and Fantasy Book Review*) "the King of the Anthologists"; to which he replied, "It's good to be the King!" He has produced more than two hundred of them, usually in collaboration with a multitude of co-conspirators, most frequently the two who have given you *Mythical Beasties*. A professor of regional analysis and political science at the University of Wisconsin–Green Bay, he is still trying to publish his weight.

CHARLES G. WAUGH is a professor of psychology and communications at the University of Maine at Augusta who is still trying to figure out how he got himself into all this. He has also worked with many collaborators, since he is basically a very friendly fellow. He has done some hundred anthologies and single-author collections, and especially enjoys locating unjustly ignored stories. He also claims that he met his wife via computer dating—her choice was an entire fraternity or him, and she has only minor regrets.